FINDING HOPE

Book Three in the Tom and Taylor Series

by

ANDREW BARRIGER

ALSO BY ANDREW BARRIGER

Finding Faith

Finding Peace

Visit Andrew Barriger Online at:

www.andrewbarriger.com

FINDING HOPE

Book Three in the Tom and Taylor Series

a Novel by

ANDREW BARRIGER

Two Brothers Press

Worldwide Distribution

This is a work of fiction. Names, characters, places, and incidents are the product of the author's imagination or are used fictitiously. Any resemblance to actual events, locales, organizations, or persons, living or dead, is entirely coincidental and beyond the intent of either the author or the publisher.

A Two Brothers Press Book
PUBLISHED BY BOOKSURGE
BookSurge, LLC
5341 Dorchester Rd, Suite 16
North Charleston, SC 29418

Copyright © 2004 by Andrew Barriger
Cover Artwork and Interior Design by Andrew Barriger
Visit the author's website at *http://www.andrewbarriger.com*

ISBN 1-59457-678-5

Printed in the United States of America

First Two Brothers Press Edition: November, 2004

DEDICATION

To my readers,
who never accepted "I'm trying to have a life" as an excuse,
and to Jason and Betty,
for giving me the last few ideas I needed to get things moving.

TABLE OF CONTENTS

BONUS ITEMS

ACKNOWLEDGMENTS

I always say, "Where would I be without my friends?" and never has that been truer than with *Finding Hope*.

After *Finding Peace* was published, I received a huge volume of email from people telling me how much they'd enjoyed it...and wondering when the next installment would appear. That taught me two very valuable lessons: 1) People really *are* reading my books, and 2) never promise another book until I have an idea for what it will be about.

That was the problem I faced with *Finding Hope*. When I finished the last book, I had a sort of half-baked idea about what the next one might be about, but no firm commitments. Then the pressure mounted as people awaited the next installment and I didn't know where to turn.

And that's where the friends come in. Jason Holland and Betty Conley, stalwart friends to the end, started sending ideas along for the kinds of things they would most enjoy seeing in the next story. As we conversed, ideas started to form in my head and an outline was born!

What you hold in your hand is the product of that outline, and those all too important ideas Betty and Jason contributed. As I recall, Café del Sol was Betty's, I *know* the hospital drama was

Jason's, and I think what happened to Gen was mine. (I figured I had to throw something in there.)

In addition to their contributions, I would be horribly remiss if I failed to mention the contributions of two other close and dear friends, Cheri Rosenberg and Kathy Conley-Aydin. Both Cheri and Kathy joined Jason and Betty in the daunting task of editing what you hold in your hands, looking for the typos that slipped by my bespectacled eyes.

Lastly, thank you to all of you, dear readers, who have taken the time out of your own busy lives to share your thoughts and experiences with me. Part of what makes writing so much fun is the feedback I receive from all of you, and it makes the work worthwhile.

Now, having learned from my previous mistakes, I won't promise another installment...but I'd say the odds are pretty good. I try to keep my website, *www.andrewbarriger.com*, up to date, and you can always reach me at *andrew@andrewbarriger.com*.

Thank you all for reading and I wish you all the best.

Andrew Barriger
October, 2004

FINDING HOPE

CHAPTER ONE

The Plot Thickens

Taylor awoke from a sound sleep, the light of day just breaking through the blinds. He felt a weight on his chest, and heard the gentle sound of breathing next to his ear. For a brief moment, he simply lay there, in the comforting warmth of his bed, and enjoyed the all too rare silence.

Five years. Time flew, that Taylor knew, and it just kept getting faster and faster. It had been five years since that fateful Sunday, when he took his golden retriever, Molly, out for a quick walk to see their new surroundings. Just a short trip up to Main Street and back, that's what he'd said. And that's when it all changed.

The first person he'd met in Pine Creek, other than his best friend, Gen, was Rob Grady. Meeting Rob had been Taylor's first experience with the uniquely welcoming—and watchful—town. It was small town America and he was the new sight to see. When Rob heard Taylor was going to Main Street, he quickly recommended he stop at the town bakery as a "great way to start the morning." Taylor still wasn't sure whether he'd made the suggestion intentionally or if it was just luck and timing.

So Taylor and Molly made the trek to the bakery. There, Taylor absently ordered a few items, without really noticing the guy behind the counter at first. He was, after all, trying to get over a bad relationship that had just ended the week before. The whole reason he had moved to live with Gen was to take a break and start anew.

Fate has its own sense of timing, as Taylor learned all too well that day. When his eyes met Tom's, that special, indefinable *something* that makes a relationship sparked and turned both their worlds upside down forever.

Over the next few weeks, the two became virtually inseparable, finding one reason after another to spend time together. The challenge for Taylor was Tom wasn't "out." Having been through enough bad relationships, Taylor decided the chance for a good one was worth the wait…and wait he did, until the Spring Dance.

The Spring Dance that year was one the town still talked about. The local bachelorette-at-large, Faith Roberts, had set her eyes on Taylor. After a few too many libations, she decided it was time to come clean with the attractive, but elusive, attorney. As Taylor tried, in his subtle, self-effacing way to let her down easy, she made enough of a scene to capture the attention of most of the revelers. As the final reality of Taylor's words hit home, she blurted his status for all the town to hear.

Angry, hurt, and panicked over what the revelation would mean for his friendship with Tom, Taylor bolted, driving back to Gen's, leaving Gen and Tom to make their way back themselves.

Faith's action, though not intended as anything more than a confrontation, also proved a watershed for Tom. For the first time in his life, he was publicly associated with who he was…and found he didn't care. His only concern was for Taylor, who had obviously been upset. He returned with Gen to find Taylor had left with another friend, feeling his place in the town was threatened. Gen was able to find out where he had gone through a mutual friend, and she and Tom went after him.

Tom's final admission, when he thought all was lost, of his love for Taylor was simply the most romantic thing Taylor could ever remember in his life. In that one moment, half-dressed in a stairwell in New York City, they created a bond that would last a lifetime.

Five years later, at the crack of dawn, Taylor smiled. Last it had, through thick and thin. "Simple" never quite seemed to describe his life, and to his immense credit, Tom found it one of Taylor's more endearing qualities. It was as though Taylor was a carnival ride and Tom had hitched on for dear life.

Taylor gently rested his hand on the golden brown arm lying across his chest. No matter how they went to bed, they invariably wound up wrapped around each other, like a puzzle that wasn't complete until they were together. Taylor smiled—that was how he felt, like a piece of a puzzle that had been lucky enough to find its counterpart out of all the billions of souls on Planet Earth.

But life for Tom and Taylor, the couple McEwan-Connolly, was not without its challenges. While studying for his Master's Degree, Tom had assumed the role of town baker, the role that ultimately allowed them to meet. However, after receiving his degree, it had turned out to be almost impossible to replace him. Ultimately, the elderly lady who owned the bakery "sold" it to them for almost nothing, hoping that it would bring them the prosperity it had brought her family.

At face value, the offer had been generous, but it turned out to be arduous for Tom and Taylor's young relationship, as they saw progressively less and less of each other. Finally, realizing he needed help, Tom ran an ad in the paper. It was answered by one of the most unlikely of sources—one of his own high school students, a senior, who wanted work to prepare for his own college degree and, as they learned later, the hope of escaping a very abusive house.

Fate again had its way with Taylor and Tom as Wayne McInerney became a permanent fixture in their life. In short order, they learned they had far more in common with Wayne than a simple understanding of how to make bread rise. As the true nature of his home life became clear, they opened their home and their hearts to him, taking him in as a member of their family.

That Thanksgiving, life again took an unexpected turn when Tom's sister, Mandy, brought a friend from college to spend the holiday with them. Eric and Wayne became inseparable, and ultimately began dating.

Everything changed on New Year's Eve. Fate's watchful eye went dark, taking the lives of their longtime friends, John and Sandy Atkins. Unbeknownst to Tom and Taylor, John and Sandy had recently executed a new Will. On his deathbed, John apologized for not having been able to talk to them before—the Will named Taylor and Tom as guardians for their three young children, Chad, Wendy, and baby Taylor. Suddenly, in an instant, Tom and Taylor had become parents.

As always, the strength of their bond carried them through, and their other long time friends came together to help with the children. That spring, Tom's parents came to spend the summer with them, and at the end of the summer announced they had decided to make their move permanent.

Since that turbulent year, life eased into a more comfortable routine. Tom took a job as a professor of writing at the local college and blossomed in his new role. Wayne started college that fall and had gone nonstop ever since. Eric, Wayne's boyfriend, moved to town for the summer, but ultimately decided his place was still at his own University. Wayne had been heartbroken, but Taylor was there for him, ever ready to be his shoulder to cry on. Ultimately, Wayne understood it was easier to get through school without the persistent worry of a relationship, and eased into an easy group of academically oriented friends, including his high school pals Emmy and Dan.

Two years later, Wayne was already a Junior, and as the full-time manager of Downey McEwan's Baked Goods, freed Tom to spend his time on classes and with his family. Wayne spent many of his evenings with his adopted family, often making use of the spare bunk in his "niece's" room to spend the night.

Another April nearly gone, Taylor thought, gently running his hand down Tom's arm, feeling the smooth skin and firm muscle below. Being near Tom always brought a smile to his lips, his quiet strength always a source of amazement to Taylor. He could just smell a hint of cologne and…soap. Tom had come home from yet another little league practice, exhausted, and had just enough energy to make a pass through the shower on his way to bed. Taylor had just held him as they quietly drifted off to sleep.

Tom stirred, a dull moan erupting from where his face was buried in the pillow next to Taylor's head. The pressure on Taylor's chest increased as Tom pulled him in a little tighter.

"What time is it?" he groaned.

"Six-fifteen," Taylor answered quietly.

"Aaagghhh," Tom sighed. "I don't wanna get up."

Taylor smiled, angling his head to take in his spouse's face. Tom had let his brown hair grow a little longer since they'd met, and it was usually the worse for wear by morning. In a few more weeks, the sun would add some highlights, making it shine when Tom molded it into a style—or spiked it into a mess, which was also a popular choice.

"You've got to get up," Taylor said. "You don't want to be late. This is your last week for the whole summer."

Tom pushed his head farther down into the pillow. "Can't I just start summer now? How about if I just pass them all?"

Taylor laughed. "What fun would that be? You *know* how you enjoy failing some of them."

Tom jumped up sharply, his gray eyes flashing. "I do not!"

"Yes, you do!" Taylor giggled as Tom poked him in the side. "Stop it!" he insisted. "You'll wake the kids."

"Mom'll be here in a little while anyway," Tom said. His mom had installed herself as their *de facto* day care provider when his parents moved to town. It was an arrangement that seemed to work well for everyone, as the kids got to spend time with their adoptive grandparents and Tom and Taylor got a break from having three kids.

Tom fell back down, lying across Taylor, his head on his chest. Taylor sat up, arms around Tom, holding him.

"Come on, Tommy. Time to go. I've gotta be in court today, too."

Making no effort to free himself from Taylor's grasp, Tom asked, "In the city?"

"Yeah," Taylor confirmed.

"What time do you think you'll be back?"

Taylor sighed. "I don't know how late it will go, but I'm hoping to be on the road by three. You can email my phone if you need me."

"I know," Tom said. It was a discussion they had often. Taylor's original plan when he bought the law firm in town was that he wouldn't have to be gone very often. Unfortunately for his plan, his previous notoriety followed him, as did the high profile cases. He and Pete had been forced to bring in an associate within a year, and had recently hired two more, and a paralegal.

Taylor was about to take the summer off, though. For the first time in almost two years, Tom wouldn't be teaching, and his parents had decided to take the kids to Florida for a month to visit their biological grandparents, with whom they had a good, if distant, relationship.

After the kids got out of school, they would have just over a month of peace and quiet, with the house all to themselves. It was going to be a blissful time.

Tom sat up and gave Taylor a quick kiss. "Okay, you're right," he said, his responsible nature getting the best of him. "Dibs on the shower," he called, then made a break for the bathroom. Taylor chased after him, and by the time they were done, it would have been a miracle if anyone in the house could still be asleep.

Monday morning traffic into the city would be Taylor's undoing. He was certain of it. Every time he thought he'd found a way to free himself from it, somehow, like a plague, it worked its way back into his life.

That summer, five years ago, when he and Tom bought their house together, Taylor was just coming off the case that truly made his career. He had secured a sizable judgment against one of the larger companies in the country for a history of sexual harassment and discrimination. His personal cut had been more than enough to secure a comfortable living for Tom and himself. Instead of continuing to work for a large firm in the city, he got together with his long time friend, Pete Madson, and they bought out the town's only law firm, Heller Highwater, when John Heller wanted to retire.

At first, they'd taken only small cases of local interest, and Taylor hired a courtroom litigator to handle the cases he didn't want to argue himself. However, fame followed him and clients with higher profile cases came asking for his help. Just as life calmed down with Tom, things sped up for him.

The firm had grown to three associates and a paralegal, and Pete was thinking they should bring on at least one more associate and possibly promote the first to partner. For his part, Taylor had never wanted to be involved in such a large organization, and told Pete he was willing to largely defer to whatever he wanted to do. Taylor hoped his summer off would be enough to get the clients more comfortable with working with the other members of the team, all of whom Taylor had trained.

But that was the future. The present was a long line of cars moving just barely over sixty miles an hour, though the signs clearly said seventy was perfectly legal. Why people felt compelled to sit in the left lane driving under the speed limit was something he still could not fathom.

His cell phone rang in its cradle and the name appeared on the display in front of him, bringing an instant smile to his face. He tapped the Send button.

"Lady Genevieve!" he greeted.

"Sir Taylor," she replied. "You're unusually chipper this morning."

"It's this Monday traffic," he said. "You know how I enjoy it!"

Gen snickered. "Yes, I do. I can call back when your blood pressure's lower."

Taylor laughed. "No need. What's up?"

They had been best friends virtually since the day they met. It had been like meeting Tom—it just happened. It didn't have to make sense, it just *was*. Over the years, they had been each others' shoulder to cry on more times than Taylor cared to think about, and had always been there when the other needed a hand.

"Miguel and I have to go to the doctor today," she said. "Will you stop over and let Molly out?"

"Of course," Taylor said. "You can probably just drop her off when you're ready to go, if Donna's there."

"Thanks. I didn't want to impose."

"It's never an imposition," Taylor replied. "How are things going?"

Gen sighed. The past few months had been hard for her husband, Miguel, and her. Gen was coming up on thirty-five, as was Taylor, and had decided the year before that she would really like to have a child of her own. Though Taylor had generously offered a long term loan on one of theirs, she was pretty fixated on the idea. She and Miguel had begun working on the process in earnest, but they became concerned when nature didn't take its course. Gen's obstetrician referred them to a fertility specialist and they'd been under her care ever since.

"You know the old saying 'no news is good news?'" Gen asked.

"Yeah?"

"They're full of crap, those old sayings."

Taylor winced. He hated seeing his friend in pain. "Still nothing, huh?"

The car to his right cut sharply into his lane, nearly colliding with the front of his car. Of course, that meant the lane to the right began moving *faster* rather than slower. Mondays!

Gen continued. "They say there are still a few more things to try. They say not to give up hope. They say it can still happen."

"They say," Taylor intoned.

"Yeah."

"I'm really sorry it's been so hard," Taylor said, expressing his genuine thoughts.

"You wanna know what else has been hard?" Gen asked.

Taylor knew he was being set up. "What?"

"Planning this doggone Spring Dance. Honestly, Taylor, you said this job wasn't going to be a lot of work."

Taylor shrugged. "It wasn't a lot of work when I was Mayor."

"I'm on the phone for two hours a night, Connolly!"

"With *who?*" Taylor demanded.

"Everybody! Half the restaurants in town are catering, the other half want to. A half dozen musicians and DJs want to provide music. There's logistics for tents, tables, and chairs…it never ends!" Gen exclaimed.

"Where's Maggie?" Taylor asked. Maggie Florence was the town's administrative secretary, but had really been more like the assistant Mayor during Taylor's two terms as Mayor.

"She keeps saying she thinks these are decisions I should make," Gen said. "You did this to me, Taylor. I kept saying I thought you were doing a fine job as Mayor, but you guilted me into taking this job and now look where I'm at!"

"The town's first female mayor?"

"Oh no, you're not pulling that diversity crap with me. Any town that can elect a gay mayor isn't going to care a whit about having a woman, Counselor."

Taylor laughed in spite of himself. "Well, I can see there's just no winning this one."

"That's what you think," Gen countered. "I'm planning to nominate you at the next election."

"Don't you dare!"

She gave him her best evil laugh. "Oh yeah, Mr. It's-Not-So-Hard, it's your turn at bat again."

"And to think we were friends," Taylor complained.

Gen laughed. "We'll be friends again in about a half hour."

"Going to the bakery?"

"It's just not a Monday morning without a croissant."

"So true," Taylor agreed. Tom's croissants had achieved legendary status, with people driving for miles around to get them on the weekend. By popular demand, he'd finally agreed to make them himself one day a week, usually Saturday morning, to keep their regular customers satisfied. Truth be told, Taylor thought the other bakers' croissants were just as good, but it kept people happy and he knew Tom enjoyed it, too. They were usually able to find someone to watch the kids Saturday morning, allowing Taylor to keep up the tradition of coming in to work the counter, too. Though he hated to admit it, seeing everyone did make it worth the effort.

"I'll let you get back to driving," Gen said. "We'll pick up Molly this evening."

"You bet," Taylor agreed. "Have a good day, Madam Mayor."

"Next election," she said, "It's all about you!"

"Bye," Taylor moaned, hitting the end key.

He had to admit, talking Gen into running for Mayor had been a bit of a coup. The job was usually ceremonial—attend a few town functions, give a few speeches, plan a couple parties. But with all the other chaos that had entered his life, even the ceremonial tasks seemed a big burden. He'd talked Gen into taking over for him about six months before the next election, giving the town more than enough time to get comfortable with her in the role. In truth, he'd never heard of a contested election—quite simply, no one else wanted the job, either.

The traffic actually thinned as he got closer to the city, as more and more of the cars moved off to the various suburban business centers. Taylor had also never figured out what was so all-fired bad about "urban sprawl." Cities hated it, as it lowered their voter and tax base, but everyone else seemed more comfortable with communities spread out over the land. The only downside he could see was that the sprawling tended to happen faster than the roads could keep up...leading to Monday Morning Commutes from Hell.

The phone rang again, and the caller ID came up "Wayne." As with Gen, Wayne's name brought a smile to his face. The young man was, at alternate times, like a younger brother and a son, all wrapped up into one very kind, very caring person. Wayne so often told them how grateful he was that they had taken him in, but Taylor wondered if he could ever truly grasp how grateful they were to have him in their lives.

"Mornin', Wayne," Taylor greeted warmly.

"Hi, Tay," Wayne said. He'd taken to using Tom's nickname for him, usually referring to his younger "brother/nephew," Taylor Thomas, by his full name.

"How are you today?" Taylor asked.

"I'm good," Wayne answered. "On your way to court?"

"Yep. What's up?"

"Are you going to Tom's game tonight?" he asked. Since Taylor had known Tom, he had always coached a town little league team. Most weeks had games on Tuesdays or Thursdays, with alternating practices, but the previous Thursday had been rained out.

"Actually, Donna said she was going to take the kids and Tom's dad is going to join them there," Taylor said.

"Cool. I was wondering if you'd like to have dinner?"

"You buying?" Taylor asked, grinning. Wayne liked to buy them both dinner from time to time, as his way of saying thank you for what they did for him.

"Of course," Wayne replied. "I wouldn't ask you otherwise."

"Dinner sounds great. What time?"

"When will you be home?" Wayne almost always referred to their house simply as "home," a fact that made Taylor very happy. His own self-doubt left him feeling like he was intruding on their lives for a long time. Taylor had finally managed to convince him that he was a welcome—and permanent—part of their family, and he took it to heart.

"I shouldn't be very late," he said. "You want to shoot for six o'clock?"

"That sounds great," Wayne said.

"Where do you want to go?"

"Alberto's?"

Taylor laughed. The restaurant was like a second home to them. Alberto had become a good friend over the years and generally made them some home cooked specialty not even on the menu, unless they wanted something specific. Tom and Taylor always made sure to slip him a little extra in the check whenever they could.

"Alberto's at six. I'll see you there. Everything okay?" Taylor asked, sensing that Wayne was unusually quiet.

"Yeah, I just haven't gotten to see that much of you lately."

"Well, I'm all yours tonight," Taylor said.

"Lucky me," Wayne retorted. "I've gotta get to class. You know how that professor can be."

"And how. Tell him I said Hi."

"Will do." Wayne hung up the phone and Taylor turned his own phone off. Between Wayne and Gen, they'd talked him all the way to the courthouse. He collected his things and made his way up the steps, ready to get the day over with.

That evening, Taylor made it back in enough time to slip home and change out of his suit into a casual shirt and shorts. The weather had just picked up enough that it was becoming shorts season again, and he eagerly tossed aside the long pants and shoes of winter for shorts and sandals, always his preferred attire.

His day had gone as he expected it to, with all of his cases making virtually no progress. In truth, he could have sent one of the associates to handle the work, but it was a nice day and he'd enjoyed getting out of the office for a little while. One of the biggest problems with the firm's success was it was rapidly turning into a job, and that was the one thing he and Pete had hoped to avoid.

He got home just in time for a quick kiss from Tom before he headed off to the ball field. Tom's parents picked up the kids and were gone, too, even taking Molly with them. Taylor was left alone in a quiet house—had dinner been with anyone other than Wayne, he would have cancelled, just to enjoy it.

But dinner *was* with Wayne, and that was enough to keep him moving. Wayne continued to amaze and impress him as he rose to every challenge he faced and overcame it with a grace few people twice his age could manage. He ran the bakery as adroitly as Tom, while going to school full time, all the time.

Whenever Taylor asked him what he planned to do after graduation, it was the only time he could see concern in the young man's face. For the first time in his life, he was truly happy and Taylor knew he feared losing that happiness more than anything. Taylor went out of his way to reassure Wayne that he and Tom would be there for him, always.

At ten to six, Taylor left and walked the four blocks to Alberto's. As usual, Wayne was early and already had a table waiting for them.

"Taylor!" Alberto greeted as he entered the restaurant. "How are you, my friend?" His speech had just enough of an accent to reveal his Italian heritage, but not enough to make him hard to understand in the least.

"Wonderful, my friend," Taylor answered warmly, shaking the offered hand. "How are you?"

"Very well, sir, thank you," Alberto said. He led Taylor to a table in one corner of the restaurant where Wayne rose to greet him with a hug and kiss on the cheek.

As they sat, Alberto asked, "Menus this evening?"

Wayne looked to Taylor, who shook his head. To Alberto, Wayne said, "Whatever you think is good tonight."

"Chicken in a lemon pepper sauce?"

"Perfect," he said. Taylor smiled in spite of himself, having Wayne order for them both.

"To drink?" Alberto asked. Though Wayne had tried wine with them several times, he tended to shy away from alcohol, having grown up with an abusive alcoholic father. Tom and Taylor respected his feelings and never made an issue of it.

"I'm just having some ice water," Wayne said to Taylor, an invitation to have something else if he chose.

"Ice water sounds fine," Taylor said to both Wayne and Alberto.

"Coming right up!" Alberto announced with his usual cheer. He shuffled away, returning briefly with their glasses, then heading into the kitchen to prepare the meals.

"So how are you?" Taylor asked, his blue eyes catching Wayne's green ones. They'd known each other long enough, and were close enough, that he was sure there was something there, something he'd heard on the phone that morning.

Wayne knew Taylor could see it, too. That was part of the strength of their friendship, that they could read each other without words. Tom had often commented to Taylor that Wayne was lucky to have found him. Though Tom had actually hired Wayne and known him first, it was Taylor's calm assuredness that had drawn him in, and helped steady him even then.

"Eric called."

It was a simple response that spoke volumes. Their relationship had been fast, passionate, and seemingly unstoppable, as only first relationships could be. Though Eric was a year older than Wayne, they were both facing their inner demons at the same time. In many ways, their time together had been therapeutic for both, but Wayne had been very hurt when

Eric announced he wanted to go back to Ohio State, where he had been attending school with Tom's younger sister, Mandy.

"What did he have to say?" Taylor asked.

Wayne stared at his glass as he spoke, his face blank. "He said his graduation is this weekend and wanted to know if I wanted to come over."

Taylor nodded, listening. Though Eric had been the one to break off the relationship, he never quite seemed to want to let Wayne go. In truth, Taylor believed Eric's motivation was exactly what it seemed—he wanted to finish his degree at a Big Ten school, then see where things went with Wayne. It had been because he cared for Wayne that he tried living with him in town, only to discover he wasn't ready for that. While Taylor had to support Wayne publicly, he also understood Eric's side.

"What did you tell him?"

Wayne looked up, his expression a little hard. "I told him I have to work. Saturday is our biggest day."

Taylor rolled his eyes. "You know darned well we can cover for you on Saturday," he said.

Wayne looked back down. "I know. I didn't know how to answer," he admitted.

"What do you want to do?" Taylor asked.

"I don't know."

Taylor pondered the situation, as he broke off a piece of Alberto's homemade Italian bread and dipped it in the spiced olive oil and parmesan mixture. He watched Wayne's pained expression and remembered all the times of confusion in his own life, when he didn't know whether to hold his ground or give in to what he wanted and see where it took him.

"You've stayed in touch with him all this time," Taylor observed out loud, trying to help prompt Wayne's thoughts.

"Yeah," Wayne said, still staring off at nothing.

Taylor sighed. It wasn't going to be the easiest discussion. "*Why* have you stayed in touch?" he asked.

Wayne looked up. "I like him. He's a nice person."

"Okay," Taylor said, taking his turn to make Wayne say more.

"I mean, we've both dated other people," Wayne stumbled.

"Is he with anybody now?"

Wayne sighed. "No."

"Is that a good thing or a bad thing?" Taylor asked.

"I don't *know*," Wayne insisted. "That's the thing—is he asking me to come to his graduation as his friend, or because he wants something more?"

Taylor leaned in. "What does *Eric* say about that?"

"He didn't. Really. I mean, he just asked if I'd like to come to the ceremony."

Alberto brought their salads, setting them in place quietly, so as not to interrupt the conversation. Over the years, he had come to know a great deal about Wayne and his situation, and he recognized when Taylor was in counselor mode, helping his young friend along.

Taylor took a bite of the leafy salad, then gestured at Wayne with his fork. "Who else did he invite?"

Wayne moved his salad around with his fork, not really paying attention to eating. "He said his parents would be there."

"Anyone else?"

Shaking his head, Wayne answered, "I don't know."

"Why would he invite *you*?" Taylor inquired.

"What do you mean?" Wayne replied, confused.

"I mean, why would Eric invite *you*? Why would he want *you* there?"

"We're friends."

"Did he invite any of his other friends?"

Again, Wayne shook his head. "I don't know. He didn't say."

Taylor nodded. "Do you think he would have said if he had?"

"Probably," Wayne admitted.

"So you're the only *friend* he wants there," Taylor concluded.

"I guess."

"And he went out of his way to invite you," Taylor added.

"Yeah."

Taylor sighed. "Wayne, do you think Eric still cares about you?"

Wayne took a big forkful of salad, chewing slowly as he considered his answer to Taylor's question. Taylor sipped from his glass, letting Wayne think. To him, the answer was fairly obvious, at least as far as Eric was concerned, but the bigger question was what Wayne wanted and how he wanted to approach the situation.

"Yeah, I think he still cares about me," he admitted finally.

And the big question, "Do you still care about him?"

Sadness descended into Wayne's eyes, and the answer was obvious, even before he said yes. Taylor reached out across the table to gently rest his hand on Wayne's.

"The decision is up to you. If you want, you can at least go as a friend, in support of your friend. It may go somewhere from there, it may not...but at least you won't be left wondering."

Wayne looked up, pain in his eyes. "I don't want to be hurt again," he admitted.

Taylor smiled, a little sadly. "That's always the chance you take. You have to put your heart out there, and see if the other person covets it or gives you use for it."

"What would you do?" Wayne turned the tables on him, forcing him to admit his own thoughts on the situation.

Taylor sighed. "Part of me would probably be stubborn, like you were when you told him you had to work. But if there really is something there, or if you really *think* there might be something there...I wouldn't want the doubt gnawing at me later."

Wayne looked away, his eyes distant for a moment. Then, with a deep breath, he turned back to Taylor. "I guess I'm going to need the weekend off."

"We need at least two weeks' notice for vacation," Taylor said with a perfectly straight face. Wayne grabbed Taylor's hand in his fist, and Taylor laughed, pulling back. "Or maybe we could make an exception this time," he said.

Wayne's mood perceptibly brightened, the weight lifted from his shoulders, and they shared the rest of their dinner together in peace. As they left, Taylor almost missed the slight breeze that touched his face, a subtle metaphor for what was to come.

CHAPTER TWO

Open Lines of Communication

With most of the staff consisting of college students Wayne's age, the bakery had to make some adjustments during finals week. Wayne actually managed to finish his finals early in the week, so he took over the morning baking responsibilities to give others time to study. Tom's schedule also allowed him greater flexibility, as he only had one final left to give that afternoon, so he joined Wayne in baking, and then let him go out and run the store while he kept the ovens full.

Thursdays were one of the busier days of the week, as people came in to buy baked goods for the weekend. Wayne initially felt guilty about leaving for the weekend, but Tom told him it was high time he took a break. Since starting college, the only time off he had was the week to two-week space between semesters. While Tom and Taylor both appreciated his diligence, they were also concerned that he would burn out.

To help cover the rush, Wayne asked his roommate, Emmy's boyfriend, Dan, to come in that morning. With school letting out, there was an above average number of students getting a quick meal on their way to study, but it tapered off as the clock reached nine, with most of them in exams.

At last getting a break, the boys took the opportunity to tidy the shelves and restock the display cabinets.

"I wish you'd reconsider going rafting," Dan complained, filling the bagel bins like the pro he had become. After high school, most of Emmy and Wayne's friends took jobs in the bakery, recognizing the great atmosphere when they saw it. Tom and Taylor were very forgiving employers, a trait they had passed on to Wayne as he took over more management responsibilities.

"It's not that I don't want to," Wayne explained again. "I'd miss the first two days of classes."

"You could make them up later," Dan suggested. "How many more opportunities like this will you get?"

"I'm only twenty years old!" Wayne protested. "I'd like to think there might be one or two more in my future."

"Maybe, but this one is here now."

Wayne piled the empty sheets back on the rack. "Classes are here now. Rafting can come next year. I should be done by then anyway."

Dan shook his head. "You're the only guy I know who will have done his undergrad in three years."

"Eric did his in three years," Wayne defended, then looked away. Dan had been a very supportive friend throughout the turmoil that followed Eric's departure, even agreeing to share the apartment with Wayne. But he had also often wondered over the connection the two continued to share. Dan, like everyone else in their circle, liked Eric, but thought it odd that the two stayed in contact while remaining so cool toward each other.

Before Dan could counter, the door opened and a customer walked in. They looked up to see Peggy, the owner of the flower boutique next door, smiling back.

"Good morning!" she greeted. "I thought I'd wait for the rush to die down before I came in."

"No problem, Peggy," Wayne said. "What can I get for you?"

"How 'bout a cinnamon roll and a coffee?"

"Coming right up," Wayne said. Dan went to fill a cup while Wayne put a roll in a bag for her. "What's new next door?" he asked, making conversation.

"Actually, I'm moving," Peggy said. "I got a great offer on a space in the new development out by the freeway."

"Moving?" Wayne repeated. "Why would you want to move out there?"

Peggy shrugged. "I couldn't pass up the deal," she explained. "I guess the developer is trying to buy up space in the downtown area to allow him to install national chain stores here. He thinks it'll be better for business."

"But the whole point of the historic district is to preserve the sort of unique stores that old downtowns usually have," Dan argued, handing her the coffee cup.

Peggy put up her hands. "Trust me, I know. But business is business and I couldn't pass up the lease offer they made. They're even paying for the move."

Dan wasn't so easily convinced, his journalist's sense that a story was brewing kicking in. "Seems like they want your spot awfully bad. Did they make you a fair offer on the space?"

Peggy shook her head. "I don't own the building, I just rent. I don't know what they're doing about the space."

"Who is the real estate developer?" Dan asked.

"Stuart DiNardo is who I rented my new space from," Peggy said.

"DiNardo…" Wayne said. He turned to Dan. "Isn't he the one who's been on the news lately?"

"The 'Liquid Landlord,'" Dan quoted. "They call him that because nothing sticks to him."

Tom came out from the baking room, dusting himself off. "Did I hear you say you're moving?"

"Yep," Peggy confirmed. "I got a great deal on a space out in the new development."

"Stuart DiNardo?" Tom asked.

"Yeah," she confirmed again.

Tom nodded. "He's been trying to make inroads downtown for the last year and a half. He bought up the old five and dime next to Alberto's. No one knows what he plans to do yet, but he's been giving Gen a run for her money as she tries to keep the chain stores out of the historic district."

"I felt bad to give in, but times have been tight and I didn't feel like I had a choice," Peggy defended.

"You've gotta do what makes sense for you," Tom agreed. "No one can fault you for that."

She turned to go. "I should get back to the shop. They're moving me in about two weeks."

"Hope it works out well," Tom said, genuinely meaning it.

"Me too," she said, then walked out.

"Well what do you think about that?" Tom said, turning to the other two.

Dan didn't hesitate. "Stuart DiNardo is a crook. My uncle had some dealings with him and the man is just slimy."

"There goes the neighborhood," Wayne said.

"Maybe," Tom said. He turned and headed toward the back door.

Unlike his beloved baker, Taylor's Thursday mornings were often quiet, unless he had to be in court. He often used them to catch up on small tasks, knowing the end of the week was only a day away and then he was free...more or less.

Their office assistant, or "administrator," as she liked to be called, usually had his desk completely organized by the time he came in. Taylor found it remarkable that she was so good at keeping the office in order, since she seemed to be in complete disarray herself most of the time. She fit the stereotype of the blonde secretary perfectly, except she actually *did* manage to do her job.

Taylor yawned broadly as he reviewed the same document for the fourth time. It had been a long week and he really was just looking forward to the weekend. With Wayne gone, they just had the three little kids to entertain.

His phone beeped, giving him a perfect excuse to finally put the pages down. "Yes?"

"Tom's on line two for you."

"Thanks, Christy," he said, pressing the line button. "Hi there," he greeted.

"Hi," Tom said. His voice was staticky and hard to understand.

"Are you on your cell phone?"

"Yeah, I'm standing outside right now."

"Where?" Taylor asked, bringing his mind back into focus.

"Out back, at the bakery."

"Why?"

"Peggy was just over," Tom said, the signal getting a little clearer. "She's moving."

Taylor's eyebrows rose. "Really? Where's she going?"

"The Pit of Prosperity." Taylor didn't remember who had first coined the phrase, but it flourished among their friends and family. The official name of the development was Prosperity Point, but it had degenerated to Prosperity Pit, and then finally the Pit of Prosperity.

"Why on Earth would she want to move out there?" Taylor asked.

"DiNardo is paying for the move," Tom said. "She didn't say what else he's doing, but it's pretty clear he just wanted to get her out of the way."

Taylor frowned. He and Gen had both taken turns battling him during their respective terms as Mayor. Stuart DiNardo had a reputation for being very aggressive and ruthless in progressing whatever agenda he had at any given time. He'd approached Tom on several occasions about buying the bakery space, making similar offers of very low rent in one of his developments. Neither Tom nor Taylor had any interest in leaving the downtown area, but that wouldn't deflect a man like DiNardo.

"So she already sold him the building," Taylor said.

"No, that's just it. She doesn't *own* the building," Tom said.

Leaning forward, Taylor rested his elbows on the edge of his desk. "Who does own it?"

"She didn't say. I only came into the conversation at the end. She was talking to Wayne and Dan," Tom explained. "Pete works with real estate, doesn't he? You guys can find out who the current owner is, can't you?"

Taylor nodded to himself. "Sure we can. But what difference does that make?"

There was a pause on the other end, then Tom continued. "I don't know. Call it curiosity. Why don't you see what you can dig up?"

Though he really couldn't imagine what good it would do them to know who owned the property at present, Taylor promised he'd find out.

"Thanks, Tay," Tom said, his voice soft as it was only for Taylor.

There was a knock on the door and Taylor called the person in.

"Is that Tom still on the phone?" Pete asked, peering into Taylor's office.

"Yeah," Taylor confirmed.

"Anita wanted to know if you guys would like to bring the kids over for burgers tonight."

Taylor listened to the voice in the phone, then looked up, nodding. "Tom says we'd love to."

"Great!" Pete acknowledged. "Gen and Miguel are coming, too."

"Quite a party," Taylor observed, still listening to Tom with one ear. Into the phone he said, "Yes, I'll ask in a minute. Let me call you back. Yes. I know. Let me call you back. Tommy! Goodbye." He hit the release key and took off his headset.

"Isn't being married fun?" Pete asked, seating himself opposite Taylor.

"A daily treat," Taylor affirmed. "Do you have time to find out some information on a property for me?"

Pete nodded. "Sure. Which one?"

Taylor wrote the address on a piece of paper and handed it across the desk. "Tom just said Stuart DiNardo is trying to make another move into town. He got the flower shop to move. However, the woman who owns the shop doesn't own the building. Tom wants to know who does."

Pete looked dubious. "Why?"

Taylor sighed, shaking his head. "I can only guess. Maybe he just wants to see if he can talk the other owner out of selling."

"It was my understanding all of you who owned property on Main Street had been presenting a pretty united front," Pete observed.

"That was pretty much true, until Mr. Monroe sold the place next to Alberto last year. Since then, DiNardo has been at everyone in town like a mosquito in a blood bank."

Pete frowned. "Why is he so hot to have the downtown?"

Taylor shrugged. "My best guess is he owns or developed most of the new stuff on the north end. He probably wants to create a monopoly. If he brings in chains and franchises, he can lease everything out and increase traffic in both locations."

"And put all the small stores out of business in the process."

Taylor nodded. "It's been working for years."

Pete stood. "We'll just have to see if there is something we can do about it."

Taylor chuckled. "Don't hold your breath."

Wayne tossed his heavily laden bag in the back seat of his Jeep, then picked up the small cooler he'd packed and put it in the passenger area next to his seat. Though he was only going to be gone for a couple of days, he'd tried to think ahead and put anything he might need in the Jeep so there wouldn't be any surprises.

"You've got plenty of money?" Tom asked, still wearing his apron in the parking lot behind the bakery. Dan had helped Wayne carry everything down from their shared apartment over the bakery, then retreated inside.

"Yeah, I stopped and got a little extra last night," Wayne confirmed.

"And maps?" Tom asked. "Maps for the whole trip?"

Wayne nodded, a little patronizingly. "Yes, I have maps."

"And you'll call us, when you get there, so we know you're safe?" Tom prompted.

This time, Wayne rolled his eyes. "*Yes*, I'll call. Will you stop worrying? You're worse than Taylor!"

Tom frowned. "Nobody is worse than Taylor. I wonder where he is?"

As though hearing the question, Taylor's black BMW X5 screeched into the parking lot from Second Street. He pulled into the empty spot beside Wayne's Jeep and jumped out.

"Whew!" he breathed. "I was afraid I'd miss you!"

"You're both obsessive," Wayne objected. "It's just a short trip. I've gone away before."

"Well…*yeah*…" Tom defended, looking to Taylor.

"You're our little boy, all grown up," Taylor said.

"Oh, for God's sake," Wayne sighed. "I'm leaving now."

Taylor reached for his wallet. "Do you have enough money? Here, take a little more."

Wayne pushed his hand away. "I am *not* taking your money."

Folding the bills, Taylor slid them into Wayne's shirt pocket. "You can always use a little more. Buy dinner for him or something. What about maps?" Taylor asked.

"Okay, that's it," Wayne said. He reached over and pulled Tom into a hug, giving him a peck on the cheek, then did the same with Taylor. Before they could say anything more, he hopped into his Jeep and started the engine.

"Don't forget to call when you get there," Taylor reminded him. "Even if it's late."

Wayne shook his head. "Did you two script this or something?"

"What?" Taylor asked, confused. Tom slid an arm around his waist as Wayne backed out, and they waved as he pulled away, watching him until he made the turn around the corner and was gone.

"They grow up so fast," Taylor said, still watching the empty road.

"Oh, come on," Tom said, taking his hand to lead him back into the store. "Did you find out anything about the owner of Peggy's place?" he asked as they made their way down the hall to the front.

"Not yet," Taylor said, plucking a donut from one of the baking racks as he passed. "Pete is working on it now, trying to search the county title records."

Emmy had come in to work the afternoon shift. She looked up and gave Taylor a little wave as she helped the customer on the other side of the counter.

"Why do you want to know so bad, anyway?" Taylor asked, taking a milk from the refrigerator.

Tom shrugged. "Just curiosity. If the flower shop's moving, the owner must already know. If Stuart DiNardo is making a move right next to us, I'd rather know now."

"The flower shop is moving?"

Tom and Taylor both stopped as they realized they were being overheard. The person standing on the other side of the counter watched them closely, awaiting an answer.

"Yes, that's what we were told today," Tom said, a little hesitantly.

"Huh," he said, taking his bag and his change from Emmy. "I hadn't heard anything about that."

Taylor and Tom exchanged glances, each wondering if the other knew who the young man was. Finally, Taylor asked, "Is there a reason you would have heard about it?"

The man on the other side of the counter looked to be about the same age as Tom, with similar medium-brown hair, and brown eyes. He wore a simple blue T-shirt and cargo shorts, and held the brown paper bag in the crook of his arm. He suddenly realized his mistake as he saw the faces of everyone watching him. He broke into a slightly embarrassed grin and held out a hand to Taylor. "Sorry," he said. "My name is Jason Harper. My grandfather owns the space next door."

Tom perked up. "Harper?" he asked. "I don't know anyone in town with that name."

Jason nodded. "It's my dad's name. Grandpa Olsen is my mom's dad."

Taylor stared, incredulous. *"Olsen?"* he asked. "Lives on Second Street, about four blocks from here?"

"Yeah," Jason said, smiling. "You know him?"

"He's our next door neighbor!" Tom exclaimed.

Jason's eyebrows shot up. "Really? Oh!" he laughed. "You must be the two guys he's told me about!"

At that they both blanched, wondering what Mr. Olsen might have said. "Probably," Tom admitted.

Jason shook his head, waving a hand. "No no, nothing bad. Actually, he thinks a lot of you guys. He kept telling me I should drop in and say hello, since we're neighbors, too."

"We are?" Taylor asked.

"Yeah, I live in the apartment above the flower shop."

"Really?" Tom inquired, surprised. "I never realized anyone was up there."

"I've been there for about seven months," Jason explained. "I moved here to help out my grandfather, and because I'd always really liked this town when I was growing up. The rest of the family lives so far away, it didn't seem right to have him here by himself."

"That's sweet," Emmy chimed in, cleaning one of the display cases.

Jason continued. "He kept telling me I should stop in here, but every time I did, you weren't here."

"We both have jobs other than the bakery, so our friends run the place most of the time," Taylor said, with a nod to Emmy.

Tom put a hand on Taylor's arm, interrupting. "So your grandfather owns the shop?"

"Well, not the shop, but the building," Jason said, setting his bag on the counter. "I guess he and my great-grandfather had some kind of store there years ago, and when they decided to shut it down, he just started renting out the space. The apartment used to be offices, but he let me convert it so I could be in town without having to commit to a house."

"And he doesn't know the flower shop is leaving?" Tom continued.

Jason shrugged, leaning lightly on one of the cabinets. "I don't know. If he does, he hasn't said anything to me about it."

Tom was on the case, and Taylor smiled as he watched him. For all his calm, relaxed demeanor, when he wanted information, he was like a pit bull. Taylor knew it was that tenacity that allowed him to have done so much in such a short time.

"Does the name Stuart DiNardo ring any bells?" Tom asked, positively interrogating their newly discovered neighbor.

Jason shook his head. "Never heard of him. Who is he?"

"He's the developer who coaxed Peggy into moving her flower shop."

"Oh," Jason said.

"We think he might be trying to buy up property here in downtown."

"Oh," Jason said again, this time with more melancholy. He looked down, as though realizing that any such transaction might significantly affect his living conditions. He looked up again. "I'll tell you what—let me check with Grandpa and I'll let you know. I was going to meet him for dinner tonight anyway," he said, picking up his bag again. "Will you be home this evening?"

Tom shook his head. "We're meeting some friends for dinner. You're welcome to come by in the morning, though. Have a croissant on the house."

Jason brightened at that. "Those things are really good," he said. "But I have to fly out of town tomorrow morning. I have to leave for the airport around eight."

"We open at seven," Tom countered.

"Tomorrow it is, then," Jason said, laughing. "I'll see you then."

They bid him good night and he headed back out to the street. Taylor turned to Tom a question on his face.

"What are you planning?" he asked.

"Planning? Me?" Tom asked with mock innocence. He headed for the baking room just in time to avoid Taylor's reach.

That evening, they met Gen and Miguel at Pete and Anita's. Pete and Taylor were working the grill, arguing over who had better grilling technique, while Miguel sat with Tom, discussing Tom's little league team's recent success. Gen and Anita were chasing the kids and Molly around the yard, waiting for dinner to be done.

All four of their friends had been a godsend in helping raise Tom and Taylor's three "orphan" children. They had all been friends of John and Sandy, the kids' biological parents, and had all taken turns helping the two often clueless men in the raising of their charges. Tom and Taylor had been particularly thankful for the positive female role model the two women were offering for Wendy.

The evening was perfect for grilling—just cool enough that the kids were in light jackets, but warm enough that Taylor got away with wearing shorts. Dusk was already slowing in its daily visit, with the sun keeping it at bay ever longer with each passing day. Overhead, a couple of puffy clouds dotted the sky, picking up the glowing yellow light as the sun crept lower on the horizon.

Pete and Anita had chosen to buy a house in the same neighborhood as Tom and Taylor, and Gen and Miguel, and wound up with one on the same street. They quickly became as much of a staple in the community as their friends, learning that everyone knew everyone else and it was easier to go with the flow than to resist.

The first summer they lived there, Pete talked Taylor into helping him build a deck. Once the project started, Pete discovered that it was actually Tom who was far more adept with a hammer, but Taylor made great sun tea and lemonade. Pete still liked to point out "the board that Taylor laid." It was perfect, down to all the screw heads being perfectly aligned. He would then point out the five boards he and Tom had put down while Taylor got his board just right.

At the grill, on the top tier of the three-tiered "homage to male ego," as Anita often called the deck, Taylor had the tongs and Pete had the spatula, with Taylor working the chicken while Pete had the meat. At last, they turned and called everyone to the table, piling plates high with barbequed food.

Anita and Tom got the kids situated at the small table the hosts had bought for just that purpose while Gen and Miguel brought the other plates out from the house. Within minutes, everyone was seated and chewing away.

"So, Tom," Pete started, "what's the story with the store next door to you?"

"What do you mean?" Tom asked, gnawing away at a corncob.

"Why are you so hot to know who owns it?"

Tom shrugged. "I figured if we know who owns it, we'll have a better idea of whether or not that person will sell." He gestured to Taylor. "Did you guys talk about the guy we met at the bakery?"

"Yes," Taylor confirmed. "Pete just confirmed what Jason already told us. Mr. Olsen owns the space and has since his own father died thirty years ago."

"Someone is trying to buy the flower shop?" Anita asked, trying to come up to speed on the discussion.

Gen looked up sharply, lowering her fork back down to the plate. "Don't tell me," she said.

"Oh, yes," Taylor affirmed.

"Argh!" Gen growled, slamming her hands on the table with unusual force, causing the other diners to jump.

Chad looked up, wide-eyed, from where the kids were seated and called out, "Aunt Gen, are you okay?"

Gen looked over to him with a nod. "It's okay, honey. Just eat your dinner." Turning back to the other surprised faces watching her, she continued.

"Stuart DiNardo." Her face wrinkled into an uncommon sneer as she said his name. "That man has been a thorn in the side of every member of the town council. He calls us constantly, wanting information about property, ordinances, zoning…it never ends. His mission in life is to bring national chain stores to the historic district, to 'redevelop' it and 'modernize' it. Taylor knows what I'm talking about," she said, gesturing to her friend.

Taylor concurred, building on Gen's comments. "I only had to deal with him for a short time before Gen took over, but I found him to be abrasive, confrontational, and downright rude. He seems to think if he just keeps barking long enough, he'll get what he wants."

"All it will take is for him to push one of his stores into the downtown district," Tom added, "and the momentum will take off. We'll all wind up with our stores in Stuart DiNardo developments."

Miguel shook his head. "At first, it might seem to make good financial sense, getting all that up front money on the property sale, but most of the businesses downtown have been there for *decades*. Over a term like that, leasing makes no sense at all."

"Exactly," Taylor agreed. "But most of the people downtown need that money for their livelihood, and for their children's livelihood. It's hard to stare down a big lump-sum check when you have kids to put through college."

"I can understand that," Pete said, raising his glass.

Taylor wrinkled his nose, turning to his friend. "How can *you* understand that?"

"Worrying about having to put kids through college?" Pete asked, eyeing Anita.

She smiled broadly in return and gave a small simple nod, which Pete turned back to her. Taking a breath, Anita spoke. "Part of the reason we invited you all here tonight was to share some news we received today."

The guests all sat up, already anticipating what Anita would say and they weren't disappointed. "I'm pregnant!"

Tom and Taylor quickly offered their congratulations, patting Pete on the back and smiling. It was obvious, however, that Gen and Miguel weren't quite as enthused. For once, Gen seemed speechless and Taylor saw a tear escape from her eye as she quickly excused herself from the table.

"What—" Pete started to ask.

Miguel started to rise to go after her, but Taylor was already on his feet, so instead he turned to explain.

"We got some news today too, I'm afraid," he said softly, lowering himself back into his chair, still a little shocked himself. He looked up, his dark eyes a little darker as he spoke. "Gen and I have been trying to get pregnant for the last few months…"

Around the side of the house, out of sight of everyone else, Gen wept, holding a hand to her face. Taylor handed her a napkin from the table, holding her as she sobbed.

"Could this day get any worse?" she cried. "First the doctor tells us it didn't take, then *Stuart DiNardo* surfaces again, and now I just wrecked the best day of Pete and Anita's life!"

Taylor chuckled at the idea that Stuart DiNardo's plans made it into the list of bad things, but it was the last item that he was concerned with the most. "You did not wreck their day, sweetie," he said gently. "They didn't know what you and Miguel have been going through. Now that they do, they'll understand."

"It's not their job to understand," Gen insisted. "This is the best day of their lives and I break into tears!"

Taylor laughed. "Genevieve, leave it to you to still be more worried about your friends," he said, smiling. "Did it occur to you that they might be worried about you, too?"

"That's why I didn't say anything," she sobbed.

"Gen, you're an amazing, supportive person, but part of being friends is letting them support you, too," he reminded her.

She dabbed at her eyes, getting what little makeup she wore out of them. "I hate being a burden."

Taylor smiled. "So does everyone else, but it's the price of being human. Do you think Tom and I like it when everyone has to help with the kids? Of course not. But without all of you, our lives would be a mess."

"It's the least we can do," Gen said. "You guys stepped up and took responsibility for them when John and Sandy died. We were their friends, too. We had to help."

Taylor nodded. "I know and that's my point. Friends help. When it's your turn to be helped, be thankful they can be there for you."

"But I hate putting on a show," Gen objected. "All these damn *hormones* have just turned me into a mess!"

Taylor laughed openly at that. "Who better than a pregnant woman and her husband to understand hormone problems!?"

Gen laughed in spite of herself. "You always keep things in perspective," she said, falling into his arms again.

"You do the same thing for me," Taylor told her. "Remember who brought me to this town in the first place."

Gen nodded. "I am pretty cool like that," she said, laughing through her sobs.

Anita and Miguel came around the side of the house, looking for them. When Gen saw Anita, she went over and hugged her tight.

"I'm so sorry to act like this on a night like tonight," she said.

Anita just shook her head and held Gen. "I'm sorry you didn't tell us so *we* could be there for *you*," she insisted. "Are you okay?"

Wiping her eyes, Gen nodded. "Yeah, I'm fine," she said. "And I am very happy for you."

"Thank you," Anita said. "I really appreciate it." She gestured toward the back of the house. "Feel like finishing dinner?"

Gen brightened, laughing through her sadness. "Of course."

As they walked back, Miguel put an arm around her and kissed her cheek. At the table, Pete rose to offer his own apologies, while the kids all came up to see what was wrong. Gen looked up at Taylor, who just nodded and smiled as she let her friends—her family—support her.

CHAPTER THREE

An Idea

Taylor awoke in the dark to absolute silence. The darkness surprised him—he usually slept through the night. As he rolled over to check the clock, he realized the problem—he was the only one in the bed. With a little moan, he ignored the clock and just let his head fall back on the pillow.

When he told Tom that Wayne was going to Eric's graduation ceremony, they decided it was a good opportunity for him to get away for a few days. There was no doubt they appreciated Wayne's attention to his responsibilities, but they agreed sometimes he was just *too* responsible for someone his age. So they made sure he would take the whole weekend, and take his time coming back, by telling him they'd cover him through Monday.

Covering the weekend wasn't such a big deal. Tom usually went in on Saturday mornings, and they didn't open until nine-thirty on Sundays, just in time for all the godless residents to slip in ahead of the church-goers who showed up just after ten. Taylor had actually laughed out loud when one of the more religious members of the town implied that they should keep the doors closed until the church let out to give everyone an equal shot. Taylor said everyone *had* an equal shot, at nine-thirty.

But, with school out, Tom was once again cycling himself into the baking responsibilities in the morning. Taylor really couldn't complain too much—he knew Tom just enjoyed doing it once in a while. Well, he wouldn't complain as long as it stayed "once in a while."

The biggest downside was he inevitably woke up early when Tom wasn't there. Tom was always very considerate, even showering in the bathroom down the hall to not wake him, but Taylor just missed having Tom beside him.

He tossed and turned, catching sight of the clock every now and then. He had nothing he needed to do that morning, but Tom's mom wouldn't be over to watch the kids until seven, so he couldn't leave.

Finally, he gave up and got up, making his way to the bathroom for a quick shower and to prepare for the day. Fifteen short minutes later, he was dressed, the bed was made, clothes in the hamper, and general disarray gone. He stood in front of the closet, arms crossed over his chest, back against the doors. Felix the cat had already taken his usual perch on the corner of the bed and was already giving Taylor the "I-Dare-You-To-Touch-Me" glare. Another normal day in his house—his work there was done.

In the hall, he crept quietly toward the back stairs, heading for the kitchen, when he heard a voice behind him.

"Dad?" Chad stood at the other end of the hall rubbing his eyes, still wearing the T-shirt and shorts he'd worn to bed. "Where are you going?"

"Dad Tom had to go to work early today to cover for Wayne, so I'm up early. I was just going to the kitchen."

"Can I come with you?" Chad asked. He was still squinting in the light, but had already started walking toward Taylor.

"Wouldn't you rather get some more sleep? You have to go to school today."

"No," Chad said simply, answering the question. He held up his arms and Taylor picked him up. Chad immediately wrapped his arms around Taylor's neck and his legs around his waist, burrowing his head in under Taylor's chin. Together, they made their way downstairs to the kitchen.

Taylor went to put him down and felt him limp in his arms— Chad had fallen back asleep. Passing through the kitchen and dining room, he went into the living room and laid Chad on the sofa, then put one of Tom's mom's homemade afghans over him.

He marveled at how much Chad looked like his parents, but also bore at least a little resemblance to his adoptive parents. Though there was no biological connection between them, Chad's parents had coloring and features similar enough to Taylor and Tom that all three of the kids looked as though they could be their own. Taylor hoped it would make the inevitable adjustments they would face as they got older somehow easier.

Taylor turned on the TV to see what the news had to say.

"In local news yesterday," the anchor announced, "real estate developer Stuart DiNardo broke ground on a new shopping mall in the town of Springfield. The new mall is anticipated to bring over a hundred new stores to the area, and hundreds of jobs. Asked how he felt about the new development, Springfield's mayor said he hoped it would draw more attention to the growing community..."

Taylor rolled his eyes. Leave it to Springfield to actually *want* DiNardo there. He understood the various economic arguments in favor of development, but experience said that they rarely played out. There may be some initial interest, maybe even for a few years, but when the novelty wore off, so did the interest.

The surrounding communities, particularly those closer to the city, were littered with empty shopping areas that had once thronged with visitors. Why did they need another one? What about the ones that were already empty? Of course, DiNardo made most of his money in the initial development and rent stage. He would sell the places off to other companies before the initial leases ran out and the existing tenants moved to other locations—usually sponsored by Stuart DiNardo! Why didn't anyone ever see his duplicity?

At six-thirty, there was a tap on the front door, and Taylor heard the sound of a key unlocking it. He got up and turned on a light as Tom's mom came in.

"Morning, Taylor," she greeted.

"Hi, Mom," he said. He and Tom had both agreed to just call their parents Mom and Dad when they first got together. Tom commented once that Taylor's Mom seemed less comfortable with the decision and Taylor replied by saying he wasn't sure she liked *him* calling her "Mom."

"I figured you'd be up," she whispered. "Tommy said he was going in early."

Taylor nodded, guilty as charged. "I was planning to go see him on my way in."

Donna smiled. "You're free to go. How come Chad is on the sofa?"

"He woke up when I did and wanted to come downstairs with me. He fell asleep before we got to the kitchen."

"He likes to be where you are," she observed.

Taylor smiled. "Works for me."

She gestured toward the kitchen. "You go ahead and go. Tell my son I'd like some dinner rolls when he comes home."

"Will do," Taylor said. He leaned over to give her a kiss on the cheek, then picked up his briefcase and made his way out to his car.

The town was already starting to move, even at such an early hour. He'd made enough drives into the city on Monday morning to know why—leave any later than seven o'clock and it was a physical impossibility to be there before eight, the fact that it was only a half-hour drive notwithstanding.

He looked over to find the lights already on in the bakery as he drove around back to park. Since they actually owned the place, they all tried to remember to park around back to leave the street parking open for customers. Tom tended to unlock the doors as soon as the cabinets started to fill, an invitation to customers to come in at their own leisure. Sure enough, he heard Dan already making sales out front as he came in the back.

Tom peeked his head out the door of the baking room when he heard the back alarm beep. His face broke into the Taylor Smile as soon as he betook his spouse.

"You're up early," he observed.

"Couldn't sleep," Taylor said, leaning in to kiss him without getting flour all over his work clothes.

"Sorry," Tom said, meaning it. "Mom made it over early?"

"Yeah," Taylor said. "She said you told her I'd be up."

Tom smiled again. "After five years, I've figured out that much at least."

Taylor snapped his fingers. "Oh, before I forget, your mom wants a bag of dinner rolls."

"No problem," Tom said, walking back into the baking room. "You just missed Mr. Olsen's grandson."

"Jason? What did he have to say?"

"He got an earlier flight, so he was heading to the airport."

Taylor rolled his eyes. "I mean, about the *store.*"

"Oh, right," Tom said, kneading bread dough. "As we suspected, DiNardo is trying to get him to sell."

"Crap," Taylor sighed. "That's the last thing we need."

"I know," Tom agreed.

"Hi, guys." Wayne came up behind Taylor and wrapped his arms around him in greeting. Taylor turned to find him dressed for work.

"What are you doing here?"

"I got in early," he said.

Tom turned from the bread to Wayne. "You were supposed to have the day off," he said.

Wayne nodded. "I just felt like getting back to work."

Taylor frowned, watching him. "How did things go with Eric?"

At that, Wayne's smile weakened and looked more forced. In an instant, he looked more like the sad kid they'd taken in a couple of years before. "We just kind of hung out for a while. His parents were around most of the time, so we really couldn't talk much," he said more quietly.

"I'm sorry, kiddo," Taylor said, putting an arm on his shoulder.

"It's no big deal," Wayne said. He looked up again. "I'm just ready to get back to work."

Tom nodded. "Okay, then. Wash up and then you can start getting this dough into pans and let it rise. It's supposed to rain this afternoon, so we'll probably get a little more traffic."

"More traffic when it rains?" Wayne asked.

"People don't want to cook for themselves," Tom explained.

"How about people who don't want to get wet?" Taylor asked.

Tom slapped him in the stomach. "Don't be difficult. Come on, since Wayne is here, I can take a break and have something to eat with you."

"I'll be right there," Taylor acknowledged. Tom walked out front, leaving him with Wayne. "Are you really okay?" he asked, still with his arm around his shoulder.

Wayne nodded. "I'm okay, Tay. I don't know what I expected. He just wanted me there, so I was there."

"Okay. I'm around if you need me."

"I know," Wayne said, smiling to him. "Now get out of here before you get flour on your clothes."

Taylor walked out front to see a steady stream of customers already making their way in and out. Emmy and Dan were holding down the fort, filling orders, and then filling the cabinets when the customers had all been helped. Tom shifted a couple of rolling racks out of their way, then took a croissant for Taylor and a bagel for himself.

"Milk?" Taylor asked, reaching into the 'fridge.

"Yeah, that's fine," Tom said.

They went and sat at one of the small tables by the window, watching as dawn broke over the town. Sure enough, the sky was overcast and looked like it might rain. Taylor noticed the meal choices Tom had made for them and gave him a quizzical look.

"Isn't this backward?" he asked.

Tom shrugged, biting into his bagel. "I'm trying to be a little more healthy, and you could use a couple of pounds," he explained.

Taylor looked down at his body. "You think I'm too *thin*?"

"I could see your ribs last night."

"What's wrong with that?"

Tom took another bite. "I could see them *clearly*. Eat."

Grudgingly, Taylor bit into the chocolate delicacy. In seconds, all objections were done. "So, what did Jason have to say about Mr. Olsen?"

"Apparently, DiNardo started in on him about six months ago," Tom said.

"About the same time he started filling Prosperity Pit," Taylor observed.

"You've got it," Tom agreed. "He started in on Mr. Olsen, then went after Peggy, figuring if he got rid of the renter, Olsen would be less likely to want the building."

"But he didn't know Olsen's grandson was in the apartment upstairs."

"Bummer that," Tom said. He sipped his milk while Taylor considered the new information.

"What does that get us?" he asked at last.

"What do you mean?"

Taylor counted off the facts. "We know Stuart DiNardo is hot to buy up space here in the downtown. He's approached most of the vendors and so far only gotten the space beside Alberto's. He managed to get Peggy to leave, but we don't know if anyone else is going. Mr. Olsen owns the place, but it's been in his family for years. Pete said his title search found Olsen owns it free and clear. His grandson lives upstairs, so he's not going to be eager to sell, but if DiNardo waves enough money around, he might still be interested." Taylor took another bite of his croissant, still thinking.

"What if we buy the place?" Tom offered.

Taylor looked up, knowing he'd been setup. "No. Tommy...no. We are trying to *save* money right now, remember? Remember that little cottage on the lake you wanted to buy? *Save.*"

Tom nodded. "I know. But think about it—if DiNardo wants it, it's gotta be worth money. Better that we have it and rent it out than have him trying to put his chain stores in there."

Taylor shook his head. "That just puts us in the same position Mr. Olsen is in now—a building with no tenant."

"What if we're the tenant?" Wayne asked as he came around the counter, a bagel in his hand, and joined them. He took a chair from a nearby table and straddled it backward, sitting between them.

"What?" Taylor asked.

He gestured with his half-eaten bagel. "What if *we're* the tenant? What if we put something there?"

"Did you suddenly become independently wealthy?" Taylor quipped, a subtle reminder that Wayne was mainly their financial responsibility.

Not to be outdone, Wayne ignored Taylor's comment. "Seriously, think about it. What if we took over the space and put a store there?"

"What kind of store?" Tom asked.

"A coffee shop."

Tom and Taylor exchanged looks, each a little perplexed. "A coffee shop?" Tom asked.

Wayne nodded firmly. "Definitely. Think about it—the college is growing fast, but the closest place for students to hang out is right here in the historic district. So why not focus on bringing some businesses here that they would frequent? The new pub across the street is already a busy place Thursday through Saturday, but not everyone is into the bar scene."

"Yeah, like us," Emmy interjected from behind. "We almost never go to the bar, but we'll drive to go get a good coffee and relax."

"Who asked you?" Taylor said. She threw a towel across the counter at him, which he deftly caught and tossed back.

"I'm telling you," Wayne defended, "It would work. College kids love to sit in coffee shops."

"College kids do not typically have a lot of money," Taylor pointed out.

"Ah, but they'll blow it on coffee before books," Wayne countered.

Tom winced. "Speaking as a professor at said college, I'm afraid I have to go with Wayne on that one."

Dan and Emmy came around, standing with them. "Actually, it's a good way to expand sales from the bakery, too," Dan commented. "Coffee shops usually sell baked goods, and they're not always that fresh. Imagine if everything is hot out of the Downey McEwan's oven?"

Taylor settled into the role of Devil's Advocate. "We can barely keep up with production as it is most days."

"So we add another baker," Wayne said. "I can have someone up to speed in no time. Besides, a lot of the customers to a coffee shop will come in the evening, when we haven't traditionally had as much volume."

Tom looked to Taylor, smiling. "It's not a bad idea," he said.

"Who's going to run the place?" Taylor asked.

"We can cover that base later."

"Don't you think it's important to at least have an idea? You're already busy, Wayne is running the bakery, and not to impinge on Dan and Emmy, but they've gotta have time for school."

Tom sighed. "Taylor, we can find a manager for the shop. That's not going to be a problem and you know it."

Taylor watched the expectant faces of the young people beside them. "We'll think about it," he said, waiting for them to take a hint and go back behind the counter. Of course, they all also found reasons to need to be out front, where they could listen in.

"We need to start having planning meetings at home," Taylor commented with a pointed look at Emmy, who was still watching him. She gave him a look in return, then went to restock the cases.

Taylor leaned in, speaking more quietly to Tom. "Seriously, Tommy, do you really think you want to get into something like this? You know how long it took us to get the bakery running smoothly, and you already knew what you were doing."

"Wayne's right, though," Tom said. "It's a great money making idea."

"Perhaps," Taylor grudgingly agreed. "But we don't know that Mr. Olsen will want to sell, or that he'll want to sell to us."

Tom leaned in, eye to eye with Taylor. "Actually, we do."

"Oh?"

Tom nodded. "Jason said Mr. Olsen wanted to know how he found out about the situation. So, he told him he talked to us and we talked to Peggy. He asked if Mr. Olsen really intended to sell."

"And?"

"Mr. Olsen said he didn't want to sell to DiNardo, but it was hard to pass up the money. I guess he's been thinking about getting a place in Florida for the winter."

"Ah," Taylor said. The other shoe had fallen—Tom already knew he could get the place. "How much?"

"Jason didn't know for sure, but he was pretty sure Mr. Olsen would sell it to us for less than DiNardo, just to keep it 'in the family.'"

"We're family now?" Taylor asked. "He usually gives me the evil eye whenever I go by."

Tom shrugged. "Well, he likes *me*."

"Oh, nice, McEwan Connolly. Keep it up."

Tom put his hands on Taylor's legs as he gazed into his eyes. "So, what do you think?"

"Did I ever really have a say in the matter?" Taylor deadpanned.

Tom smiled. "Of course you did."

Taylor sighed again. "Since he likes *you*, why don't *you* talk to Mr. Olsen and see if you can get it settled. If so, give me the details and I'll ask Pete to draw everything up."

"Yes!" Tom hissed, then caught himself and gave Taylor his best Smile. "I mean, uh, thanks honey." Taylor stood, and Tom followed him. "Really, Tay, I think this will be good." He put his arms around him and gave him a discrete kiss.

"Woooo," Dan and Emmy called from behind the counter. "Go Tom, go Taylor!"

Taylor again gave them the eye. "I hope you three realize you're involved in this now, too. That means more work for all of you."

"Cool!" Dan said.

"Sounds like fun to me," Emmy agreed.

"Wouldn't have it any other way," Wayne concluded.

"Good," Taylor said. He picked up the empty tray from the table and headed behind the counter, dumping the leftovers in the trash. "I'm going to go to work now," he announced, "to balance my checkbook." He gave Wayne a little wink on his way by, and Tom followed him out the back door to his car.

"Thanks, Tay," Tom said again, holding him in front of the open door.

"You know I can't say no to you. Never have been able to," Taylor said, smiling.

"The feeling's mutual," Tom said, smiling back. "This is going to be fun, though."

Taylor nodded. "It's going to be work. And DiNardo will be back with a vengeance. Mark my words, this isn't the last we'll hear of him—and we can't afford to buy out the entire downtown."

"We'll figure it out, honey," Tom said. "We always do."

"So confident today," Taylor noted. "Be sure to bring some of that home for later."

Tom's cheeks reddened just a little—a rare event for the usually unflappable Mr. McEwan. "I'll bet I can bring home a few other things, too."

"I can't wait," Taylor said. One more kiss and he hopped into the car, letting Tom close the door behind him. He rolled down the window. "If you talk to Mr. Olsen, just get me the figures. We'll do everything else. Pete already has the title info."

"Got it. I'll give you a call in a little while," Tom said.

Taylor backed out and then was gone. As he watched the buildings recede in his back window, he wondered just what they were getting themselves into.

Later that afternoon, with Tom out of the store to run some errands, the three junior culprits milled around behind the counter. Sure enough, it was raining outside, but contrary to Tom's original theory, business was slow. Wayne figured it would probably pick up as the time drew nearer to five, but at two-thirty, the place was empty.

"When did you really get the idea for a coffee shop?" Emmy asked, sipping her cup of tea.

Between classes and working in the bakery, Emmy didn't have a lot of time for the finer things in life. She usually opted for a simple Downey's T-shirt and shorts for attire, her sandy blonde hair pulled back in a ponytail. One day, though, she had tried some of Tom's tea, and rarely a day went by when she didn't have a small cup in the afternoon. Dan usually made some comment about her being an Anglophile, and then they would go back and forth for a while about who was more traveled, literate, etc. Wayne always expected the debates to one day get heated enough to cause a rift, but they only seemed to pull them closer together.

"I started thinking about it a couple weeks ago," Wayne admitted, biting into a sandwich he'd thrown together after the last customers left. "Then the trip back and forth to Eric's gave me more time with no distractions and I realized it would be a really good way to expand."

Dan leaned on a broom, having just swept the dining area on the other side of the counters. "But Peggy just told us she was moving last week. What did you plan to do before that?"

Wayne shrugged, swallowing another bite of his sandwich. "I hadn't really thought it through that far," he admitted. "Peggy's move just hit at a really good time."

"I'll say," Emmy agreed, raising her cup. "At the rate the college is growing, this town is going to turn into a college town in no time."

"And it's not college without coffee," Dan repeated, looking to Wayne. "After all, who needs books?"

Wayne smiled. "What else are we going to do besides sell coffee?"

"Baked goods, obviously," Dan offered.

Emmy piped up. "What about music? Most good coffee shops have a great selection of music."

Dan nodded. "And most have places where live bands can perform some of the time."

Emmy's face brightened at the prospect and she turned to Wayne. "*Live* music! That's a great idea! We should make sure to leave enough room right up by the window, so everyone knows they're there."

"What about people who want to study?" Wayne asked.

"Who studies on a Thursday or Friday night?" Emmy countered. Dan and Wayne exchanged glances and she regarded them both, nonplussed. "Present company excepted."

"What about equipment?" Wayne asked. "What do we need to provide?"

Dan made a dismissive gesture, still leaning on his broom. "They'll bring whatever they need. A lot of them may go acoustic for the setting."

"What's the setting?" Wayne inquired.

Dan smiled. "Cool coffee shop with a band," he said. "Obviously."

Emmy looked to Wayne. "Will Tom and Taylor go for something like that?"

"They both like music," he answered. "They're going to want to do whatever they can to draw in business."

Before anyone else could speak, the front door opened. The three of them immediately went back to what they should have been doing, expecting it to be Tom back from his errands. Instead, a young man stood on the other side of the counter, waiting to be served. Emmy and Dan exchanged a knowing glance, then both headed toward the back, leaving Wayne up front.

Wayne realized what they'd done as he quickly chewed and swallowed the last bite of his sandwich, then smiled a little self-consciously.

"Hello," he greeted, turning to the sink to wash his hands. "Something I can get for you?"

The young man smiled back, nodded slightly. "I hear these are the best baked goods for miles around," he said.

Drying his hands, Wayne nodded. "Sounds like a fair assessment to me," he agreed. "Who sent you over?" he asked, making conversation. The man was quite attractive, so it wasn't a difficult task on which for him to embark.

With a chuckle, he replied, "You did."

Wayne looked up, taking a more direct interest in the conversation. He looked more closely at the young man, trying to recognize him. "I did?"

"Well, sort of," the man said. "Actually, I just overheard you talking about where you worked and how good the food was."

Wayne leaned forward, naturally curious. "Where was that?"

"At school. We had undergrad core math together."

"We did?" Try as he might, Wayne couldn't place the other man's face, and he felt sure he would have noticed.

Nodding, the man replied, "You probably don't remember me. We were on opposite sides of the room, and I hadn't had a haircut in about a year."

His hair, though still longer than Wayne's, was a rich, dark brown color, bordering on black, and was tussled casually into small natural curls. It shimmered with whatever product he had put in it.

"Of course!" Wayne exclaimed. "You sat over by the coat rack, near the back."

At the sudden burst of recognition, the man smiled broadly. "That's me," he said. "I'm an art major. I don't know why we had to take a stupid math class. I'm really bad at it, so I just sat in the back."

Wayne shrugged. "I just did what I had to do to get by." He reached over the counter and held out a hand. "I'm Wayne, by the way. Wayne McInerney."

"Pedro Aguilar," he said. "Nice to meet you."

They shook hands and Wayne snapped his fingers in a moment of recognition. "Now I remember! Sorry to have been so slow."

Pedro shook his head dismissively. "Don't worry about it. Like I said, I look a little different than I did last semester anyway."

He did indeed look different, as Wayne looked a little more closely. The light bulb finally on, he remembered Pedro…and having noticed him a few times before. Truth be told, even with longer hair, he would have been hard to miss. His complexion was fair, but still a nice shade of tan, no doubt aided by the recent bout of good weather the town had enjoyed. His eyes, like his hair, were a deep brown, almost black, giving his gaze a penetrating effect. He was not one to stare, however, and those same dark, penetrating eyes were surrounded by the early marks of smile lines. Wayne realized they were nearly the same height, though Pedro somehow felt smaller because he was thin, and not as muscular as Wayne had become. He was dressed in casual summer attire of a white T-shirt and cargo shorts, leaving his toes peaking out from the ends of his sandals.

Pulling himself back to the present, Wayne asked, "Are you taking classes now?"

"They start next week," Pedro replied.

Wayne nodded. "Right. I've got two each term."

They proceeded to compare their schedules. It turned out they were both far enough along in their majors that most of their classes were different, but they did have one shared history class where they would be together, starting the following week.

Pedro didn't look excited about the class. "I hate taking history. I'm not a very good writer and they always expect these brilliant essays. I'm an art major—ask me to create something and I can do it. Ask me to name the presidents and I'm in trouble."

Wayne laughed. "I'm an English major. I'll be happy to help when it comes to writing."

"Really?" Pedro asked. "That would be great! Trust me, I can use the help. I just hope you don't regret offering."

Wayne watched him. "I don't think I will."

Pedro's face darkened just a bit, but he didn't back away. Instead, he asked more questions. "You're the kid who took another boy to the prom, too, aren't you?"

Surprised, Wayne said, "That was two years ago!"

Pedro nodded. "I know. I remember because I was a freshman then. I remember thinking how cool it was that someone had the courage to do that...and wishing that I'd been that person the year before."

Wayne caught the subtle message. "You mean you wished you'd taken a boy to the prom?"

Pedro smiled again, a little embarrassed. "It might have been more interesting than Martina Fredericks. Nice girl, but you know..."

Wayne nodded. He knew.

Pedro looked at his watch. "Anyway, I'm meeting a friend on campus to go over some stuff before next week, so I should be going." He looked at the array of food before him. "Just give me whatever is best," he said with a smile.

Wayne handed him a croissant drizzled in chocolate. "These are usually everybody's favorite," he explained.

"What do I owe you?" Pedro asked, reaching for his wallet.

"This one's on the house," Wayne said.

"No, let me pay," Pedro objected.

Shaking his head, Wayne said, "Nope. It's on me for not remembering your name."

"Okay," Pedro chuckled. "Thank you." He took a bite of the croissant and then closed his eyes with delight. "Delicious!"

"Thought you might like that," Wayne said.

Finishing the bite, Pedro looked at him a little closer and asked, "Would you like to have dinner?"

Surprised, Wayne said nothing for a moment, then broke into a smile. "Sure, why not?"

Pedro brightened noticeably. "Great! How about Thursday?"

Wayne nodded. "Thursday it is."

Shaking his hand again, Pedro said, "I really do need to run, but I'll look forward to seeing you on Thursday."

"I'll be here," Wayne said. The moment the screen door closed, Emmy and Dan reappeared from the back.

"A *date?*" Emmy asked. "Waynie's going on a *date?*"

"Sounds that way, doesn't it?" Wayne said, blushing.

He wondered what he'd gotten himself into. He and Eric had spent the weekend together. While they really didn't get to spend much time alone, being with him rekindled some of the old feelings he'd had for him. Though there was still a spark, Wayne didn't think Eric had felt the same thing. The quick hug goodbye certainly hadn't held much more than friendship. Maybe it *was* time to get back out there. He'd been out with a couple of guys since their breakup, but the most recent had been months ago. It was time to get back on the horse, as it were.

Wayne smiled. It would be fun...he hoped.

CHAPTER FOUR

A Coffee Shop

Lightening flashed outside, offering brief brightness in place of the waning night. The rumble of the thunder followed a short time later, gently reverberating through the house. The first summer their adoptive children came to live with them, the slightest storm brought the two oldest ones running into Tom and Taylor's room. They had quickly learned to either be prepared for such visits...or to keep the door locked. Fortunately, by the next year, as they had grown accustomed to their new lives, that was no longer a problem.

As the torrent of rain hit the roof, Taylor pulled the bed covers a little tighter around himself. Unlike earlier in the week, the temperatures had dropped off with the sun, leaving the mornings cool and comfortable. He had always preferred cool sleeping weather, so he wasn't that disappointed.

Tom rustled beside him, pulling the covers a little tighter around himself as well. As he moved, Taylor caught a just a hint of sweat mixed with cologne. He had returned home the night before, exhausted, after coaching a little league game. He had baked that morning and not gotten much of a break throughout the day, as Emmy had the day off. He stopped in the kitchen just long enough to have a sandwich, then said he was going to take a quick shower and a nap. Taylor had come upstairs to find him passed out on his stomach, his arms wrapped tightly around his pillow, still in his uniform. Not wanting to wake him, Taylor just quietly slipped into bed next to him.

As he looked over, the uniform was gone and Tom was under the covers. He had a vague memory that Tom had gotten up at some point in the middle of the night, but really didn't know when. As though realizing he was being watched, Tom opened his eyes slowly and smiled at Taylor.

"Hi," he said.

"Good morning," Taylor replied, smiling back.

Tom rolled over, pushing back against Taylor so Taylor could put his arms around him. "Raining?" he asked

"Actually, it's a pretty good thunderstorm," Taylor reported. "Started about ten minutes ago."

"Mmm," Tom mumbled. "You're up early."

"The rain woke me," Taylor said. "And it's a big day."

"Yeah," Tom said, pulling Taylor's arms tighter around him. "I think we got a pretty good deal."

"I hope so," Taylor agreed. "You're really sure this is what you want?"

"Definitely," Tom confirmed, a little more awake. "The coffee shop is going to be a great idea and Wayne has really run with it. I'm looking forward to it."

"So am I," Taylor said. He kissed Tom's neck and shoulder, just as he had the first night they'd been together, after Tom and Gen came to retrieve him from New York. Tom sighed, turning his head to expose his neck even further. Taylor accepted the invitation, shifting his position just enough to move up toward Tom's jaw. Still in Taylor's arms, Tom slowly turned until their lips met.

A sudden loud clap of thunder made them both jump, and Tom started laughing. Not to be outdone, Taylor fell back, still holding him, and ran his hands along Tom's back as the rain continued. Tom's hands did a little roaming of their own and Taylor made no move to stop them.

A half hour later, they both once again lay immobile, entwined in each others' arms. The rain let up and just enough light came through the blinds to allow them to see. Tom glanced at the clock and realized it was later than they had thought. His mom would be over to watch the kids in a half hour.

"We should get up," Tom said, making no move to do so.

"Yep," Taylor said, also making no move to go.

"I need a shower," Tom continued.

"I'll say," Taylor agreed.

Tom poked him in the ribs. "You're no flower of loveliness yourself."

"I was before you woke up and deflowered me," Taylor countered.

"Ha!" Tom said. "You didn't exactly resist."

Taylor smiled. "I'm not stupid."

Tom sat up and pulled Taylor along with him. "Come on, we'll have you smelling pretty as a peach in no time."

Twenty minutes later, they emerged clean, refreshed, and ready to face the day. Tom went to the closet and pulled out a shirt and slacks for Taylor, then selected a polo and khakis for himself.

"Do you mind if I just wear this?" Tom asked, showing Taylor the outfit.

Taylor shook his head. "I don't mind. You can just wear shorts and a T-shirt if you want."

Tom pulled the shirt over his head. "I figured I should at least look a little presentable, since I'll be at your office," he explained.

Taylor buttoned his own shirt. "Everyone knows you. You don't have to do anything special."

"Still," Tom said, pulling on a pair of socks.

"Whatever makes you happy," Taylor reiterated, putting on his slacks. They had been together long enough that Tom often just selected an outfit for him, rather than waiting for him to go through the inevitable decision making process. Tom had realized long ago that Taylor turned fashion selection into an ordeal, but didn't mind if someone else did it for him.

The front door opened and Tom's mom called "good morning" up the stairs.

"See you downstairs," Tom said with one last kiss, then left Taylor to finish arranging his attire.

It was indeed going to be a big day. Tom had approached Mr. Olsen Tuesday morning, mentioning that he'd talked to Jason about the situation with Peggy. However much they joked, it was true that Mr. Olsen liked Tom. His wrinkled, haggard face always brightened just a little when he saw the town baker. Whatever it was that made Tom special, Taylor was just glad there was something.

When Tom mentioned DiNardo's name, Mr. Olsen had become a bit more animated, telling him a long story about how "that swindling real estate developer" was trying to steal his building for a song. Even as DiNardo's offer rose to become more competitive, Olsen refused to sell—he wanted nothing to do with the man.

Mr. Olsen then asked Tom what his interest was in the situation. He could understand how his neighbors might be interested in someone buying the space next to their store, but had DiNardo approached them? Tom answered that DiNardo had made a few casual inquiries, but that they'd been able to fend him off. Tom explained that, if Mr. Olsen was truly interested in selling, they might be interested in the property.

At that, Olsen became more engaged. He admitted he really had enjoyed the idea of getting away for the winter. His biggest concern was Jason—Mr. Olsen explained that Jason was his youngest grandson and he'd always felt a certain responsibility to look out for him. Jason, he said, had always been the one to look out for *him*.

Tom understood, having been close to his own grandfather, and assured him they had no need for the space upstairs. As far as he was concerned, Jason could stay there almost indefinitely. Olsen explained that he didn't charge rent, but thought that Tom and Taylor should if they were going to own the building. "Responsibility builds character, after all," he'd said.

So Olsen agreed to sell, they agreed to buy, and the deal was done. Tom left Mr. Olsen's and met with Taylor and Pete, who drew up the contract. Mr. Olsen had reviewed it the day before and agreed with the terms. He was to meet them at Taylor's office that morning to close the deal.

Taylor picked up the discarded clothes from the night before and tidied the bedroom. He'd always tried to leave a neat room, but when they realized Tom's mom had a habit of cleaning while the kids were away or asleep, they both put forth a little extra effort, feeling guilty. The bedroom once again presentable, he made his way down the back stairs to find all three kids, Tom, and Donna sitting around the kitchen table.

"Hi, Dad!" Chad greeted. Wendy gave a greeting of her own, with a mouthful of Cheerios. Little Taylor didn't have a whole lot to say, eating his breakfast one "o" at a time.

"Morning all," Taylor greeted. He poured himself a bowl of cereal and joined them at the table.

"So you're closing on it this morning?" Donna asked.

"Yes," Tom said. "Mr. Olsen is meeting us at Taylor's office at nine o'clock sharp."

"Is Wayne going?" she asked. Before anyone could answer, the back door opened and Wayne came in, wearing a fresh Downey's polo and khakis.

"Wayne!" Wendy greeted. He gave all three kids a hug and a kiss, then stopped between Tom and Taylor, a hand resting on each of their shoulders.

Taylor answered Donna's question. "I told him he'd gotten us into this, so he deserved to be a part of the action."

"Isn't it going to be cool?" Wayne asked.

"Did you have breakfast yet?" Tom asked him, looking up.

Wayne nodded. "I ate before I left the bakery. Mrs. Johnson's in covering things while I'm gone. Kyra was due in any minute to help her."

"You two are meeting with the architect this morning?" Taylor asked.

"He'll be there at eight," Tom confirmed. "Peggy said she didn't mind if we stopped by."

"When is she vacating?" Donna asked.

"End of May," Tom said. "It actually works out okay—we'll need more time than that to get the plan in motion anyway. Taylor and Gen have already started the permits, so we should be able to do most of the build-out while you guys are away with the kids."

"You think you can do a build-out in one month?" Donna asked.

"That's what we're going to determine today. It looks promising, though," Tom said.

"Gen and Maggie are helping to keep the permits flowing," Taylor explained. "By getting things lined up now, it makes the process smoother when they're working. Ted Johnson, Mrs. Johnson's husband, is the town inspector, so he's agreed to be available whenever we need him."

"Helps to know people, doesn't it?" Donna observed. She rose to clear the table.

Taylor checked his watch. "I'm going to head in. Pete should be there shortly. We'll see you guys in a couple of hours?"

"We'll be there," Tom confirmed. Taylor gave him a kiss on the cheek, then kissed each of the kids as they ran up the stairs to get ready for school. Donna followed them up, waving a quick goodbye to Taylor as he turned to go.

"What about me?" Wayne asked, arms out.

"*You* I will see later, troublemaker," he said and gave him a wink, then left.

Wayne turned from the door to face Tom, who was finishing the dishes at the sink. "So, what kind of décor are we going for?"

"Lots of plastic and chrome," Tom answered.

"What?" Wayne demanded. "What kind of décor is that?"

Tom rolled his eyes. "We're going for the coffeehouse look, obviously."

"Whew. Okay, so I was talking to Emmy and Dan the other night," Wayne started.

Tom turned around. "Talking to Emmy and Dan is what got us into this in the first place."

Wayne sat at one of the vacated spots at the table. "Not really. *You're* the one who wanted to buy the store. We just came with an idea for what to sell."

"And now you have more ideas?" Tom asked.

"Exactly!" Wayne was not one to be easily assuaged. He looked at Tom more closely. "Aren't you supposed to be excited about this? You're starting to sound like Taylor."

"It's still early, Wayne," Tom sighed.

"You're usually the morning person."

"Me? You've obviously been living away for too long, my young apprentice," Tom laughed.

"Good point," Wayne said.

Tom gestured toward him. "Okay, what else have you got?"

Wayne went on to explain the idea of creating a space for performers to give live shows. He pointed out how they thought it might be good to have the performance area up near the front, where people would see it from the street. He said they needed to have a large coffee bar where people could get their orders, and then have lots of chairs and couches for them to relax and listen to the music.

Tom just let him go until he was done, quietly listening. At last, when Wayne had fully made his case, Tom spoke. "That's your plan?"

"Yeah," Wayne said, a little uncertain.

"So, to summarize, you want it to be a coffeehouse," Tom concluded.

"But with music," Wayne pointed out.

"Coffeehouses have music," Tom said.

"But it's new here," Wayne defended.

"The whole thing is new here," Tom replied.

Wayne pursed his lips, breathing out through his nose. "You know, you're *really* starting to sound like Taylor."

"It's something he puts in my food when I'm not looking," Tom said. He rested his hand on Wayne's shoudler. "Come on, music man, let's go meet with the architect. You guys can figure out where you want the stage."

Wayne hopped up out of his chair. "Cool!"

Tom called a goodbye up the stairs to his mom, then gave all the kids a hug and a kiss as they came running down to see him off. Promising to see them at dinner, he and Wayne left, bound for the new store.

Taylor sat at his desk, reviewing the purchase document one last time. Everything was in order. He'd gone to the bank the day before and arranged the financing, then had Tom join him to sign everything. Though they could have bought the space, Taylor preferred keeping their funds in reserve and having a mortgage on the store. Tom freely admitted the finer details of the financing were more than he really needed to understand, so Taylor took care of it.

Pete came in, a steaming cup of coffee in his hand, and sat down in one of the chairs opposite him, as was their usual morning ritual.

"Everything all set?" he asked.

"Looks that way," Taylor said. "The docs are ready and I have the check here from the bank."

"And Tom is already meeting with the architect?" Pete asked, sipping from his mug.

Taylor nodded. "You know how he is. I've never known anyone with as much energy as him."

"I know I envy him," Pete admitted.

"Speaking of energy, how's Anita?"

Pete brightened at the mention of his pregnant wife. "She's doing very well. Everything is on track. The baby should be born sometime around the first of the year. They're still waiting before they give us an actual date."

"It shouldn't be that hard to calculate, should it?" Taylor asked. "Nine months from…"

"Yeah," Pete agreed. "Anita could explain it better. With four kids of your own, I'd have thought you'd understand by now."

"Funny!" Taylor sneered.

"Have you talked to Gen?" Pete asked. "I still feel bad about that."

Taylor shook his head. "She's fine. It was just bad timing. You know she couldn't be happier for you guys."

"I know," Pete said, a little less than certain, as he took another sip.

Taylor's phone beeped and their receptionist spoke. "Taylor?"

"Yeah?"

"Mr. Olsen and Mr. Harper are here."

Taylor nodded. "Show them to the conference room, will you?"

"Will do," she said and hung up.

"Time to go, huh?" Pete asked, standing.

"Sounds like it," Taylor said. He checked his watch. "Tom and Wayne aren't due for another ten minutes. Want me to just have Christy give you a buzz when they get here?"

"Sounds good," Pete said. He followed Taylor out, then turned off at his office as Taylor went on to the conference room to meet his neighbors, old and new.

Christy had just finished giving them coffee, and Taylor thanked her as she closed the glass inlaid French doors behind him. Both Mr. Olsen and Jason sat facing the doors, with their backs to the windows and the forested space beyond. Taylor and Pete had leapt at the opportunity to have space in the building, where one whole end faced national forest land. A year later, they had bought the building outright, guaranteeing they would stay for some time to come.

"Good morning," Taylor greeted, shaking hands with both of them. He took a seat at the end of the table nearest them, allowing them to talk while still letting him see the office beyond. "How are you?"

"We're good, Taylor," Jason replied, smiling. He watched Taylor intently. "I'm impressed you have a cappuccino machine," he said, gesturing to his mug.

"Pete's an addict," Taylor explained. "It's the only thing that wakes him up in the morning. It's cheaper than having to pay court fines if he's asleep."

"I'll bet," Jason said. "I love the layout of your office. The color choices are great. Who decorated it?"

"Tom and our friend, Gen Pouissant. I got to pick the doors," Taylor said, gesturing to the double French doors to the room. "Tom even let me put a set in my office at the other end. Other than that, they pretty much went hog-wild by themselves."

"It must be nice," Jason observed. "I don't have an office— I'm on the road most of the time. When I'm home, it's to do laundry before I go on the road again."

"Tough life," Taylor said. "But at least you get to travel."

"Even that doesn't always make it worthwhile when you come home to an empty house," Jason said.

Mr. Olsen spoke up. "I keep telling him it'll work out in the end."

"Sounds like sage advice to me," Taylor agreed.

Tom and Wayne appeared at the door, and Pete came down the hall to join them, file folders in hand. Everyone said their hellos and then settled in to sign the necessary documents. At last, Taylor passed the check over to Mr. Olsen, who turned it over and slid it in his folder without even examining it—an old fashioned sign of trust that was not lost on his neighbor.

"That's all there is to it?" Jason asked.

"I was thinking the same thing," Wayne admitted.

"That's it, boys," Mr. Olsen said. "I've bought and sold enough property in my time. The scary thing is it just seems to get easier."

"More money helps," Taylor observed.

Mr. Olsen laughed. "That it does, son. That it does." He looked to Jason, resting a hand on his arm. "Come on, old man, let's get out of these folks' hair so they can get some work done."

"Sure, Grandpa," he replied.

"Where are you off to?" Tom asked, rising.

"I'm going to check out this place called Sun City in Florida. I guess there are a bunch of old farts like me hanging out there. Sounds like a good place to visit," Mr. Olsen said, uncharacteristically happy.

"When are you going?"

"Tomorrow," he said. "Jason here is going to be in town for a week, so he'll look after the place while I'm away. I figure I've got all this money, so the least I can do is take a trip."

Taylor nodded. "Sound logic, if ever I've heard it."

"Darned right," Mr. Olsen said. "Best of luck to you boys."

"Thank you, sir," Taylor said, shaking his hand again. Tom and Wayne said their goodbyes to him as well, while Taylor turned to Jason. "And we hope to see more of you around town."

Jason brightened at the invitation. "I hope to see more of me around town, too," he agreed.

"Stop in and have breakfast once in a while," Tom added.

"I will," he promised, then followed his grandfather out the door.

Pete excused himself and went back to his office to finalize the transaction, leaving Taylor and his family in the conference room.

"Seems like a nice guy," Wayne observed.

"Yes, he does," Taylor agreed, turning to Tom. "He approves of your decorating style, too."

Tom's brows rose. "Is that so?"

"Single, doesn't get out much, always on the road..."

"You think he plays for our team?" Wayne asked.

Taylor shrugged. "I think it's at least a possibility."

"Should be interesting," Tom agreed. He pulled his chair back out and sat. Wayne followed suit and Taylor moved to sit opposite them, where Mr. Olsen and Jason had been. "The architect thinks we can be up by the first of July."

"Really?" Taylor asked, surprised.

"Yep. He said having you clear the way with the town was a big help. He already has a builder in mind and did some preliminary budgeting before we met. He's well within our budget."

"That's good news," Taylor said.

"He said he should be able to open the wall between the two stores with minimal disruption of the bakery. He's proposing an archway with glass doors that we can use to close off one from the other if we don't want to operate them on the same hours," Tom explained.

Taylor nodded. "That's a great idea."

Tom handed him a hand-drawn sketch. Taylor's brow wrinkled in concentration as he examined it. He'd left his glasses in his office, so he squinted at the small print without even realizing it. "What's this?" he asked. "It looks like it says, 'stage.'"

"It does," Tom confirmed.

Taylor looked up, his blue eyes inquisitive. "You're building it with a stage?"

Tom looked at Wayne, who picked up the cue. "It was my idea," he admitted. "Well, actually it was Emmy and Dan, but I brought it to Tom. I thought the town could use a place for live music to perform."

"Cool," Taylor said.

"You really think so?" Tom asked.

"Yeah," Taylor approved. "I think it's a great idea."

"Really!" Wayne said, backhanding Tom on the shoulder. "*Somebody* was doubting me."

Tom backhanded his shoulder back. "*Somebody* accused me of being like Taylor," he said.

Taylor frowned. "Hey! When has being like Taylor become a bad thing?" he complained. "As far as I'm concerned, you can both just go home."

"It's only because we love you, honey," Tom said.

"Yeah," Wayne seconded. "Honey."

"Humph," Taylor said. "So, what do you want to do?"

Tom spoke first. "We're meeting with the builder tomorrow. If he can work within our budget, we'll go. The architect said they should be able to start work in two weeks."

"That's before the kids go," Taylor said.

"I'll help manage it while they're here," Wayne offered.

Taylor considered the plan. At least on the surface, it seemed viable.

"Okay, let's do it."

Later that afternoon, Wayne lay on his bed, contemplating the ceiling. It wasn't that often that someone asked him out and he couldn't remember a time it happened on the first meeting.

To date, his dating track record was less than stellar. After Eric came Nate, the runner, who ultimately ran away from him and into the arms of some circuit boy from the city. That one had been harder for Wayne to understand than Eric—on the one hand, he could understand Eric wanting to put his education ahead of a relationship, but for Nate to leave him just to go out with some kid who was just strung out on drugs and using him as a paycheck? Taylor had laughed as Wayne voiced his confusion, and ultimately told him the story of his last long term relationship before Tom. While Ryan hadn't been involved with drugs—at least none that were illegal—his med students were a whole different story.

Then there was Brian, the sweet one, who decided to answer his calling to work as a volunteer somewhere in Africa. He'd tried mightily to get Wayne to come with him, but Wayne finally just explained that wasn't where his life was going. Since Brian, he'd been on several dates, but none of them amounted to anything, either by Wayne's choice or the other guy's.

Pedro's face entered his mind's eye again. He'd seemed like a nice enough guy, and he initiated the date, which always made Wayne a little more comfortable—after all, it was already a sign he was interested.

Against his will, another face replaced Pedro's. Why couldn't he get Eric out of his mind? Their weekend had been very casual—dinner with the family, watching TV, hanging out. Nothing at all like when they had been a couple, spending hours together just talking and sharing each others' company. Where had that Eric gone?

Wayne took the current Eric's continued lack of interest as a sign, too—they were just friends and it was time to move on. Perhaps that was why he'd been so willing to go out with Pedro?

It occurred to him that he didn't even know where they were going. He hoped it wasn't anywhere fancy—he *definitely* wasn't up for fancy. A first date should be casual, he thought. Of course, it rarely turned out that way, no matter how hard either party, or both, tried.

"Shouldn't you be getting ready?"

Dan stood in Wayne's doorway, licking an ice cream cone. He was still dressed for work, shirt still bearing the telltale sign of flour and sweat. Working in the baking room in the summer was always fun—even the slightest dampness sucked the flour out of the air and on to one's shirt like magic.

"I'm working on it," Wayne said. He was clad only in a fresh pair of boxers, lying with his bare feet on the floor, hands behind his head.

"You look like it," Dan commented. "What's the dilemma?"

Wayne sighed. "Nothing. I was just thinking."

"About?"

"Relationships," Wayne said. He sat up and turned, facing Dan, who leaned against the doorframe. "The good and the bad."

They'd been friends long enough that Dan knew exactly where Wayne was going. "Any one in particular?"

Wayne gave his shy smile when he'd been caught. "I just wish I knew what last weekend was about," he complained.

Dan held out his hand. "Sometimes a cone is just a cone," he prophesized.

"Maybe, but I'd feel better if I was sure."

Dan took another lick. Wayne could tell it was Chunky Monkey, his favorite. "What do you think?" he asked.

"I think we're just friends," Wayne admitted.

"So just be friends," Dan said.

"That simple?"

He shrugged. "Why not? You said he invited you as a friend, you went as a friend, and you did friend things. Sounds an awful lot like just a cone to me."

Wayne smiled. "You know, you're pretty good at this...for a straight boy."

"I've had good teachers," Dan said. "Now you'd better get ready. He seemed like a nice enough guy, and he was pretty into you."

Again, Wayne blushed a little. "He did seem nice, didn't he?"

"Yep," Dan said, taking a big bite from his cone as he walked away. Wayne was very glad Emmy and Dan had stayed together after high school. Dan had been a good friend after they met his senior year and their friendship had only grown stronger as they worked together and ultimately shared Tom's old apartment above the bakery.

Wayne went to his closet and took out a black polo and khaki cargo shorts. Pedro was in college—hopefully that would mean he didn't want to go anywhere expensive. Dressed, he hit his nearly dry hair with some styling products, then arranged it to look a bit messy. It never ceased to amaze him how much trouble it was too look disheveled. He stopped at his dresser long enough to hit himself with a couple spritzes of Ralph Lauren Romance— it never hurt to plan ahead. He'd no sooner pulled on his sandals when he heard a knock at the door.

"I'll get it," he called down the hall. Dan was already sprawled out on the couch, one leg up, remote in hand.

Wayne caught one last look at himself in the mirror near the door. Satisfied he was presentable, he put on his best smile and swung open the door. "Hi ther—" he stopped cold.

The person in front of him looked equally surprised by the somewhat magnanimous greeting, his head a little low, regarding Wayne through his brows. At first, neither seemed to find the words, but finally, Wayne spoke:

"Eric?"

CHAPTER FIVE

Turmoil and Chaos

"Hi, Wayne."

Eric was pale as he looked up apologetically through his tightly drawn brows. Wayne could never remember seeing him more self-conscious or unsure of himself. One of the things Wayne had most appreciated about Eric was his self-assuredness, his self-confidence. To see it missing was disconcerting, to say the least.

When they were together, Eric's personality reminded him of Taylor. Since the moment Wayne had met him, when Taylor saved him from his father's abusive home without so much as a second thought, Wayne had felt an innate trust for him. It had been the same with Eric—he knew Eric loved him and wanted the best for him, and as long as they were together, nothing could hurt him. The day Eric announced he wanted to finish his education out of state had been like a five ton weight dropped on Wayne's shoulders. He had been speechless for days.

Over the next two years, they had stayed in touch, largely at Taylor's advice. Eric made it clear he still cared about Wayne, but that they needed to focus on their education first and let everything else wait until they were done. Intellectually, Wayne understood his argument, but he didn't really agree with it. With no real choice, however, he had just gone along.

Then there was last weekend, Eric's graduation, where they'd "talked." They'd talked about what was going on in town, the weather, Eric's job prospects, their family situations…anything to avoid the most obvious, and dangerous, topic. One pat-pat-pat-on-the-back hug was as close as they'd gotten to any meaningful contact and Wayne still sensed a feeling of embarrassment coming from Eric as they hugged in front of his parents. True, he didn't know how he'd feel if he was with another guy with *his* parents, but his instinct was he wouldn't care as much—at least, not after so many years with the Tom and Taylor support structure behind him.

"Sorry I didn't call ahead." Eric spoke again, still watching him, pulling him back to the present. As Wayne observed him, he realized Eric was downright terrified—but of what?

"What are you doing here?" Wayne asked, trying hard not to make the most obvious question also sound like a condemnation.

Eric started to speak, then stopped, taking in a short, uneven breath, his lower lip trembling ever so slightly. He watched Wayne, his face an ever-changing pattern of emotion. Wayne didn't know whether to feel compassion for his obvious angst, or anger at him for showing up without warning, without any apparent concern for Wayne's feelings.

"I—I had to talk to you," Eric stumbled, wracked with emotion.

Wayne looked back into the apartment. Though Dan was out of earshot, he still didn't want to talk to Eric in front of him. Jaw set, he stepped out onto the landing and pulled the door closed behind him.

"Were you going somewhere?" Eric asked, suddenly realizing the greeting at the door hadn't been meant for him.

"Actually, yes," Wayne said. "I'm having dinner with someone."

At that, Eric looked nearly panicked, but he kept himself together. "Who with?"

Wayne frowned. "It's a date, Eric, okay? Look, I'm sorry that you drove all the way out here, but I didn't know you were coming. Where are you staying?"

He looked down, unable to meet Wayne's gaze. "Actually, my company has put me up in a hotel."

"Your company?" Wayne asked. "You found a job?"

Eric nodded, still looking down, his voice quiet. "Yeah. They're based in the city. I was hoping to tell you last weekend, but I didn't find out until yesterday."

Wayne's eyes narrowed. Last weekend? *Had* Eric planned for it to be more than just his graduation?

"Why didn't you tell me anyway?" Wayne asked.

"I wanted it to be a surprise," Eric explained. "I wanted to tell you I was coming back here, but I didn't know for sure and I knew my parents would be upset that I wasn't coming to live near them and I didn't want to cause a scene..." His face wrinkled and a tear escaped. He lowered himself to sit down on the first step. He looked up at Wayne, his eyes glistening. "I had to do this, Wayne, to finish my education."

"I know," Wayne said. "We've talked about it."

"But do you know how *hard* it has been? This wasn't what I wanted," Eric insisted.

Wayne knelt down, resting back on his ankles. "It wasn't what I wanted either," he admitted.

"I had no *choice*," Eric insisted.

"What do you mean? You're the one who made the decision," Wayne reminded him.

Eric shook his head. "My dad made the decision. He called, a few nights before I left. You were working. He told me my first priority was my education and that he was going to do what he had to do to look out for me. He said I'd thank him later."

Wayne watched him, confused. "You're saying your *dad* made you go back to Ohio State?"

Eric looked up, tears flowing freely. "He told me as long as I was on his dime, he was going to make me do what was best for me. He told me to go back to Ohio State, to finish my degree. He didn't leave me any choice."

It suddenly became obvious what Eric meant. "He threatened to cut off your money," Wayne concluded.

"He hasn't exactly been...happy...about my 'recent behavior.' However, as long as I played along, he didn't say anything."

"He didn't want you shacked up with some small town gay kid," Wayne said.

Eric looked up, his eyes pleading. Wayne just shook his head, incredulous.

"Why didn't you ever say anything?" he asked.

"I couldn't open the door," Eric explained. "I couldn't take the chance that you would say something or do something to talk me out of it. I just had to go and finish—as fast as I could. That's why I pushed myself so hard, why I graduated a year early."

Wayne stood again, slowly pacing away, gently massaging his forehead with his right hand. Just as he thought he was getting over Eric, *this* had to happen. He swung sharply, angrily toward Eric.

"Do you know what the last two years have been like?" he demanded. "You just up and *left!* Sure we stayed in touch, we were 'friends,' but that was it. You put yourself ahead of *us*, without ever even considering the option that there may have been other solutions."

Eric shook his head. "I considered it. I considered it a lot. You don't know what my dad is like," Eric insisted.

"For God's sake, Eric, my dad and my brother used to *beat* me!"

"You think it's any different for me?" Eric asked. "Sure, he didn't hit me with his hands, but he did it all the same with words and with actions! I always had to live up to his expectations, and if I didn't then there would be hell to pay."

Wayne shook his head. "You could have said something— *anything*—to let me know what was going on. God, Eric, there we were, *last weekend,* and you still didn't say anything! Your dad wasn't there the whole time—*why* didn't you say anything?"

"You don't understand!" Eric cried. "He may not have been there every moment, but he was there all the same. He would see it, in my face, in my voice, he would know. I mean, I took enough of a risk, just by having you there. I told them we were just friends now, that it was okay. But we had to *be* just friends."

Wayne watched the agony in his eyes, the pain on his face, the tension in his body. As angry as he was, he still felt pity for Eric. At least *his* father's abuse had been overt and direct. There was no subtlety, no hidden meaning, no cloaked contempt. When his father was drunk, he hit. He lashed out with fists and with words, but he said what he meant—that he thought his son should be more of a man, the man he wanted him to be. For Eric, the abuse was far less obvious, far easier to cover up, and like anything so easily hidden, always there.

At last, Wayne broke. He didn't know what else to do, so he bent down and pulled Eric into his arms from behind, resting his head lightly on Eric's shoulder. However complicated their relationship may have become, there was no question Wayne still had feelings for him, and Eric apparently felt the same way. Weeping openly, Eric rose up and turned, clutching at Wayne tightly. He sobbed, his head resting on Wayne's chest thanks to the lower step he was standing on.

"I never stopped caring," Eric said.

Wayne froze, once again unsure of his own feelings. "It's going to take some time to work through this," he said gently, not wanting to hurt Eric, but not wanting to leave the door wide open either. "There is a lot to talk about," he said.

"I know," Eric said, looking up at him. "Just promise we can talk."

Nodding, Wayne said, "We can talk."

Eric stood up, wiping away the tears on his cheeks. "I'm sorry, Wayne."

"So am I," Wayne said, genuinely so.

Eric brushed at the dark spots on his shirt. "I've messed up your clothes."

Wayne shook his head. "It's okay. I don't think I feel much like going out right now anyway. I'll go take care of it. You look like you could use some rest."

"I'm tired," Eric admitted.

"Is your hotel far? Do you need a ride?"

Eric shook his head. "No, I can get there."

Wayne nodded. "Alright. Be careful, okay?"

"I will," Eric said. "Sorry again to drop all of this on you."

Wayne chuckled in spite of himself. "I just wish you'd told me sooner," he said. "It might have helped both of us."

"Maybe it still will?" Eric asked.

"Maybe."

He looked sad again, but not as bad. "I'll talk to you soon," he said.

"You have my number," Wayne answered.

"Good night."

"'Night."

Eric made his way down the stairs and back to his car. Wayne watched him go, all the way until he made the turn and disappeared around the corner. Behind him, the door to the apartment opened and Dan leaned out.

"Eric?" he asked.

"Yeah," Wayne sighed. "It's a long story."

Dan stepped out. "I'm here for you if you need me."

Wayne smiled. "I know."

"Not to add stress to your life," he said, "but the bakery just called. Pedro is waiting there—he wasn't sure where to meet you."

Wayne nodded. "I figured. I'll go take care of it. I'll be back in a minute."

"I'll be here," Dan said, silently acknowledging Wayne's message.

Wayne headed down the stairs, already forming the words in his head to let Pedro down easily. Eric had just dropped a whole plane's worth of bombshells on him, and he needed time to think...a lot of time...

The next morning again brought rain. For a town that was so often sunny, frequent rain seemed almost an omen. Wayne relaxed at one of the tables in the front, having completed the lion's share of the baking earlier that morning.

It had been a late night for him as he considered what to do next about the situation with Eric. Dan, ever the faithful friend, had been with him every step of the way, never once even implying that Wayne was keeping him. Of course, the faithful friend was consequently dragging tail, just as Wayne was, but he put on a happy face for Wayne's benefit and quietly explained what had happened to Emmy, to keep her in the loop and avoid any inappropriate questions.

He sipped at his orange juice, picking at a cinnamon bagel, lost in thought. He'd spent so long angry and hurt by Eric's actions—or lack thereof—that he wasn't sure how to come to terms with the revelations he'd made.

On the one hand, he wanted to be angry that he was so misled. Why hadn't Eric said something? Why did it have to be such a big secret when it was a burden they could have borne together?

But, as Eric had said, his own painful past was at least a reasonable analogy. Hindsight was always twenty-twenty, and it's always easier to look in from the outside. The dynamics of actually *living* in the situation, especially with family involved, were something else entirely.

So he pitied Eric and felt pain at what he had been forced to endure...but what about *his* pain, Wayne's pain? He had endured it, too, but without the comfort and knowledge that it would one day come to a close. How many nights had he lain in bed, anguished over the love he lost, wondering why his own love hadn't been enough? How could he reconcile that sense of loss with the revelation Eric had made?

And should he try? That was the other question that rolled through his mind. Did he need to reconcile it, or simply accept it for what it was and move forward, seeing if he and Eric could work through their shared pain. Did he want to risk his heart again? What promises would Eric give—could Eric give—that they would not repeat the same mistakes? Now that he was done with school, would his father stop trying to manipulate him?

In Wayne's mind, that didn't seem likely. While his own father had virtually no contact with him, Eric's dad didn't seem similarly inclined. In his mind, he *was* trying to do what was best for his son. The fact that he did it through manipulation and heavy-handed control was irrelevant to him. Was Eric prepared to stand up to his father, to show him the man he was, regardless of who his father may want him to be?

The questions just poured out of his mind, as they had all night, since the moment Eric left. Wayne had gone down to let Pedro down gently. To his credit, he understood when Wayne explained that an old friend had come into town unexpectedly, and they agreed they would meet for lunch the following week. Pedro seemed to just want another friend in his life, and that sounded very good to Wayne. While he had little doubt that he was interested in him, he also felt that they could move forward as friends. Time would tell and Wayne resolved to be honest with him, to try to spare his feelings. He certainly knew what it was like to feel alone in the world, and he was glad to offer friendship to any who wanted it.

"Hey there." Tom jolted him from his reverie, taking the other seat at the small table. He had a toasted bagel with cream cheese and a tall glass of water. "What's new?"

Wayne glanced in the direction of the back, but there was no one to be seen. Emmy must have been in the baking room with Dan.

"You haven't heard?"

"Heard what?" Tom asked, breaking off a piece of bagel. "Taylor just dropped me off. The Jag's in for an oil change right now."

"Eric's in town," Wayne said. "He came by last night."

"Came by here?" Tom asked.

"The apartment."

"Oh. What did he want?"

Wayne looked down. "He wanted to talk."

"Did you want to talk?"

Wayne chuckled a little ruefully. "I'm still working on that."

Tom sipped from his glass. "Do you want to talk about it now?"

Shaking his head, Wayne said, "Not really."

The door to the bakery opened and a person rushed in from the rain. Wayne and Tom looked up to see Jason fanning his shirt in a futile attempt to shake off the water. Dripping, he stood on the rug in front of the door.

"Good morning," he greeted.

"Hi, Jason," Tom said. He started to rise, but Wayne put a hand on his arm.

"Have your breakfast," he said. "I'll help Jason." He walked behind the counter. "What can I get for you?"

Jason glanced at their table. "Those toasted bagels look pretty good," he said. "Wheat with cream cheese? And whatever the strongest coffee you have is."

"Coming right up," Wayne said. "Are you eating here or taking it with you?"

"I think I'll dry out a little," Jason said.

Wayne nodded. "Have a seat, then. I'll bring it out to you."

"Thanks." Jason sat at one of the other small tables and Tom turned to make conversation.

"How goes the traveling life?"

At once, Jason's face fell. He crossed his arms over his chest, rubbing them to warm up in the chill the air conditioning produced on his cool clothes. "I don't expect to be doing a lot of traveling for a while," he said.

"New job?" Tom asked.

"No job," Jason said. Wayne handed him his meal, then retook his seat. "Thanks to the Republicans and their lovely economic management, I got downsized."

"Ouch. Any prospects?"

Jason shook his head. "Everything is tight right now. Nobody is hiring—at least, nobody local."

"What is it you do?" Wayne asked.

"I manage the installation of computer networks," Jason answered, biting into his bagel.

Tom's brows went up in surprise. "And with experience like that, you can't find a job?"

Again, Jason shook his head. "Nothing local. The market is just really tight. If I want to move, there are some options, but they're all places where I don't want to live."

"That's rough," Tom said. "When did you find out?"

"Yesterday. It was kind of a long day."

"Seems to be going around," Tom said, taking his leftovers to the trash. He turned to Wayne. "Speaking of a long day, I heard from the architect last night."

"Oh?" Wayne perked up.

Tom nodded, walking behind the counter as he talked. "He already has contacts with the town planner, thanks to Taylor. So, while he was out here, he took the preliminary idea to him. Of course, he still has to present formal plans, but the planner said everything looks okay."

Wayne brightened. "Really? So we can open the wall between the stores?"

"Looks that way," Tom affirmed. "The builder should be by in a little while to have a look, too. They're working together on the final plan."

"That's great!" Wayne exclaimed, looking from Tom to Jason, who nodded politely. "When do we open?"

Tom laughed as he restocked one of the cases. "Don't get too far ahead of yourself there," he cautioned. "Remember, we haven't even seen the plans yet. Then there's the small matter of selecting what we want to sell, hiring a staff, buying furniture, painting…"

Wayne sighed. "You could at least play along."

"I *am* playing along. Remember, I voted with you at our little impromptu family meeting," Tom reminded him, amusement in his eyes.

"Oh yeah," Wayne said.

"So you're going to open the wall between the two stores?" Jason asked, having quietly listened to the conversation.

"That's the plan," Wayne confirmed. "We thought it would be good to let people move back and forth between the bakery."

"Don't forget the stage," Emmy interjected, carrying a fresh tray of croissants from the baking room.

"Stage?" Jason asked.

"Yes," Tom said. "Wayne and a couple of his little friends came up with an idea to have live musical performances in the coffee shop in the evening."

"Little friends?" Emmy echoed. "We're *your* little friends, too," she said, giving him a punch in the arm on her way back to the baking room.

"Live music will be cool!" Jason agreed.

"We're putting in some acoustic insulation so it should still be quiet in your apartment," Tom added.

"That's awfully nice."

"We have to be considerate," Wayne seconded.

"The next thing we need to do," Tom said, "is figure out who's going to run the place."

Wayne looked at him. "I thought I would."

"You're running the bakery and going to school," Tom reminded him. "Whoever is running the coffee shop will need to be around during operating hours."

"Good point," Wayne agreed.

"What are the skills needed?" Jason asked.

Tom shrugged. "I don't know. It would probably help to have someone who likes coffee. Truth be told, it's not something

Taylor and I have much of an affinity for. There will be management of the retail side, then back office work keeping the books and ordering, which I can help with. Then there's day-to-day personnel management, payroll, etc., which we can probably handle the same way we do here…" He broke off. "It's a lot to get rolling in not a lot of time."

Jason nodded. "Sounds like you need someone with retail project management experience."

Tom sighed. "And how. Problem is we can't afford it right now."

"So you'd need someone whose expenses were low and just wanted a fun challenge."

Tom looked up, a little more pointedly. "Yeah…?"

"Perhaps someone who recently lost his job and needs enough to cover his expenses for a while?"

"You wouldn't be asking a question, would you?" Tom asked.

"Depends on if you're interested," Jason countered.

"Jason, are you interested in running the coffee shop?"

Jason smiled, getting up to stand across from Tom, in front of one of the cases. "I'd love to."

Tom and Wayne exchanged a quick glance and Wayne said, "Cool."

"Yes," Tom agreed. "I think you and Wayne will be co-managers. You can coordinate both stores together so we can operate them as one as much as possible."

"Works for me," Jason said.

"Me, too," Wayne acknowledged.

"Okay, then, welcome aboard," Tom said, reaching across to shake Jason's hand.

"Thanks," Jason said, taking his hand.

Tom reached for the pad of paper he'd left behind the counter when he got there. He and Wayne joined Jason at his table. "The first thing I want the two of you to work on is getting a list of everything we need to do in the next couple of weeks. I know it won't be complete, but it'll be a start. Think of things we can start doing now, while the architect is still getting the plans ready. We're going to need vendors, equipment, supplies, etc."

Tom scribbled away furiously at his pad, handing Wayne and Jason each a sheet of paper and a pen so they could work as well. As far as Tom was concerned, there was no point in waiting, when work could be done. It was a motto that everyone respected, though, since he usually put the lion's share of the work on himself.

Later that day, Taylor sat at his usual table at Alberto's, quietly sipping a glass of iced tea. He knew summer was upon them when Alberto started slipping him iced tea instead of water. He still found it refreshing to have a place where the owner knew him so well that he didn't even have to order half the time.

"Are you sure I can't get you something while you wait?" Alberto asked.

"Nothing at all," Taylor reiterated. Alberto had already insisted on bringing a basket of bread, which Taylor picked at unconsciously, dipping the still warm morsels in the plate of olive oil, parmesan, and fresh ground pepper Alberto had prepared.

"Is Tommy joining you?" Alberto asked.

"I think so," Taylor said. He had been waiting for almost ten minutes, partly due to the fact that he was early. "His car is still at the shop, so he said he would meet Gen and me."

Taylor and Gen had tried to get back into the habit of a standing lunch date. They typically met on Fridays, when Gen was in town working on her Mayoral duties. Where Taylor had generally spread his responsibilities out over the week, Gen tried to keep it all to one day—preferably one morning, if she could swing it.

Fridays were usually light days for him, especially as he managed to get more and more of his caseload moved over to the other attorneys in his office. With Pete's help, Taylor was becoming less and less of an office presence and more and more of just a courtroom litigator. Not that working in the courtroom was a great way to reduce his workload, but it did free him up a little more.

No sooner was he really starting to wonder if both his spouse and his best friend were going to stand him up at the same time when he saw Tom's form pass by the window and turn to come in the door.

"Hi," Taylor greeted him with an unobtrusive kiss. He realized Tom was sweating, his hair plastered to his forehead, his T-shirt damp.

"Hi," Tom breathed. "Whew! Does it feel good in here," he said, referring to Alberto's cool air conditioning. "What a morning!"

"What's going on?" Taylor asked, watching as Tom visibly decompressed.

"Big rush order came in at the last minute. Wayne, Jason and I were planning some stuff for the coffee shop and Emmy came out to tell us someone had just called in an order for ten dozen dinner rolls and two cakes."

Taylor tried to process the barrage of information. "Wow. Big order," he said. "Is Mrs. Johnson available to make the cakes?"

Tom shook his head. "No, that honor fell to yours truly. Emmy is pretty good, but since I was there, she wanted me to do it."

"Fun for you," Taylor agreed. "Jason was helping plan the coffee shop?" he asked.

Tom nodded. He reached over and took Taylor's iced tea, taking a long sip. "Yeah, Wayne and I hired him to be the manager," he said, as though it was ancient history.

"I should just accept that I'm out of the loop, shouldn't I?" Taylor asked, watching his drink disappear.

"Sorry, honey," Tom consoled. "You're there in spirit."

"Humph," Taylor grumped.

"But I still love you," Tom reminded him.

Alberto appeared at his side, another glass of iced tea in his hand. "Can I get you anything, Tommy?" he asked.

"I'll wait for Gen, Alberto. Thanks."

"My pleasure," he said, then disappeared back into the kitchen.

Tom gently laid his hand on Taylor's. "Hey, speaking of out of the loop, did you know Eric was in town yesterday?"

Taylor frowned. "No, I didn't. He came to see Wayne?"

Tom nodded. "Yeah. I don't know what the story is. Wayne just mentioned it to me in passing this morning, but he didn't want to talk about it."

"That's interesting," Taylor said.

"You might want to check in with him later," Tom suggested. "You're usually the one he talks to."

Taylor looked up. "He talks to you," he reminded.

Tom shook his head. "No, I just mean you're the one he *talks* to. It's okay, Tay, it doesn't bother me."

"I'll check on him later," Taylor agreed. Truth be told, he knew very well that Wayne usually talked to him more than Tom. Wayne loved Tom, as he did Taylor, but just gravitated toward Taylor more than Tom. As far as they were both concerned, it was fine since Tom was usually busy with the rest of their gaggle of kids anyway.

The door opened again, this time admitting the ever-fashionable Gen Pouissant. She had opted for an unusually bright pink sleeveless blouse and Capri pants, with white sandals that set off her matching pink toenail polish. The bright colors made her skin look unusually dark, and her hair pulled back in a clip made her look like a Nubian fashion model. She came to the table nearly as breathless as Tom had been moments before, slipping her glasses off and setting them beside her place. She stopped long enough to give them both a kiss on the cheek, then sat.

"What a morning!" she said, echoing Tom's comment as well.

"Busy?" Taylor asked.

"And how," Gen said, grabbing up a glass of water. "And the air conditioning is out, so it's about eighty-five degrees in the office." She gently fanned herself with a menu. "Whew. It feels a lot better in here, I'll tell you that."

Taylor watched her from across the table. "How'd the doctor's appointment go?"

Gen sighed. "Par for the course. They're running out of options, but they don't want us to know," she said. "We have another meeting with them next week. Honestly, most of the time I just try not to think about it."

"I understand," Taylor said. He glanced at Tom, who leaned forward, changing the topic to something less likely to depress her.

"Did you hear about our latest purchase?"

"I heard you bought the flower shop building," Gen said, glad for their understanding. "When did you decide to do that?"

Taylor and Tom looked at each other, talking at the same time. "I don't know…it was what…Monday? Yeah, Monday." Tom turned back to Gen. "We decided on Monday," he said.

"On Monday!?" she exclaimed. "You two never waste any time, do you?"

"We had to beat out Stuart DiNardo on the purchase," Taylor explained, proud of himself.

Gen shook her head. "Well, get ready boys, 'cause we have more than just a building to beat him out on now."

"What do you mean?" Taylor asked.

Gen looked up, eyes dark. "He turned in his application this morning. He's having a big fundraiser in the park this weekend."

Tom leaned in still closer, remembering his last-minute order. "Fundraiser for what?"

Gen positively glared as she spoke. "Stuart DiNardo is running for Mayor."

CHAPTER SIX

It's All About Who You Know

Wayne awoke to the sound of pounding coming from somewhere. At first, he started out of his bed to see what Dan might be doing, but then remembered the reason he got to sleep in in the first place was Dan had agreed to do the morning baking for him. What was that racket?

Wearing only his boxers, he padded into the front room, where the sound was the loudest and realized it was coming from below. It wasn't until he looked out the window that he remembered—they were starting demolition of the space between the stores. Wayne took small solace in knowing Jason was bearing the worst of it—the builders had started structure installation the week before, fully a week ahead of schedule.

In order to allow the store to stay open during construction, they had removed one full section of the counter where the new pass-through would be, and taken out all of the tables and chairs, storing them in the office space Peggy had used in the flower shop. Though the space was slated to be demolished and rearranged as well, it would not need to be touched until after the changes were made between the two buildings. By then, they could put the tables back until construction was complete. Tom and Taylor had spent several days trying to decide how to lay out the store, since they were losing space where the large entry was going.

The current plan was to flip-flop the cabinets, leaving just enough room by the front door to allow the door to open. They felt it was likely many patrons would pass through the coffee shop anyway, and Taylor had promoted the idea of closing the Downey's entrance entirely, to increase traffic to the shop.

Tom and Jason had conspired to replace the front windows in the flower shop space with French doors, but Taylor had nixed the idea in the near term. He felt it was important to get the shop up and running first, and then make additional improvements later. Though Tom had been disappointed, Jason had been forced to concede Taylor's point, so they settled on putting in just one set of French doors for the main entrance. Much like Downey's, they would stand open on nicer days, with just a simple screen door to keep the bugs at bay.

The pounding grew louder and Wayne realized they must be attacking the wall from both sides. His understanding from meeting with the builder was the two buildings were truly separate, though there was no actual space between them. So, in essence, it was a double-thick wall they were breaking through. The builder had agreed with their idea to save as many of the bricks as possible for the new opening—they were designing it as an old-style bricked archway that would be just slightly shorter than the Downey's ceiling, as it was higher than the space on the other side and they needed to leave room for the fixtures that would adorn the coffee shop.

The coffee shop ceiling itself would be an interesting structure. They had wanted to leave the beams exposed, but that would make providing sound insulation to Jason's apartment difficult. So they had opted for a classical tinned ceiling, complete with cove work and decorative trim around the lights. Above was enough acoustic insulation to quiet all but the loudest of performances. Ultimately, they decided it would be up to Jason to determine what was acceptable, since he was in charge anyway.

Wayne and Jason had been charged with much of the day-to-day management of the project. Since DiNardo's announcement of his intention to run for Mayor, Tom and Taylor had spent a great deal of time networking with the other owners of stores in the historic district, as well as town residents, lobbying to keep Gen in office. They were finding DiNardo's promises were attracting a lot of attention. Many of the residents in the newer parts of town felt it was time to offer a fresh breath to the historic district and encouraged the current owners to consider allowing the spaces to be developed. So far, no one else seemed willing to sell to DiNardo, but they all figured it was just a matter of time.

The pounding continued and Wayne realized it wasn't going to let up anytime soon. He took a quick shower, then dressed for work and headed down the back stairs. Once inside the bakery, he found it was even louder as the masons chipped away at the wall. Jason stood with Emmy and Dan by the baking room, wincing as the sound permeated the place.

"How long is this going to take?" Wayne yelled.

"They promised it wouldn't take very long," Jason replied, equally loudly over the racket. "They're coming at it from both sides. They're already through in one place."

Wayne shook his head. "And *this* is the morning I decide to sleep in!"

"Don't you think it's going to drive away the customers?" Emmy asked.

"It might," Wayne agreed, "but we had no choice. It had to be done and it would cost a fortune to do off hours."

"Maybe we should have closed for a day or two," Dan offered.

"We would have if it was going to be longer than a day or two," Tom said, coming up from behind to stand between Wayne and Dan, his arms on their shoulders. "Demolition will only take a few hours, then they'll build out the arch and work on installing the doors," he explained.

"Then what?" Dan asked.

Tom smiled. "Then we start working on rearranging everything in here. Long nights, kiddo."

"Great," Dan deadpanned, rolling his eyes. He and Emmy went back out front, restocking the cabinets in the din. Tom walked into the baking room, followed by Jason and Wayne.

"Taylor and I have to meet with Gen at noon to discuss mayoral strategy, but I've got a couple errands to run. Will you guys be able to cover things here?"

"No problem," Wayne said.

"We've got it," Jason added. His warm brown eyes watched both men, still learning how they interrelated. Since he'd started working for them two weeks before, he'd already learned how to make himself a part of the team and integrated quickly.

Tom smiled. "Thanks, guys. Let's meet for lunch at Alberto's, say, around twelve-thirty? Emmy and Dan should be able to hold down the fort."

"We'll be there," Wayne confirmed.

Tom turned to him. "Are you planning to be there for the talent show this afternoon?"

Wayne smiled. "Are you kidding? Chad called last night, just to be sure."

"Great. I know he's been worried that something would keep us, but I promised him we'd all be there," Tom said. Chad was in the second grade talent show and had spent the last couple of weeks working on his routine with Emmy and Gen, getting it perfect. As much as Wayne tended to gravitate to Taylor, the younger kids all gravitated to Tom. They loved Taylor, but Tom's natural comfort around kids conveyed itself to them.

Wayne nodded. "Jason and Dan are going to cover the store while Em and I go to the show. That way, if there are any issues with the construction, Jason can handle it, and Dan can run things for the afternoon."

Tom stood taller, proud. "You guys really have it together. I don't even know why I come in anymore."

"Neither do I," Wayne said straight-faced. He couldn't hold it, though, and broke into a grin as Tom smacked him in the stomach.

"I've gotta run. I'll see you this afternoon," he said to Wayne. "Jason, thanks for keeping things covered."

"Not a problem, Tom," Jason replied, and then as fast as that, Tom was gone. "Where does he find the energy?" he asked Wayne.

Wayne shook his head. "Nobody knows."

The hammering continued out front, but it wasn't nearly as loud in the baking room. Jason turned to Wayne. "Hey, there was something I wanted to talk to you about," he began.

"Okay. I had something I wanted to talk to you about, too."

"Oh? You want to go first?"

Wayne shook his head. "No, you can."

Jason leaned back against one of the counters. "It's about the coffee shop," he said. "I think there's a marketing opportunity we're missing out on."

Wayne looked up sharply. "The bookstore?"

Jason broke into a broad grin. "Yeah! How'd you know?"

"I was about to raise the same topic!"

"Great minds!" Jason said, high-fiving him. "Do you know who owns it?"

"Sure, it's Liz Ryan and her sister-in-law, Sherry," Wayne confirmed.

Jason checked his watch. "Do you think they're open yet?"

Wayne started for the front. "Dan and Emmy will know. They stop in for a cinnamon roll every morning."

Emmy looked up from the counter she was cleaning, just having caught the tail end of Wayne's statement. "Liz and Sherry?" she asked.

"Yeah," Wayne said. "Have they been in?"

"About five minutes ago," Emmy said. "Hey, you know, we should see if—"

Wayne nodded. "They want to open their wall, too?"

Emmy nodded emphatically. "Yeah!"

"We're already on it," he said, nodding to Jason. "We were just talking about it."

"Do Tom and Taylor know?" Dan asked.

Jason shook his head. "Not yet. We'll bring it up if Liz and Sherry are interested."

"You should go and talk to them," Emmy insisted. "See what they think!"

"You've got the store 'til we get back?" Wayne asked.

"Sure, no problem," Emmy said. "Dan and I can keep it going for now."

"Great, then we'll see you in a few!" Wayne said. He and Jason made it through the mess and left through the front door, happy to leave the hammering behind.

The rain had finally abated and left in its place cool, sunny weather. The builders had covered the windows of the old flower shop with paper and there had been a lot of speculation about what might be going in.

When they had to rearrange the bakery storefront to facilitate demolition, everyone knew the Downey's people had to know what was happening. Word of the new coffee shop had spread like wildfire and the town was abuzz, much to the chagrin of

Stuart DiNardo's forces. Even as he tried to rally the townspeople around bringing his chain stores into the historic district, the district was responding by expanding its own unique presence. If word got out about what Wayne and Jason were about to propose, Wayne shuddered to think what the response would be.

They opened the door to Uniquely Books and went inside. The store was, like every other store on the street, two stories. However, Liz and Sherry had used both floors, removing a large section near the front to allow the upstairs to be seen from below. A staircase ran up in the center, with a curving stair at the back of the store. The open space allowed light to come in from windows on both levels, offering a bright, airy feel, complimented by the skylights and well positioned halogens. Tom had explained that Liz's husband did all the construction while Sherry's husband completed the finished carpentry. They had opened the store almost ten years before, just before Tom arrived in town.

Sherry was coming down the front stairs, a stack of books in hand, when she saw her two guests.

"Wayne!" she greeted. "How are you?"

Wayne smiled at her natural good humor. "I'm great, how are you?"

"Wonderful!" she answered, setting the stack down on a nearby table. She eyed Jason. "Who do we have here?"

Wayne turned to Jason. "This is Jason Harper. He'll be running the coffee shop," he explained.

"So you're the one making all the racket next door," Sherry observed, shaking his hand.

"Guilty as charged," Jason replied, looking guilty.

Sherry shrugged. "Well, it can't last too long," she prophesized. "Anyway, I'm Sherry, and up there in the rafters is Liz, my sister-in-law. We try to keep this place going as best we can."

Jason's eyes continued to take in the store, where every nook and cranny held something different. "It looks fabulous to me," he said.

"Fabulous, huh?" Sherry asked, glancing at Wayne. "Well, I suppose it does. So, what brings you boys over here? Looking for something in particular?"

Wayne nodded. "Actually, we wanted to talk to you and Liz," he said.

"Oh?" Sherry asked. "Hey, Liz, come on down here. Wayne wants to talk to us," she called.

"Coming," Liz replied. She made her way down the stairs as well, meeting up with them by the counter. "What's up?"

"We wanted to run an idea by you," Wayne explained. "You know we're putting in a coffee shop next door..."

Liz chuckled. Though nowhere near as loud as in the bakery, the banging was still audible. "How could we miss it?"

Wayne nodded. "I know, sorry. But it may not be for nothing—we had an idea: would you be interested in opening a connection from the coffee shop into your bookstore, too?"

The two women exchanged looks, then turned back to Wayne and Jason. "Can't they just come through the front door, like everyone else?" Liz asked.

Jason answered. "Of course. But these days, people like to browse back and forth while they shop. They pick up a coffee and maybe something sweet, then they browse into the bookstore and look around, then back for more coffee... That's why all the big chain stores started adding coffee shops and cafes."

Sherry nodded. "I'll admit, the idea has crossed our minds from time to time. We had thought about doing something down here, but we hated to give up the floor space. Then when we found out you guys were putting in a shop right next door, we figured it didn't really matter since your shop would be there."

Liz spoke next. "However, it *is* interesting to consider joining up with your store. So, in theory, people could walk all the way from the bakery to the bookstore and back without ever going outside?"

"That's the idea," Wayne agreed.

"Interesting," Liz said. "What would we do about checking out, though? How would people know they needed to pay in each place?"

Jason smiled. "Actually, that's where I come in," he said. "I haven't even had a chance to discuss this with Wayne yet, but I was thinking we could install a retail management system to allow customers to check out in any of the stores. We each maintain our own separate inventories and the computer tracks who buys what. We add it all up at close of business, split out the difference, and pay each place."

Sherry shook her head, as if to clear it. "Sounds pretty complicated. We still add things up by hand."

Jason was in sales mode and Wayne knew it, so he let him talk. "The nice thing about the computer is it would actually be able to maintain your inventory, let you know if something was getting low, track and place orders, etc."

Liz was a little more computer ready than her counterpart. "So with this system, if someone wanted to buy, say, a loaf of Downey's bread and the latest copy of People, they could do it in either place?"

Jason nodded affirmatively. "Exactly. You've got it."

"What about hours? We don't usually stay open real late, especially during the week," Sherry said.

"Just like the bakery, there would be doors you could use to close off your store from the coffee shop. I think you'll find, though, that if you stay open, people will come. We could probably help staff the store, if you wanted to," Jason answered.

Sherry turned to Liz. "Tom and Taylor have always been good neighbors, and it certainly wouldn't hurt to try increasing the business."

"What will it cost to have the wall opened up?" Liz asked.

Wayne stepped in. "First we have to run the idea by Tom and Taylor, then we'd have to ask the builder."

"You haven't asked them yet?" Sherry inquired.

Wayne and Jason both looked a little guilty. "We wanted to see what you thought first."

"They put us in charge of the project," Jason added.

"Sounds like you two had better go check with the boys," Liz reprimanded. "If you wanted to know if we're interested, we are. But you need to make sure Tom and Taylor will want this, too."

"I think they're going to be thrilled," Wayne said.

"Let's find out first," Liz reminded him.

"We'll let you know," Jason said, leading Wayne back to the door.

"We'll be here," Sherry said. "Bye, boys."

"See ya," Wayne said as Jason shoed him out.

Shaking her head as they disappeared from sight, Sherry sighed, "Kids!" She and Liz made their way back upstairs, eager to get back to work.

Gen had called Taylor that morning, insisting that they needed to get together at lunch. She didn't have time to talk, but she wanted to meet with both Tom and him at lunch. Taylor sensed urgency in her voice, so he agreed, telling her they'd meet her at Alberto's at noon. He'd called Tom, who agreed they'd meet there, after he ran some errands.

So Taylor was, once again, the first person to show up, and sat waiting while Alberto fretted around his restaurant, wanting to bring Taylor food.

"You're sure I can't get you anything?"

"I'm great, Alberto," Taylor said, shaking his head. "Honestly."

"You know, I just can't get used to having people around who aren't eating," Alberto admitted. "It's an Italian thing."

"This low carb craze has got to be driving you crazy," Taylor observed.

"Ah," Alberto sighed with a dismissive wave of his hand. "It'll pass. We Italians have been eating pasta and drinking wine for centuries, and we live very long lives. Instead of counting carbohydrates, people should be worried about where their food came from. Learn to eat fresh, you know?"

Taylor nodded. "That's why we eat here," he said.

Alberto smiled proudly. "And my food will give you a long and happy life!"

Tom came in with Gen right behind him. "Look who I found," Tom said, greeting Taylor and Alberto.

"Madam Mayor," Alberto greeted with mock severity. "What can I bring for you today, ma'am?"

Gen brightened as she always did, but not as much as usual. "Just water, please," she said.

"Water it is," Alberto said and he was off. Tom was about to stop him, but saw iced tea already waiting at the place beside Taylor.

"I guess I'm having iced tea," he observed. Like Taylor, he enjoyed Alberto's tendency to decide what was best for them on his own.

"Gen, you sounded positively upset on the phone," Taylor recounted. "What's up?"

"You did not hear this from me," she said in a low, hushed tone. There was no one else in the restaurant besides Alberto, and he was in the kitchen. "Stuart DiNardo inquired about building permits today."

Tom leaned in, speaking quietly as well. "Is that unusual?" he asked.

Gen shook her head. "Of course not, he's a real estate developer. What was unusual was that he was so specific." She looked at Taylor, knowing he would recognize what she was about to say. "Mixed use retail with limited food service."

"Next door?" he asked.

"Yep," she confirmed as Alberto brought her water.

"May I bring you a menu, Madam Mayor?" he asked.

Gen shook her head politely. "No need, Alberto. I would love to have whatever you're bringing for them," she said, gesturing to her two friends. She had picked up on the fact that they rarely ordered anymore, yet what showed up in front of them always looked divine.

Alberto smiled at her trust. "Gladly, ma'am. I'll have it for you, right away!"

"Thank you," she said and he disappeared back into the kitchen.

"What's his theme?" Taylor asked as soon as their friend was gone.

"Fence and Edges."

At that, Tom jumped like he'd been shocked. "You're kidding!" he gasped.

"Biggest chain bookstore in the nation," Gen confirmed. "Right here next to Alberto."

"That no good, son-of-a—" Taylor rested a hand on Tom's arm, reminding him to stay quiet.

"What's the city's position?" Taylor inquired.

Gen looked down. "Ron said there is little they can do to block it. The space is retail and as long as DiNardo meets all the codes, he can basically use it for whatever he pleases."

"He's retaliating for us buying the flower shop space," Tom hissed. One of the few things that could ever get Tom worked up was apparent unfair behavior from the people around him. Needless to say, DiNardo had him worked up a lot of the time.

"Probably," Gen agreed. "In a way, that was to be expected. He's had his eye on the historic district for the last two years, so anyone he perceives as blocking his objectives will become a target."

"Fence and Edges makes Liz and Sherry a target, too," Tom observed.

"Don't I know it," Gen said.

"How long can Ron keep them tied up in planning?" Taylor asked, pondering the situation as he ran his finger through the condensation on his glass.

"Well, *legally*—" Gen began.

Taylor glared at her. "Gen," he said, stopping her disclaimer.

"Several months at least," she said. "Ron is, of course, willing to work with us on it. Of course, I also can't be seen as being involved," she reminded them, "or else we might as well open the doors to city hall for him."

"Of course," Taylor agreed, still thinking.

"You're already plotting," Tom observed, watching him.

Taylor smiled back at him. "It's what I do," he defended.

Alberto appeared with three plates—chicken breast on focaccia with mixed vegetables and a very light strip of homemade aioli—a relatively healthy, light lunch for summer.

"Looks wonderful," Gen praised, and Tom and Taylor joined her. Alberto sensed that their discussion was not something he wanted to overhear, so he made his way back to the kitchen.

"So?" Tom demanded as soon as the door had swung closed. "What are we going to do?"

Gen seemed equally interested in whatever scheme Taylor had dreamed up, knowing how difficult it would be to battle DiNardo if he was entrenched.

"We talk to Liz and Sherry," Taylor said, taking a bite of his lunch.

"You want to tell them?" Gen asked.

The light went on over Tom's head. "No, he wants to partner with them," Tom answered, giving Taylor a wry smile.

Taylor's blue eyes positively twinkled as he looked back at Tom. "You've been hanging around me too long," he said.

Gen still wasn't quite there. "Partner with them how?" she asked.

Tom turned to her. "What's the big difference between their bookstore and the big chain stores?"

"Usually the chain stores are cheaper and have a bigger selection," Gen said.

"Ah, but they have a very large store, with a great selection. Price might be a factor, but these days the chains aren't as competitive as the internet," Tom said. "What else?"

It was Gen's turn to join the wave. "Coffee shop!"

"Bingo," Taylor said, taking another bite.

Tom continued. "They need a café, we need a bookstore, and the two combined with Downey's will put a real crimp in DiNardo's plan."

"We need to make sure Fence and Edges knows about the existing competition in this little one street town," Taylor added.

Gen nodded. "I think I can make that happen. Maggie wondered if the person she talked to had a clue. I'm sure she wouldn't mind asking."

"We have to be careful and not get ahead of ourselves," Taylor warned. "This is not a time for mistakes."

The door to the restaurant opened again and Wayne and Jason appeared. They saw Tom and Taylor seated with Gen and made their way over.

"Sorry we're early," Wayne said.

"It's okay," Taylor replied. "Have a seat."

"We have a great idea we just had to share with you and we didn't want to wait," Wayne explained. Alberto appeared with two more plates.

"Taylor said you'd be coming a little later," he explained, handing them each identical meals to what their hosts had "ordered."

After Alberto left, Jason looked up. "We don't order here?" he asked.

"I'll explain later," Tom said.

"So, guys, listen," Wayne interrupted, brimming with excitement. "We've got this great idea. We talked to Liz and Sherry and we were thinking we should open the coffee shop to their bookstore!" He sat up, smiling broadly, as though it was the best idea he'd ever heard.

The three senior members of their little party eyed each other quietly over their lunches. Finally, Taylor shrugged and said, "Okay."

Wayne was stunned. "Okay? That's it?"

Tom nodded. "Sounds like a good plan," he said, just barely able to contain himself.

"You don't even need to think about it?" Jason asked, incredulous.

Taylor shook his head, nonchalant. "Nah. What's to think about?"

Wayne wasn't giving in so easily. "Okay, what's the story? Tay, I know for a fact you would never give in so easily."

Tom couldn't contain himself any longer and he started giggling. Gen followed suit and Taylor looked at them both. "What?"

Gen burst out laughing. "He's right!" she said.

Wayne looked distinctly annoyed, but Tom put a reassuring hand on his arm. "I'm sorry, we aren't laughing at you," he said. "We had just discussed the idea not two minutes before you two showed up."

"Really?" Jason asked.

"Really," Taylor confirmed.

Wayne smiled a little ruefully, realizing he'd been had. "You know, Emmy and Dan came up with the idea this morning, too. I guess we're all there, huh?"

"Great minds," Tom agreed.

"Well, I'll bet your great minds haven't come up with Jason's idea for managing it," Wayne said, turning to his co-manager. Jason took the cue and explained his concept for computerizing the operation of the business while the three non-technical people listened with rapt, if often puzzled attention.

That evening, after Emmy and Wayne got back from little Chad's talent show, they spotted Dan and Jason, letting them have the rest of the evening off. The bakery was due to close in an hour, and they would use most of that time to get everything ready so they could lock up promptly at closing time.

It had been awhile since Wayne had closed. He almost always worked an early shift, taking responsibility for the baking. Since he was used to being in the baking room anyway, he told Emmy he'd take care of that if she wanted to get the cabinets ready.

He stood at the sink, washing the paddles for one of the large mixers, steam from the hot water riding around him.

"Hey, Wayne."

Wayne jumped, splashing water on the floor and down the front of his apron. He stopped the faucets, quickly reaching for a towel to wipe himself off.

"You scared me!" he yelled. Eric handed him another towel, taking the other one and tossing it into the dirty bin.

"You still run the hot water like crazy," Eric observed. "It always dries out your hands."

"I don't usually have to close anymore, but Dan did me a favor, so I felt I should do the same," Wayne explained, still dabbing at his wet clothes. "What are you doing here?"

"I came to see you," Eric answered. He still looked sad, like it had taken all of his energy to work up the courage to come visit him.

"Still didn't want to call ahead?" Wayne asked, turning back to clean the last of the paddles.

"I called," Eric said from behind him. "You didn't answer your phone."

Wayne reached for his pocket, then remembered. "I must have left it in my Jeep," he said. "Emmy used it while we were driving back."

"See?" Eric said.

"How was home?" Eric had spent the previous week at home, bringing things back with him to start his new life on his own.

"I was glad to leave," he said honestly. "It's not home anymore."

Wayne gave him a grudging smile and Eric's whole face lit up. "So what's up?" Wayne asked.

"I met with my new employer this week," Eric said, his voice a little stronger. "The project I'm supposed to work on isn't going to start until the end of the summer and they don't have anywhere for me to go in the meantime."

"What does that mean?"

Eric shrugged. "They told me to check in once a week, but I have the next few weeks off. They said it would give me a chance to get settled in anyway."

Wayne turned off the water, placing the last of the equipment in the rack to dry. "So you have nothing to do?"

"Pretty much."

"Except come bug me," Wayne finished.

Eric laughed. "Is that so bad?"

Wayne shook his head. "I don't know yet."

Leaning back against a wall, Eric said, "I was actually thinking it might be kind of fun to come work with you guys again for a while." Wayne turned to look at him, surprised. Eric continued, "Come on. I'm experienced. I know everybody. You're going to need the help with the coffee shop."

"What do you know about that?" Wayne asked.

"Emmy told me about it," Eric explained. "The construction is kind of hard to miss."

"How do I know you won't run off again?"

Eric looked hurt, but he understood the concern. "I won't," he insisted. "I promise you."

"Eric…"

He walked across the room, facing Wayne, looking him straight in the eye. "Give me a chance to make up the last two years to you. Give me a chance to explain everything that has happened. Let me make it up to you and show you the friend I can be. Please, Wayne."

"Aggh!" Wayne moaned, turning away. He tossed the last towel in the bin, then turned back, his face tight. "I suppose everyone deserves a second chance."

Eric's face lit up like a Christmas tree, and the tension visibly drained from him. "Thank you!" He moved as though to hug Wayne, but Wayne took a step back.

"Hey! Not so fast. You have a significant amount of groveling ahead of you before hugging privileges will be restored."

Eric smiled in spite of himself, and took one step back himself. "Got it."

"And you will be here *promptly* at eight o'clock. Dan and I will be baking. You can help Emmy out front."

"Will do," Eric affirmed. It was all he could do to keep himself from floating off the floor.

Wayne thought for a minute, then nodded to himself and looked up. "Okay, that's it for now. I'll see you in the morning."

Eric looked disappointed that they wouldn't be talking more, but he knew to quit while he was ahead. "I'll be here."

"Good night," Wayne said.

"See you tomorrow!" Eric said brightly, then turned to go.

Wayne leaned back against the edge of the sink as Emmy came in from the other room. She walked over and put her arm around him, as she often did when no one else was around.

"How are you?" she asked.

He gave a humorless chuckle. "Vexed and perplexed."

She smiled, leaning her head on his shoulder. "For what it's worth, he seemed pretty sincere when he talked to me."

"He talked to you?" Wayne asked.

"Yeah," Emmy confirmed. "He wanted to know if I thought you'd be okay with him asking you. Honestly, he seemed to care."

Wayne looked down at her. "You were the one who wanted to burn him in effigy when he left."

Emmy nodded. "Yes, I was. But I'm also the one who has seen you pining for him for the last two years, and I see the way he looks when he talks about you. Dan told me a little about what his father did and that's not fair at all. I guess I'm saying it won't hurt to at least talk to him, let him tell his side of the story, and see what you think."

"And then?"

Emmy shrugged. "Either you get back together and you're happy, or we burn him in effigy."

Wayne smiled. "Either way, I'm going to hold you to it."

Emmy hugged him once more, then stood up. "No problem, Waynie. I'll be there." She looked back toward the door. "You going upstairs?"

"Yeah," he said, hanging his apron on a coat hook. Together, they walked out, turning off the lights behind them.

CHAPTER SEVEN

A Second First Date

It was just over two weeks until the grand opening of the coffee shop. In honor of the fact that it was originally his idea, Tom and Taylor decided to leave it to Wayne to name the new store. After a great deal of thought, he settled on Café del Sol, enjoying the spoken double-entendre with "soul," given that live music would be a key component of the new establishment.

And so the café was born. Dan and Wayne did the art for the windows, menus, and any other printed material in the shop, while Emmy and Jason partnered on the visual look. As was relatively common, they opted for rich, deep colors offset with warm earth tones. Tom insisted on state of the art halogen lighting, while Taylor focused mostly on ensuring the couches were all suitably comfortable for lounging. Wayne even brought Eric into the fold, having him work on the stage backdrop. Eric offered the idea that they might also consider a stand-up comedy night, and everyone agreed the idea may have merit. Building on the thought, Emmy pointed out poetry readings were a sure draw as well, particularly since the opening of the wall to the bookstore.

Liz and Sherry had quickly agreed to the idea of connecting the stores, even before Tom and Taylor gave them the news about DiNardo's pending agreement with Fence and Edges. They arranged to free a large section of wall directly across from the main staircase, inviting visitors from Café del Sol to browse on both levels as they came through the double French doors that were installed. The way Tom and Jason had positioned the doors, it almost looked as though the two businesses were actually one, and that was exactly what all concerned had wanted.

Life in the bakery had slowly settled back into a routine. The crew spent one whole weekend completely renovating the space, arranging the counters, tables, and other surfaces, then putting up a fresh coat of paint before rehanging the numerous mementos from decades of business. When all was said and done, virtually everything fit that had before, with one table and set of chairs having to go into storage for the time being.

The town was fascinated by all the changes, more than any could remember in recent memory. Virtually all the customers had to stop and look through the windows in the doors to see how progress was going on the coffee shop. Liz and Sherry reported similar interest from their establishment. Everyone wanted a peek, though all the windows were…mostly…covered with paper. Tom and Wayne had agreed to leave just enough gaps to tantalize the most interested viewers.

Life in the bakery also settled into a routine with the people working there. With Eric's return, it felt like everyone was back in the nest, along with a few new players to keep things interesting.

Wayne and Eric were still working through their issues, but they'd talked a few times, and their friends tried to support them. To their credit, while Emmy and Dan were ever supportive of Wayne, they also tried to be there for Eric. While Wayne wasn't being overtly unkind, he wasn't throwing his arms wide, either. Everyone understood that the kind of emotional trauma Wayne had suffered throughout his life didn't leave him one to trust quickly when a trust had been broken. Taylor reminded him that it was okay to be angry, but not to let anger rule his actions. Anger was an indicator, a warning bell, but it should never be allowed to triumph over logic or love. Both were more powerful, and ultimately, more valuable.

Wayne had taken the words to heart, letting Eric participate in more and more of their activities, but always keeping his distance. Wayne knew Eric wanted to be closer, to have what they shared before he left, and Eric knew Wayne wanted it to. So they just had to find their way through the maze that was their shared pain together, to find the prize waiting at the end.

Taylor arrived one morning to find Tom and Eric covering the front. Emmy had finally gotten a morning off, with Dan and Wayne doing their usual shift in the baking room.

"Your mom called," Taylor said, taking the bagel Tom handed over the case to him.

"How are they?" Tom asked. His parents had taken the three younger children to Florida to visit their biological grandparents for a couple weeks. It was a double gift because it also gave Tom and Taylor some much needed time on their own.

"She said everyone is having a great time. They're all going to Disney World tomorrow, and the Gulf on Friday," Taylor recounted. Tom stayed behind the counter, knowing he had just stopped in for breakfast on his way to the city for hearings. "We need to get them a really good Christmas present for this," he reiterated.

"I'll say," Tom agreed. "You'll be home tonight around five?"

Taylor nodded. "Should be," he said.

"It's home cooked meal night at the McEwan-Connolly house," Tom said with a smile.

"I can't wait," Taylor replied. He leaned over to give Tom a quick kiss on the lips, then headed for the door. "Call me if you need me."

"Will do. Drive safe," Tom said.

"Love you," Taylor answered, opening the door.

"Love you, too," Tom said. Taylor stopped to hold the door for a customer, then was gone.

"Aren't you sweet?" Eric chided, knocking elbows with Tom. He turned to greet the customer. "Can I help you?"

The young man offered a friendly smile and nodded. "Actually, I was wondering if Wayne is working?"

Eric's brow wrinkled. It was rare any of them had people ask to see them personally. "Actually, he is. May I give him your name?"

"Pedro Aguilar," he answered.

"I'll let him know you're here," Eric answered politely. He glanced in Tom's direction as he turned to walk to the back and the look on Tom's face told him there was more to Pedro than met the eye. He couldn't remember Wayne having mentioned him.

At the entrance to the baking room, Eric said, "Hey, Wayne? Pedro Aguilar is here to see you."

The look on Wayne's face said there was more to the story than met the eye, too, and he saw Dan give the slightest of glances in Wayne's direction as Wayne dusted off his hands to go out front. Eric stood aside to let him pass, then cornered Dan in the back of the room.

"So who's Pedro?" he asked, trying not to let the question sound as pointed as it was. He wasn't particularly successful.

Dan gave a nonchalant shrug, trying to make it look like it was no big deal. "He's a friend of Wayne's from school," he answered.

"A close friend?" Eric quizzed.

Dan glanced at him. "You'd have to ask Wayne. I don't know."

Eric gave him a look. "Come on, Dan-o. You two have been living together for two years."

Dan looked up, and Eric couldn't tell if he was annoyed or just uncomfortable. "Eric, don't put me in the middle of whatever is going on with you and Wayne. I consider myself a friend to both of you, but I can't do that if I start choosing sides, or if I start being asked to choose sides. You two need to talk, to figure out what the heck you're doing."

Eric nodded, understanding. "I've been trying to do that for the last couple of weeks. Every time we get close, he backs away."

"Still, you need to talk," Dan reiterated.

Eric turned and walked back toward the front, nearly running into Wayne as he rounded the corner. The expression on his face perfectly matched what Dan had said—they needed to talk.

Wayne nearly ran into Eric as he headed back to the baking room. He regarded Eric silently for a moment, seeing the pain once again in his eyes. While he and Pedro had settled on a solid friendship, he knew it would look wrong to Eric. Taylor was right—it was time for them to figure out what was next.

"Hey, we're going to take a couple minutes out back," Wayne called to Tom. "Will you and Dan be okay for a few?"

"We're fine," Tom assured him.

In an uncharacteristic motion, Wayne reached out and took Eric's hand, leading him out the back door and into the sunlit parking lot. Still with Eric's hand in his, he led him to one of the shade trees in a grassy island of the parking lot and they relaxed on the grass.

"Pedro is a friend from school. We have a history class together," Wayne explained, answering the most obvious question first.

"Okay," Eric said simply, playing with the blades of grass between his legs.

"That's all there is to it, Eric," Wayne reiterated.

"I believe you," Eric said.

"I hear a 'but' in your voice," Wayne observed.

Eric looked up. "I saw the look on his face, Wayne. He's more than a little into you."

Wayne let out his breath, looking up through the leaves of the tree to the bright blue sky beyond. Nodding, he said, "Pedro was the date I was supposed to go on the night you came back."

Eric's face froze, a thousand questions flying through his mind. Wayne continued. "However, I cancelled that date and told him I wasn't in a place to date anyone right now."

Eric took a couple heavy breaths, then looked up at Wayne, his lower eyelids glistening. "I can't keep doing this, Wayne. I can't keep playing this game."

Wayne closed his eyes, nodding. "I know."

"I came back here for *you*," Eric insisted. "I came back to make it up to you, to show you how I feel, so that you would consider...me...again." His gaze was pleading as he looked at Wayne. "I care about you so much, but I can't keep this up. I can't keep wondering."

"I know. Really, I do," Wayne said, leaning back to let the tree support him. His own expression was pained as he looked back at Eric. "What are you going to do when your dad finds out?"

There. There it was, out there, on the table. Eric said it was fear of his father's retribution that broke them up before. Wayne had to know how he would handle it this time.

"I will never go through this again," Eric promised. "I told you I never said anything because I knew you would turn me back." He looked deeply, piercingly into Wayne's eyes. "I was right. You turned me back. As sure as I knew you would, you turned me back. I promise you, with everything that I have, if you'll let me, I'm here to stay. I did what I told them I'd do, and it's my life now."

Wayne sat back, considering. No matter what Taylor said, two years of anguish was a lot to overcome. But, for possibly the first time, he knew he wanted to overcome it, and he was sure.

"Okay."

"Okay?" Eric asked, leaning forward.

"Okay," Wayne said again. "Take me on a date."

Eric cocked his head. "A date?"

Wayne nodded. "Yep. We never actually really went on a date before. We just kind of happened. If we're going to do this, we need to start over, from scratch. Let's start with a date."

Slowly, Eric smiled. He saw what Wayne was proposing—he didn't want to just pick up where they'd left off, he wanted a chance to let them start completely anew, to wipe the slate clean and have a fresh, new beginning.

Smile broadening, he said, "Okay, a date. Wayne McInerney, would you go out with me?"

Wayne returned the smile. "I'd love to," he said graciously.

In an aside voice, Eric asked, "Where do you want to go?"

Mimicking the voice, Wayne answered, "You asked, you pick."

Eric thought for a moment, then said, "Shall we go tomorrow?"

Wayne winced. "Ooh, I can't," he said. He put a reassuring hand on Eric's knee. "We promised to help Tom with the little league game, remember."

"Oh yeah." Eric did remember. "Okay, how 'bout Friday?"

"For a second first date? Isn't Friday a little familiar?" Wayne asked, playing coy.

"Only a little," Eric dismissed.

"Friday it is," Wayne agreed. "What time?"

"Seven o'clock?" Eric asked. "I'll pick you up."

"Wonderful," Wayne said, rising. Eric rose to meet him and they regarded one another. "I'm looking forward to it," Wayne admitted.

Eric watched him, a dictionary of emotions passing across his face. Finally, he breathed, "Wayne," as he reached out and pulled him into a tight hug. Eyes closed, he clung to Wayne like he was the only thing holding him to the ground. Wayne didn't resist, holding Eric tight as he fought back tears. It was time for them to move on, past their pain, to grow, and to experience life together as adults. They held one another for several moments, in the shade under the maple tree, then they let go and walked back inside, together.

Wednesday afternoon, the final work was completed on installation of the ceiling at Café del Sol. Jason had supervised much of the work himself, ensuring that various electrical and data installations were completed prior to installation of the tiles. His philosophy was it was better to take the time to do the job right once than to go back and have to do it over a second time.

The last of the tiles finally in place, the electrician connected the lighting and began positioning the various hanging lights. His assistant turned off the work lights, and for the first time, they started to see how the coffee shop would come together.

The more subdued, directed lighting went a long way toward bringing out the color in the walls. The entire McEwan Connolly crew had spent a very long evening applying paint. Of course, Tom and Emmy, ever the fashion mavens, would not *hear* of flat wall colors, so everything had to have an effect applied, doubling or tripling the labor involved. To their credit, everyone pitched in, including a few of Tom and Taylor's friends, to get it done.

Standing in the space, with the lighting active, Jason had to admit the effect was stunning. He couldn't wait to see how it merged with the library green of the bookstore. He already knew it worked with the colors in the bakery, since he and Emmy had planned it that way.

"Impressive."

Jason turned to find someone standing in the doorway, someone he didn't know. He'd forgotten he left the door open when the builder called him in to inspect the ceiling.

"It is," Jason agreed. "Can I help you with something?"

The man smiled, shaking his head. "Nope, I just had to see this place. I'm a friend of Tom's, from the college. We teach in the same department."

"You're an English professor," Jason remembered.

Nodding, he said, "Guilty as charged." He held out a hand. "My name is Adam Brown."

"Jason Harper," he said, shaking hands. "I've heard Tom talk about you a few times."

"Nothing good, I suspect," Adam said. He was about Jason's height, and his blue eyes twinkled behind his fashionably rimless glasses. Unlike Jason's casual attire, he wore a smart summer blue shirt and beige slacks, with cordovan tassel loafers—he looked every bit the part of a college professor out in town for the day. His light brown hair had a natural wave to it and Jason could tell it had been moved around by the wind outside.

"Not too bad," Jason dismissed. "If Tom's here, he'll probably be in the baking room. They just finished the ceiling, so I was checking it out." He gestured to the door. "If you'd like to come back, I'll see if I can find him for you."

Adam smiled softly. "I'm in no hurry," he said. His voice was truly disarming, not soft, but not harsh at all. He seemed the sort of person who was entirely at ease with himself. "When will you be open for business?"

Jason regarded the store, still very much under construction. "We're planning to have our grand opening next week, on the Fourth. We figure everyone will be off work and the town is always busy for the fireworks, so why not offer coffee and apple pie?"

"Sounds like a good plan to me," Adam agreed. "Maybe I'll have to bring my students over here a time or two. Might help spread the word about this place."

"That would be great," Jason agreed. "We never turn down a little free publicity."

Adam nodded. "It's the least I can do. Tom's a good guy and I'd like to see him succeed."

"Did I hear my name?" Tom asked, peeking his head through the door. He smiled as he saw who was standing with Jason. "How did you get in here?"

"I kind of let myself in," Adam admitted. He shook Tom's hand, then gestured to Jason. "Jason was just telling me you think you're going to be open by next week?"

Jason found himself glad to hear Adam acknowledge his name. Tom nodded and said, "Jason has been riding herd over the whole project. He and our bakery manager are sharing the responsibilities. Jason comes from the tech industry, and he's going to fully automate both of our stores, as well as the bookstore next door. Their systems are already in and he's been bringing up the bakery all week."

"You never do anything small, do you?" Adam asked Tom, who gave a friendly laugh in response. Adam continued, "Listen, I was wondering if you could cover a class for me on Friday afternoon. I need to fly out for a book signing in Cleveland and it would really open up my schedule if I could leave earlier."

"Sure," Tom said. "Friday is one of the few days I have open right now."

"Are you sure? I don't want to overload you."

Tom shook his head. "Think nothing of it. You covered for me for a week while Chad was sick last winter. I'll be there. What time?"

"Twelve-thirty."

"No problem."

Adam smiled and shook his hand again. "Thanks, bud. I've gotta run, but I'll be in town on the Fourth, so I'll stop by."

"See you then," Tom said.

"Jason, nice to meet you," Adam acknowledged, and with a wave, he was off.

"Book tour?" Jason asked.

Tom nodded, following him back into the bakery and closing the door against any other surprise guests. "He just published his third novel. He teaches creative writing and English lit at the college."

"He was talking about wanting to hold an occasional class *in* the café."

Tom shrugged. "I won't turn down the business."

Jason nodded. "That's what I said."

Tom gave him a pat on the back. "Good contact," he said, smiling. Jason almost missed the sidelong look he gave him as he turned away to go back to whatever it was he was doing. Jason watched him go and wondered what was coming next.

Taylor sat behind the store, waiting for Tom to come out. He had planned to go inside, but his cell phone rang as he was getting out of the car, and the display said it was Gen. He flipped it open, and before he knew what was happening, Gen was railing on about Stuart DiNardo—her recent favorite topic.

"I'm telling you, Tay, people are talking about this guy like he's going to be the next president of the United States!" she exclaimed.

"Who is talking about him?" Taylor prompted. He sat on one of the cement blocks in front of a vacant parking spot, resting his elbows on his knees. He held his phone to his right ear, while he held his head with his left hand.

"Everywhere I go—the supermarket, Target, dinner, it's all the same. People whispering and commenting. Some people just come right out and ask whether or not I'm going to beat him in the election!"

Taylor sighed. "What do you tell them?"

"I say, 'Of course I'm going to win.' But it never seems like they think so."

Tom came up behind him, the door to the bakery slamming closed. He put his hands on Taylor's shoulders, offering him a gentle massage. Taylor leaned back against his legs, allowing Tom to support him.

"Why would they think someone like Stuart DiNardo would win against an incumbent mayor who has lived in the city for a decade?" Tom knew immediately who was on the phone and just kept his hands on Taylor's shoulders. Taylor reached back with his left hand, gently resting it on Tom's.

"He's very popular, Tay," Gen explained. "He's practically buying votes! He's had events at all his properties, hosted two big free parties down at the pavilion, and he's on the move every weekend."

"So why don't you do that?"

"What, do you think I'm independently wealthy? I didn't even want the stupid job—you made me take it!"

Taylor shrugged. "So, leave."

"Hell no! I'm not letting that conniving, backstabbing, swindling, no good, developer weasel take over my town! On a cold frickin' day in Hell, Taylor. On a cold frickin' day!"

He held the phone away from his ear as she went on her tirade, and it was loud enough that even Tom could hear. He snickered in spite of himself, but stayed quiet.

"Then what do you want to do about it?" Taylor ventured.

"If I *knew* what to do about it, I wouldn't have called you!" Gen exclaimed.

Taylor laughed. "So you want my advice?"

"That would be nice," she said.

"Are you on hormones again?" Taylor asked.

"What do you think?"

"Got it. Okay, here's what you need to do. DiNardo is going around town putting on a big show, telling everyone how wonderful he is, and how he's going to do all these wonderful things for the town, right?"

"Yeah?"

"How's he going to make that happen?"

"How should I know?"

"Do you think it might be a good idea to ask him?" Taylor asked.

"You think he's going to tell me?" Gen quizzed.

Taylor smiled. "I think if you put him in the right position, he won't have a choice."

There was a pause on the other end, then Gen spoke. "I'm listening."

He pressed on. "You know better than anyone, certainly better than Stuart DiNardo, the real issues affecting the town, right?"

"I would hope so," Gen answered.

"Then if DiNardo thinks he has a better plan, it's time for him to lay it out. How do you get him to do that? Challenge him to a public debate."

He heard as Gen took a breath on the other end of the phone. "A debate..." she pondered. "A debate! Of course! Taylor, you are brilliant."

"Yes, that's true," Taylor agreed.

"Smarty pants," Gen chided. "I will positively roast that man in a debate. It's the perfect thing to do. For once, everyone is interested, so people will turn out to hear it. Where do you think it should be, the pavilion? I think we should do it there. We can get a moderator, compose a list of questions and let him tie his own noose. That man won't know which end is up by the time we're done with him..."

"Sounds like you have a plan," Taylor said, standing and putting his arm around Tom.

"But we have to plan!" Gen insisted.

"Not tonight. Tonight I have to have dinner with my spouse and enjoy a house free of anyone between the ages of two and twenty. We can discuss it tomorrow."

"Okay, I'll start tonight," Gen said. "Miguel and I can work on it. He should be home soon. He'll love this..."

"Sounds good. Hey, I'll talk to you tomorrow, okay?"

"I'll be here," Gen said, happier than she'd sounded in days. "You're my man. Love you!"

"Love you," Taylor said. "Bye." He closed the phone and returned it to his belt.

"Love you," Tom said, putting his arms around Taylor and planting a long slow kiss on him.

"Mm, I'll take more of that at home," Taylor breathed.

"Count on it," Tom said.

*   *   *

Two days later, late in the afternoon on Friday, Wayne lay on his bed again, contemplating an entirely different relationship situation than the last time he found himself in the same position. Before, he'd been trying to convince himself that Eric had moved on. Now, he had to convince himself to move on with Eric.

No, that wasn't true—that part was pretty much taking care of itself. After all, if he was to be completely honest with himself, he'd never left Eric in the first place. And even two years later, he still hadn't let go.

The problem was he had to convince himself to trust. He was very sure Eric believed he was ready to commit in the way Wayne needed, but he was less sure his resolve would maintain itself once he had to face his father.

Wayne thought back to his senior prom, when Eric had insisted they get their picture taken, then deliberately chosen a pose that was very intimate and close, with Eric sitting on a box, and Wayne in his lap. He smiled in spite of himself—he'd been so mad when he saw what Eric did, but then Tom had changed his whole perspective by asking, "Would you rather look back and smile about enjoying yourself or wish you'd taken the opportunity while you had it?" Well, Wayne was smiling, so he figured he made the right choice.

But what happened to that Eric, the one who was so confident, so comfortable, so adjusted? How, in just a few short weeks, did he become so frightened, so withdrawn, and cave in so completely to his father's whims?

It was hard for Wayne to imagine or understand. He'd spent a lifetime fighting his father mentally, emotionally, and ultimately, physically. There was nothing his father could have said or done to cause Wayne to capitulate to his wishes. Yet there was Eric, so strong, so sure, and one phone call pushed him over the edge.

In the end, Wayne knew it was that fact, more than any other, that was rekindling his love for Eric. He knew how it felt to be abused, mistreated, manhandled by another person. For Eric, there were no bruises for some shining white knight to see and rescue him, but the bruises were there all the same.

Still, Wayne felt he owed it to himself to not rush back at the first sign Eric had reopened the door, either. So far, he had done a good job of keeping him at arm's length, even if he did let the hug go the other day. Again, he smiled. He'd wanted to hug Eric so bad at his graduation, to tell him how he felt, but he'd let Eric keep him at arms length there. Wayne didn't believe in retribution, but he did feel it was best to let things happen slowly.

He'd thought about their dinner date the rest of the week. He was flying by the seat of his pants, but it felt good. In truth, he didn't know exactly where things would lead, but he was pretty confident the trip would be worth taking. As he came to terms with his feelings, he also came to terms with his expectations.

As he'd told Eric, their relationship had grown at an uncontrolled rate before. They met at Thanksgiving, and by Christmas, Eric spent the entire holiday with them. It was, as far as Wayne was concerned, one of the happiest times of his life, but he wanted to create something that would last longer than a holiday, longer than a few weeks. Knowing how he'd felt the last two years, he couldn't imagine how he'd feel if he let Eric back in and it happened again…but for reasons he was just starting to understand, he knew he would take that risk.

"Shouldn't you be getting ready?"

Dan was an echo of himself from Wayne's last attempted date. Wayne knew Dan secretly found his situation at least a little amusing, since he and Emmy had been together since high school. Theirs was the sort of relationship many married people never achieved, where they just worked, so they both felt a responsibility to help Wayne achieve the same goal. With Eric back in the picture, their allegiances were a little murkier, but Wayne knew they had his best interests at heart.

"I'm working on it," he answered, repeating what he'd said before.

This time, Dan was sans ice cream, with his arms just crossed over his chest. The corners of his eyes wrinkled, belying his good humor as he watched his friend.

"You still going?" he asked, breaking from the previous script.

"Of course. I was just thinking," Wayne answered.

"Waynie, you think too much," Dan said.

"It's a curse," Wayne agreed.

Dan walked in and sat on the edge of the bed, facing him. "Wayne, my friend, I have watched you mope around about Eric for the last two years. He's back, he's apologized, and he wants to be with you. Stop counting your chickens, get off this bed, and go out with him."

Wayne watched him, listening.

"Come on," Dan said, taking his hand and pulling him upright. "You know you're looking forward to it, if you just stop planning for the worst. You're going to have a good time. Lighten up on him a little. You know he's going to be tense—give him a break."

"I did," Wayne defended. "I let him take me out."

"Wayne!" Dan snapped. "Be nice."

Wayne laughed, standing to face him. "Thanks, bud," he said, hugging Dan.

"You're welcome," Dan said, hugging him back. "You know, it's not every straight man who could hug a gay man in his underwear and not feel weird."

"That's why you're so doggone *special*," Wayne said, letting him go.

There was a knock at the door, making Wayne jump. "Crap, he's early!"

Dan gave him a pat on the shoulder, walking to the door. "Just get dressed. I'll talk to Eric until you're ready." He pulled Wayne's door behind him.

Wayne made short work of his outfit. Eric had told him they'd go somewhere comfortable, so shorts and a polo would be fine. Wayne opted for a navy blue and khaki combo, with the sandals he'd bought while shopping with Taylor the day before. A quick splash of Ralph Lauren Romance and he was on his way...to exactly where he wanted to be—his second first date.

CHAPTER EIGHT

Grand Opening

As with any good, well-managed project, when it all comes down to the wire, people are left scrambling to make sure everything is done. It was no different at Café del Sol on the third of July.

With Tom's blessing, Jason had taken out ads in all the local newspapers, as well as posted signs around town and in most of the stores in the historic district. The message was simple—come see the new shop for an opening night party. As with every previous year in recent memory, the town would be hosting fireworks at the park, meaning people could stop by on their way to see the fireworks and check out the newest store on the block. They were anticipating a large crowd.

Jason and Wayne had agreed the paper should remain in the windows until the last possible moment—they wanted the town to see the store when it was ready and not a moment before. So, though they planned to have the logo art etched on the glass, it wouldn't be done until after the grand opening. Their plan was for all the players to meet that evening, after hours, and take the paper down when everything was finally in place.

To that end, Jason was driving himself crazy running from store to store, trying to get all the details in order. The furniture had come in late, causing the final layout to slip by two days. The espresso machine still wasn't working correctly, resulting in a service tech taking up much of the space behind the counter. Supplies still had to be organized, tables prepared, and to top it all off, Jason's pièce de résistance computer software was not working correctly.

"I don't understand what's wrong with this thing," he complained, tapping at the colorful LCD panel. "I put the order in, and then it goes away!"

"What if you try this here?" Eric asked, pointing to another key.

Jason shook his head. "No, I've already tried that. I tell you, I've installed these systems dozens of times. It shouldn't be this hard."

"It's not actually deleting it, though, is it?" Eric asked.

"No, it's just not printing. The other station works just fine, but this one won't print."

Dan appeared from the bakery entrance, carrying a box. "Hey, Jason, they delivered this to the bakery, but it's supplies for you. Where do you want them?"

Jason ran a hand through his hair, confused by the computer, and overwhelmed with the work.

"Just put it in the storeroom for now, Dan," he said. He punched several more keys, to no avail. "I swear, I'm going to throw this thing out a window!"

Taylor came through the door from the bakery, plate in hand, a single, golden chocolate croissant in the middle of it.

"Hungry over here?" he asked, handing Jason the plate.

Confused, he accepted it. "Why did you bring me a croissant?"

Taylor handed him a long stream of thermal register receipts. "You've ordered about fifty of them."

Jason took the slips, then suddenly realized his error. "We never told this station to point at *this* printer, did we?" he asked Eric.

"How should I know? I'm an engineer, not a computer guy," Eric answered, making his way out from behind the counter.

Jason glared at him, but he disappeared around back. As Jason made the necessary changes to the computer, Taylor leaned on the counter with his elbows, watching.

"So, how's it coming?" he asked, making conversation.

"There are so many things left to do, and every time I make a little headway, something like this happens," Jason complained, tapping the screen.

"Anything that will keep the doors from opening tomorrow?" Taylor asked.

Jason glanced at him, still tapping. "I suppose not, but we still want it to be perfect to make a good first impression."

Taylor shook his head, smiling. "Jason, look at this place," he said, gesturing with his head toward the room beyond. "How could we not make a good first impression?"

"Losing customer orders would be a good start."

Taylor gestured to the screen. "If the computer isn't up by four o'clock, plan to use paper in the morning. There is no point worrying about it. Orders will still be placed and customers will still be served."

"But we want it to be perfect," Jason reminded him.

"Look at the people around you," Taylor said. "Do you notice anything unusual about them on a day to day basis?"

Jason frowned, not following him. Taylor continued.

"They're *happy*. When Tom and I first got together and started all these businesses, our top priority was to be *happy*. If people are miserable at what they're doing, they're just wasting their time. Why do something you hate? So, we do the best job we can, produce the best product and service we can, and have a good time while we're doing it. I promise you, no one is going to come down on you if the computer doesn't print or the lights in the corner don't turn on, or the sound system automation isn't ready," Taylor said.

"I forgot about the lights!" Jason exclaimed.

"Jason! You're missing my point," Taylor glared. "You look like you're about ready to kill someone. Relax. That's an order."

Though he didn't appear to want to follow the order, Jason finally relented, and even let a grudging smile pass his lips. Beneath the counter, the printer finally printed up a receipt for his croissant, and he just laughed.

The next evening, the time had finally come, and Taylor's usual optimism paid off. All of the equipment was working, the lighting repaired, the furniture arranged, the i's dotted, and the t's crossed. They had closed the bakery early, at three o'clock, to give everyone a chance to get back to their relative homes to relax.

The formal unveiling would be at six o'clock, and it was the talk of the town. Virtually every person they saw eagerly planned to attend the much-anticipated event. Taylor had gone so far as to invite some of the local media, making a point of the continued investment and commitment to the historic district, much to the chagrin of Stuart DiNardo. At his insistence, Gen had provided one of her reelection signs to adorn the front window, making it clear where their loyalties lie.

Standing in his bedroom, Taylor buttoned his pants and arranged the white linen shirt Tom had left for him, enjoying the cool, airy feeling the cloth allowed. They had decided to go with a casual theme in keeping with the new store and, as usual, Tom had selected Taylor's wardrobe to save him an hour of tossing clothes on the bed.

Tom came out of the bathroom, the navy blue sleeves of his own linen shirt properly tjuzs'ed, and stopped to look Taylor over. His gray eyes caught Taylor's as he smiled.

"Not bad, if I do say so myself," Tom observed.

"And say so you do," Taylor replied. "I think I can be seen in public with you."

"Oh, you only *think* you can?" Tom asked, adjusting Taylor's collar.

Taylor shrugged, pulling Tom to him. "It's always open to debate."

Tom leaned into him, his arms around Taylor, though only loosely, so as not to wrinkle them. "Big night," he said. "You looking forward to it?"

Taylor smiled. "Definitely."

There was a knock at their door and Tom went to answer it. Eric stuck his head in, his hair still damp from the shower, a towel around his waist. His tan skin glistened with water, a field of tiny stars in the light, giving him an astral radiance.

"Uh, hey guys," he greeted, a little self-conscious. "I forgot to bring a belt. Do you have one I could borrow?"

"Brown or black?" Tom asked.

"Black, thanks," Eric answered.

They had invited him to spend the evening at their house, since his hotel was quite a bit closer to the city. Tom had gently asked how the apartment search was coming, but had only gotten a vague response in return. He had no doubt that Eric was hoping the situation with Wayne might improve sooner rather than later, but he and Taylor had agreed to stay as far out of it as they could.

"The towel is a nice fashion choice," Taylor observed as Tom went to the closet. "Of course, out here, it might get you more girls than guys."

At that, Eric outright blushed. "I'm on my way to change," he said quietly, not giving in to the humor.

"Taylor, don't tease him," Tom admonished, handing Eric a thick, plain belt. "Here you go—will this work?"

"Perfectly," Eric breathed. "Thanks, Tom."

"Not a problem," Tom said, offering a reassuring smile.

Taylor turned back to Eric. "Hey, do you want to just ride down with us?"

Eric nodded. "That would be great. I'll be ready in about ten minutes."

"No hurry," Taylor said. Eric left to change and they both finished getting ready. Minutes later, they waited in the living room as a gentle knock sounded on the door. Tom opened it to find Gen and Miguel waiting for them. He invited them in while they waited for Eric.

"We wondered if you'd like to walk down with us?" Miguel asked, his arm gently draped around Gen.

Tom glanced at Taylor, then answered, "We were planning to take the car."

"You're welcome to ride with us," Taylor added. "Eric is here, but we can easily take five people the whole four blocks to the store."

Gen shook her head. "We don't mind walking. It's a beautiful evening."

Eric came down the stairs, wearing a black cotton shirt and light beige slacks. He'd arranged his hair in a trendy style and Taylor caught a light whiff of cologne.

"We're walking?" he asked.

"Gen and Miguel invited us to join them," Tom explained.

"Walking is fine with me," Eric said, ever ready to go with the flow.

Taylor nodded. "Walking it is, then."

*   *   *

A scant two hours later, the coffee house was alive with activity. At Taylor's insistence, Tom had prepared and presented the grand opening speech, making special mention of all their friends who had contributed so much of their time and energy to the successful opening. His eyes had fallen on Wayne with special pride, as he recounted Wayne's efforts to convince them that the town needed a place for people to relax and hang out.

Though the evening was officially focused on opening Café del Sol, they had kept the bakery open, and Liz and Sherry kept Uniquely Books open as well. All three spaces were filled to overflowing, with people milling outside in addition to standing in the three stores. It was all Taylor and Tom could do to make sure they saw all of the people who had come to wish them well.

Tom found Pete and Anita sitting off to one side, complimentary cups in hand, watching the crowd. Anita's abdomen had started to show in the last couple of weeks, and she patted it happily as he inquired as to the status of the pregnancy.

"It's going very well," Anita answered, raising her cup in thanks. "Everything is on track and the doctor assures us it's all normal right now."

Tom smiled broadly. "That's great news. With Taylor here so much lately, I haven't gotten much of a report."

"We knew you guys were busy," Pete said. "He'd been planning to take time off this summer, so we thought we'd keep out of the way."

"You're never in the way," Tom objected.

Anita waved a hand. "He means he was trying to keep from getting called in," she explained. "If he could have worked, you know I'd have made him."

Tom nodded. "I know. It's extenuating circumstances of the best kind."

"Hey, guys!" Gen greeted, appearing from behind Tom. She leaned in to give Anita a hug and waved to Pete. "You look radiant!" she said, smiling to Anita.

"They tell me that's normal," Anita deadpanned.

"I think so," Gen said, nodding. "Everything still going well?"

"Very well," Anita affirmed. Though Gen had initially been sad about the pregnancy, thanks to the unfortunate timing of the announcement, she had quickly rallied to her friends' happiness and showed no hesitation in her support.

Tom rose from his chair and gestured to Gen. "Here, why don't you have a seat? I need to mingle."

Gen nodded and gave him a pat on the shoulder. "Looks great, sweetie," she reiterated, referring to the very popular new store.

"Thanks," Tom said. "I'll see you all later."

"Have fun," Pete said.

Tom made his way into the crowd, looking to see who else he knew and realized the answer was everybody.

Jason filled a cup with the flair of someone who had been working on espresso machines for years, not just days. At least he could put on a good show. Smiling, he handed the beverage over to the person who ordered it and thanked her. Unlike the owners, he knew only a few of the people in town. After having worked in the bakery for the last few weeks, he'd met many more people, but he was still getting to know most of them. He'd decided to work behind the counter, allowing him to keep a relatively low profile.

Business was booming on their first official night. Taylor had given many people coupons for free food and beverage, but many others were buying, and many were buying extra. As they'd hoped, access to the myriad of baked goods from Downey's was proving just as strong a seller in the new store as the old.

As he handed another warm cup to a waiting patron, Eric turned to him. "Hey, Jason, will you run and get more small cups? We're almost out."

"It may take a minute," Jason answered, looking at the crowd between him and the storeroom.

"That's why I warned you now," Eric acknowledged with a grin. Though he was technically working for the bakery, Emmy and Dan had been available to work with Eric, so he'd bailed Jason out as he worried over having enough experienced people to work opening night.

Absently wiping his hands on his apron, Jason made his way into the throng. Some people he knew, many he didn't. It amazed him the number of friends Tom and Taylor had. He'd once commented on it to Taylor, who answered that most of the friends were really people who knew Tom, and that he'd come along later. He was quick to point out, however, that they'd accepted him just as readily, and would likely do the same with Jason.

The three stores had become a virtual who's who of the town's residents. Liz and Sherry had made it over earlier in the evening, but had opted to make their way back to their own shop, eager to put a smiling face on their place as well.

Jason had to admit, it had gone far more smoothly than he'd expected. His personal responsibility had been the integration of the three operations. Wayne had managed much of the construction, while Tom and Taylor kept a finger on the details. Looking back from the hall to the storage area, it was hard to believe the three stores had ever *not* been connected.

Taking his key out, he opened one of the closets and pulled out a long package of cups. Giving it a second thought, he reached in and took a second set. As he closed the door, he was startled to find someone standing behind it.

"Jason," the man greeted calmly, smiling. "I didn't mean to startle you."

Standing in the glare from the store, it had taken him a minute to recognize Adam, Tom's friend from the college.

"That's okay," he replied, blushing slightly. "I was just getting some cups," he said sheepishly, holding up the cups.

"I see," Adam said. His voice was like warm butter—rich and smooth, soothing yet strong, confident and reserved at the same time. He was a modern day Robert Redford.

"So, how are you?" he asked, watching Jason.

Shaking himself from his thoughts, Jason answered, "I, uh, I'm...I'm good."

"Good?" Adam asked. "I thought you'd be better than good on opening night."

His topaz eyes wrinkled at the corners as he teased Jason, belying his good humor. He held out a hand to take one of the bundles of cups.

"Here, let me give you a hand with that, now that I've distracted you."

"No, it's okay," Jason objected. "It's no trouble."

"It's the least I can do," Adam insisted. He took one of the packages, then led the way back toward the counter. Where Jason had waded through the crowd, it just seemed to naturally part for Adam. Several people stopped to glance in his direction, men and women both. It reminded Jason of the old quote: *women want him, men want to be him.* He couldn't remember who had said it, but it seemed appropriate...at least, the second part. Some of the men wanted him, too, that much was sure.

Adam was one of the most disarming people he'd met in a long time. It was amazing to Jason how he simply materialized out of nowhere both times they had met. The first time had been a casual, accidental meeting. This time, this visit, seemed a little more targeted. What other reason would Adam have had to wait behind the door, except to see him?

Jason shook his head as he followed Adam through the crowd. Why would Adam seek him out? Jason was his own definition of average, a point his friend Natalie usually took exception to whenever she could. His luck with relationships had been the stuff of legend, if a sad story to tell. Two relationships since college, both poster-children in their own right for disaster—nuclear bombs would wreak less havoc, especially in the emotional and financial categories. So what did this—rather well built—friend of Tom's find interesting about him?

"Somebody looking for these?" Adam asked, smiling radiantly as he handed the package over to Eric.

"Thanks, Adam," Eric answered. Jason was even more confused—Eric knew Adam, too?

"Here, Eric, I brought another pack," Jason said, handing his cups over.

"Cool," Eric acknowledged. "Thanks."

Adam reached out to gently move Jason out of the way of the patrons and back out into the crowd. "Looks like a good turnout tonight, hmm?"

"Not bad," Jason agreed. "It's certainly kept everybody hopping."

"Better than only having a couple of customers," Adam commented, smiling again.

"Definitely," Jason seconded, trying to return the smile.

Adam turned to him, gesturing toward the window. "Hey, listen, I've only been in town for the last year. I'm still kind of new to the area. What are the good places to have dinner?"

Jason considered his question. Where to offer up? "Truth is," he answered, "I've never spent much time eating out here, either. My old job had me on the road most of the time."

"Ah," Adam said. His face broke into an impish grin, as though Jason had said exactly what he'd expected. "Then I guess the only answer is to try them all, huh?"

"Umm...sure," Jason stammered. "I suppose that's one approach."

"Seems like a good one to me," Adam said with a shrug. "Care to join in the research?"

Wait a minute. Was Jason hearing him correctly? Had he just been asked out on a *date*? It had been so long, he barely remembered, so he had to process it a little longer than he might have otherwise. But it sure sounded like a date. And when it walks like a date and talks like a date...

"Research does work better with a control, doesn't it?" Jason countered. If Adam was going to ask him out on a date, he might as well play along.

"So what's the first place to check out?"

"Depends on the kind of food you want," Jason said. "There's always Alberto's."

Adam shook his head. "Been there. I was thinking that new place, Rainbow Pronto, sounded kind of interesting. They've got that nice *al fresco* patio in front."

Jason was sure it was a date. Rainbow Pronto was owned by a couple of men, both friends of Tom and Taylor. Adam Brown, professor and author, was asking him out on a date. It was *definitely* a good night.

"As long as this weather holds, *al fresco* sounds like a great plan," Jason agreed.

"What's a great plan?" Taylor asked, appearing from one side. He shook hands with Adam.

"Jason has agreed to join me in testing some of the local eating establishments. Turns out neither of us has a lot of experience with them."

"Tom and I are partial to Alberto's," Taylor offered.

"We're going to try Rainbow Pronto," Adam answered smoothly.

"Oh?" Taylor said, with a quick glance to Jason. "Another good choice. Tom and I know the owners. In fact, they were just here, but had to leave. I'm sure you'll run into them, though— Mike and Tim Tilakis. Let them know you're friends of ours and they'll make any dish you can dream up."

"Sounds perfect," Jason said.

Before Taylor could say anything more, another woman Jason didn't know came up and stole him away.

"Taylor, how are you?"

"Faith!" Taylor greeted, managing a smile. In the years since their infamous run-in at the Spring Dance, he'd come to understand the person Faith was, and ultimately to forgive her for what she did when she outed him in front of most of the town. It had been the catalyzing event to push him together with Tom, so it would be hard to hold a grudge. Not that Tom didn't still feel a bit of a grudge toward her, but even he had softened in the years since. "Thanks for coming tonight," Taylor said.

"We wouldn't have missed it," Faith responded, her arm wrapped in that of a tall, mildly good-looking man. "I've been wanting to introduce Patrick to the people in town."

"Patrick?" Taylor asked, extending a hand.

"Patrick Bailey," he said, smiling as he took Taylor's hand and gave it a firm shake.

"My husband," Faith added.

Taylor did a double-take, then broke into a smile. "Husband? Congratulations!"

"Thanks, Taylor," she said, smiling.

"I'm surprised I didn't hear about it sooner. When were you married?"

"About a month and a half ago," Patrick answered with a smile toward Faith. "It was just a small ceremony. We've both been married before, so we didn't want anything big."

"Still, that's great news," Taylor said.

"We think so," Patrick agreed.

"So, where are you living now?" Taylor asked.

"Actually, we got a very nice house over on Fourth Street East," Faith said. "Mrs. Hess' place."

Taylor nodded. Mrs. Hess had been a good, regular customer of the bakery for years, until she had a stroke during the winter. Her daughter had been forced to place her in a nursing home. He knew the house was up for sale, but didn't know who had bought it.

"It's a lovely old Victorian," Faith continued. "Patrick is very handy, so we've been remodeling it for the last few months."

"It's the sort of remodeling that never ends," Patrick said.

Taylor laughed. "I know the feeling. Instead of remodeling the house, though, Tom always wants to add another business."

"You guys always do so well at it, though," Faith offered. "Café del Sol is beautiful. Great places like this will make it harder for Stuart DiNardo to call for redevelopment of the historic district."

Taylor sighed. "Harder, but not impossible, I'm afraid."

"It'll work out, Taylor," Faith said, resting a reassuring hand on his arm.

Tom appeared as if from thin air, gently pulling Taylor up next to him. "Faith Roberts," he greeted, a little less warmly. "How are you doing?"

"Actually, it's Faith Bailey, now," Taylor said, introducing Patrick.

"You don't say?" Tom said, brightening slightly as he shook hands. "Congratulations."

"Thanks," Patrick said, watching him.

"Honey," Tom said, turning to Taylor. "Steve and Rick are here, but they're going to have to leave to head up to the city. Did you want to see them?"

"Yes, I do," Taylor answered. He said his goodbyes to Faith and Patrick, then followed Tom into the crowd, headed toward the opening to the bookstore. There, Rick and Steve waited, cocktail plates in hand, talking with Rob and Mel.

"Hi," Taylor greeted warmly, giving each a hug. "Thanks for coming."

"The pleasure is ours," Mel said. "Amanda couldn't make it tonight," she explained, referring to their daughter. "A bunch of her friends are driving into the city for fireworks."

"She wanted to be here," Rob continued, "but you know how kids are."

"Oh yes, we do know that," Tom agreed, standing with Taylor.

"How are yours doing?" Steve asked. He had been integral in helping Wayne overcome many of the issues he faced from his dysfunctional childhood. He'd also spent a fair amount of time with their three younger children, helping them to deal with their own issues from losing their parents at such a young age. As far as Tom and Taylor were concerned, Steve and Rick were another branch in their very extended family.

"They're all very well adjusted," Taylor said with a laugh.

"That'll change," Mel assured him.

"I don't doubt it," Taylor agreed.

"Great night," Rick said. "I can't remember the last time I saw a crowd like this down here."

Tom nodded. "We just have to keep them coming back."

Rick held up his cup. "With coffee like this, it shouldn't be hard. Besides, the other restaurants are really starting to draw people in. Wayne said you're going to be hosting live music here. I'm sure that'll bring in even more people."

"Tom's been trying to book some bigger name acts," Taylor said. "Sort of along the lines of a surprise—people buy tickets without knowing who will play and then, all of a sudden, they're three rows away from a big name act."

"Let me know where to sign up," Steve said, raising his cup to Tom.

Rick took his plate and cup and put them in a nearby waste receptacle. Rob did the same for Mel, who turned back to their hosts. "Well, we all need to be going, too. Turns out we're both going over to Springfield Hill for their fireworks. We just wanted to wish you well."

Tom and Taylor hugged them all again, and then they were off. As the two turned back to their new store, they saw the crowd had thinned noticeably, as people made their way out to various functions around town, or to head in and call it an evening. It had been a very long few weeks for them, so they were as eager as anyone to get a little time to themselves.

"Well, we did it," Tom said, leaning back to rest against Taylor, pulling Taylor's left arm around him.

"That we did," Taylor said, resting his other arm over Tom's. "Wayne really did an amazing job, didn't he?"

"Yes," Tom readily agreed. "They all did. This place belongs to all of them, you know?"

"Yeah," Taylor sighed, resting his forehead against the back of Tom's head. If he could have, he would have gone to sleep, right then and there.

*　　*　　*

"Where have you been?" Dan asked as he rolled a cart back to the baking room.

Eric helped him empty the few remaining loaves of bread off and bag them for sale in the morning.

"I was next door. You guys had things covered here, so I was helping Jason."

"You just wanted to be with all the new stuff," Dan complained.

"Ha!" Eric objected. "I was busting my butt over there. Jason went off and spent half the evening chit-chatting with Adam Brown, meaning I had to keep the counter moving with the newbies."

"Dr. Brown? Jason? *Really?*" Dan asked, eyeing Eric.

"What about it?"

Dan shrugged. "Nothing. Just a lot of people around campus have tried to figure out whose team he plays for."

Eric rolled his eyes, shaking his head. "Who *cares?*"

Frowning, Dan said, "Well, you know, it's just one of those things."

"Yeah, I know," Eric grumbled.

"Hey, it's the long lost baker!" Wayne greeted, pulling the last cart of leftover items through the door. "Done playing with all the new toys?"

"You knew where I was," Eric defended, a crease forming in his brow.

"He said the coffee people are more fun," Dan incited.

Eric glared at him. "I did not!"

Wayne shrugged. "Don't worry, Dan, I know how fickle he is."

"That's a pretty low blow, McInerney," Eric said, face serious.

"Relax, Driskell," Wayne countered. He turned to Dan. "Hey, we can wrap things up here. Em already took off. Why don't you go ahead and go, too? We'll catch up with you guys at the park."

"Thanks, Wayne. I'll be done in the bathroom by the time you come up," Dan said, pulling his apron over his head on his way out the door. Tom had promised they would be able to close in time to catch the fireworks in the park, and Dan and Wayne had decided to turn it into a double date.

As Wayne turned back to Eric, he saw Eric was still unhappy. "Come on, Eric. I was just kidding."

"We worked awfully hard over there tonight," Eric reminded him.

Wayne smiled. "I know. I slipped over to see you, but you didn't even get to look up. I saw Jason was off in the crowd with Dr. Brown. That's why I didn't bug you."

"I was just trying to help in the place where I thought I was needed most," Eric defended. "I'd have rather been with *you*."

Wayne moved to stand in front of him. "You were. Here," he said, pointing to his heart, "by helping make that place a huge success."

"It was a success, wasn't it?" Eric said, a thin smile on his lips.

"A *huge* success," Wayne agreed.

"This was your baby," Eric said. "Congratulations, Wayne."

Wayne couldn't stand it any longer and pulled Eric to him, kissing him deeply. Eric held him tightly, tears escaping his eyes as he returned the kiss. It was the first time they'd really kissed since that afternoon behind the store. Wayne had wanted to take it slow as they worked through the issues that had remained between them. Since that time, they had shared almost every dinner together, and had many heart-to-heart discussions. But Wayne had still been distant, the pain something he was fearful to let go. Eric knew that, and he was patient, letting his actions speak for him as words never could.

"Do you want to go to the fireworks show?" he asked.

"Not so much," Wayne breathed, resting his damp forehead against Eric's.

"Do you want to go upstairs?" Eric asked.

"*Definitely*," Wayne agreed. They finished the cleanup in record time, then made their way up to Wayne's apartment, both of them finally determined to make up.

CHAPTER NINE

Conflict of Interest

Two weeks after the grand opening, life had settled back into something approaching a routine. As they'd hoped, the store was an unmitigated success, and Tom anticipated even better business once the students returned en masse to the college in the fall. For the summer, the smaller crowd gave them time to work out the remaining kinks. Fortunately, there were relatively few—they had all done their jobs preparing and the combined operation of the three stores was proceeding according to plan.

Tom's parents had kept in regular touch with them while traveling with the kids. Taylor was surprised how strange it felt to come home to a quiet house. After almost three years of having the kids, he had expected it to be a welcome reprieve, but in the end, it just felt vacant. It was nice to have some time to himself with only Tom requiring his attention, but he'd be glad when the kids got home.

Of course, Wayne and Eric had seen to it that they didn't have to spend *all* of their time by themselves. Taylor smiled as he remembered the look on Wayne's face the morning after the grand opening. He had recognized it as soon as he saw it, and the way Wayne's gaze just melted when he saw Eric come in a few moments later confirmed it. Later that morning, when the rest of the team was off working out in the store, he'd slipped into the baking room to talk to Wayne, and learned the two of them were officially back on. Taylor was glad for them—Wayne had been a virtual basket case without Eric, and he had the distinct impression Eric hadn't been much better off. They were each others' soul mates, and he was just glad for their sake that they had found each other.

The biggest surprise had been the ever-unpredictable Jason. More than Wayne and Eric's resumption of their relationship, Jason's pending date with Adam Brown had been the talk of the morning after the grand opening. When Taylor arrived, Emmy and Tom were positively interrogating the young man, eagerly soaking up any details he would reluctantly share. Since they had never formally discussed Jason's orientation, Taylor tried to run interference for him a bit and fend off the hounds. Emmy and Tom were not easily dissuaded, however, and it was ultimately Taylor who relented.

With Café del Sol open and operating successfully, Taylor had pulled back from his involvement in what he still largely considered Tom's businesses. He knew Tom liked thinking of him as a part of them, too, as a way to further express his love for Taylor, but Taylor tried to let him run them himself whenever possible—it wasn't like he was wanting for things to keep him busy, either. Business had picked up at the firm again and Pete reluctantly asked if he would be willing to forgo some of his time off to help with client meetings. Pete and Sam were handling the court appearances to keep his time requirement to a minimum.

When he wasn't working, Taylor assisted Gen with her reelection campaign. He knew of no time in the history of the town that two people had fought so vehemently for a position that had previously been a virtual booby prize. For Gen and the rest of the people in the old part of town, it was an expression of their distaste for the development that was threatening to impinge on their quaint way of life. For the residents of the new part of town, it was no doubt an attempt to continue to forward their goals of expansion and growth. DiNardo had begun yet another development, this time of what Tom called, "McMansions"—very large houses on very small lots, priced far higher than they were worth, with militant, nazi-like "neighborhood associations" to pick the pockets of residents. In just over three years, the town would have two hundred twenty five additional residential properties, with probably a good five hundred or more registered voters. Tom contended DiNardo planned to win by sheer force of numbers, if nothing else.

The beep of the phone intercom interrupted his reverie, and he quickly lowered the volume on the music playing in the background from his computer.

"Sorry to bother you, Taylor," Christy greeted.

"What's up?" Taylor asked casually.

"Pete was supposed to be back from court a half hour ago. His ten o'clock appointment is here, and she's been waiting for twenty minutes. Have you talked to him?"

Taylor sighed. The best laid plans almost certainly went astray for them lately. "No, I haven't heard from him. Is this a new client or an existing one?"

"She's new, coming in for her first interview."

Nodding, Taylor rose and reached for the sport coat hanging from the back of his chair. "Why don't you show her to the conference room and I'll talk to her, okay?"

"Will do. Thanks, Taylor."

Christy hung up and he picked up a pad and pen. Tom still thought he ought to put his notes directly into his laptop, but he thought it was more personal to just write on a pad as he conversed with a client. He also found he retained the information better when he transcribed it by hand.

He entered the conference room to find an attractive woman in her mid-thirties, well dressed in a pin-striped navy blue suit with navy blue pumps. Her thick blonde hair was arranged in a professional style, falling in large curls from the clip she used to hold it back from her face. Her eyes were a rich blue, not too different from Taylor's own, and they watched his every move as he entered the room. Her presence and demeanor was of a confident person who felt somewhat uncomfortable with her surroundings as she sat on the opposite side of the table, facing the door.

"Good morning," Taylor greeted, reaching across to shake her hand. "I'm Taylor Connolly."

"Good morning, Taylor," she replied smoothly, taking his hand and giving a firm, professional shake. "I'm Maxine Reynolds."

"Nice to meet you, Maxine," Taylor said. "I'm sorry for your long wait and that Pete isn't here to meet with you. He's apparently tied up in court. If you don't mind, I'd be happy to talk to you now, though, and then we can bring Pete in if he gets here in time."

Maxine nodded. "I don't mind at all. I'm well aware of your record. Actually, it makes me feel better just to know you're involved."

Taylor gave a self-deprecating smile. Even after all the years of notoriety, he still wasn't comfortable with it. "Well, I'm happy to do what I can. What brings you to us today?"

She shifted in her seat, clearly uncomfortable with what she was doing, but resolved to do it anyway.

"I want to bring discrimination and harassment charges against my employer," she said, putting it as bluntly as she could.

Taylor blinked, not prepared for the stark honesty of what she'd said, but then started taking notes. "Okay, we can help you do that. Why don't you tell me a little about what is going on? First, who is your employer?"

She looked up, and for the first time, he saw anger, possibly hatred, in her eyes and she said two words, five syllables, that rang like gunshots...

"Stuart DiNardo."

Taylor coughed, sitting up in his chair, and dropped his pen on the pad, next to the large ink spot he'd made by pressing it into the paper. He watched Maxine, her eyes unblinking as she regarded him, and they sat for a moment in silence, until at last, he spoke.

"Uh, Maxine," he began slowly, "I'm bound to tell you of any conflicts of interest I may have before we go any farther."

She frowned, shaking her head slightly. "Okay?"

"Are you familiar at all with the mayoral race going on in this town right now?"

Maxine shook her head. "I live in the city," she said. "I know Stuart is running for mayor, but that's about all I know. I came here based on your firm's reputation for success in these cases."

Taylor nodded. "We appreciate that," he said. "But you need to know that I'm working very closely with the current mayor of this town, Gen Pouissant, to keep her in office. Part of my job has been to discredit Stuart DiNardo and show that Gen is the better choice to continue to lead the town."

Maxine leaned forward across from him, her frown deepening. "How would that make you a danger to my case? If anything, it should mean you already know at least something about the kind of person Stuart is, and you should understand why I would want to come forward to stop him."

Taylor nodded. "I can certainly understand that. My point is I must be honest and open with you to let you know that I am working on other matters related to him and give you the opportunity to decide whether you want me involved in your case."

"Is there a reason I should be concerned?" Maxine asked.

He considered her question, explaining his logic out loud as he went. His job in helping Gen with her campaign, he explained, was to discredit DiNardo as a viable choice to be mayor of the town. Certainly, having someone provide him with inside information about DiNardo's business practices would be enticing. However, privilege would dictate he should not use that information, in most cases. Further, if they weren't careful, DiNardo could argue that he had gone fishing for Maxine, trying to use her case, whatever it may be, to discredit him in the eyes of the town. That could weaken Gen's position with people who were on the fence, and it could weaken Maxine's position in court, should the matter be brought before a jury.

"What if Mr. Madson were handling my case?"

Taylor nodded. "That would certainly add a solid layer of protection to both of you."

"Does having him handle the case going forward mean we shouldn't talk now?"

He considered the question. While it could be brought out that he conducted the initial interview, the fact that he took himself off the case should balance that fact out. In effect, he was merely providing backup for his partner, who was delayed.

"I think it's okay if we talk now, but we do so with the understanding that Pete will handle your case going forward."

"Fair enough," Maxine agreed.

Taylor picked up his pen again. "Okay. So, tell me what you feel Stuart has done to break the law…"

Business was booming at Café del Sol, but afternoons were relatively quiet and Jason had come to relish them as a respite from the morning to lunch rush. He was finally getting a hold on the staffing needed to keep things moving, and Wayne and the bakery team continued to offer assistance when he got slammed. Sherry had even slipped over the day before, toasting bagels and preparing lattes on an unusually busy morning.

Afternoons, though, were usually calm, with a few students and one or two residents of the town coming by to read the paper, a magazine, or do a little homework. Adam had brought some of his students over on a couple occasions, taking over some of the couches and chairs across from the stage, where they had relocated it at the back of the store. Jason found their discussions fascinating and tended to shadow them a bit. If Adam kept it up, he might have to enroll in college again, just to get to attend all the lectures.

That afternoon, Jason was working with Sally, who Taylor called their Token Goth Pierced Lesbian. Sally had taken to the title immediately, and spent the next week with extra dark blue hair pulled back into two ponytails, heavy eye shadow, and a bright silver sphere protruding from her lower lip. The image broke down whenever someone spoke to her, though, as her face immediately brightened into a huge smile.

Sally was making her way around the restaurant, collecting spent trays and disposing of trash. She checked in on the group of four who had collected in the far corner. They were eagerly and animatedly discussing some topic, oblivious to those around them, and Sally politely took their spent cups, offering to bring more for any who wanted it. Two of them ordered an additional cup and Jason started filling the order.

"What are they on about?" he asked as Sally walked by him to put the spent trays away.

"Some professor one of them likes. Honestly, who would want to date some old professor?" she asked, picking up a fresh tray to return the cups.

"Who is it?" Jason asked. "Maybe it's someone my friend Adam knows."

Sally shrugged, taking the tray. "I think they said 'Dr. Brown,' but I'm not sure."

Jason froze, turning to her. "Dr. Brown?"

"Yeah. Know him?"

"Adam's last name is Brown."

Sally's eyebrows shot up and she giggled. "No kidding? Boy, it looks like you've got some competition."

The front door opened and Adam appeared. He walked swiftly toward the group, giving Jason a quick wave as he passed. Jason could hear his voice as he announced to the students that he had been delayed and was sorry for being late.

"Give me that," Jason demanded, taking the tray from Sally. He walked to the group and handed out the beverages, catching Adam's eye as he did.

"Can I bring you anything?"

Adam smiled, a little more reserved in front of his students. "My usual would be great."

"You have a usual?" one of the students teased. "Has the place even been open long enough?"

"I guess so," Jason countered. "I'll be right back," he said to Adam, then turned and walked back behind the counter.

The students continued to banter with Adam while Jason got his coffee. Sally came up behind him, leaning in to whisper in his ear. "That's the one."

"What?" Jason asked, leaning away.

"The mouthy one," she said. "He's the one who likes Adam."

Jason looked over and saw the student had positioned himself to have to share the couch with Adam, and he wasn't doing a good job of keeping to his end of the space.

"What are you going to do?"

Jason glared at her, capping the cup. "What can I do? I don't own him, and we're not a couple of teenagers."

"Wimp."

"What would you have me do? Take him out to the playground?"

Sally clapped her hands, her eyes twinkling. "I love a good bitch fight!" she cheered gleefully, though quietly enough that the customers wouldn't hear.

Without another word, he walked back to where Adam's group was sitting. As he approached, he once again heard the conversation, and it was clearly off topic. The girl was eagerly interrogating Adam, and Jason could just make out her voice as she asked, "So, *would* you date one of your students, Dr. Brown?"

The boy beside Adam leaned in a little closer, watching him expectantly for a response.

"Not a chance," Adam said.

"Oh, come on," the boy said. "It would be fun."

Before Adam could respond, Jason appeared at his side. He handed him the cup of coffee and gave a quick smile. "Can I bring you anything else?"

Adam looked up and shook his head. "No, thanks. That's great."

"Hey, Jason," the girl called. She must have read his nametag, since he couldn't remember ever being introduced to her.

"Something I can bring you?" he asked, trying to keep his contempt for her from his gaze. The last thing he wanted was some nineteen year-old trollop trying to fix Adam up with one of her little friends.

"No no," she answered, shaking her head. "We were just talking, thinking it would be really nice if Dr. Brown had a date. Keith's available," she said, gesturing to the puppy sitting next to her. "What do you think?"

Who was this chick? Was she serious? Did she know something Jason didn't? Quickly, he tried to compose an answer. "Aren't there rules about that?" he managed.

"Rules schmules," the girl answered. "Rules are meant to be broken, right? Come on, you're not *that* old, are you?"

Jason felt his blood pressure skyrocket. He was only twenty-seven, but that was six years too close to thirty, as far as he was concerned. The last thing he needed was for some snot-nosed, penny-ante, troll-faced *English student* to remind him!

"I don't know about my age," Jason began, "but if it was something that meant my job, I'm pretty sure I'd be careful. You'll understand when your mom and dad aren't paying for you anymore, *dear*." He felt simultaneously righteous and annoyed with himself that he'd given in. Oh well.

The people seated around her snickered and Adam repressed a little grin. Clearing his throat, he interjected, "There, an excellent point. Thanks, Jason."

"No problem," Jason said, turning to head back to his counter. Behind him, he heard the girl grumble some comment, but Adam drowned her out with a call to order as he flipped open his book.

At the counter, Sally was waiting for him. As he poured himself a coffee, she came up behind him and said, "Way to pick on the little kid, big guy."

"Don't start or you'll be next," Jason glared. He positioned himself where he could see Adam. As he watched, the young professor interacted with his students, guiding them into their discussion and keeping them on track. Clearly, "Keith" wasn't going to be dissuaded so easily. Jason felt a lump form in his throat and knew there was more to come.

* * *

Taylor stirred his signature tomato sauce, waiting for Tom to get home. He'd called around lunchtime, telling Taylor he was going to stay late at the bakery to go over some management stuff with Wayne. With both stores open, Tom had to split his time and rely more and more on Wayne's skills. As usual, Wayne rose to the challenge and exceeded their wildest expectations.

Still stirring without really paying attention, he pondered his meeting with Maxine. Pete had shown up a short time after their discussion started and Taylor recapped what Maxine had told him, then excused himself. He would work with Pete on the case in the background, reviewing material and offering advice, but it would be for Pete to take the lead, hopefully helping to insulate all of them from the charges that DiNardo was bound to level against them.

From what Taylor learned before Pete's arrival, he felt they had a good case. She had only worked for DiNardo's company for about nine months, but in that time, she had amassed a sizable amount of material. It would be up to the court to determine what would and would not be admissible, but Taylor was confident a large portion would be.

Judging from what Maxine had said, if there was a law, there was a good chance DiNardo was breaking it. Off the top of his head, the only topic Taylor could really think of that she hadn't covered was illegal drugs, and it was entirely possible that had come up after he left. Pete had another meeting and they didn't get a chance to talk before Taylor went home.

Outside, the weather had taken a turn for the dark, with thick storm clouds rolling overhead. Though many people around town had complained about the weather, Taylor was thoroughly enjoying it. For the first time in many years, it was not sweltering hot and humid outside. Of course, the flipside was it had rained more than he could remember in recent years, too, but that just meant all the yards stayed green with no extra waterings. The rain hadn't impacted any of the regular town events, including the recent fireworks and their grand opening. What more could he ask for?

Tom pulled up to the garage, waiting for the door to swing out of the way. Though it was still fairly early, his headlights were on in the darkened skies. It certainly looked like thunder and rain would not be far behind. Tom came in from the garage, his T-shirt and shorts baking attire a stark contrast to the Jaguar he drove. Taylor smiled, thinking back to how much Tom had fallen in love with the car when they first met. Sometimes he wondered if Tom was more impressed by the car or him. He tried to stay optimistic.

"Whew! Made it!" Tom said as he came through the back door. He tapped the button to close the garage, then sat down to take off his shoes. "What a day!" he exclaimed, smiling brightly at Taylor as only he could.

"Good?" Taylor asked.

"Busy!" Tom answered, setting his shoes aside by the door. "The ad ran in the paper yesterday and we really had a bumper crowd today. More work for the coffee shop means more work for the bakery keeping it stocked, in addition to the overflow *from* the coffee shop…but I can't complain."

"You can try," Taylor said as Tom came over to look in the pot.

"You'd just tease me," Tom said, kissing him casually as he reached for the lid. "What's for dinner? Smells good."

"Spaghetti," Taylor replied. "Seems good for the weather."

Tom nodded. "Sounds perfect. Is Waynie joining us?"

Taylor continued preparing the meal, now that Tom was home. "I was going to ask you that."

"He didn't say," Tom said, leaning back against the counter. "You know, now that he and Eric are back on, they're pretty well inseparable."

"Just like old times," Taylor reminisced. He started plating their dinners, assuming Wayne wasn't making an appearance. Since he had let Eric back into his life, he truly *hadn't* been around much, but Taylor figured that was probably for the best, too.

"So how was your day?" Tom asked, watching him.

"Not bad." Taylor turned to look at him, realizing he might as well come clean on the new case, rather than have it come up later. "We picked up a new client today."

"Someone we know?" Tom asked, joining him at the table, which Taylor had already set.

"Not the plaintiff," he answered.

"Someone is suing one of us?" Tom asked.

Taylor shook his head. "No, not us. Stuart DiNardo."

Tom did a double take, a shocked expression on his face. "DiNardo!?"

"Yeah."

"What are the charges?"

Taylor added sauce to his pasta. "I'm really not supposed to discuss a pending case."

"Taylor!"

He looked up, shaking his head. "Tommy, you wouldn't believe it. It runs the gambit. I've never seen anything like it."

"Harassment?" Tom asked.

"Yep."

"Discrimination?"

Taylor nodded. "Wrongful termination. Fraud. Intent to commit fraud. Inciting others to commit fraud. Perjury. Intentional misrepresentation. Theft."

"Oh, come on," Tom complained, incredulous.

"I'm not kidding," Taylor promised, holding up his hands. "And let me tell you, we're not even stretching the bounds of believability. She has paperwork."

"Can you use it?" Tom knew Taylor had been forced to ignore evidence on a number of occasions under various laws regarding work papers removed from a job site.

"Probably not all of it," he dismissed, "but I'll bet more than a little"

"Wow," Tom said. He sat back, considering the charges. "Can you prosecute the case? I mean, you're hardly a disinterested party as a business owner and key figure in Gen's campaign."

Taylor shook his head. "Pete is taking this one. I'll advise him, but I don't plan to do anything active in the case, for those exact reasons."

"When does DiNardo find out?"

"He'll be served tomorrow," Taylor confirmed.

Tom looked at the back door, unlocked as it usually was. He got up and locked it, flipping the deadbolt for good measure.

"What are you doing?" Taylor asked.

"Are we going to be safe?" Tom asked. He wasn't kidding. Outside, a crack of thunder sounded, adding emphasis to his question.

"Of course we are," Taylor reassured him. "DiNardo is the sort of person to take financial risks, not criminal."

"But those *are* criminal offenses," Tom reminded. "Taylor, honey, don't be naïve. We're not exactly at the top of Stuey's Christmas list as it is. Your firm suing him on so many fronts isn't going to increase our popularity."

Taylor smiled, resting a calming hand on Tom's. "I had lunch with the Chief this afternoon," he said simply.

"You did?" Tom asked, visibly relaxing.

"I did. I told him what is going on and asked him what he thought. He said he doesn't think DiNardo is the sort of person to do anything, either. But, he said they'll be sure to spend a little extra time on our street. After all, they can keep an eye on all three houses from just about any vantage point."

Tom took Taylor's hand in his. "That does make me feel a lot better," he agreed.

"I knew it would," Taylor said. "You're getting predictable."

"Then I guess I'll have to shake things up a bit," Tom said, pulling his hand back to take another bite of spaghetti. "Have you told Gen yet?"

Taylor shook his head. "Not yet. I thought I'd stop over this evening."

Outside, the rain poured down in earnest, bringing on an early dusk. The back door shook as someone impacted it, making them both jump. After the discussion they'd just had, Tom reflexively jumped back, reaching for the baseball bat he'd left standing in the closet.

"Relax," Taylor said, sliding past him. Another bolt of lightning lit the yard and he saw a form standing in front of the door—a form far smaller than Stuart DiNardo, and certainly smaller than a hired goon.

Taylor quickly unlatched the door and threw it open. Gen rushed in, shaking her umbrella outside in a futile attempt to leave the water there.

"Why is the door locked?" she asked, annoyed. "It's pouring out!"

"How did we know you'd be coming over?" Taylor asked.

"Taylor, this is Pine Creek—no one locks their doors!" she exclaimed, as though he'd just made the dumbest statement she'd ever heard.

"It's kind of a long story," he said. "Would you care to join us for some spaghetti?"

Gen let out a breath, taking a seat beside Tom. "That sounds wonderful, actually," she said. "Miguel won't be home until later this evening and I haven't cooked."

"So you figured you'd come see what we were having?" Tom asked.

"What are friends for?" she replied, taking the plate Taylor handed her. "So, why the locked door? Does this have something to do with Stuart DiNardo? I heard he's being sued."

Tom and Taylor retook their seats, staring at her in amazement as she loaded her plate with pasta and sauce. Word traveled fast in a small town, but this was ridiculous.

"What? I'm the mayor. You know how it is. People talk." She took a bite, giving Taylor an approving nod. "Very nice," she complimented, stopping just long enough to swallow. Continuing, she explained, "The Chief came by earlier. He told me he had lunch with you and that there was going to be some litigation against Stuart. He said I shouldn't be concerned because his staff would be watching all of us."

Gen talked about it like police protection was an everyday thing for them. True, with her a mayor and Taylor an ex-mayor, it wasn't unheard of, but it certainly hadn't risen to the level of an everyday occurrence...had it?

"So you're not worried?" Tom inquired.

"Worried? Heck no! This is the best thing I can think of," Gen said. She turned to Taylor, eyes expectant. "So, what have you got on him? I want *dirt!*"

Taylor shook his head. "Genevieve, you know I can't talk about it."

"You've already told Tom."

"How do you know I've already told Tom?"

She shrugged. "You can't keep a secret. Besides, you just admitted to it."

"No," Taylor said, his tone final.

"Come on, Tay. This is the best possible news for my campaign. Bringing Stuart's behavior into the light will finally show people the kind of man he is."

Taylor shook his head, leaning forward. "No, Gen. You have to distance yourself from this. If it looks like you're involved in any way, it will make it look like we just dug up something to defame him. Pete is handling the case and we must stay as far away from it as we can, or it'll blow up like a nuclear bomb."

"Taylor, I can't just pretend it's not there," Gen said, frowning.

He nodded. "That's *exactly* what you must do. The press will be sure it's in everybody's face. They'll call you, they'll want comments. You need to either be prepared to answer them in a neutral, indifferent manner, or refer them to me."

Gen looked genuinely annoyed. "What do you want me to say?"

Taylor thought for a moment, then answered. "You have to stay away from it. Say something like, 'I understand there have been charges made against Mr. DiNardo. The court will decide the merit of what the lady has to say.'"

"So it's a lady?" Gen asked.

"Genevieve!"

"What if they ask my opinion?"

Again, Taylor shook his head. "Don't engage. You keep the ammunition out of DiNardo's hands if you won't open up the gates. If they ask, 'But what do you think?' answer, 'It's a decision for the court to make, not me. I'm not a judge, I'm just running for mayor.'"

"And when they ask if I think he's guilty?" Gen inquired.

"I'm not privy to the facts of the case to form an opinion," Taylor supplied her answer.

"What about when they notice your law firm is handling the case?" Tom asked.

Again, Taylor supplied an answer. "I'm aware that Taylor's firm is handling the case, but Taylor is not directly involved in the matter himself. His partner, Pete Madson, is the lawyer on the case."

Gen watched him, her dark eyes narrow, as she considered his plan. "That's really what you want me to do?" she asked.

"It's what you have to do, at least for now. Be the better person, Gen. It's your greatest strength," Taylor insisted.

"I hope you're right," Gen said, taking another bite of spaghetti as the sky flashed and the rain poured on.

CHAPTER TEN

Faith, Treachery, and the Red River

Some days just start off on the wrong foot and never seem to pick up.

Just before lunch, after a long morning of client meetings, Taylor sat behind his desk, considering the previous day. His back was slightly achy from having spent most of the night at an awkward angle, having held Tom in his arms as they slept. As much as Tom would put on a brave face, situations like the one with Stuart DiNardo made him uncomfortable, and Taylor felt bad for having been forced to involve him in it.

It would have been worse if he'd tried to shield Tom from knowing about it. The case was going to be high profile. There was no getting around it. With all the connections to their town, people were going to talk about it—a lot. If he hadn't said something right away, Tom would just have been angry with him for not trusting him. Of course, it wasn't that Taylor didn't trust him, not even for a minute. Taylor just tried to protect him, much as Tom tried to do the same in return.

Gen had stayed for dessert, then gone home after the rain let up. In the end, Taylor realized she'd already known about the case, thanks to the Chief, and she was just trying to get more information. After more discussion, they'd managed to bring her around to the idea that she had to avoid the topic as much as possible. Her greatest advantage was being an observer, like the rest of the town.

Taylor knew DiNardo's lawyers would try to stall the case, or kill it outright. Maxine had insisted she wasn't interested in publicity, and she wasn't interested in a settlement. She wanted DiNardo, and she would settle for nothing less. That worked out well in the sense that she would take the case all the way to trial, but it also gave DiNardo a chance to put on a show himself. It was something Pete would have to handle with the utmost care. Fortunately, he planned to use Sam for much of the public interaction, and Sam was an accomplished speaker. Further, as a woman, she would force DiNardo's team to be more reserved in their comments, since harassment and discrimination figured so prominently in the charges. It was going to be a long game of cat and mouse, and the jury was still very much out, literally as well as figuratively, on who would be the victor.

His phone chimed and Christy's voice rang in. "Taylor?"

"Yeah?" he answered, making no effort to conceal his fatigue.

"Phone call for you. It's Faith Bailey."

Faith? What on Earth could she want? Taylor got the impression his morning wasn't going to improve.

"Okay, I'll take it. Thanks," he said. Christy put the call through and he picked up the receiver. "Good morning, Faith."

"Hi, Taylor, how are you?" Faith greeted.

"I'm well, thanks," he answered, playing the role of polite "friend." "What can I do for you?"

"Actually, I was wondering if you'd let me take you to lunch?" Faith asked. "It's been forever since we talked and I'm sure there are some very interesting things for us to discuss."

Faith's voice was cheery, but to Taylor's mind, it was almost too much so.

"Oh?" he asked, against his better instincts. Was she already gearing up for divorce? He hoped not—aside from the fact that he preferred people to have successful relationships, he was not remotely interested in handling divorces.

"Yes," she said again. "Lots to catch up on. Are you free?"

She seemed to be deliberately vague, yet insistent. Taylor couldn't remember the last time he'd said more than a few words to her at a casual function. They certainly weren't close. What was she up to?

Curiosity got the better of him and he answered, "Sure. What time?"

"Well, I'm in Shelbyville right now," she said. "And it's about eleven thirty. There's a great restaurant here, if you wouldn't mind the drive. The Shelbyville Hotel. Heard of it?"

"Yes, I've eaten there a couple times," Taylor confirmed. "I could meet you around noon."

"Wonderful!" Faith said. "I promise, you'll have a great time."

"Sounds like fun," Taylor said, not really meaning it.

"See you then," Faith said, then the line went dead. Shaking his head, Taylor returned his own handset to the cradle. What on earth was she up to?

He rose and pulled on his sport coat, then went to Pete's office. The door was open, and Pete was at his computer, reviewing some document. Taylor rapped lightly on the door.

"Hey, buddy," Pete greeted. "Going somewhere?"

Taylor nodded. "I just got invited to lunch…by Faith Roberts, who is now Faith Bailey."

"Faith? Really? Why?" Pete asked, turning to face Taylor.

"That's the question I'm asking," Taylor confirmed.

"Weird. Okay, well, if you're not back by a reasonable time, we'll send out the hounds."

"We're going to the Shelbyville Hotel," Taylor informed him.

Pete's eyebrows went up. "Not exactly local, huh? I wonder what she's up to?"

"Beats me," Taylor said.

"Hmm," Pete pondered. "Well, in any event, I'm in court this afternoon, so I guess we'll catch up this evening."

"This evening?"

"Tom's team is having a playoff game," Pete reminded. "Anita thought it would be fun for us to come along."

"Having trouble keeping yourself entertained?" Taylor asked, giving him a look.

"*Anita* thought it would be fun," Pete emphasized.

"Got it. I've gotta run if I'm going to get there on time," Taylor said.

"Have fun."

"Yeah." He headed for his car, butterflies fluttering lightly in the depths of his stomach.

As good as her word, Faith was already seated at a table waiting for him when he arrived. Shelbyville was a twenty-minute to half-hour drive from Pine Creek, depending on traffic and the route taken. Taylor opted for a choice that would get him there just in the nick of time.

Unlike Pine Creek, Shelbyville was even smaller. There was one traffic light at the center nexus of town, but it consisted of just four blocks, one on each corner. Tom had once commented that they only put the light in to make themselves feel better, since it was rare there was even anyone waiting at it.

The Shelbyville Hotel, by contrast, was one of the better restaurants in the area. Though no longer operated as an actual hotel since the train depot was moved to Pine Creek, the restaurant continued to prosper. Its Victorian themed dining rooms and five star cooking drew in diners from as far as two hours away.

Given the town's size and location, it was not conducive to a large lunch crowd. The only other occupied table in the restaurant was four blue-haired ladies, obviously out for a social gathering. They paid Faith and Taylor little attention as they shared a small table on the other side of the room.

The waiter came and politely took their drink order, his gaze lingering just a second or two longer on Taylor as he smiled and said he'd be right back. Inside, Taylor rolled his eyes. The kid was twenty if he was a day. Flattering, yes. Enticing, not a chance. But it would make Tom jealous later…

"I'm glad you were able to make it on such short notice," Faith said, drawing him back to the present.

"I was supposed to be off the last few weeks," Taylor admitted. "But the firm has been so busy, I've been covering a lot of the office stuff while Pete and Sam are out."

Faith nodded, sipping her water. "That's what I understand, at least as far as you guys being busy. I saw an interesting article in the paper this morning."

"Oh?" Taylor asked, sipping from his own glass.

"Seems Stu DiNardo is being sued again by one of his ex-employees."

"Really? I haven't seen the article."

Faith's eyes narrowed. "And the law offices of Heller Highwater are representing him."

Taylor smiled, accused. "It's possible our firm may be involved."

"More than possible, though Pete Madson had no comment," Faith said.

Taylor leaned back in his chair, arranging his napkin on his lap. The waiter returned, gingerly placing his iced tea with lemon in front of him, then serving Faith her Diet Coke. The fact that he was served first did not escape Taylor's notice, but he said nothing.

"Have you decided what you'd like?" he asked, looking to Faith, but eyeing Taylor.

"The *foie gras*," Faith said.

"Excellent choice. Sir?" Though he tried to hide it, he looked Taylor up and down.

"The chicken," Taylor answered, deadpan. The boy did a double take, but Taylor was able to keep his face perfectly neutral.

"Of course, sir," he said, taking Taylor's menu with a little less bravado. He headed back to the kitchen, leaving Faith to continue her subtle questioning, completely oblivious to the interaction before her eyes.

"So what's the story?" Faith asked, sipping her beverage.

"I really can't say," Taylor answered. "I'm not directly involved in the case, and even if I was, I wouldn't be able to discuss it."

Faith nodded. "That's a good answer, Taylor. Exactly what I expected."

"It's the truth," Taylor assured her, unsure of where she was going with the conversation.

"Of course," Faith repeated. "I used to work with Stu DiNardo a number of years ago."

"Oh?" Taylor prompted.

Faith smiled. "Thank you for not asking how *many* years ago." She laughed at her own little joke and Taylor smiled thinly. Another sip, and she continued. "Truthfully, I was just starting out and he was a few years ahead of me. At that time, he liked to take on apprentices, to show them the ropes."

"So you apprenticed under him?" Taylor asked, regretting the way the question came out as soon as he'd said it.

Faith simply nodded. "I wasn't the first, nor the last. Stu was a mover and shaker in the business. He already had many contacts in the commercial world, and whoever was with him tended to get to make use of those contacts as well."

"I see," Taylor said, not fully seeing just yet, but having a pretty good idea.

"As I said, I wasn't the first and I wasn't the last. It became a sort of club, where I first worked. The older ones looked out for the younger ones."

"How bizarre," Taylor commented as their salads were delivered. He took a healthy bite of leaves, still listening to Faith.

She watched him, picking at her own plate. "It has been a number of years…well, more than a number now…but we've all stayed in touch."

"Really?" Taylor asked. If the relationship between DiNardo and the other agents was what Taylor thought it was, it seemed particularly odd that they would all keep in regular contact. But then, he'd seen stranger things in his years of practicing law.

Faith's bravado wavered and she seemed to grow uncomfortable with the revelation she was making, but she pressed on.

"I'm sure you can imagine how surprised we were to see the headlines in the papers this morning."

Taylor shook his head. "Honestly, Faith, I didn't see the paper this morning."

"It's all over all of them—the Pine Creek Gazette, and the big papers from the city. They're all carrying it, front page, above the fold."

"Not again," Taylor moaned.

"What do you mean?" Faith asked, confused.

Taylor set down his fork. "Every time we get involved in the big cases, the news media starts hounding us. Usually, the first shot is an above-fold story."

Faith laughed. "You've gotta be the only attorney I've ever met who dislikes front page coverage."

"Maybe," Taylor agreed.

The waiter exchanged their entrees for their salads, then disappeared into the back again.

"Well, my *point* was to tell you how excited the former DiNardo apprentices were to hear about the case."

"Oh? Why is that?" Taylor asked.

Faith looked puzzled. "He's a horrible, awful person."

"Then why didn't any of you do something about him?" Taylor inquired, a bit mystified himself.

She considered the question, apparently unsure of how to answer it. She chewed a bite of her lunch before speaking again.

"You'd have to know how it was to work with him. It was truly a love hate relationship," Faith said. "And as much as we hated him, we loved him, too. So, in some strange way, none of us wanted to go through it."

"And now?"

"Now...your client has burst the bubble, I guess," Faith said. "He needs to go down. He *deserves* to go down. He's a lowlife, a bottom feeder, a man who wants nothing more than to stand on the backs of anyone and everyone before him."

"That bad?" Taylor asked.

"That bad. He's filled with hate and it's what drives him. He hates women, hates minorities, ardently hates gays, and will do virtually anything to achieve his goals."

"Anything? What do you mean by anything?" Taylor asked, hearing Tom's worried voice nagging at him in the back of his mind.

Faith rolled her eyes. "Not *anything*. I mean, he's not a murderer…at least, not that I know of," she said, laughing. "But when it comes to business, he's relentless."

Taylor considered her comments, formulating how they might fit into a prosecution strategy…for Pete.

"So, what do you want, Faith? What involvement do you want?"

"I want to take him down," she said. "We all do. We're willing to come forward, to provide information, to testify. Whatever it takes."

"The statute of limitations has probably run on a lot of it," Taylor said.

"Can't we at least testify as to character and our experiences with him?"

"Maybe," he said. "I'll need to have you talk to Pete, though. I really am trying to keep my hands off this one," he reiterated. "Between my connection to the stores downtown and my efforts to get Gen reelected, I have to be careful to avoid even apparent conflicts of interest."

"I'm not creating a problem for you, am I?" Faith asked.

Taylor shook his head. "No, it's okay for us to talk. But when it comes to any actual matters related to the case, testimony, etc., you will have to talk to Pete."

"Can he talk to me?"

Taylor nodded. "I do know his client has authorized him to discuss the case with other parties who may come forward. His client anticipated other people may want to be involved and is okay with that."

"Good," Faith said. "It has to stop. I'm sorry none of us ever came forward before, but it has to stop. I will do whatever I can to help."

They had both finished their lunches as the discussion progressed and the young waiter appeared to take their plates. Neither of them wanted dessert, as they had covered the topic they came to discuss. Faith insisted on picking up the check, so it would not appear that Taylor had in any way bribed her to come forward. He appreciated her concern and let her buy.

"Thank you, ma'am," the waiter said, taking the book back from Faith. "If there is ever *anything* I can do for you, please don't hesitate to call. Again, my name is Aaron."

His eyes stayed on Taylor the entire time he spoke, but his gaze was broken as they rose. Taylor followed Faith to the door, and they walked out to the porch.

"Taylor, I think that boy was flirting with you," Faith confided quietly.

"Really?" Taylor asked. "I hadn't noticed."

She let the subject drop, shaking Taylor's hand. "I'm really glad you came," she said. "I'll look forward to hearing from Pete."

"I'll bet he will call tomorrow," Taylor said, explaining they wouldn't be able to talk until that evening, with Pete tied up in court.

"Until then," Faith said, and gave a little wave as she walked to her car.

Taylor returned to his own car, deciding to head back to town by the quickest route. Whatever he might have expected from Faith, a revelation about Stuart DiNardo never crossed his mind. She never ceased to amaze him.

Some days just start off on the wrong foot and never seem to pick up.

Anita Madson sat behind the wheel of her sport utility, stuck in traffic. She was supposed to be home over an hour before, in order to meet Pete for dinner before the first playoff game for

Tom's little league team. Since she was the one who had insisted they go, she felt particularly angry that she was the one stuck a half hour from home in traffic that *would not* move.

The phone rang and she saw it was their home number. She pressed the send button and heard her headset click on.

"Hi, honey." Pete sounded genuinely sorry she was stuck.

"Hi," she grumbled. No one hated traffic worse than Anita, since she had to drive in it so rarely.

"Any progress?" Pete asked apologetically.

"Not a bit. I heard on the radio there's an accident ahead. They've just about got it cleared, but it had all three lanes shut down," Anita explained.

"What efficiency," Pete complained, trying to be sympathetic.

"Tell me about it."

Pete cleared his throat. "Tom just called to say they're heading over. Do you want me to go with Tom and you can just meet us there? I guess Taylor is running late, too. Tom sent him to pick up something."

Anita rolled her eyes. She wasn't dressed to sit out in the bleachers, but at least Pete could go support Tom. "Yeah, that's fine."

"Why don't you give a call when you're close and I'll come meet you in the lot?" Pete asked. Whatever she could ever say about him, she would never say he was inconsiderate.

"All right, I'll do that," Anita said. Her tone softened as she talked to Pete—he was always able to calm her down.

"See you in a bit," he said. "Love you."

"Okay. Love you," she said. She waited and Pete hung up the phone. They'd gotten over the "no you hang up first" thing years ago, and usually agreed the last person to speak waited while the other hung up. It worked for them.

The car ahead of her crept forward a few feet and she followed suit, then pressed the brake again. She'd just gone for a checkup with her doctor, the only thing that would get her in the city at a time when she would have to drive back in traffic.

The good news was all was well with the baby. The doctor had given her a clean bill of health. She and Pete had decided not to learn the sex right away. The doctor told her it wasn't time yet anyway, but she could already tell she wasn't going to last. Each time, she came a little closer to asking.

She couldn't wait to be a mother, and Pete couldn't wait to be a dad. They were a little older to be starting a family, but they'd both agreed that would work out best for them. Together with Pete, she'd traveled to all the continents but Antarctica. They'd talked about trying to go seven for seven, but it just didn't work out.

Ahead, the cars were finally moving, the obstruction completely gone. She gratefully pressed the accelerator, hoping to at least catch part of the game she'd insisted they attend. Tom was so proud of his team and their success. She hoped that their son or daughter would one day want to play on the team. Anita had never played sports much as a kid, but felt it was important for the younger generation. She read the studies and knew kids were becoming more complacent, and getting fatter in the process. She didn't want her own child to face those challenges.

Thankfully, traffic was moving swiftly. Anita anticipated all the other travelers were equally eager to get to their destinations, having been caught in the jam nearly as long as she. Though it was hardly a record setting trip, she made her way to Main Street without much interruption. Both downtown lights were green, but she had to stop at Red River Drive.

Watching the town, and the people out enjoying the unusually temperate weather brought a smile to her face. The bad day was behind her. It was going to be a beautiful evening.

A car pulled up behind her and she recognized it as Wayne's Jeep. Eric was at the wheel, no doubt taking it to meet Wayne and Tom at the field. Wayne had become a sort of assistant coach, helping Tom out while he was so busy with all the other business they had undertaken.

Anita gave a little wave and saw as Eric smiled in return.

Some days just start off on the wrong foot and never seem to pick up.

Eric rolled over and found his bed empty. Of course, that was hardly unusual, since he was still living out of a hotel room, but that morning, it just caught his attention and set his mood for they day.

Things were going well with Wayne, that much was certain. They had officially announced themselves as a "couple" again, and were dating regularly. Wayne was definitely interested in him, but he'd still largely drawn the line at them spending the night together.

Eric's hotel room, paid for by the company he would be working for in a couple more weeks, was near the city—a half hour drive from Pine Creek. Wayne's apartment, of course, was directly above the bakery.

On the fourth of July, Eric hinted it might be nice if he stayed over. At first, Wayne seemed to be somewhat receptive to the idea, but then he cooled off. He said he didn't know how Dan would feel about it. Eric tried using logic, asking if Emmy spent the night, but learned that she didn't stay very often. Leave it to Wayne to have old-fashioned friends. It wasn't that they didn't spend nights together, but Dan had tried to be considerate of Wayne and not rub his relationship in Wayne's face.

Eric was not one to pressure him to do something he didn't want to do, so he invited Wayne to come back to the hotel with him. Wayne had politely declined, reminding Eric of the long drive, as though he'd forgotten, and saying he wanted to be in town in case he was needed. Though Eric couldn't imagine what they would need Wayne to do on a moment's notice, he played along.

And so he'd been playing, for the last two weeks. They'd spent a grand total of two nights together, when Dan went to stay with Emmy when Emmy's roommate went home for a weekend. To say he was a little frustrated was to put it mildly.

He was due to be at the bakery in an hour. He quickly showered, shaved, and dressed. Wayne had to help Tom at a little league game that evening, so he brought a change of clothes. At least it was okay for him to change at the apartment, saving another hour-long drive to and from the hotel.

Luckily, his drive was always opposite the direction of the heavy traffic. Eric made it to town in a little under a half hour and came in the back door to find Wayne already covered in flour, managing the baking while Dan and Emmy were out front.

"Good morning!" Wayne greeted, giving him a quick kiss.

"Hi," Eric answered.

Wayne stopped, a bag of flour over his shoulder. "What's wrong?"

"Just tired," Eric said, taking the bag to store on one of the racks.

"Really?"

"Yeah," he said. "What do you want me to work on?"

Wayne could barely contain himself. "That'll wait. I have something to tell you."

"Oh?" Eric asked, nonplussed.

"Come on, cheer up. Listen, Dan said he's staying over with Em tonight." Wayne was positively beaming.

"Oh?" Eric repeated, a little more interested.

"You know what that means!" Wayne cheered.

"Sitting around in your boxers watching the Simpsons?"

Wayne put an arm around him. "With you right next to me!"

"I guess," Eric agreed, still reluctant. He was glad he'd get to stay with Wayne, but they were going to have to discuss the situation sooner or later.

Wayne looked a little hurt. "You guess?"

Eric couldn't upset him. "Sorry, I'm still waking up. You know how the drive can be."

"I know," Wayne said, pulling him closer. "But you won't have to drive tonight."

"That'll be cool," Eric agreed.

Wayne froze, then looked at him, face guilty. "Actually, would you mind driving tonight?"

"What?"

Shaking his head, Wayne clarified, "Not to the hotel. I mean, could you bring a car down to the ballpark? Tom asked if I wanted to just ride down with him, rather than take a bunch of cars."

Eric shrugged. "Yeah, that's no problem."

"Thanks, babe," Wayne said. "I can't wait to have you here."

"Me, too," Eric said.

They went on with the day's work, meeting the increased demand from the coffee shop. Eric had to admit he wondered what they were going to do when everyone had to go back to school and he started working, but he figured that was Tom's concern. He just did what he was told and went where he was told and waited for Wayne to let him know what to do next.

To Wayne's credit, he was working through his lingering issues and things really were improving. His reaction to Dan's night away was a perfect example—he didn't waste time asking Eric to come spend the night with him. They just needed to get to that next step, where they decide what they want to do, together.

Though it started off slow, the day positively flew by. Taylor had dropped by to have a quick chat with Tom, then went home to change. Tom seemed to have a little extra spring in his step after the talk, so Eric wondered what was up. Whatever it was, Tom didn't comment, and he didn't want to be nosey.

Near the end of the day, Tom and Wayne left Eric and Dan to do the final cleanup. They made short work of the task and Dan left to go meet Emmy for an evening out together. Eric went upstairs and took a shower, happily leaving his clothes in Wayne's room, neatly piled on his overnight bag at the foot of the bed.

He checked the time and saw he was right on schedule. Knowing how Wayne loved his Jeep, he took the spare keys and headed down. Wayne always parked right behind the store, where he could keep an eye on his vehicle. Eric got in and the engine roared to life.

Town was quieter than usual, but people were milling around on the sidewalks. He'd taken Second Street to Main, then headed north toward the ballpark. The light at Red River Drive changed and he stopped, a white Volvo station wagon ahead of him. He looked again and recognized Anita waving to him. He waved back, giving her a big smile. It was going to be a nice night.

Taylor was exhausted. What a day. Some days start off on the wrong foot and just never seem to pick up, and try as it might, it had been one of those days.

Coming back from Shelbyville, he'd opted to take the freeway, cutting a good ten minutes from the drive. However, he'd no sooner gotten on and there was a big accident right in front of him as a sports car cut off a tractor-trailer, causing it to jackknife, blocking all lanes of traffic.

Taylor had pulled off and rushed to see if there was anything he could do. Both the Shelbyville and Pine Creek police responded. The truck driver was okay, with bruises and scrapes, but the sports car driver was a little less healthy. An ambulance whisked him away, back to the city, but righting the tractor-trailer took longer than expected.

Once again on his way back to town, Taylor heard on the news that the backup stretched for miles. He was thankful to have at least been near the start of it, so he was able to leave more quickly. Since the police from both towns knew him, they said they'd get a final statement from him later. Fortunately, no one had asked why he was there—the last thing he wanted was to draw more attention to his lunch meeting with Faith.

The day was shot, so he called the office to let Christy know he wasn't coming back in. He stopped at the bakery to fill Tom in. Tom was positively delighted by the news from Faith, and for the first time, Taylor thought he might truly forgive her for her past transgressions.

He went home, hoping to catch a quick nap before the game. At home, Tom's mom called to give them an update on the kids. All was well, and they were making their third trip to Disney World. He couldn't imagine what he and Tom would do to entertain them when they got home, but he was glad they were enjoying their time with their grandparents.

After a far too short nap, he pulled on a fresh T-shirt and shorts, then headed out. Traffic in town was fairly light, possibly due to the traffic congestion that was no doubt still plaguing the freeway. A few people were walking around downtown, enjoying the great weather. It was nice to see families on the sidewalks— he hoped those families would keep in mind how nice it was to have good places to walk to when they cast their vote for mayor!

The light at Red River Drive turned and he stopped. Ahead, he saw Wayne's Jeep, and a car that looked a whole lot like Anita's station wagon. He didn't know who was in front of him, or he'd have honked and waved.

The light changed and they started forward, headed for the ballpark.

The light changed and Anita released the break as she looked to see if anyone was coming. A lot of people seemed to be walking to the park that night. She had to agree—if she wasn't so late, she'd have loved to walk, baby and all.

There were a number of cars coming into town on the other side of the street. Anita was always glad to see traffic—it meant people to shop downtown and keep people like Stuart DiNardo at bay. The last thing they needed was that crook gaining a foothold on the town.

Anita gently accelerated, pulling into the intersection. A family was walking on the sidewalk beside the road, their toddler carrying a ball that was a little too big for her. In the blink of an eye, she dropped the ball and ran out in front of Anita to catch it.

She didn't have time to think. She just reacted, pulling the wheel hard to the right. There was too much traffic on the other side of the street. She just hoped against hope that she wouldn't hit the edge of the bridge...and she didn't. But instead of stopping, her car slid down the side of the embankment, toward the water.

The light changed and Eric let up on the brake, waiting for Anita to pull away. He followed her, keeping an eye on the traffic around him. A few cars were passing in the opposing lane, and a number of people were walking across the bridge, no doubt on their way to the park.

As he watched, before his eyes, one of the kids dropped her ball into the street, right in front of Anita's car. Eric slammed on the breaks even as Anita swerved to the right, trying to avoid the family without pulling into oncoming traffic.

At first, he thought it would be okay, but her car slipped on the wet grass from the earlier rain and slid forward, precariously toward the river. In an instant, he accelerated, pulling onto the grass, where he stopped and leapt from the Jeep.

Anita's car was in the water, where the current was strong enough that it would keep her from easily freeing herself. As he slid down the embankment, he looked for signs of movement, but saw none. Her airbag had deployed and she appeared stunned.

Eric ran into the cold water, reaching for Anita's door. Thankfully, it was only partially submerged, but he couldn't see any way to get the window open. To do it, he was going to have to open the door.

He slapped his hands on the window, trying to get Anita's attention. At last, she looked up, still dazed.

"Are you okay!?" he shouted.

"Yes," Anita replied weakly.

"Unlock your door!" Eric called. He repeated it again. Slowly, she moved and pulled the handle.

Water rushed into the car, but Eric moved at the speed of light. He released her seatbelt and pulled Anita from the car, just as the water caused it to slip.

The cold against her skin helped Anita become more aware and she caught hold of herself against the car, rising. Taylor and someone else came down the embankment to help. Eric was soaked and stayed in the water to help Anita up. Taylor and the other man each took an arm and pulled her to safety.

As they did, the car shifted again and Eric was pulled back into the water. He tried to catch himself, but his hands were wet and slid on the car. The current carried him out into the river.

"Eric!" Taylor shouted, watching as the current pulled him farther into the river. "Eric!"

"Taylor!" he coughed, trying to keep his head above water.

Taylor took off along the embankment. The river was moving faster than usual, thanks to the recent rainfall. The land along the riverbank on the south side of the river was all natural and wooded, leaving uneven, often rocky surfaces for Taylor to run on in the dim light. Tree limbs pulled at his shirt and scratched his arms and legs as he ran.

"Don't fight the current!" he called to Eric. Above, he heard the sirens of emergency vehicles and he desperately hoped someone had sent them in his direction.

Eric wasn't moving, but Taylor couldn't tell if it was because he was following his advice, or because he was unconscious. As he ran, he tried to look ahead in the waning sunlight. He knew the river got narrower, but that would also tend to cause the water to move faster. He had to think of something.

He was running faster than the water was moving, but just barely, and the uneven surface was causing him to fall behind. Pushing himself faster, he saw his best chance ahead.

Eric was just slightly behind him. Frantically, he looked down and found a large tree limb. He grabbed it, then ran to the water where a single large trunk tipped out over its surface. The tree was dead, but all he needed it to do was give him a place to balance against the current.

As fast as he dared, he went into the water, feeling it move up closer and closer to his waist. Eric was there, and he wasn't moving.

"Eric! Can you hear me?"

There was no response. Gaining precarious purchase against the steady current, Taylor reached out with the tree limb, and snagged Eric's shirt. His motionless body spun in the rapidly moving water and Taylor struggled to keep the small swatch of fabric in the limb's grasp while slowly pulling him in. The fabric slipped, but stayed on the tip of the limb, just barely.

The large limb that was holding Taylor from falling was also preventing him from pulling Eric any closer. Slowly, with all the care he could muster, Taylor waded farther out into the current, his shoes slipping on the river rocks below, the water crawling up his abdomen to his chest as he slowly made his way down the stick, praying to not lose his hold on Eric, nor slip in himself...

CHAPTER ELEVEN

Disaster...Again

The town ball field was alive with activity as two young teams duked it out to see who would move ahead in the playoffs. Friends and family lined the stands, split down the middle between the Shelbyville Raiders and the Pine Creek Pioneers. The weather had broken and left them with a beautiful evening of puffy clouds and bright sun, just warm enough to be comfortable, and with a slight breeze to keep the bugs away.

Tom watched as Amanda slid into home, right before the ball made it to the catcher. The crowd erupted in applause as she rose and dusted herself off. They had one out left, but she'd put them ahead again, after two innings without scoring.

As Ricky, one of her classmates, stepped up to bat, Tom again scanned the stands. Where was Taylor? He'd promised he was going to attend. Tom checked his phone again, but there still hadn't been any calls.

Wayne glanced in his direction, frowning, and made a gesture as if to say, "where are they?" Tom shrugged in response. The only person he saw in the stands was Pete, who was sitting with Amanda's parents, Rob and Mel. As far as Tom knew, Anita was supposed to be there, too. Was something going on in town?

"Strike two!" the umpire called.

Tom returned his attention to the game. Ricky was usually one of their best hitters, but he hadn't been on his game all evening. Wayne had mentioned hearing a couple of the team members talking about him having broken up with his longtime girlfriend of two months. He told Tom he'd talk to the boy later, being able to commiserate all too well on the pain of a breakup.

The pitcher lined up another pitch, watching both Ricky and the players on the surrounding bases. Tom called out to his player.

"Come on, Ricky! Watch that ball!"

As the pitcher made his move, a motion in the corner of his eye distracted Tom. Reflexively, he turned to see the chief of police standing with Wayne, face dour. Wayne turned to Tom and waved him over.

His eye still on the motion on the field, Tom joined them.

"What's up, Chief?" he asked.

The Chief didn't mince words. "There's been an accident."

Tom felt a rock form in the pit of his stomach. "Taylor?"

"He should be fine," the Chief said quickly.

"Should be?" Tom repeated urgently. The game continued behind him, but his attention remained squarely on the chief. Wayne stood right beside, his attention equally centered.

The man rested a reassuring hand on Tom's shoulder. "They just took him to the hospital for observation." He looked at Wayne, his expression as gentle as Tom had ever seen it. "I've never seen anyone move that fast. He ran for all he was worth."

"Ran for what?" Wayne asked.

"He was trying to save your friend."

Wayne became unsteady on his feet, teetering close to falling, and Tom reached out to support him.

"Chief, you'd better take it from the top," Tom said.

Before the chief could answer, Pete pushed through the crowd and ran up to Tom.

"Tom, there's been an accident!" he breathed. "Anita ran off the road into the river! Eric saved her, but then he got caught in the current! Taylor pulled him out, but I can't get any word on any of them! We need to go! Now!"

"That's it," the Chief said, gesturing to Pete. "Come on, I'll take you over myself."

The other assistant coach ran up, seeing the crowd around Tom. The game had ground to a halt as everyone watched what was happening.

"Tom? Is everything okay?" he asked.

Tom shook his head. "There's been an emergency. We have to go. Take over, will you?"

"Sure," he said hesitantly. The Chief leading the way, the three men followed him to the large sport utility he drove. Tom climbed in the front seat, while Pete and Wayne sat in the back.

The chief started the car and headed out of the parking lot as he explained what had happened. "Witnesses said Anita was coming up the bridge when a child ran out in front of her car. She swerved to the side to miss the kid and then slid on the wet grass. The current pulled her car farther into the river and it was pure luck that Eric was able to get her out."

"How is she?" Pete demanded. "She's pregnant, you know!"

"We know," the Chief assured him. "We'll get a report when we get to the hospital." He reached down to activate the flashing lights on his car, moving effortlessly but safely through traffic.

"So Taylor tried to save Eric?" Tom queried.

The chief nodded. "After Eric got Anita out, the current pulled him back in and he was caught in it. We lost sight of them as Taylor chased him, until they were just about to the Shelbyville Road bridge. We found them there, on the bank. Somehow

Taylor had managed to pull them both out, though they swallowed a good bit of water."

"Is Eric okay?" Wayne asked, tears flowing freely from his eyes, his hand in Tom's.

"Again, I don't know. The paramedics took them both to the hospital," the Chief reiterated.

Tom hated waiting, and even though they were running with lights and siren, it was the longest wait of his life. He thought about calling Taylor on his cell phone, but he knew it would be docked in his car, not with him. Even if it was with him, the hospital wouldn't allow him to use it, so he would just have to hope everything was okay.

At last, after what seemed to be several centuries of travel, the hospital loomed ahead of them. Tom felt his pulse quicken as they pulled up, his hand already on the door handle. The Chief drove past the emergency entrance, then parked his car in an official space. He didn't even have a chance to put the vehicle in park before his three passengers ran for the door.

"Whoa!" one of the doctors called, holding out his hands. "Can I help you gentlemen?"

"We're here to see the people who were just in an accident," Pete said breathlessly.

"What's your relationship to the patients?" the doctor asked.

"Family!" Tom snapped. He was in no mood for the "friend or family" debate.

"Who is with whom?" the doctor asked.

"Taylor Connolly," Tom said, holding up a hand.

"Anita Madson," Pete said, following suit.

"Eric Driskell," Wayne called out.

The doctor nodded, acknowledging each of them in turn. "Mister...Connolly?"

"Tom," Tom said, waving a hand to prompt him along. The chief appeared behind them, quietly listening to the interaction.

"Tom. Mr. Connolly is with Mr. Driskell in Triage Room Two. They're just making sure all the water is out of Mr. Driskell's lungs. If you'll wait in the waiting room—"

"Think again, Doc," Tom said. "We want to see them *now.*"

"Sir, they're being treated—" the doctor began again, trying to keep them calm.

"Where is my wife?" Pete asked bluntly.

The doctor turned to him, glancing quickly at Tom and Wayne as he spoke. "Mr. Madson, your wife is okay. They're running an ultrasound right now to make sure nothing happened to the fetus. At this time, we have no reason to suspect anything is wrong, it's just a precaution."

"Thank God," Pete breathed, visibly relaxing.

"As soon as the ultrasound is done, I'll ask the nurse to come get you," the doctor assured him. "Now, if you'll just please go to the waiting room…"

Taylor appeared in the hall, his clothes still damp and dirty from his marathon down the riverbank. Tom ran to him and pulled him into a tight hug.

"Ow!" Taylor said. "Easy there. I guess I bruised a rib or two."

"Sorry," Tom said, still holding him.

"How's Eric?" Wayne demanded.

Taylor shook his head. "They think he'll be okay, but he's asleep right now."

"I want to see him," Wayne said.

"It would be best if you waited—" the doctor began again.

The chief stepped up, his stature intimidating to the small doctor. "Raymond, take the boy back," he said simply.

"Chief, Mr. Driskell needs time to—"

"Raymond," the chief growled, face set.

The doctor turned to Wayne. "This way," he said, leading Wayne away.

Tom guided Taylor back toward the waiting room, with Pete right behind them. The chief joined them, standing before them as they sat.

"You look like hell," Tom whispered, the terror of the past few minutes having left a strong smear of worry across his face.

"Thanks, honey," Taylor managed, leaning into him over the arm of a chair. "You didn't happen to drive did you?"

Tom shook his head. "The Chief brought us."

Taylor looked up to the man. "Thank you."

"Don't mention it, Mr. Mayor," the Chief said. Even though Taylor was no longer mayor, he insisted on calling him by his former title.

"Taylor, what happened?" Pete asked, turning to face him. Taylor recounted the accident again, from his angle behind both Anita and Eric. Pete became visibly pale as he heard Taylor describe how Eric pulled her from the car. He was relieved she'd been conscious, but concerned that she couldn't free herself. Taylor then described chasing Eric, and vaguely recalled pulling him from the water. Even as he spoke, he realized the memory was fading into a blur.

"I don't know how to thank you for helping my wife," Pete said, taking Taylor's hand.

Taylor smiled, giving his hand a squeeze. "You'd have done the same for mine," he replied, with a nod toward Tom.

"Funny," Tom deadpanned.

For his part, the Chief snickered, too. "Well, boys, seems like everybody's okay. I can give you a lift back to town if you'd like."

"We shouldn't leave Pete," Tom said.

"I'll stay with Pete," Taylor promised. "You go get one of the cars and some dry clothes, will you?"

"Where is your car?" Tom asked, realizing it must have been left near the river.

Taylor looked to the Chief, the obvious question on his face. Smiling, the Chief held out Taylor's keys. "It's parked at the church. I moved it myself."

"Thanks, Chief," Tom said, taking the keys. He rose and turned to Taylor. "Do you still have a bag in the back?"

"Yeah," Taylor confirmed.

"Okay. I'll be back in a few minutes, then." He turned to Pete. "Do you want me to stop and get something for Anita?"

Pete handed him a key. "That would be great, thanks."

Taylor looked up. "You should probably get something for Eric, too. I don't think he'll be wearing his clothes again after tonight."

"His car is with Taylor's," the Chief said, handing Eric's keys to Tom.

"You're a good man, Chief," Tom said.

The Chief gave a shy smile, turning toward the door. "Just part of the job."

"I'll be right back," Tom said. He gave Taylor a quick kiss, and gave Pete a reassuring pat on the back, then followed the Chief back to his car.

Wayne followed the doctor, Raymond, down the hall. Raymond's demeanor said he was anything but happy about having *his* rules ignored, but for some reason, the Chief's command was enough to put him in motion.

They reached a closed door and Raymond stopped, his hand on the lever.

"Now listen, Mr. Driskell is asleep. You can sit with him, but understand it may be a little while before he awakens."

"I've got it," Wayne said with a nod. If Raymond didn't move, Wayne felt like he might be forced to move him.

Fortunately, no such intervention was necessary. Inside, the room was relatively small, and dark, with just a light on behind the bed. Eric lay there, his head on a pillow, clad in a blue hospital gown, sheet loosely covering him.

"His breathing appears to be normal," Raymond reported, slipping into doctor mode. "We'll want to observe him until he's conscious and able to move freely."

"I'll stay with him," Wayne said quietly. He walked to stand beside the bed, then quietly lowered himself to a chair.

"We'll monitor him. So far, it's a quiet night, so hopefully we won't have to move him," Raymond said. Without another word, he slipped quietly from the room, closing the door behind him.

Wayne took Eric's hand in his, gently running his thumb over its smooth back. For the first time, Eric's hand felt small. Wayne knew it was his imagination, that nothing had happened to cause it to feel any different then it ever had, but seeing him lying there, helpless, made Wayne feel very protective.

According to the Chief's story, Eric hadn't even given a second thought to chasing Anita's car to the river. As soon as he saw her swerve off the road, he'd followed her, parked his own car, then chased her into the water. He'd single-handedly pulled her out, then helped get her out of the water while Taylor and another good Samaritan pulled her back to dry land.

In his mind, Wayne could see Eric's bravery as though he'd been there himself. He suddenly felt very foolish for his behavior over the past few weeks. The man lying before him was an honest, caring, loving *good* person. He'd been forced to make a decision that would have caused him great pain, no matter which course he'd taken. In the end, the path he chose probably made life easier on everyone, including Wayne, by allowing them both to focus on what they were supposed to be doing—finishing their educations—and letting time pass.

But Wayne's feelings were for more than just what happened in the past. Lying before him was a man who was willing to risk his own life to save the life of someone he barely knew—if, in fact, he'd known it was Anita at all when he ran to provide aid. That kind of selflessness was rare, and it was something Wayne recognized as very valuable.

A tear escaped and his hold on Eric's hand tightened as he realized how close he could have come to losing Eric forever. How could he have been so self-centered? Eric had expounded, over and over, on the anguish he'd felt for the decisions he'd been forced to make, and how he hoped Wayne would forgive him. All Wayne was worried about were his own feelings of abandonment and rejection. In his mind, Eric had to *earn* his way back into Wayne's heart.

As he sat there, Eric's hand in his, Wayne knew that task was completed. The horror he'd felt when he heard what happened confirmed that. There was another task ahead of them, though— one that might prove equally daunting: Wayne had to earn *his* place in *Eric's* heart. It wasn't enough that Eric offered it freely; Wayne had to give back what Eric had given him.

"I'm sorry," he whispered, biting back tears as his eyes beheld Eric's quiet face. His skin looked so pale in the harsh fluorescent light, and his chin and cheeks were peppered with thin five o'clock shadow, already several hours past its deadline.

"I'm sorry for putting you through the past few weeks," Wayne continued. "You didn't deserve to have your feelings treated so casually. You made your case and told me how you felt, and I hid behind my fear."

He sobbed, his grip on Eric's hand firm. "The truth is, I was scared. I was scared to let myself love again." The tears flowed freely as Wayne spoke. "Until I met Tom and Taylor, I wasn't even sure I knew *how* to love. It's not an excuse, just the truth. Then there you were, this perfect person, and you *loved me*. I mean, it was like a dream. In just a few months, I went from living with my hate-filled family, to living with Tom and Taylor, and loving you. You were everything I'd ever wanted, everything I'd ever dreamed."

Wayne looked away, wiping his eyes. "It wasn't your fault, what happened to us. You did what you had to do. I know that now. If you can forgive me for being an ass these past few weeks, I can forgive you for having to leave when you did. Can we just move forward? Can we just move on?" Gently, he held Eric's hand to his lips, kissing it softly. "I need you," he begged. "Come back to me and I promise, we'll never be apart again."

Eric's hand tightened and he drew in a deep, cleansing breath as he forced his eyes open. Slowly, his gaze fell on Wayne and he smiled.

"Waynie," he managed.

"Eric?" Wayne answered with a sniff, wiping his eyes.

Eric frowned. "Why...crying?" he coughed.

Wayne choked a laugh. "Why do you think?"

"Me?" Eric asked.

"Yeah."

Eric groaned. "Silly. I'm okay."

"I hope so," Wayne said.

With a moan, Eric tried to sit up, then fell back on the bed. "I may need a ride back to the hotel."

Wayne shook his head. "We're done with the hotel."

At that, Eric's eyes opened. "Oh?"

Again, Wayne shook his head.

"What about Dan?" Eric asked.

"He'll just have to adjust."

This time, Eric did sit up and Wayne leaned onto the bed to help hold him up, wrapping his arm around the man he loved. "Really?"

"Can you forgive me for being such a jerk?" Wayne asked.

Eric smiled, wiping a tear from Wayne's cheek. "How about if we both agree that we're forgiven for everything in the past?"

Wayne smiled. "Sounds good to me."

"And we look forward to the future," Eric continued.

"Done."

Eric sighed, his eyes fluttering closed again. He leaned heavily into Wayne, his head on his shoulder. "I thought I was dreaming," he whispered.

"Dreaming?"

"When you said you needed me."

"I need you," Wayne repeated.

Eric smiled, looking deeply into his eyes. "I need you, too."

Wayne kissed him gently, sealing the deal.

The next day, everyone was clean and rested. Wayne had taken Eric home that evening, and they spent their first night together, once again officially a couple. Tom and Taylor stayed with Pete until they were sure everything was okay with Anita. Anita's car had been pulled from the river, but would be in for repair for at least a couple weeks, so Tom drove them all home, finally getting Taylor to bed around midnight.

Pete had insisted that they all come over for dinner that following evening, and Gen and Miguel joined them, curious to find out what had happened to their friends the day before. Gen was absolutely incredulous about the timing—she had passed through the same intersection not a minute before, and even remembered seeing the family of the child who had run in front of Anita's car.

To their credit, the family had been mortified about the chain of events that followed their daughter's simple action, and had offered to do anything they could to help any of the people affected. Fortunately, other than some water damage to Anita's car, no one was really the worse for wear. She had a couple of bruises on her arm and a small bump on her forehead, but that was the extent of the damage. Though the impact had been enough to deploy the airbag, it hadn't been enough to harm the baby.

After dinner, everyone had gone their separate ways. The baby was fine, but Anita still needed her rest. Gen and Miguel headed home, as did Wayne and Eric. Earlier in the day, Taylor had quietly asked Dan what he thought of the situation between his two friends, and to his credit, he thought it was great. As he'd explained to Taylor, Wayne had been an emotional basket case without Eric, so he viewed it as an improvement. He told Taylor he and Emmy had discussed getting their own place, so as not to bother Wayne and Eric, but Wayne wouldn't hear of it, so he was staying.

The evening sky darkening, Taylor turned on the television while Tom bustled around in the kitchen. Over the summer, he'd become hooked on the cooking show with the blonde haired guy with glasses who explained the science of various meal preparations. Taylor was an adequate cook, but with the additional information, he was starting to branch out and experiment more.

"What's he cooking tonight?" Tom asked, sticking his head out the door from the kitchen.

"Cookies," Taylor answered. He was sitting on the couch, but had his feet up on one of the ottomans from the chairs. After Anita, he was probably the worst looking after their harrowing ordeal—he hadn't even felt it at the time, but his skin had taken quite a scraping from various twigs and branches as he ran along the shoreline. He'd do it all again, though, and he figured he might as well milk it while he could.

"Ooo, that sounds good!" Tom said. "Cadbury bar?"

Taylor sighed. "Sure." Being with Tom was doing his waistline no favors. Tom had it in his head that Taylor was too thin, so he kept doing what he could to fix that. Tom, of course, was one of those people who could eat a whole table of food and feel no ill effects. Taylor, on the other hand, was going to have to buy some new pants if he wasn't careful.

"Here you go," Tom said, handing him one of the chocolate treats. On the screen, the host had a large green puppet expounding on the virtues of various ingredients in the cookie making process.

"You know," Tom continued, "I've been thinking about trying some new recipes."

"Is that so?" Taylor said through a mouthful of Caramello.

"Yeah. The coffee shop is selling stuff like crazy. I thought it might be fun to try some new recipes."

Taylor swallowed his candy, then asked, "Is that your idea, or the boy wonder?"

Tom laughed, nudging him in the side. "Wayne had nothing to do with it."

"No?"

Tom shook his head. "No. He wants to start offering caramel corn."

"Oh, for cryin' out loud," Taylor groaned. His waist would never be the same again.

Before Tom could say anything more, the phone rang and he reached to answer it. "Hello? Hi, Mom, what's new?"

Taylor watched as the various ingredients were assembled. There was some dilemma about whether to use a mixer or not, but he couldn't catch everything with Tom talking. As far as

Taylor was concerned, people who didn't have a Kitchenaid mixer were simply a glutton for punishment. He'd learned that from Emeril.

"You're where?" Tom asked. Taylor could hear his mom talking to him in the phone, but it wasn't loud enough for him to make out what she was saying. "Oh," Tom continued. "So you think you'll be home tomorrow?"

Taylor looked over, questioning. Tom shrugged, still listening. Quietly, he said, "They're on their way back." Back into the phone, he said, "Yeah, Taylor's here. No no, it's no problem." To Taylor, he added, "Dad got the bug, huh?"

Taylor shook his head. His conversations with his mother tended to last a minute or two at most. Tom could be on half the night.

"Yeah, we'll be glad to see them, too," Tom said. It had been strange to have the kids gone for so long, but by the same token, the time had positively flown by with all the action that had happened.

"Hi, Chad," Tom continued. The kids always wanted to talk to them. Though they spent a lot of time with Tom's parents, there was no doubt who they considered their parents to be. It had been hardest for Chad, since he was the oldest and thus had the best memory of his biological parents, but even he had stopped talking about them much after a time. Wendy would ask questions once in a while, or look at the photos of John and Sandy that Taylor had put on the mantel, along with their own family pictures. Little Taylor, the baby, really had no memory of his parents. He'd been only a couple of months old when they died and he still wasn't old enough to realize he didn't have a "mommy," no matter how many jokes Tom made at Taylor's expense, and vice versa.

"Three pictures with Mickey Mouse?" Tom asked, over emphasizing his excitement for their son's benefit. "You did? He did? No! It was? How scary? *That* scary? That's pretty scary. Do you think Dad Taylor could have taken it? No, me either."

"Hey!" Taylor complained in the background. "What was so scary?"

Tom handed him the phone and Chad started to recount his last trip to Disney World before they left, when he got to ride on a couple of small roller coasters. Taylor let him talk for a couple of minutes, then talked to Wendy for a couple of minutes, too. At last, Tom's mom took the phone back, telling the kids they'd have to tell the rest to their parents when they saw them the next day.

"Hi, Taylor, how are you?" Donna asked.

"Not too bad," he answered. "Somebody is nursing me back to health."

"Wayne's over?" Donna chided.

"I heard that, mom," Tom said, leaning in close enough to hear his mother's side of the conversation.

"He's so nosey," Donna said. "Just like his dad." Taylor heard a complaint in the background on the other end as she kept talking. "We didn't say anything about it here, so no one would be upset."

"Thanks," Taylor said, meaning it. No pun intended, but they had already planned to give the kids a *very* watered down account of why Taylor had so many scratches and why Aunt Anita had a big bump on her forehead. They were going to keep Eric's near drowning down to just the part where he helped Anita out of the car. The kids could get the details when they were older...like, twenty.

"Anyway, we just wanted to let you guys know we'd be back tomorrow. The kids are really excited to see the coffee shop, and of course, their parents."

"We're looking forward to seeing them," Tom said, turning the handset so they could both hear it.

"Tomorrow then, boys. Love you."

"Love you," Tom and Taylor said at the same time. Taylor clicked the phone off, then handed it back to Tom, who set it down on the couch beside him.

"I guess the peace and quiet is over, huh?" Tom observed.

"It was never really that quiet," Taylor reminded him. "Nor that peaceful," he added.

"The glass is half empty?" Tom asked, looking into his eyes.

Taylor shook his head. "Always over half full...as long as you're here."

Tom laughed, wrapping his arms gently around him. "You're so full of it!"

"Hey!" Taylor objected. "I was being genuine."

"You were being full of it," Tom countered.

Taylor sighed. "You know what that means."

Tom nodded. "Last night of no kids."

"I think we should make the best of it."

Tom rose and helped him to his feet. "I'll break out the Haagen-Dazs, you get the fudge."

"I'm there," Taylor said. As he followed Tom into the kitchen, he reflected on the changes their lives had seen in just five years. When had a night without the kids become a food fest? And when, really, had he quit objecting to it?

As he followed Tom, he just smiled. People said life was too short and they were wrong. There was always time, it was just a matter of using it to the fullest. It started with overpriced ice cream shared with a loved one over a kitchen table. It would end upstairs a few hours later, with that same loved one in his arms as they both drifted off to sleep.

CHAPTER TWELVE

A Time for Action

Eric wiped the counter for the umpteenth time, thinking over the changes the past few weeks had brought him. It seemed hard to imagine, just over two months ago, he'd graduated from college, gotten a job, and promptly been put on leave while they "got ready for him." What was to get ready for?

But there was a bigger question and he'd been quietly trying to answer it for weeks—was *he* ready for *them?* The time for him to answer that question was getting closer all the time, and he still didn't have a clue. Had he gone to college, pushed himself harder than he'd imagined possible, and gotten his degree, all to run a coffee shop in Pine Creek? Or, on the days he wasn't helping in the coffee shop, to bake at Downey's?

He didn't know how to ask Wayne, and the fact that Wayne hadn't raised the issue himself spoke volumes. They were doing very well together, and that was the best thing that had happened since graduation. His parents suspected something was up, but he played off the story about his department not being ready to ramp up for a few more weeks. He made sure they had his cell phone number and told them that was the best way to reach him.

He'd checked out of the hotel the day after Wayne brought him home from the hospital, and hadn't looked back. On the question of what he was going to tell his parents, Wayne had been a little more vocal, but they agreed it wasn't something Eric had to handle right away. As much as Wayne wanted him to say something, he understood why Eric was hesitant to do so and didn't push. For his part, Eric just made sure Wayne knew he wasn't going anywhere and that any decisions he needed to make would be made with Wayne's input.

And he knew he was already breaking that promise. The fact was, his job *was* going to start up in a couple of weeks and he *did* need to talk to Wayne about it and he was scared. Of course, his promise to stay with Wayne was not in jeopardy—if nothing else, he would start working, as he had expected to do, and drive to the city every day, as many people already did.

The question that plagued him, though, was if he *wanted* to. Did he want to work an eight to five job? Did he want to get up each morning, quietly rush out of the house, drive forty-five minutes, sit in a cubicle, drive an hour home (it always took longer in the afternoon), and spend the evening holed up in the apartment? Wayne's schedule varied—some nights he would be home; others, he had to work, and he still had classes for another year before he graduated. Summer baseball was nearly done, so at least that would be off the schedule, but did Eric want to be the one who broke up their little family?

It plagued him, haunted him, and left him with no answers. He straightened the condiments area, throwing away used stirrers and napkins. Was he meeting his potential? He knew what his father would say—*that* was a foregone conclusion. "I didn't pay for a college education to have you filling coffee cups!"

Was it his father who still haunted his thoughts? If it didn't mean telling his father he was going to stay in Pine Creek with Wayne, working for Tom and Taylor, would he do it? Eric just didn't know. He wasn't the sort of person to think he was too good for one job, or that one had more merit than another. He was just at a crossroads, where more than one option existed and he didn't know which one would lead to greater happiness for him.

It occurred to him it might be *good* for him to be gone some of the time. Wasn't there an old saying about absence making the heart grow fonder? He sighed. That old saying had nearly blown up in his face, in a big way. If anything, it was the opposite—he was afraid *not* working in the coffee shop or the bakery would leave him feeling left out, cut off, no longer a part of the little family they'd all created. He already knew how that felt, and wasn't eager to repeat it.

He thought about Emmy and Dan. Though they were still only coming up on their junior year of college, sooner or later, they would have their degrees. Were they going to stay in Pine Creek? Would they keep working in the McEwan-Connolly family businesses? It didn't seem likely, at least to Eric.

His own ties to the businesses were, in many ways, a little closer. Wayne was part of Tom and Taylor's family. Eric had no idea what financial arrangements the guys might have made for him, but there was no doubt they considered him one of their own. So, in some ways, they were like his in-laws. To be fair, he knew Tom tended to think of Emmy much the same way, having worked with her since just before her fifteenth birthday. But Emmy's family was well off and Emmy was a very smart girl. Eric was sure her aspirations went beyond the town, and he seriously doubted Dan would be far behind. In the past few weeks, he'd heard Emmy talk about following her dad's interest in medicine. Dan's interests were more artistic, tending toward writing and reporting for the school paper, but that didn't seem to bother Emmy at all. Eric suspected they'd be married, unless something major came along to throw a wrench in the works.

That brought to mind another question he'd half asked himself, but not come right out and considered—was he married? After everything he and Wayne had gone through, it sort of felt that way, and yet it didn't. They were sharing the apartment again, and in closer surroundings than they had before, but just what *was* their relationship? And what did Wayne want it to be?

Eric chuckled to himself. He knew the questions were all things he should be asking Wayne, but they'd been so *happy* lately, he hadn't been able to do it. It was time. He needed to just bite the bullet and come out and ask the questions and work them through, together.

"Hi."

He looked up, so lost in thought he hadn't noticed the person standing across from him, and he jumped when he saw it was Wayne, his apron showing the marks of the day's baking.

"Hi," Eric answered.

"You look surprised," Wayne observed, smiling. "Thinking about me?"

Eric flushed, caught. "Yes, actually."

"Anything *good*?" Wayne inquired.

Eric felt his face go redder. "No."

"Liar."

Attempting to deflect the topic, Eric asked, "Something to drink?"

Wayne shook his head. "No, thanks. I just came to see you."

"Here I am," Eric said, holding out his hands.

"Not bad," Wayne said, causing him to blush yet again.

"Don't you have work to do?" Eric asked.

Wayne nodded. "Unfortunately, yes. Mrs. Johnson has me baking cakes by the dozen. I guess there is some ladies' group and they're having a raffle or something."

Eric watched his irritation, but knew it wasn't real. Like Tom, Wayne enjoyed the simple work, and the challenge each new batch created, to best the last one. "Fun," he said.

"Yeah," Wayne agreed. "So anyway, how late are you working."

"I'm here until about seven. I guess Sally had something she had to do tonight," Eric answered.

"Getting something else pierced?" Wayne asked.

"Probably," Eric agreed.

Wayne put up his hands. "I don't want to know. I'm done about the same time. Want me to bring you a sandwich?"

"That would be great," Eric said, genuinely glad to not have to worry about dinner.

"Dinner at seven," Wayne said. "Done. I should get back— the next round of cakes will be done in a couple of minutes."

"Don't forget to wear your mittens," Eric said, absently wiping the counter again.

"I never do," Wayne replied, then disappeared back into his domain. As he pondered what his own domain might be, Eric resolved to start the conversation with Wayne that evening. They had plans to make, and it was time they start making them together. As he continued cleaning, Eric saw Jason come in from the office in the back, then stop to talk to a customer.

After his last relationship ended less than smoothly, Jason promised himself he would never again find himself pining for the man he couldn't have. Yet there he was, pining away, eyes firmly set on the great Adam Brown.

What had happened? How had his resolve faltered? Jason knew the answer—when Adam had all but followed him the evening of the grand opening, he knew he was in trouble. It had nothing to do with Adam himself—Jason had fallen for him, and there was no looking back.

The trick was figuring out what to do next. Adam had stopped by a couple of times, usually immediately before a meeting with his students, and there hadn't been a lot of time to talk.

On the one hand, Jason thought it was a little presumptuous of Adam to meet his students in their shop, but on the other, he knew the professor was a friend of Tom's, and the students usually did buy something to eat or drink. Besides, Jason knew the more comfortable they were, the more likely they were to keep coming back.

Running the shop was going very well—better than he'd ever hoped. It seemed Wayne's words were prophetic—the people of the town were indeed happy to see a coffee shop on Main Street. Jason, ever the pragmatist, wondered how long it would be until the next one popped up. From what he knew of Stuart DiNardo, he was guessing it wouldn't be too long.

He didn't know the details, but he knew Taylor had partially funded the shop, and gotten outside funding for part of it. If the spreadsheets before him were remotely indicative of what was to come, the time until they were in the clear would be measured in months rather than years. It was incredible.

With a yawn, he leaned back in his chair and stretched, his back tired. Like many managers, he also wound up working long hours when employees didn't show up for work. One of their students had something come up the night before, meaning he'd been forced to work with Sally. The high point was seeing Adam drop by with yet another cadre of kids. The low point was not getting to chat with him as he had to go meet someone for dinner. Wasn't Jason supposed to be meeting him for dinner, somewhere along the way?

He rose, heading out to the store. He needed a little of their flagship product to put some wind back in his own luffing sails.

Eric was covering for Sally, for which Jason was eternally grateful, but he didn't want to leave him to do all the work.

As he entered the store, he saw Wayne just walking away from Eric, whose mind appeared to be elsewhere as he straightened the various items in the counter cabinets. Jason was going to help him when his eyes fell on the man seated in the "living room" area—a couple of couches and some comfortable chairs, circling a low coffee table, in front of a gas fireplace. It had been Jason's idea, seconded by Tom, as a way to bring people in to have discussions and share ideas. In the mid afternoon, it was only Adam sitting there by himself, no doubt waiting for students to show.

Jason took the opportunity. "Hey, stranger," he greeted.

Adam looked up, a stack of papers in his lap, a red pen in his hand. His dark-rimmed glasses were balanced on the end of his nose, giving him an aged, regal haute as he gazed over the rims at Jason.

"Hi there," he replied, smiling. He reached up and removed the perched lenses, setting them on the couch next to him. "How have you been, Mr. Harper?"

Jason smiled, both at the greeting and the acknowledgment of his name. "I'm well, thanks. You?"

"Midterms," Adam groaned, gesturing to the stack. "As much as students hate to write them, they forget that we professors have to *read* them. There are days when I would love to just drop a scan-tron in front of them and pretend that was really a gauge of learning."

"That's what my professors did," Jason said.

"Did you learn anything?" Adam asked.

"Not really," he admitted.

Adam nodded. "So, for the next three days, my eyeballs pop out of my head, and I run through a pen or two, telling them what they need to learn to pass finals."

"Are they that bad?" Jason inquired, slowly sitting on the edge of the couch across from him.

Adam quoted from the paper in his lap. "Aldus Huxley wrote his masterpiece novel, *Brave New World*, to tell people all about how dangerous it was to use drugs. By using analogies, he made you think about how social classes are bad, but people don't think about them. Without books like *Brave New World*, people might not think to ask important questions like this."

"Wow," Jason breathed.

"That's one of the better ones," Adam assured him. "These are from one of my intro classes. Honestly, I don't know what some of these schools are teaching kids anymore." Jason shook his head—he didn't know either. Adam continued. "You know what's really funny? I remember when Tom was teaching public school. For a couple years, the kids who came through from his classes really seemed to *care*. Not all of them, but many. The girl they got to replace him isn't bad, either, but the kids who knew both of them said she's not as entertaining."

"But can she teach?" Jason asked.

Adam nodded. "Of course. Tom kept the kids engaged, though. I've seen him in his college classes and I've talked to people who had him before. He was always telling stories and putting on little shows as he acted out scenes from the books— he made them more than just stories."

"Sounds like Tom," Jason agreed. How had they gotten on Tom? That wasn't what he wanted to talk about.

"So, what's new—" Adam started to ask. Before he could finish, Keith and the other girl appeared behind Jason.

"Hey, Dr. Brown," the girl greeted. "Your office said you'd be here."

Jason turned to watch them and saw the way they both eyed Adam.

"What can I do for you?" Adam asked.

Keith spoke up. "We were wondering if you'd had a chance to read our papers."

"Actually, I was just going over yours now," Adam said. Jason nearly choked as he realized what they'd just been saying about it.

"It's pretty good, isn't it?" Keith asked, nodding expectantly.

"You'll see on Thursday," Adam answered.

"Oh, come *on*, Dr. Brown," the girl whined. "A hint?"

"I haven't read yours yet, Katie," Adam answered.

She wasn't easily swayed. "We can wait."

Adam shook his head. "Sorry, guys." He rose, checking his watch. "Actually, I need to head off to an appointment anyway. I'll finish them this evening."

"Okay," Katie huffed. Keith gave Adam one more glance, then followed her to the door.

"Thanks for the chat," Adam said to Jason, who also rose. "We'll have to catch up once these finals are out of the way. There are still more restaurants that need to be tried."

"I'd like that," Jason agreed.

And, just like that, Adam Brown, the great author and professor, was gone. Jason half expected to see swirling patterns of dust behind him as he moved, but there was only carpet. He made his way behind the counter, where Eric waited.

"How's it going?" Eric asked.

Jason looked up, his mouth cocked to one side as he considered his answer to that question. "Still can't make contact," he said.

"How's that?"

Shaking his head, Jason sighed. "Every time I try to talk to him, something happens to keep it from working. Today, we talked about how his students can't write, then, as he started to change the subject, that pain in the butt from his class showed up. Then, poof, he was gone again."

"Poof?" Eric asked.

"Poof," Jason repeated.

"You just need to bite the bullet and say something," Eric advised.

Jason's expression was vacant, as he looked off at some invisible object in the distance. "That's what Sally said, too."

"Sally? You asked *Sally*?"

Jason shrugged. "She's always got a girlfriend," he pointed out.

"And yesterday's usually isn't the same as tomorrow's," Eric clarified.

"Still a better track record than mine," Jason observed.

"You may have a point."

At that, Jason shot him a look, but didn't argue. "Maybe I'll call him tonight."

Eric nodded. "That's the spirit!"

"Knowing would be better than wondering, wouldn't it?" Jason continued.

"Exactly!"

"Then that's what I'll do," Jason concluded. He looked up. "Why don't I feel better about it?"

Eric laughed and put a reassuring arm around his shoulders. "That, my friend, is called being human."

Taylor flipped the patties one by one, trying to ensure each had just the right grill marks on both sides of the burger. He had no doubt it was yet another expression of his anal retentive tendencies, trying to achieve the perfect burger when no one would even notice.

Behind him, Gen and Tom relaxed in the late day sun, watching as the three kids chased Molly around the yard, or were chased by Molly, depending on the moment. Tom and Taylor had agreed to take the evening off, glad to finally see their kids again after so long apart. They invited Tom's parents to join them, but they politely declined, as Taylor had guessed they would. A month of carting the kids around would try the patience of the very best of grandparents, and he had no doubt that they would appreciate a little time off. Tom had arranged to be off for a couple of weeks, or at least alternate whatever work he needed to do with Taylor's schedule, to give his mom a break.

Gen, using her patented Dinner Radar, had stopped by when she saw Taylor starting the grill. In near record time, she tricked him into asking where Miguel was so she could point out that he had to work late and then look like a sad puppy. Taylor, playing his part, had promptly invited her to join them, which she politely declined. He then insisted, as he was supposed to do, and Gen quickly relented, offering to bring a fruit salad...which she just *happened* to have conveniently already prepared. Taylor smiled. It was her ritual, and one she seemed intent on continuing.

"Food's on!" he called. The kids ran for the deck, cheering as they came. Molly trotted to a stop and dropped to the grass, finally free of her three mini human charges.

To Gen's credit, she was as quick to get up and help as anyone, and took a plate for Wendy, who insisted on sitting next to her at the table. As usual, they alternated kids and grown-ups, making sure everyone was comfortable and well fed.

"This looks great, Tay," Gen said.

"So does your fruit bowl," Taylor answered, returning the compliment. "Isn't it great how the timing worked out?"

"Amazing," Gen acknowledged, giving him a brilliant, devilish smile.

"Gen was just asking how your DiNardo case is going," Tom said, biting into his perfectly prepared burger without a second's hesitation.

Taylor prepared his own sandwich, hand hovering over the patty an extra second before letting loose with the mayo. "It's not *my* case," he insisted. "Pete is handling it. I'm only advising him on a few matters of law."

Gen nodded. "That's great, Tay. But Pete won't *tell* me anything!"

"He's not *supposed* to tell you anything," Taylor said, biting into his sandwich.

"But I have to debate that guy!" Gen complained. "The more ammo I have, the better."

Taylor shook his head. "Genevieve Pouissant, we have already had this conversation. You're not going to win this battle with mud slinging."

She shrugged. "I *know*. The question is what facts might be useful in debating the man. How do I prepare? He's evil, I'm not. How do I share that with the town?"

"By not *being* evil," Taylor concluded. "The town isn't stupid. DiNardo may put on a dog and pony show, but even the best illusionists are figured out sooner or later."

"Tay's right, Gen," Tom interjected. "People in town already know you. They know the kind of person you are, and the kind of leadership you bring to us. Just be yourself and you'll do fine."

Gen sighed. "If being myself is all it's going to take, then why are there so many Stuart DiNardo signs around?"

Taylor considered her question as he chewed, then chased the bite with a sip of water. "People like to ally themselves with money. They perceive it as a connection with success. It's how the Republican Party gets votes from the poor, minorities, and immigrants. When was the last time you saw a Republican out there pounding the pavement to help the underclass? Yet there was the little shrub, getting nearly fifty percent of the vote! It's the same thing with DiNardo. Some people think a vote for him is a vote for success. It's not fair and it's not logical, but it's the truth."

Tom shook his head. "God, Gen, don't get him started on voting strategies," he begged. "We'll be here all night."

Gen laughed, while Taylor shot a look in Tom's direction. "The only voting strategy I'm interested in is how to keep DiNardo out. I swear, I don't even want this job, except that it scares me to death to think of what that man could do to this town."

"There's still the town council," Taylor observed.

"How many times did they step in to stop you?" she inquired.

"How many times did I give them a reason to?" Taylor countered.

"The point is we can't rely on them to do it," Gen said.

"Unless we got appointed to town council," Tom offered. He jumped as they both glared at him. "It was just a thought," he defended, leaning back.

"Gen, it will be fine," Taylor insisted. "You'll debate. You'll be a shining star. People will naturally trust you because you're not a sleazy middle aged man with greasy hair and a bad dye job, wearing an ill-fitting double-breasted suit from nineteen ninety-two."

"Don't forget the mustache," Tom added, helping little Taylor with his cut up hot dog pieces.

"And you don't have a big furry mustache," Taylor added.

"Thank God for that," Gen agreed. "But really, there's nothing you can tell me from the case? Maybe I should talk to Faith. I still can't believe she's helping."

"Neither can I," Tom said, taking a bite from his burger while he watched Taylor.

"No, you should not talk to Faith. Am I speaking French here?" Taylor demanded. "You need to argue on *your* merits, not argue against his issues. Keep the ball in your court, where you can control it."

"Not a bad sports analogy, hon," Tom said, raising a forkful of fruit in Taylor's direction.

"Will you stop?" Taylor said, again giving him the eye.

Gen considered his advice, clearly not convinced, but recognizing the merit it presented. "Maybe you're right."

Taylor nodded. "I'm telling you, if you give him the rope, he'll hang himself. Have I ever steered you wrong before?"

Wayne appeared at the door between the café and the bakery, two containers in hand. Eric saw him and flashed a smile as he reached to take off his apron. Wayne set the containers on the counter and turned to close the doors between the two spaces. The bakery was officially closed for the day, but the café wouldn't close for hours.

"Hi there," Eric greeted. Sally had returned a few minutes before, and thankfully did not find it necessary to tell him where she'd been. Jason was running back and forth between the stock room and the counter, making sure they were prepared for whatever rush the evening may bring.

"Hiya," Wayne greeted. He retrieved the boxes from the counter and followed Eric to a couple of the low-slung chairs near the doors to the bookstore. Sherry and Liz were keeping their store open late, too, and according to Jason sales were up.

"How was your day?" Eric asked. He'd been amazed how easily he and Wayne had started to fall back into a comfortable rhythm, enjoying each others' company and listening to each others' stories.

"Once I got those doggone cakes done, everything went well," Wayne said. "Emmy and Dan were both in, so that kept things moving. How was yours?"

Eric shrugged. "The usual. Fill cups, wipe counters, counsel Jason."

Wayne laughed. "How's he doing?"

Eric rolled his eyes. "Adam Adam Adam. You know how it is."

"Any progress on that?"

"Not so far," Eric said, munching on his sandwich. Wayne had a nearly perfect track record for selecting things he would enjoy...or maybe it was just that he enjoyed whatever Wayne gave him...

"That's too bad," Wayne said. Jason had become their pet project. Though he was older than both of them, and theoretically had more experience with relationships, his experiences had been bad enough that they both felt compelled to protect him. Eric didn't really know Adam, but Wayne did. Wayne liked him, but said he was afraid Adam wasn't as ready to settle down as Jason was.

"Yeah." Eric made a point of eating his sandwich, quietly looking toward the front windows, watching the street.

"So, you ready to talk about the work thing yet?" Wayne asked.

Eric felt the question like a jolt of electricity passing through him, caught completely off guard.

Wayne smiled. "I know it's been on your mind the last few days. I figured that's why you looked so relieved when I said I'd bring dinner."

Eric was shocked. It never ceased to amaze him how well Wayne could read him—it had been the reason, after all, that he so studiously avoided him while he finished school. He simply couldn't hide anything from Wayne, and he didn't know why he tried.

"I don't know what to do." There. He'd said it.

Wayne kept smiling. "Do what you want to do."

"But I don't know what that is."

"Then give the job a try and see what you think."

Eric made a sweeping gesture, looking at the store. "What about the café? Between you and Jason, I've been pretty busy."

Wayne shrugged. "You have to do what is right for you," he insisted. "Don't get me wrong, I love having you around all the time." At that, Eric grinned openly. "But I can get by with just having you night and weekends if that's what you want."

"The thing is, I *like* working here," Eric insisted. "I just don't know if it's what I *should* do. I mean, we're all one big happy family. But sooner or later, some of the kids are going to leave the roost."

Wayne nodded. "And you don't want to be the first."

"Would you?"

"No," Wayne agreed. "But sometimes, that's the price of being the oldest."

Eric laughed, setting his empty sandwich box aside. "What are you going to do?"

"What do you mean?"

"Next year," Eric said. "You're going to graduate. What do you want to do once you're done?"

Wayne looked down, suddenly a little more closed off himself. "I haven't figured that out yet," he admitted. "Obviously, there is plenty of work to do here, but it seems silly to go all the way through school and never use any of the stuff I've learned. Some of Adam's friends are in publishing, so you never know what may come along."

"Would you move?"

At that, Wayne's expression suddenly vanished, his face hard. When he looked up at Eric's eyes, there was the slightest hint of panic in them. "Not if I have a choice."

"I feel the same way," Eric assured him. "But my point is we need to identify the boundaries we're willing to accept and then work within them."

"It's exhausting," Wayne complained, sitting back in his chair and resting his face in his hand.

Eric took Wayne's other hand in his and held it. "Yes, it is. But it's better that we discuss it now."

Wayne's grip firmed up. "Don't you forget it," he said, eyeing Eric from under his hand.

The front door opened, interrupting their discussion. Adam entered, with two students in tow. He gave a wave and said hello as he passed, heading for their usual hangout in the back.

As Wayne and Eric watched, Jason looked up and saw Adam, then caught sight of the students a split-second later. His expression went from excitement to sour distaste just as fast.

"This should be interesting," Wayne said, his hand still holding Eric's.

Jason looked up at the trio and tried to keep his face neutral. Sally quietly turned and headed for the back room, forcing him to acknowledge the new arrivals.

"Good evening, everybody. What can I get for you?"

Before either Adam or Katie could speak, Keith pushed his way forward, edging up next to Adam. He cocked his head to one side, gesturing to the items on the menu behind the counter. "The Professor will have his usual, of course, and Katie wants an iced tea. I think I'll have an iced mochachino with extra whipped cream, K?"

He was being extra flamboyant that evening and Jason truly had to restrain himself as he watched the display before him. He had no doubt that at least some of it was for his benefit.

"We'll have those right up for you," Jason replied happily, making change. "If you'd like to have a seat, I'll bring them out."

"No problem, sweetie," Keith said. Adam rolled his eyes as he followed the insistent students to the sofas.

Sally conspicuously returned just as they left the counter and busied herself helping Jason prepare their order.

"Aren't you going to do something about him? He's moving in on your turf."

"He's not my 'turf,' Sally," Jason hissed. "We're just friends."

She snickered. "Friends who you melt for every time he walks in the place. I may not like your kind, but it doesn't mean I can't see what you're thinking. Woman's intuition works for both teams, you know."

"Good lord," Jason moaned, picking up a tray. "Don't even start." He put the three cups on it and headed out to serve the customers.

He handed Katie her iced tea and Adam his latte. He turned to Keith and what happened next was like a slow motion film of a fast moving disaster. Adam had set his ever-present briefcase next to the low coffee table in just the right position where it wasn't obvious, but was in the way of someone walking by. Jason's foot caught the edge of it, and he tripped forward, managing to catch himself before he fell on Adam. The cup in his right hand wasn't so lucky. The action of catching his fall caused him to tighten his grip just enough to pop the lid and it flew off. The cup's contents, frozen and slushy, were then free to observe the laws of physics, particularly the pesky one about objects in motion tending to stay in motion. The frozen drink spewed from the glass and landed in a large brown smear...down the front of

Keith, where he was sitting too close to Adam, with the lion's share landing in a satisfying pile in the boy's lap.

To his credit, the kid tried to back out of the way of the onslaught, but his reflexes weren't fast enough, and he gave a high pitched squeal as the icy cold drink quickly passed through the thin material of his T-shirt and shorts, touching skin. He then jumped up, causing what hadn't bonded with his clothing to fall onto the floor, covering his bare feet and flip-flops.

Keith blurted a string of expletives, standing with his arms out in shock as frozen coffee dripped down the front of him. Adam took a napkin from the table and wiped the few drops that had fallen on his own slacks, trying to keep from laughing at the situation.

Sally came up behind them, several dry rags in her hands.

"I am *so* sorry," Jason said, trying to offer the rags to the kid.

"Dude, what the hell was that?" he exclaimed. He swiped the rags from Jason's hand. "I'm a mess!"

"I'm very sorry," Jason said again, trying really hard to mean it.

"Shit," Keith exclaimed, still cursing like a sailor. "Now I've gotta go home and change."

"Come on, Keith, it's not that bad," the girl said.

"Katie, I'm *covered* in it," Keith yelled. He turned to Adam. "Dude—Dr. Brown—can we go over this stuff later?"

Adam smiled and nodded. "You're the one who's been hounding *me*."

Keith glared at Jason one last time, then stormed from the shop. Jason turned to Adam.

"I'm really sorry."

Adam smiled, placing a reassuring hand on his shoulder. "Don't worry about it." He turned to Katie. "I'll be in my office tomorrow. If you want, you can come by for office hours and I'll talk to you then. How's that?"

"Works for me," she said. "I'll see you then." She turned and was gone. Adam helped Jason clean up the mess while Sally kept fresh rags coming their way. Eric and Wayne joined them, assessing the damage.

"That was impressive," Adam said, wiping off the side of the sofa.

"I'll say," Sally agreed, sponging the floor with a mop.

"I didn't do it on purpose," Jason defended.

"Sure you didn't," Sally said, rolling the mopping bucket back to the storeroom.

Adam looked up, the sofa once again clean thanks to the fabric protector. "You know what they say, timing is everything."

"Not the best way to build repeat customers," Wayne observed, handing Sally the rest of the rags.

Adam laughed. "Are you kidding? Keith drives them all nuts. They'll drag him back here, just to see if they can get a repeat performance."

"We'll see," Jason grumbled.

"Speaking of timing," Adam continued, "I seem to have my evening free again."

Jason shook his head. "I'm on until close."

"Oh," Adam sighed, looking down.

Sally appeared from behind. "Go," she said.

"What do you mean, 'go?' You can't run this place by yourself," Jason said.

"Why not? Wayne is upstairs if I need anything. I'll hold down the fort until Ethan gets here." She looked from Jason to Eric and Wayne. "Is that okay?"

Before Jason could object, Eric shrugged. "Sure. We're just hanging out over there right now. We're not in any hurry."

"Are you sure?" Jason asked.

"Go," Eric said. Wayne nodded behind him. They returned to their chairs while Sally reached behind Jason to untie his apron. She pulled it over his head, leaving him in just the usual work attire of shorts and a T-shirt.

"I need to change," Jason said, noting Adam's button down shirt and slacks.

"Actually, I'm the one who needs a change of clothes," he said, gesturing to the stains the coffee had left. "I've got a spare set in the car. Can I use a bathroom?"

"Jason lives right upstairs," Sally offered helpfully.

"Oh?" Adam asked.

Jason eyed Sally, but recovered quickly. "It's true. You're welcome to change there."

"Great," Adam said. He retrieved his bag from the car, then followed Jason out the backdoor. Sally and the other two exchanged smiles and she gave them a group high-five as she went on about cleaning the tables, her boss safely away.

CHAPTER THIRTEEN

The Devil You Know

The tension hung in the air, thick as the summer humidity, as people milled around the entrance to the Town Hall. Residents and spectators had begun showing up over an hour before the event was due to begin, some to get seats, others to be seen on one of the local news stations covering the event. Nothing drew people out to make fools of themselves like evening news cameras.

To describe the day as humid was an understatement. After a highly temperate, rather cool summer, the heat had reasserted itself with a vengeance. The temperature had climbed into the low eighties by lunchtime and was into the nineties by the time the reporters started appearing in their news vans.

Taylor had made his way quietly into Gen's office earlier in the afternoon, seeking to calm her jittery nerves. Unfortunately, the usually unflappable mayor was not to be soothed that day. In the end, he'd left her to her work and slowly made the rounds with the various news trucks, listening to their reports and even conceding a couple of interviews, provided the reporters stick solely to the election and make no mention of the lawsuit against DiNardo.

One of the more prominent city stations, a subsidiary of one of the national networks, had sent their biggest field gun, Ellen Malone, to cover the story. Taylor stood off to one side, watching her prepare for her live report. As some unseen voice prepared her, she suddenly stood straighter and positioned her handheld microphone while the cameraman stood in front of her, allowing a shot of the town hall and some of the younger residents behind her.

"This is Ellen Malone, coming to you live from the Pine Creek Town Hall. As many of you are aware, Pine Creek has been the center of an unusually hot race for the position of town mayor. Tonight, the two candidates, incumbent Mayor Genevieve Pouissant, and her opponent, real estate developer Stuart DiNardo, will square off. Sources close to the event expect an intelligent, articulate debate on the issues facing this typically quiet town. KRP9 will follow this breaking story and bring you updates throughout the night. Stay tuned to KRP9 for our ten o'clock news, when we'll bring you highlights from this charged event. I'm Ellen Malone, back to you, Ted."

Malone continued to pose for the camera for a few more seconds, until the cameraman indicated they were clear. She immediately pocketed the mic and started to remove her sport coat. Then her eyes made contact with Taylor and she mumbled something to the cameraman and headed his way.

"Excuse me," she said. "Aren't you Taylor Connolly?"

"Yes?" Taylor asked. Ellen Malone was not one of his personal favorite news personalities, having broken several rather insensitive stories on civil unions and defense of marriage acts over the past couple of years.

"You're Mayor Pouissant's campaign manager, right?"

Taylor nodded. "Yes, that's true."

"Would you be willing to give an interview? We're going to air a report on this debate on the evening news. I wouldn't mind having a few words from you to add in."

He wanted to say no. He was hot and tired, and knew the debate would start shortly and he really did need to be with Gen. However, he also knew his voice carried political weight with the community and it was important to use it whenever possible. He'd been a popular mayor and he hoped his endorsement of Gen would help her chances at reelection.

"Sure," he said.

"Great!" Malone agreed. Her makeup person appeared from out of nowhere and quickly worked to improve Taylor's appearance, dabbing the sweat from his forehead, rearranging his hair, fixing his tie, giving him a quick dab of makeup, and finally a friendly pat on the shoulder as she returned to the truck.

The cameraman returned, this time to take the interview on tape for later use. Malone positioned herself next to Taylor, again with the town hall as a backdrop.

"You've been interviewed before, right?" she asked.

"Once or twice," Taylor affirmed. One of the first things he'd been forced to understand as a high profile attorney was privacy was a thing of the past.

"Great, then let's roll. Eddie?" she said, addressing the cameraman.

"You're on," he replied.

"This is Ellen Malone. I'm with former Pine Creek town mayor Taylor Connolly. Mr. Connolly is acting as current Mayor Genevieve Pouissant's campaign manager." She turned to Taylor. "Mr. Connolly, how is it that you're managing the campaign of your successor?"

Taylor put on his best TV smile. "Gen is one of my oldest friends. When I needed to step down from the mayorship to

spend more time with my family, she quickly accepted my request
that she take over. She won the last election uncontested."

Malone played her roll as interviewer. "Yet in this election,
just two years later, she is facing a serious contender, real estate
developer Stuart DiNardo. To what do you attribute her fall in
popularity?"

Taylor shook his head, thinking fast to spin the question. "I
wouldn't characterize it as a fall in popularity at all. Her last
election was uncontested—that means no one else ran against
her. This time, she has an opponent who has a rather well known
name in our community."

Ellen leapt in. "A name that has recently come under fire
from several ex-employees," she said. "Would you care to
comment on the lawsuits your firm has filed against Mr.
DiNardo?"

Taylor's face froze. With the heat and his fatigue, he hadn't
warned her to stay away from that topic. He tried to beg off. "I
can't comment on matters related to pending litigation."

Malone shook her head, giving him her best inquisitive
reporter gaze. "Is there any conflict of interest by having your
firm involved in litigation against Mr. DiNardo while you
represent his political opponent?"

Taylor shook his head. Better to answer the question directly.
"The plaintiff in the case is aware of my political involvement. I
am not directly involved in any of the pending litigation, having
specifically removed myself for that reason. We believe that
satisfies any concerns with regard to conflict of interest."

Ellen Malone had single-handedly pulled out the one issue he
did not want covered. Their entire game plan was to show
DiNardo as the unscrupulous character, while Gen was just a
citizen of the town, trying to do her civic duty. If the media tried
to spin that he and Gen were using the courts to attack DiNardo,
it would be a political disaster. Worse, he couldn't say anything to

Malone after the fact, or she would just run with it that much faster.

"Mayor Pouissant has made a point of avoiding any discussion of Mr. DiNardo's business dealings, insisting that she wants to run a clean campaign. In that regard, what is it you feel most differentiates the mayor and makes her the person to lead Pine Creek?"

Taylor nodded, relieved to be off the lawsuit topic. "Gen Pouissant has been a resident of this town for ten years. In that time, she has consistently shown her civic responsibility and participated in town functions. Since taking over as mayor, Pine Creek has seen a consistent pattern of growth and development, in both the new commerce district and the traditional downtown historic district. That development has been led by Mayor Pouissant, and when she is reelected, we can expect more of the same compassionate, caring leadership."

Malone flashed her reporter's smile. "I guess she has your vote?"

Taylor nodded, returning his own TV smile to his face. "She does indeed," he agreed.

"Thanks for talking with us tonight, Mr. Connolly." She turned back to the camera. "This is Ellen Malone, reporting for KRP9 News from Pine Creek."

Eddie the cameraman waited a couple of seconds, then dropped his camera and headed back for the truck. Malone held out her hand to Taylor, who shook it.

"Sorry about that lawsuit question, but it's what everyone has wondered about and I had to ask."

"I understand," Taylor said.

"I wonder if you'd be willing to give a follow up interview after the debate. I'd like to get your feedback for my report. If Mayor Pouissant is available, that would be great, too."

"Of course," Taylor agreed. Rule one to getting elected was keeping the media happy. After all, he'd called them there in the first place...

Gen paced her small office, stopping to glance through the blinds every couple of passes. Miguel sat in front of her desk, looking calm and composed as ever. Tom sat in the chair beside him, watching as Taylor tried to get Gen to relax.

"There are an awful lot of cameras out there," she commented, squinting out the window.

"There are a lot of people in town who can't come see the debate. Getting positive media attention will help," Taylor explained.

Gen glanced at him. "As long as it's positive."

"It will be," Taylor assured her. "Why don't you sit down and relax for a few minutes?"

"How am I supposed to relax?" Gen asked. "If I screw this up, DiNardo will get to run willy-nilly through the town."

Tom shook his head. "Now that's not the right attitude to have. You're setting yourself up to fail."

"I agree," Miguel chimed in. "There is nothing to screw up. You are the best candidate for the job, and as you answer the questions, people will recognize that for themselves. All you have to do is be you."

Gen turned to her husband. "That's sweet, honey. You're full of it, but it's sweet."

"Genevieve!" Taylor barked. Miguel and Tom both jumped. Both of them knew better than to get between Taylor and Gen when Gen was having a moment. Taylor continued, "Sit down and chill out. You're going to be fine. The person who should be worried is DiNardo. How can he possibly hope to compete with you? You're smarter than him, nicer than him, and a *way* better dresser."

At that, she laughed. She'd called Taylor earlier in the day to inquire about what he thought she should wear. Taylor, usually so indecisive when it came to clothing, told her *exactly* what to wear, in less than thirty seconds. He rolled it off the top of his head, like it was the easiest question in the world: Charcoal suit, cream blouse, black patent leather heels, a simple gold broach, the diamond solitaire necklace Miguel had given her for Christmas, and her wedding ring. No more, no less. Gen had taken his advice, then gotten her hair done in a subdued yet trendy style that made her look professional, hip, and entirely approachable. When they saw DiNardo enter the building in one of his typical silver double-breasted suits, hair slicked back, and aging wingtips, they'd exchanged a high five.

"I am cooler than him," Gen agreed.

"And don't you forget it. This is going to be fun. You're going to have a good time. Remember, you're smarter than him and you're going to make him show his true colors by using your intelligence against him," Taylor coached.

Gen nodded. "I let him get comfortable, get confident, get cocky, and then get arrogant. Then I throw the board in front of him and let him trip and fall on his face," she recited.

"Now you've got it," Taylor said.

Gen looked at the clock. "I guess we should be going."

Miguel and Tom rose, both somewhat relieved. Miguel had to be present for obvious reasons, but Tom had offered to join them to lend moral support as well. Wayne and Eric were spending the evening at their house, watching the kids.

Outside Gen's office, reporters clustered at the entrance to the meeting room. By agreement of both participants, the local cable access channel would provide simultaneous feed to all television stations, eliminating the need for five or six cameras in the room. Of course, the print photographers were under no such sharing agreement, so the flashbulbs flashed and shutters clicked in earnest as Gen and her team entered the space.

As they made their way to the seats that had been reserved for them in the front, many of the people in the room cheered Gen. She smiled self-consciously, unsure of how to respond to the limelight. Many of the townspeople reached out to shake her hand and she readily accepted their support. Taylor surveyed the audience and saw many, many faces he knew. It was as though someone had made a point of calling all their friends the night before, between the hours of six and nine, to remind them of the debate and ask that they attend.

At the front of the room, two podiums had been set up, facing a centered table. By mutual agreement, the chief of police had been selected as the moderator of the event. He sat in the center seat reviewing his note cards. He caught the mayor's entourage as they moved to their places in the front row and Taylor caught the single, subtle wink he gave them.

Tom and Miguel each gave Gen a hug, then took their seats as she and Taylor approached the podium. They had already had an opportunity to visit the location earlier in the day, as had DiNardo's team. His office manager was acting as a sort of campaign manager for him, though he had officially been managing his run himself. Together, the two of them were prepping him for his participation as well.

"Here we go," Gen breathed as Taylor helped her arrange her materials in front of her. One of the cable station personnel came over to wire her microphone, explaining how to turn it on and off as he helped her position it on her skirt, then tucked it out of sight behind her. She left it off until it was time to speak.

"You're going to be brilliant," Taylor anticipated, smiling.

"Yes I will," she agreed, with a little more bravado than she really felt.

The chief left his table and approached them.

"Are you ready to go?" he asked.

"Absolutely," Gen responded. Taylor gave her a hug, then turned to join Tom and Miguel.

DiNardo indicated his readiness as well. The event set to begin, both candidates left the stage. The planned program called for them to be announced and walk up simultaneously, shake hands at the middle, then each move to his or her respective podium.

The chief stood facing the audience and activated his own microphone. The lights were dimmed and a light shone squarely on him.

"Good evening, everyone. As most of you know, I am Martin Embry, Chief of Police for Pine Creek. By mutual agreement of the candidates, I have been selected to moderate tonight's program."

The audience clapped politely, then the room was silent once again.

"Tonight's debate will consist of a three part program. Each candidate will have four minutes to present a prepared speech discussing his or her unique qualifications for office. We will then have a twenty-six minute session where I will ask a series of prepared questions and each candidate will have forty-five seconds to give her or his response. Finally, there will be a half-hour open session where members of the audience will be invited to submit questions for the candidates to answer."

The chief flipped his cards and continued.

"Without further adieu, I present Mayor Genevieve Pouissant and Mr. Stuart DiNardo."

Both participants walked to the center and executed the planned greeting perfectly. DiNardo stood at least four inches taller than Gen, but she was unflinching in his gaze and gave him a small smile. They both turned and assumed their speaking positions while the chief returned to his table.

"Madam Mayor, Mr. DiNardo, good evening," the chief greeted. "You've just heard me present the speaking program as decided previously. Do either of you have any questions with regard to how the program will go?"

Both speakers indicated they did not.

"Very well, then. By a flip of a coin that occurred earlier, Mr. DiNardo has won the right to make his speech first. Mr. DiNardo, if you'd like to begin…"

Wayne helped Wendy with her pajama top while Eric got little Taylor into a fresh diaper and shorts. In the waning days of summer, the kids tended to want T-shirts and shorts rather than pajamas. Of course, little Taylor already watched everything his older brother did and wanted to be exactly the same. Wendy usually paid attention to what she saw Gen do when she spent time with her. When she saw Gen had satin pajamas, Wendy insisted Tom buy her the same. When she saw Gen's pink fluffy slippers, Taylor was at Target the next day, getting her a pair to fit her little feet. Wendy seemed to instinctively understand that she was the only girl in the house and could get special treatment when she wanted it.

"Waynie, will you play with us?" Wendy asked.

"Eric and I want to watch Auntie Gen on TV," he explained.

"Is she on now?"

Wayne nodded. "Yep. It started a few minutes ago. If we hadn't had to change your clothes, we'd be watching it now."

"It was Taylor's fault," Wendy complained. "He shouldn't throw food." She gave her brother a stern look, which Wayne realized she must have picked up from Tom.

"Sorry," Taylor said, holding up his arms for Eric to pick him up.

"Do I have to watch?" Chad asked. "I'd rather play with my Legos."

"Do you want to bring them downstairs?" Eric asked.

"Okay," Chad said. Taylor climbed down to "help" him, which was to say he started grabbing the parts he wanted, then took off for the living room.

Tom had asked them earlier if they would be free to watch the kids. He knew Taylor had to be with Gen, but he thought it would be nice to be there, too. Wayne and Eric knew who they were voting for, and they could watch the debate on TV if they were interested.

Eric had agreed they would be there. Truth be told, he enjoyed the kids and always got a kick out of spending time with them alone with Wayne. They hadn't discussed it in a long time, but he always thought it would be nice to have kids, too. Of course, before they did that, he and Wayne needed to stop *being* kids, but that would come with time.

After they got everyone situated and filled a sippy cup for little Taylor, they settled in to watch the debate. They'd missed the speeches, but Wayne had a pretty good idea of what Gen planned to say, having sat through several drafts with her, Tom, and Taylor. They'd used the stage in the café to their advantage, preparing her for what it would feel like to stand in front of the town. She had given many speeches during her time as Mayor, but once the question and answer session started, she had to be on her toes.

As they watched, Gen and DiNardo answered a series of prepared questions presented by the chief. The questions included their thoughts on development of the town, expansion plans for new subdivisions, ways to improve education, traffic flow issues, and a host of other minor topics.

The kids played on the floor, staying quiet to allow their babysitters to watch the event. As the clock reached the bottom of the hour, the chief asked his final question, then opened the floor to allow questions from the audience. Several people Wayne recognized asked follow up questions based on the answers Gen and DiNardo had given to the chief's questions. Finally, Rob Grady rose and was recognized.

"Mr. DiNardo, do you feel it's appropriate for a person whose stated goal is the redevelopment of the historic district to be the mayor of the town? Doesn't that present a conflict of interest?"

DiNardo faced him, answering the question from his podium. "We're all members of the town. As I've explained this evening, I think it is in the best interests of all the town residents to explore any opportunities available to bring additional revenue to Pine Creek. As Mayor, my job will be to represent the town and its interests."

The chief turned to Gen for rebuttal. "Rob, I feel there is a clear conflict for someone who is seeking to radically reconfigure our historic area to be in a position to help take his projects through without outside competition and oversight."

DiNardo retorted. "With respect, ma'am, the former mayor—your campaign manager—is a property holder in the historic district and recently expanded his holdings to include a large section of the space between second and third streets. He held property while he was mayor, as well."

"But he did not expand his holdings while mayor, nor did he have a stated objective to redesign downtown," Gen corrected.

"I'm sure it was useful to have his friend as mayor, though, when he did expand. Wasn't it?"

"Mr. DiNardo, please," the chief cautioned. "We have strayed from the topic, and bordered on making personal accusations, which is beyond the bounds of this forum. Let's move on…"

Wayne turned to Eric. "What a jerk. He can't answer the question about himself, so he tries to drag Taylor into it and make it look like he and Gen are in cahoots."

Eric shrugged. "It's a good way to deflect interest from himself," he pointed out.

"Who's side are you on?" Wayne demanded.

Eric gave him a doe-eyed look. "Yours honey, always." He pulled Wayne closer to him, holding his hand.

"Hmph," Wayne grumbled, but didn't move away.

Taylor watched the action with a decidedly neutral face, in case the camera should happen to pass over him. He had coached Tom and Miguel to do the same, and for the most part, they were successful. Tom was always defensive of both Gen and him, so it was harder for him, but Taylor just offered him an occasional reassuring smile to remind him to keep the commentary in perspective. As the clock continued it's inevitable countdown, the chief indicated the next question would be the last. Steve, their long time friend, and town psychologist, rose and was acknowledged.

"Mr. DiNardo, there have been a number of allegations in the news recently, regarding your treatment of employees in your organization. I understand that you're not at liberty to discuss the cases themselves, but I wonder what thoughts you have on ways to continue to make Pine Creek an open, inviting place for minorities and people with non-traditional families?"

Was it Taylor's imagination, or did Stuart just get a shade redder?

"As Mayor, I would view it as my duty to continue to promote inclusion and diversity for all of our town's residents. Rather than focus on any one group or set of groups, I would focus on our town population as a whole."

The chief turned to Gen. "Madam Mayor, we have enough time for your rebuttal, and then your closing comments. Mr. DiNardo will then have an opportunity to make his final comments, and then we will bring this event to a close."

Gen offered a warm, inviting smile to contrast DiNardo's radish-like complexion. "Thank you," she acknowledged, then turned back to the man in the audience. "Steve," she said, addressing him by name, as she had each and every resident who asked a question, driving home the fact that she knew all of them personally. "I would continue my program of diversity education in our schools, and continue to promote the sense of inclusion that this town has had since the first time I crossed its borders, over a decade ago. As I believe my track record will show, I have appointed representatives of a broad range of minorities and classes to positions within the town, and have encouraged the growth of ethnically and racially diverse single-owner businesses in the historic district." She looked at the crowd as a whole and made her final statement. "I live in this town, and will continue to do so for many years. I know almost all of you, and most of you know me. My door has been and always will be open. I ask that you allow me to continue to work for you and with you, growing our community into the sort of place we want to live in and raise our children in. Thank you for your consideration."

The chief turned to DiNardo. "Mr. DiNardo, your final comments."

Stuart turned to the audience, smiling thinly, which did nothing to offset his grim expression. "I ask that all of you consider the thoughts you have heard tonight. Like my opponent, I am a resident of this town and have the best interests of the town at heart. I believe, with continued growth and development, the town will prosper, making us all stronger. I hope you'll agree with me and I ask for your vote when you cast your ballot. Thank you."

The chief acknowledged them both with a nod, then rose and turned to the audience. "That concludes our session for this evening. Thank you all for attending and have a good night."

Gen and DiNardo again met between the podiums and shook hands, then turned and walked to the sides of the stage. The crowd broke into applause as people rose to leave. Gen turned off her mic as she walked to meet with her men.

"Well, that was interesting," Tom commented as she approached.

"How do you think she did?" Miguel asked.

"I think she did fine," Taylor concluded.

"Really?"

The expression on Taylor's face said he was a little less sure than he was letting on, but he kept a smiling face for Gen's sake.

"How'd I do?" she asked.

"You did great. You couldn't have done better," Taylor said.

Gen looked disappointed. "I tried to set him up, but just when I thought I had him, he'd back down."

Taylor shrugged. "Don't worry. You did great. You were poised and collected. You answered all the questions without having to stop and think about them first, and your answers made sense. Really, you were great."

She hugged him. "Thanks, Tay." Miguel leaned in to give her a kiss and Tom gave her a peck on the cheek. "So, what now?"

Taylor looked toward the door, where the news media was already waiting. DiNardo had gone to meet with his people. One of the cable operators was there, helping him remove his mic.

"I told Ellen Malone we'd give her a couple minutes after the debate. Let's go smile and be happy, then we can call it a night," Taylor said.

"I am so tired of interviews," Gen said.

"I know. So am I. Just one more."

"Okay."

The foursome headed for the door, trying to look the part of the victors in a dubious battle.

Later that evening, after having had to give short interviews to most of the assembled media, they stopped at Alberto's for a quiet dinner, then made their way home. Gen complained over having to deal with the media. She had hoped for a more decisive victory over DiNardo, but no matter what she did, she couldn't get him to respond.

Taylor reminded her that he'd invited the media to allow the rest of the town to see DiNardo in action. Though they hadn't gotten the rise from him they'd hoped, his message had still been clear. And, to Gen's credit, her team had spent more time with the media than DiNardo had, and the reporters had been more responsive to her.

At the house, Wayne and Eric sat on the porch swing, having gotten Taylor and Wendy to bed a few minutes earlier. Chad had lobbied for an extra half hour, but Wayne knew Tom and Taylor would be tired when they got back, so he told Chad he could stay up a little longer, as long as he played quietly in his room.

As Gen's Jag appeared on the street, they both ran to the driveway, eager to meet the returning victors.

"Way to go!" Wayne cheered.

"You did it!" Eric called out.

The town's dream team looked worn and haggard as they got out of the car. Gen managed a smile for her young friends, appreciating their enthusiasm.

"We'll see how it goes next week," she said.

Wayne and Eric exchanged a puzzled look. "Next week?" Wayne asked.

"How could anyone vote for him after tonight?" Eric asked.

Taylor turned to them. "You'd be surprised what people will accept in a candidate."

Wayne and Eric still looked confused. "But after a comment like *that*, he can't hope to think people will forget."

It was the others' turn to look confused. "What comment?" Miguel asked.

"Didn't you hear?" Eric inquired.

"Hear what?" Gen asked.

Eric looked to Wayne, who started laughing, as they realized they both knew a secret the others weren't in on yet. "You'd better come in the house," Wayne said.

"What is it?" Tom asked.

Wayne shook his head. "It's all over the news. Come inside and listen."

Tom, Taylor, Gen, and Miguel followed them inside. Wayne reached for the TV and set it to KRP9, where they were carrying a special report.

The screen showed the customary red "Breaking News" logo that had gone from a legitimate announcement of major importance to a ubiquitous local news ploy to make a fender bender seem somehow interesting. The screen swirled and faded to show the face of the evening anchor.

"Good evening, I'm Clarke Lane. On tonight's edition of the Ten O'Clock News, we have a special live report coming in from Pine Creek, and reporter Ellen Malone." The picture changed to show Malone, in the dark, standing in front of Town Hall.

"Thanks, Clarke," she acknowledged, taking her cue. "Good evening, everyone. We're broadcasting to you live from Pine Creek, where an unexpected turn of events has led to a stunning outcome in an already hotly contested race.

"As those of you watching our six o'clock newscast will recall, we have been covering the scheduled debate between mayoral incumbent Genevieve Pouissant and her opponent, real estate developer Stuart DiNardo."

The image changed to show pictures of Gen and DiNardo, respectively, both silently talking into the camera as their names were mentioned.

"The debate occurred as scheduled and the candidates discussed a series of questions, some prepared, some from town residents, and responded to questions about how they could best provide leadership to the town. During the debate, both conducted themselves according to the rules of decorum and common human decency."

Sound bites of Gen and DiNardo answering questions played in the background as Malone spoke. The focus returned to her and she continued.

"I had the opportunity to speak with Attorney Taylor Connolly, former mayor of Pine Creek, and Ms. Pouissant's campaign manager. I asked if the incumbent mayor had any comment about litigation pending against Mr. DiNardo for harassment and racial discrimination. Here's what Mr. Connolly had to say."

Taylor's words were replayed in the form of a quick sound bite: "The plaintiff in the case is aware of my political involvement. I am not directly involved in any of the pending litigation, having specifically removed myself for that reason. We believe that satisfies any concerns with regard to conflict of interest." The image jumped as a clip occurred and Taylor's answer to the next question was played immediately after what he had just said. "Gen Pouissant has been a resident of this town for ten years. In that time, she has consistently shown her civic responsibility and participated in town functions. Since taking over as mayor, Pine Creek has seen a consistent pattern of growth and development, in both the new commerce district and the traditional downtown historic district. That development has been led by Mayor Pouissant, and when she is reelected, we can expect more of the same compassionate, caring leadership."

Gen looked at Taylor. "You didn't tell me they asked about that."

He looked like a little boy caught with his hand in the cookie jar. "I didn't want to distract you."

"I thought we weren't talking about the litigation?" Gen asked.

Taylor gestured to the screen. "She took the response out of context."

"Shh!" Tom said, hushing both of them, watching what Malone was saying.

"...carried by the local cable station," Malone said. "By agreement of all parties, the feed was given automatically to the local news stations as well. Following the debate the candidates shook hands and parted ways. What came next was shocking to those of us who had assembled to report the story. Even we did not know what had happened at first, until we had the opportunity to review the feed sent by the cable company."

The picture changed to show the debate area, obviously an unedited feed from one of the cameras in the room. The shot was from one side of the stage area, facing where Gen had been standing, nearer to DiNardo's side. Gen and DiNardo shook hands and made their way off stage.

As DiNardo cleared the stage area, his voice was unmistakable: "F(*beep*)n' n(*beep*)r."

Malone spoke. "Obviously, we have edited the content for television, but we can report to you that Mr. DiNardo was, in fact, heard to use both the 'F' word and the 'N' word. It is not clear whether he believed his mic was no longer active, or that recording had stopped, but we in the media were shocked and appalled to hear Mr. DiNardo's comments, which were broadcast, unedited, over the local cable station."

"I'll say," Eric commented.

"You heard it?" Taylor asked, turning to him.

"Wayne and I both did," Eric confirmed. "Fortunately, the kids were playing and weren't paying attention. They were sitting right here in front of the TV."

Malone continued her report with background on the litigation pending against DiNardo. The friends stood stunned, unable to believe what they'd just seen.

"I guess you got him worked up after all," Miguel observed, wrapping an arm around Gen's shoulders.

Tom turned to Taylor. "What does this mean?"

Taylor took in a deep breath. "I'm not quite sure. The town has a very strong antidiscrimination policy. It's entirely possible we could sue to block him from running. I'm just not sure if we'll have to." He watched the screen, which had cut back to the studio and another story. Taylor looked up. "I can't believe he said that. I mean, the election is enough, but it will be used against him in court, too."

"So what do you think?" Gen asked, expectant.

Taylor shrugged. "I think you got him to show his true colors. Congratulations."

She smiled broadly, for the first time that evening, and gave a simple nod in response. The night had indeed gone well.

CHAPTER FOURTEEN

No Contest

Sunlight streamed through the window, giving the room a soft, early-morning glow. Eric squinted in the light, turning to face away from the window. As he moved, he bumped Wayne's sleeping form stretched out next to him. He still wasn't used to Wayne being home in the morning when he woke up. Though it wasn't every morning, Wayne and Dan had agreed to take turns at the early shift, allowing each to sleep in some of the time. Since Wayne and Eric had been out late watching the kids, Dan and Emmy had volunteered to take the early shift in the bakery.

Wayne was still out like a light. He told Eric he used to be a very light sleeper because he never knew when his dad or his brother might come home and decide to use him as a convenient punching bag. Since he'd lived with Tom and Taylor, and later been on his own, he'd slowly adjusted to the idea that he was safe. With Eric back, he slept like the proverbial log, which Eric took as a compliment.

By the time the shock of DiNardo's unexpectedly candid comment and the related news attention wore off, it was nearly midnight. Taylor had fended off a number of requests for comment, saying they would release a formal statement in the morning. Gen had pointedly asked Taylor, "Can I call him a 'jerk' now?" and Taylor reminded her that it was her own grace under pressure that made him look that much worse. They agreed Taylor would write a statement for her and that she'd hold a press conference in the morning.

Eric watched Wayne and smiled. Since his return at the beginning of the summer, Wayne had let his hair grow out again and it tended to turn into a wild mess during the night. Wayne hated it, but Eric thought it gave him a sense of realism that was appealing. His dark lashes gave his eyelids an almost mascaraed look, while his thin brows framed his eyes perfectly. Wayne never looked more serene and at ease than while he was sleeping.

As he shifted the sheets that had become tangled around them during the night, Wayne moved, throwing his arm over Eric's chest and coiling a leg around his bare thigh. Smiling, Eric lightly ran his finger down the side of Wayne's chest and he jumped.

"Hey!" he moaned, opening one emerald green eye to squint at Eric.

"Hi there," Eric greeted.

"Hey," Wayne repeated, with less enthusiasm.

"Sleep well?" Eric asked.

"I was sleeping fine until you woke me," Wayne complained. Eric smiled. "Yeah?"

"Yeah," Wayne said, adjusting his position again. "I was having a nice dream, too."

Eric's smile broadened. "Was I in it?"

Wayne gave a little snort. "No."

Eric poked him in the side again, making him jump. "Stop that," he objected, yawning as he poked Eric back.

"Don't start what you can't finish," Eric said, poking him again. Wayne fought back and they wrestled like five year olds for a couple minutes, laughing and enjoying themselves. Finally,

Wayne managed to pin Eric, holding down his arms while he straddled his chest.

"You were saying something about not finishing what you start?" he said.

Eric answered by pulling Wayne into a long good morning kiss.

"Whew," Wayne breathed. "Maybe I need to get Dan to work every morning."

Eric smiled again. "It wouldn't hurt my feelings."

"Probably would Emmy's," Wayne sighed.

"What time do we have to be down there?" Eric asked.

"Eight."

"It's only seven now," he observed.

"Yeah?" Wayne asked.

"Maybe I can think up another reason to get you to stay home in the morning," Eric said, then kissed Wayne again...

One story down, in the bakery, Dan rolled a rack of empty shelves into the back room, then returned to the front to help Emmy with the morning rush. They'd gotten a little feedback from Wayne and Eric the night before, and the morning paper gave them some more. Stuart DiNardo, it seemed, had crammed his foot so far down his throat that it was protruding from another part of his body and he was kicking himself with it. As far as the two young people were concerned, he had gotten his just reward.

Apparently, a large percentage of the town agreed with them. The morning rush had been unusually heavy as people hoped Tom or Taylor might be working and have something to say about what they'd witnessed the night before. Emmy and Dan had both told more people than they could remember that they hadn't been present at the event, nor had they seen it on TV. All they knew was second hand information they'd gotten from friends or read in the paper.

"It was amazing," Rob Grady was telling Emmy. "None of us even knew it had happened."

"But weren't the mics on? That was how they got it," Emmy pointed out.

Rob shook his head. "They'd already turned off the feed to the room's speakers. What they got was only from the television feed the cable station had. Gen turned her mic off, but DiNardo forgot about it."

"Do you really think it'll be enough to knock him out?" Dan asked, making change.

"I sure hope so," Rob said. "I was really hoping to hear what Taylor thinks about it. You guys haven't talked to him?"

Dan shook his head. "Nope. All we know is what Wayne and Eric said when they got back and what we saw in the paper this morning." Times he's repeated the statement: six hundred fifty-two.

"Weren't they with Tom and Taylor, though? We ran into Pete at the debate and he said the boys were watching the kids."

Dan nodded. "They did, but Taylor swore them to secrecy. I guess Gen is holding a press conference this morning."

"Where will that be?"

Dan looked to Emmy. "Gen's office," Emmy said. Though she would never admit it to anyone other than Dan, she had talked to Taylor that morning and knew about the planned meeting. He'd specifically asked that none of them make any statements, even to their friends.

Rob shook his head. "Too bad—I have to go to work. I guess I'll just find out what happened later."

"It'll be all over the news," Emmy assured him.

Rob wished them a good morning and made his way out of the bakery as the phone rang. Emmy left Dan at the counter and answered the call.

"Downey's," she said, still using the old name as she always had. "Yeah, it's ready. Now? Sure." She hung up the phone and reached for an inconspicuous box sitting on the counter. To Dan, she said, "I'll be right back," and headed for the back door.

Behind the bakery, Taylor and Tom sat in Taylor's black BMW. He'd pulled right up to the door to minimize the chance they would be spotted. When he'd talked to Emmy earlier in the morning, he couldn't believe the uproar surrounding DiNardo's comments. He'd never seen the town in such a furor. It was alternately gratifying and frightening at the same time.

Emmy came out the back door and handed him the box through the window.

"Half donuts, half bagels. I don't think anybody saw me."

"Has the press been here?" Taylor asked.

"Oh yeah," Emmy confirmed. "I just told them what you said. I'm sure they're all over town hall by now."

Taylor smiled. "Great job, Em."

"Taylor, what *is* Gen going to do?" Emmy asked.

He shook his head. "Exactly what I said. She's going to hold a press conference."

"But what is she going to say?"

Taylor shrugged. "I'm not sure yet."

"What?"

"I'm still waiting for a call from Pete."

Emmy looked puzzled. "Why Pete?"

"We've gotta see what 'ole Stuey is going to do next," Taylor explained.

She nodded and wrinkled her nose. "I don't want to know, do I?"

Taylor shook his head. "Not really."

Emmy backed up so he could pull away. "See you tonight, then."

"Thanks, Em," Taylor said again. He handed the box to Tom and they both gave her a wave as he pulled away.

They didn't even make it back to Second Street before Taylor's phone rang. He pressed the button on his steering wheel and Pete's voice came over the car speakers.

"Good morning," he greeted.

"Hi, Pete. Tom's with me."

"Hi, Tommy," Pete greeted.

"Morning, Pete. What's new?"

"You were right, Tay. Stu's attorney just called."

Taylor smiled, exchanging glances with Tom. "And?"

"Settlement with payout if we drop the charges."

Taylor's eyes narrowed. "What did your client say?"

"She's interested."

"What else did they offer?" Taylor asked.

Pete continued. "No admission of guilt. DiNardo will finish the two existing developments he has in Pine Creek, then will pull out of the area. He understands the town has strong anti-discrimination language and doesn't want the lawsuit to prove it." Pete paused for a moment, then continued. "He's dropping out of the race."

"YES!" Tom cheered next to Taylor, slapping him on the shoulder in excitement.

"Anything else?" Taylor asked, reserving comment for the moment.

"Actually, yes. He's offered to sell the downtown property, too. Apparently, he never completed the Fence and Edges deal—the city has been dragging its feet." Pete paused for a beat to let the message sink in, then continued. "He's prepared to concede not developing the space and sell it for what he paid for it, offering it first to any current downtown owner who wants it."

Taylor looked at Tom. "Don't even think about it."

Tom tried to look innocent. "I didn't say a word!"

As Taylor turned into the parking lot outside town hall, Pete continued. "Actually, Taylor, I thought the firm might want to consider it. We're going to need more space and it's right there with your other businesses."

Taylor rolled his eyes. "What do you two do, *conspire* while I'm not looking?"

"Never," Pete said unconvincingly. "Anyway, what do you think?"

Taking a breath, Taylor pondered it. "Basically, it sounds like DiNardo knows we have him in every possible way. Rather than try to take it to court, where he knows he already has a bad reputation, he'd rather cut his losses and walk away."

"That's the gist of it," Pete agreed.

Taylor shrugged. "Then it really just comes down to whether or not your clients accept. If they're okay with it, it certainly sounds beneficial to everyone else. However, given the various potential conflicts, you should advise them they might want to have someone else review the settlement."

"I've already discussed it with Maxine. She said her only goal was to put a stop to his behavior. She's confident this will do it. Apparently, the county prosecutor has already been in touch with her about criminal litigation."

"DiNardo's lawyers must be anticipating that," Taylor observed.

"I agree. I'm sure that's why they'd rather not have this case come to trial. No need to air the dirty laundry before they have to, and I'm sure they don't want a civil judgment to be out there against him."

Taylor nodded. "Work it out, Pete. As long as the clients are satisfied, I have no problem with it."

"There's one other thing," Pete said.

"Yes?"

"They know you're about to hold a press conference. They've asked that you not discuss the situation in the media."

Taylor frowned. "That's going to be a little hard to do."

"The offer is complete, Tay. All we have to do is sign it. They've asked that you announce DiNardo's intent to drop out of the race and leave it at that. He's willing to do that publicly and immediately. You announce we received a call from him, and that he has indicated he is no longer running for public office. You make a point of saying no admission of guilt was given. When asked about the pending litigation, you say a settlement has been reached, but do not comment on the terms."

Taylor and Tom looked at each other, surprised by the speed with which DiNardo had moved. "Your client has signed off?"

"She has," Pete confirmed.

"I mean, really signed off?"

"She was here not five minutes ago."

Taylor thought it over, then made his decision. "Fax the settlement to Gen's office. I'm going in there now."

"It's on its way."

"I'll call you back," Taylor confirmed. He hung up the phone, then removed it from its cradle. "No comment to the press yet," he said to Tom.

"Got it," Tom said. Together, they got out and headed for the building. The chief met them on the way.

"They've been camped out here all night," he said.

"I'm not surprised," Taylor admitted, moving swiftly through the throngs of reporters. He recognized several faces from national media outlets and was amazed at the attention their little town was drawing. As they neared the door, he turned and stood at the podium.

"Ladies and gentlemen, my name is Taylor Connolly and I'm Mayor Pouissant's campaign manager. The mayor has authorized me to tell you that we'll have a statement for you shortly. Please bear with us. Thank you."

Without another word, he followed the chief and Tom into the building. Gen was waiting inside, a number of people milling around her.

"Pete just called," she said, holding out a stack of paper. "He said it was important no one saw this except you."

"Thanks," Taylor said. "Let's go to your office for a minute."

Together, the three of them went into her office and closed the door behind them. Taylor took a chair, reviewing the settlement agreement to the case Pete had filed, as well as the other related documents including the agreement to drop out of the race in exchange for Gen and her team agreeing not to discuss the accidentally recorded comments publicly.

"Amazing," Taylor sighed. He handed the parts related to Gen to her and let her read them.

"What do you think?" Tom asked.

"It looks fine. Basically, DiNardo walks away and we all agree to forget anything ever happened and not to talk about it."

"What if he's sued criminally?"

"They can't keep us from testifying if we're subpoenaed. Basically, they're in damage control mode, trying to keep us from telling everyone what happened so he won't be tried in the media."

"You're okay with it?" Gen asked, looking up.

Taylor nodded. "Pete has settled the civil case, provided we agree not to sue on what happened last night."

Gen shook her head. "So he drops out, settles everything, and leaves town, and that's it?"

Taylor shrugged. "That's it."

Gen stood behind her desk, staring out her window. "Why don't I feel better about it?"

Taylor watched her as Tom watched both of them. "It still feels like he's getting away with something. We get everything we wanted, but he doesn't have to say he did anything wrong."

"And he can do it all over again," Gen said, turning to Taylor.

He nodded. "There is that possibility. But he can't do it here."

She held up the documents. "You're sure?"

"Part of the settlement is you agree not to sue for his comments made last night and he agrees to withdrawal all business from Pine Creek and not to conduct any business here, openly or tacitly, in the future. If, at any time, he violates the agreement, your oath of silence is abrogated." Taylor looked at her. "It's a good deal, Gen."

"I know," she sighed.

"It's the best we can get without dragging this thing out a lot longer than anybody wants to."

"I know," she repeated. Resigned, she walked to her desk and picked up a pen. "Where do I sign?"

Taylor started pointing to the various lines where her signature was required, and signed himself in several places. In a matter of minutes, it was all done and he dropped them in the fax machine, back to Pete.

"Mr. DiNardo has phoned my office and indicated he is withdrawing from the race," Gen recited. "Though there was no admission of guilt, he felt withdrawing was in the best interests of all concerned."

"That's it," Taylor agreed. Tom rose to stand with them. "I'll answer any questions regarding the litigation. If asked directly, you can honestly say you have no information other than what I told you, that an undisclosed settlement had been reached."

"Okay," Gen said. Taking a deep breath, she continued, "Let's do this."

They walked back out front and took their positions at the podium. Tom stood at the back next to the chief and watched as his spouse and his spouse's best friend faced the firing squad, with heads held high.

Refreshed from their morning exercise, Wayne and Eric made their way down to the store to relieve Emmy and Dan. As they came through the back door, they knew it was going to be a busy day—there was already a line in the front.

"Good morning," Wayne greeted Emmy as he pulled on an apron and washed his hands. "Busy?"

"Very," she said, tossing him a towel. "Everybody and their brother has been in here wanting to know about last night."

"What's our story?"

"We don't know anything," Emmy said.

"Got it." Wayne went to help take orders while Eric washed up behind them.

Dan gestured to the small TV he'd placed on the back counter. "I thought we might want to see the news," he said. The local news had broken in from network coverage, with Ellen Malone's face centered on the screen, in front of Town Hall.

"Turn it up, Dan," Emmy called. The customers closed in, also eager to see what was happening.

"Good morning. I'm Ellen Malone, reporting for KRP9 News. We're live at the Pine Creek Town Hall, where Mayor Genevieve Pouissant is about to comment on the stunning comments from competitor Stuart DiNardo, a local real estate developer. Here's the mayor…"

The camera shifted on-air and centered on Gen. Taylor was standing beside her and they could see the chief of police and Tom in the background. Gen smiled broadly, her hands resting lightly on the sides of the podium as she spoke.

"Good morning, everyone, and thank you for coming. As most of you know by now, some candid comments were made following the mayoral debate last night, and those comments were inadvertently received and broadcast by the local cable station.

"First, I want to apologize to those residents who heard the comments in their unedited entirety. Obviously, no one at the event, nor the cable company, had any way to anticipate those things would be said and everyone involved asks your forgiveness for any upset the words may have caused.

"Second, my office has received official communication from Mr. DiNardo, through his attorneys, that he is withdrawing his candidacy from the mayoral race—"

The bakery was filled with cheers and clapping as Gen announced DiNardo's withdrawal. Most of the patrons were locals and most of them favored Gen over DiNardo. Emmy shushed them, wanting to hear what else Gen had to say.

"…no admission of guilt on Mr. DiNardo's part. He simply felt the interests of the town would be best served by his withdrawal."

"Does this have anything to do with the litigation that was pending against him?" one of the reporters called out.

Gen shook her head. "I have no information about the litigation, other than what Taylor told me this morning. A settlement has been reached, but the terms of it are sealed."

"What about you, Taylor," the reporter called. "Can you comment?"

Gen turned to Taylor and he stepped forward. "I'm sorry, but the terms of the settlement are private. As I've said before, I am not directly involved in the case, but I did confer with my office this morning and was made aware that our client chose to accept Mr. DiNardo's offer."

"Mr. Connolly, was the lawsuit just intended to put pressure on Mr. DiNardo to withdraw?" another reporter asked.

Taylor shook his head. "Quite the contrary. As I've indicated before, the two events are separate. However, given the nature of the litigation and the recorded comments last night, Mr. DiNardo thought it would be preferred to simply reach a settlement, and that is what we have done."

"What about Mr. DiNardo's other projects in Pine Creek?"

Taylor shook his head again. "I'm sorry, but the terms of the settlement cannot be discussed. I recommend you contact Mr. DiNardo's attorneys and inquire of them what his plans might be."

Ellen Malone spoke up. "Mr. DiNardo's withdrawal means Mayor Pouissant is once again unchallenged, correct?"

"That's true," Taylor agreed.

"Ladies and gentlemen, that's all the information we have," Gen said, nodding to Taylor as he stepped back.

"Yes!" Wayne exclaimed, hugging Eric in excitement.

"Very cool," Dan said, smiling.

"It's about time," one of the customers said. The bakers went back to serving them, reenergized as their nemesis met a fitting end.

"Do you think he's gone for good?" Emmy asked.

"I sure hope so," Wayne said, handing a bag across to one of their regulars.

Dan was keeping the register moving, as they tried to handle the throng of people. "Hey, Waynie," he called.

"Yeah?" Wayne asked, filling another bag.

"Where's Jason?"

Wayne looked at the door between the coffee shop and the bakery and saw it was closed. Frowning, he went over and saw the lights were off.

"I have no idea," he said. Jason was usually very reliable and prompt, and usually took the early shift to make sure everything was handled properly.

Wayne reached for his keys and opened the door. He walked through the dark store and flipped the light switches in the back, bringing the place to life. Outside, several people were in front of the door, waiting for them to open. Fortunately, most of what they would need was already prepared.

Eric stood in the door, watching Wayne. "Want help?"

"Yeah. Why don't you open up and bring over some stuff from the bakery. I'll start getting orders moving. Have Em call Mrs. Johnson and Sally and see if they can come in a little early," Wayne said.

"I'm on it."

Fortunately, much of the services offered by the café overlapped with the bakery. They didn't have the full menu available that morning, but most customers were able to make due, and they all understood the pressures the family had been facing in light of the night's events.

For once, Sally didn't give them a hard time about calling her and even rushed to join them and help keep things moving. Mrs. Johnson showed up a short time later, and in no time, both stores were operating and the customers thinned out to the usual weekday crunch.

Wayne went to Eric, who was busily filling cups as Sally took orders. "I'm going to go see if I can find him."

"Got it," Eric acknowledged.

Wiping his hands on his apron, Wayne headed for the back door and the stairs that led up to Jason's apartment over the coffee shop. At the top of the stairs, he rapped on Jason's door and waited.

The door pulled open to reveal the young man, pulling on his shoes and trying to tie them. His hair was disheveled and it didn't look like he'd shaved that morning.

"Hi, I'm sorry I'm late. I forgot to set my alarm last night," he explained.

Wayne watched him as he fought with his shoes, waiting to see what was really going on. As Jason looked up, Wayne caught the redness at the edges of his eyes and knew it was more than oversleeping.

"We've got it covered," Wayne said. "Sally and Mrs. Johnson came in."

"Oh," Jason said, breathing fast from rushing. "Okay. I don't usually over sleep, but I just woke up about ten minutes ago."

Wayne nodded, acknowledging the obvious. "We've got it covered," he said again. "Take a breath. Why don't you go ahead and get ready? There's no hurry."

Jason shook his head. "No, it's okay."

Wayne both didn't want to ask and felt like he had to. "Are you okay?"

Jason froze. "Yeah, I'm just running a little behind."

Not buying, Wayne commented, "You never run a little behind. You're the one who's always early."

"I can have an off day now and then."

Wayne just watched him and Jason returned his gaze. It was a technique Wayne had seen Taylor use many times and he suddenly understood why. As they stood there, Jason's resolve cracked and he said what he really wanted to say.

"Adam came over last night and told me he's going to England for a year."

There it was. Wayne nodded as the pieces fell into place.

"Why England?"

Jason sighed, leading Wayne back inside. "He applied for some kind of associate professorship at Oxford and got it. I don't know the details, but it means he's going to be gone for a year."

Wayne frowned. "Tom never said anything to you about it?"

Jason shook his head. "Neither of them did. I asked Adam why he'd never mentioned it and he said he didn't think it would happen. Then, when it did, it was something he was simply unable to pass up."

"Wow," Wayne said. "I'm really sorry to hear that."

"Me, too," Jason agreed.

Wayne gave a little chuckle at the irony. "What is it about colleges screwing up our plans?" he asked.

Jason smiled, understanding his point. "At least yours came back."

"Yours may, too," Wayne offered.

Jason shook his head. "I don't think so. The great Dr. Brown isn't going to want to be cooped up forever in Pine Creek."

"Being cooped up here isn't so bad," Wayne pointed out. "And besides, you didn't used to be cooped up here all the time, either. Maybe he'll go out into the real world and find Pine Creek isn't so bad after all."

"Maybe," Jason agreed.

Wayne sat forward in his chair, facing Jason. "One of the things I've learned over the last few years is you always have to stay optimistic. Taylor and Tom taught me that. When I came to them, I was down and out. They taught me the world can be a good place, if we just open our eyes and let it."

Jason sighed. "Sounds good to me."

Wayne smiled. "The thing is, you have to actually live it. You have to believe the glass is half full, and when you do, you'll find it's actually overflowing."

Jason looked up. "You really have been hanging around them too long, haven't you?"

Wayne laughed. "They got me through the problems with Eric. That was worth its weight in gold alone. You never know what the future may hold. It may be Adam, or it may be someone else entirely. That's both the challenge and the excitement."

Jason considered his words quietly, staring off into space. Finally, he looked at Wayne and said, "Thanks."

"Anytime," Wayne replied.

Jason stood, heading for the door. "We should get to work."

"We can cover it," Wayne said. "Take your time and freshen up. It'll make you feel better, trust me."

Jason nodded. "Thanks."

Wayne smiled. "Don't mention it. See you in a little bit."

"That you will."

Wayne headed to the bakery, once again ready to face the day with a smile on his face.

CHAPTER FIFTEEN

Life Continues

Taylor walked into Alberto's and promptly ran into someone waiting by the door. As he excused himself, he realized the place was full to overflowing, and there was a line. He couldn't remember the last time there was a line on a Wednesday night.

"Pardon me," he said, moving around a couple of people he didn't recognize. The realization that he didn't recognize them brought another frown to his face. How was it there were people in town he didn't recognize?

"Taylor, my friend!" Alberto greeted, moving between the largely full tables to make his way over. "How are you?"

"I'm great, Alberto," Taylor answered. "How are you?"

"Busy," he half complained, leading Taylor toward the back of the restaurant. "Ever since all the publicity, we've been getting busier all the time."

"Publicity?" Taylor asked.

Alberto nodded. "The news reports about Gen. People started coming to town and they've kept coming. Surely business has been up for you, too?"

Taylor shrugged. "Whenever we close a big case, it tends to bring a few taggers-on." They reached the large round table in the back, where Gen, Miguel, Tom, Wayne, and Eric waited.

"But what about the bakery?" Alberto queried, curious.

"I don't know," Taylor admitted. He'd spent most of the last day helping Gen work through the last of the fallout from the debate.

"What about the bakery?" Tom asked.

Alberto gestured to the crowded room. "Has business picked up for you as well?"

"And how!" Wayne groaned.

"Really?" Tom asked.

Wayne nodded. "You've been so busy getting ready for school, you haven't been down there much. We've been swamped." Beside him, Eric sat with his arm loosely draped over the back of Wayne's chair, and nodded his own emphasis on the statement.

Tom and Taylor exchanged a glance and smiled. "Cool," Tom said, looking at Wayne.

"For you," he complained. Eric gently patted his shoulder, and Wayne smiled back at him.

Taylor laughed, sitting down. "It keeps your tuition paid, sonny-boy."

"Well, there is that," Wayne agreed, relenting.

"I'll be back with a water," Alberto said. "Anything special for dinner?"

Taylor shook his head. "The usual."

"Beef tonight," Alberto said.

"Wonderful," Taylor agreed and he was off.

Tom poured him a glass of wine, then raised his own glass. "To Gen, still our Mayor!"

"To Gen!" they all agreed, clinking glasses.

Eric was the first to speak. "It's official?"

Gen nodded. "With no other names on the ballot, it turned into the sort of vote the town is used to. There were about a thousand ballots cast."

"At least you got that much turnout," Taylor said.

Gen smiled at him. "It's okay, sweetie. When you were mayor, they weren't used to voting."

Pete and Anita made their way through the crowded restaurant to join them at the table, taking the last two seats. Alberto came back with glasses of water for all three of them.

"We were just toasting Gen," Taylor explained to the new arrivals.

"To Gen," Anita said, raising her water glass.

"To Gen!" they repeated again.

Miguel leaned in. "I really have to thank all of you for the work you did to get Gen reelected. It's funny the amount of effort we all went to for a job she didn't even want."

"Hear hear!" Taylor agreed.

Miguel continued. "It really does mean so much to us, though, that you pulled it off. The town can breathe a collective sigh of relief."

"And how," Pete agreed.

"Anything new?" Eric asked, joining in.

Pete shook his head. "Not really. I think there's a good chance DiNardo will see some criminal charges brought forward. We were contacted today by a forensic accountant who has been brought in to review the financial allegations. Conceding Pine Creek just kept one small part of the bigger picture out of his way."

Gen sipped her wine. "It wouldn't break my heart to see him face the music."

Taylor looked at her. "What happened to gracious?"

"Meh," she dismissed with a shrug.

Pete turned to Tom. "So, business is picking up now?"

"Actually, we were just discussing that," Tom said.

Pete eyed Taylor. "Any discussion of picking up the space next door?"

Tom glanced at Taylor, too. "Somebody hasn't exactly jumped at the idea."

"You know," Taylor defended, "Every now and then, I get this idea we ought to *save* some money."

"Save schmave," Tom said, waving a hand.

"With all this extra business, it ought to be a breeze," Pete added.

Taylor turned to him. "If you want that space, the firm is going to have to pay for it. Can we afford it?"

"Yes."

Pete's answer surprised Taylor. "Really?" he asked.

Pete nodded. "I actually discussed it with the bank already. We really are going to need more space, so I thought I'd do the homework and save you the aggravation."

"Really?" he said again. "And the bank said yes?"

"The bank said yes."

Tom wrapped an arm around Taylor. "And just think, you'll be right next door to me."

Taylor looked back at him, nonplussed. He knew a sell job when he saw one and they weren't even trying to hide the fact from him. In fact, he should have expected it when Tom made extra sure to position him so Pete would be on the other side of him.

"Aren't you supposed to be professing or something?" Taylor asked, referring to Tom's job at the college.

"Well, you'll be right next door to me part of the time."

Taylor shook his head. "I'll have Pete move to the downtown office."

Pete shook his head. "No way. I'm not getting in the middle of this."

Taylor laughed. "Okay, we'll look at it tomorrow then," he promised. "If it's that easy, I know it would break Gen's heart for us to take the space from DiNardo."

"Ha!" Gen said.

"How's the café working out?" Anita inquired. In the few short weeks since the accident, her midsection had blossomed out to the point that she almost had her own shelf between herself and the table, and she rested her hands gently on it.

"Very well," Tom affirmed. "Wayne and Jason have the two stores operating like a well-oiled machine."

"Good job," Anita said, nodding to Wayne. To Tom, she continued, "I heard Jason and Adam Brown didn't work out?"

Tom nodded. "Adam got a job at Oxford. Jason was pretty disappointed, but he's doing okay. Wayne and Eric have been keeping an eye on him."

"That's too bad," Anita said.

"He'll be okay," Eric assured her. "Besides, it gives Sally a chance to try to set him up with her friends."

Anita's eyes went wide. "You've got to be kidding."

"If only," Tom sighed, shaking his head.

Alberto appeared, trailed by one of his waiters, plates in hand. Everyone but Anita had rolled the dice and taken Alberto's recommended beef dinner. "Beef" hardly did the plates justice. He'd prepared filet mignon, stuffed with a garlic, onion, and bleu cheese combination, served with steamed vegetables and a light sauce. In contrast, Anita had ordered a grilled cheese, saying it was the only thing that sounded good to her. Though her pregnancy was going well, her diet had been curtailed by nausea. As the friends ate, she did steal one bite from Pete's plate, but otherwise left well enough alone.

Dinner lasted for about an hour, until Alberto served a dark chocolate torte with a light drizzle of fresh heavy cream. Stuffed and barely able to move, everyone split up for their last evening of summer. Tom and Wayne were to resume full-time classes the next morning, and the McEwan-Connolly children would be back in school. Tom's mom would be there around eight to help get them ready, meaning it was their last sleep-in morning of the summer.

Wayne and Eric walked slowly down the street, waving as their friends passed in their cars. They cut back down the alley to their apartment. As they reached the stairs, Dan came out the back door of the bakery, carrying a garbage bag.

"Hey, guys," he greeted. "How was dinner?"

"Good," Wayne answered. "Everything okay at the store?"

"Sure is. Mrs. Johnson said she'll be in bright and early to open. That new kid you hired is already coming up to speed, so they should be fine."

"Sounds good," Wayne said.

"See you in a little while," Dan said, heading back inside.

Eric led the way and they headed up. Inside, they changed into more comfortable clothes and headed for the living room. Wayne checked their phones and saw Eric's had a message. He tossed it to him and Eric listened to it. As Wayne watched, Eric frowned and his face fell.

"What is it?" Wayne asked.

"That was Cassie, at my office. They're ready to start me next week. They want me to come in tomorrow for some orientation stuff."

"Tomorrow?" Wayne repeated.

"Yeah." He set the phone down on an end table and sat down on the couch. Wayne sat beside him, resting a hand on his knee.

"We knew it was going to happen soon," he said.

"I know," Eric said. "I just wasn't ready to go yet."

Wayne looked at him. "Think of it this way—I have to start back to school, you're starting work. It's not like it would be the same as the summer anyway."

"I still don't know if I even *want* to do the job anymore. I got that degree because it's what my dad thought I should do. But is it something I *want* to do?"

"Try it for a couple months. If you find you don't want to do it, leave. Otherwise, you'll be happy, so it won't matter."

Eric didn't look convinced. Wayne reached out and hugged him, then stood up. "Come on."

"Where are we going?" Eric asked, rising slowly.

"Who do we always go to for advice?"

"Miss Cleo?"

Wayne smacked him in the stomach, laughing. "Funny! Let's go talk to Taylor. If you're going to have to go back, we'll need to cover you anyway."

"Okay."

They took Wayne's Jeep to Tom and Taylor's house. The night air was refreshing and a little cold as they made their way along the quiet residential streets. As was becoming the norm, Main Street was alive with activity, but the side streets were all quiet.

They pulled up to the house and parked around back.

"Waynie! Eric!" Little Taylor stood at the back door, already in his pajamas, jumping up and down to see his two favorite uncles show up.

"Hey, kiddo!" Wayne said, picking him up as they entered.

Tom walked in from the living room, a book in his hand. "Didn't we just leave you guys?"

"We couldn't get enough of you," Wayne countered.

Tom took one look at Eric and said, "What's wrong with you?"

Eric looked up sharply, surprised. "I got the call tonight."

"Ah," Tom said, leading them back into the living room.

"Eric sad?" Little Taylor asked.

"No, I'm okay," Eric said, patting him on the head where he sat with Wayne.

"Good," Taylor said, sliding off Wayne's lap.

"Go get Dad," Tom told him. "Tell him Wayne and Eric are here."

"Okay!" Taylor said. He ran up the stairs, yelling "Dad! Dad! Waynie and Eric are here!"

Tom rolled his eyes. "They've been pretty excited to get back to school. Tay is getting Chad and Wendy ready for tomorrow. I was keeping Mini-T occupied."

"Sorry to barge in," Eric said.

Tom laughed. "You're family—it's not barging. So what's the problem? Not sure what to do?"

"Yeah," Eric admitted.

"What do you think?" Tom asked.

Eric looked at Wayne. "Wayne thinks I should give it a try."

Tom nodded. "Okay, that's fair. So give it a try. What's to lose?"

"I'm just not sure I want to be back out there, in the corporate world. I like it here, with all of you."

Tom smiled warmly, almost—almost—his Taylor smile. "We like having you here, too. It's not like you have to move away. It's just working in the city. You're still living out here with us." Eric nodded, listening. "Besides, Wayne and I will be back in school tomorrow. Wayne and Jason are planning to hire students to backfill and cover the larger crowds. They can cover for you, too."

Taylor, the older, came down the stairs. Apparently, his junior namesake had found something to do upstairs, no doubt harassing his brother and sister.

"Hi, guys," he greeted. "What's going on?"

Tom filled him in, explaining Eric's dilemma. Taylor nodded understandingly, sitting across from them in the waning light of the evening. Tom turned on a lamp as they talked.

"It's not fun when you have to go back to work after a summer like this one," Taylor said. "And we're certainly not going to push you away. But you worked so hard to get your degree, I'd hate to see you not at least try it. If you decide you don't want to do that job, you can always come back. You're part of the family, too."

Eric seemed to visibly relax at that. He and Taylor had shared a long conversation once things settled down between Wayne and him. Taylor wanted him to know that no one harbored any ill will toward Eric for what had happened. They understood the situation he had faced and were just glad he was back. Taylor always liked Eric, and he thought he was good for Wayne, with the obvious exception of the college situation. Taylor told him he'd learned over the years that honest and open communication was the best path to keeping a relationship healthy.

"I guess I can try it," Eric said.

Taylor nodded. "Give it some time. We're all going to be on our own little projects for a while. It sounds like *somebody*," he looked in Tom's direction, "has gotten the idea that my firm needs to take space in town. So, I'm going to be tied up working with Pete on that. Tom's going back to teach, Wayne's going to wrap up his senior year of college, and then Chad and Wendy are back in school. If you want to feel bad for somebody, think of poor Jason—it's like we're abandoning him."

"I think he may be relieved," Wayne said, laughing.

"I know the feeling," Tom added.

Taylor just gave him a look, then continued, "We're all still here and we'll all see each other evenings and weekends. Don't worry about it. If anything, it'll give you a chance to make some new friends and find new customers to come buy things from our stores!"

Eric laughed. "Okay, I'm convinced. I'll start schlepping bagels in the morning."

"That's the spirit!" Taylor agreed.

"Thanks, guys," Eric said. "Your support means a lot to me."

"To both of us," Wayne added.

"We're always here for you," Tom said.

Eric stood and Wayne followed him. "Looks like you guys have to get the kids ready. I guess I need to figure out what I'm going to wear tomorrow," he said.

"If you need to borrow anything," Taylor said, "just let me know."

"Thanks, Taylor."

They all exchanged hugs and walked to the back door. With a final wave, they climbed back in Wayne's Jeep and headed home.

The next morning, Taylor lay in bed quietly, listening to the soft sound of Tom's breathing, enjoying the total silence of the house. What a summer it had been.

How had time passed so quickly? It seemed like just yesterday that he'd been in the same place, pondering the last few years. Things were going well then, as they were now, but so much had happened in between.

He thought of Eric and his concerns over starting a new job. Pine Creek was an amazing place, and not somewhere easily left behind. Unfortunately, it wasn't always possible to stay there all the time. Working in the city would be good for Eric—he liked his own time, too, though he didn't realize it yet. Taylor had no doubt he was committed to Wayne and that their relationship would be fine, but Eric needed to get out in the world a little more.

As Taylor thought about Wayne, he wondered what his young friend would do when he graduated. As important as he thought it was for Eric to pursue his dreams, he thought the same for Wayne. The difference was Wayne was still more fragile, even as strong as he had grown. Where Eric would be fine in the colder, grittier confines of the city, Wayne almost needed the warmth of the town to support him. Taylor would not say anything unless Wayne brought it up, but he hoped Wayne knew he was more than welcome to stay. He didn't need to feel obligated to leave, just because his education was done.

But then, Taylor had no doubt Wayne *would* bring it up when he was ready. One thing he knew about their relationship was how much Wayne valued Taylor's openness and support of him. For Taylor, it was like getting to sit back and actually watch a flower bloom. Wayne had gone from a tiny, shriveled bud to a beautiful bright blossom before his very eyes. Without a doubt, it was one of the most rewarding experiences of Taylor's life.

Tom stirred beside him, rolling back into Taylor's embracing arms. He took a deep breath, resting his own arms over Taylor's.

"Good morning," he greeted.

"Hi honey," Taylor replied. He rested his cheek on Tom's neck, enjoying the sweet smell of his cologne mixed with his own scent. Tom moved his legs so they were entwined with Taylor's.

"Sleep well?" he asked.

"Very," Taylor replied. "You?"

"Like a baby," Tom said. Once they'd gotten the kids off to bed, they decided to make it an early night. Tom didn't have to get up too early, but his mom had said she'd be there by eight and they tried to be ready before she got there. They spent a little time with each other before drifting off into a relaxing, restful sleep.

"Big day," Taylor said.

"Another class, another paper," Tom replied. The truth was he really enjoyed teaching at the college level. His Ph.D. was nearly completed, meaning he would probably finish the year as Dr. McEwan, a fact that made Taylor very happy.

"How many classes this semester?"

"Five now," Tom said. "I took one of Adam's and they gave the rest to a couple grads."

"Darned Adam," Taylor commented.

Tom turned to face Taylor. "Can you blame him?"

"Would you leave me to go to England?"

Tom's eyes brightened. "Heck yeah!"

"Where is the love?" Taylor asked.

"Right here," Tom said, and kissed him.

"That's better," Taylor replied. "You coming by for lunch?"

"Of course. My afternoon classes don't start until one-thirty."

Taylor smiled. "Good. I think Pete arranged to have the architect join us."

"Really!?" Tom exclaimed. "Oh, I can't *wait*. Anita and I talked about colors and themes. She thinks Pete should move to this office, too. Let Sam run the other one. Maybe you can split the cases between them or something. Anyway, we were thinking we should put you guys upstairs so the storefront is still available—"

Taylor put a single finger over Tom's lips and smiled. Tom stopped rambling and he said, "We're *meeting with the architect*. You and Anita can pick out wallpaper once we're sure the space will work."

Tom smiled and Taylor moved his finger away. "Okay," he said. "But really, if we keep the storefront open so we can rent it out—"

Taylor just laughed as he rolled back and rubbed his eyes. Tom rested on his chest, still talking about the various ideas he and Anita had shared in anticipation of his agreement to buy out the space. What a summer indeed.

Taylor wambled across the quad on his way to Tom's office. For a change of pace, Tom had invited Taylor and Gen to join him in the college cafeteria for lunch. It wasn't nearly as fancy or tasty as downtown, but it was a beautiful campus and there was no better way to end the summer than a lunch on the green.

In the building, he made the short trek to Tom's office and found the door open. Unlike the man he awakened to every morning, Professor McEwan was the picture of college propriety. For the start of classes, he'd chosen a conservative blue button down shirt, beige slacks, and brown square-toed shoes. As Taylor expected, one of his navy blue blazers was tossed over one of the chairs opposite a floor to ceiling bookshelf.

"You know," Taylor began as he walked in, "Every year, I expect to come in and find you wearing a cardigan."

"A cardigan?" Tom asked, giving him a quick kiss in greeting.

"Yep. Every year, the shelves get a little messier, the stack of books you hope to read one day gets a little taller, the salt in your hair gets a little more prominent, and I prepare myself for the day when you decide to wear a cardigan."

Tom just laughed. "You are nuts, you know that?" He thought for a moment and then added, "And I do not have any gray in my hair."

"Been plucking again?" Taylor countered. He sat down on the couch under the window.

"What's got you all fired up?"

Taylor gave him an evil grin. "We already met with the architect."

Tom's face fell. "What? I wanted to be there, Tay. I wanted to see the space."

Taylor shrugged. "I guess you'll just have to wait."

"Wait?"

"Pete's making the offer this afternoon. Part of the settlement was the price DiNardo paid. We're offering the same."

Tom leaned forward in his chair, eyes wide. "Really?"

"We should know shortly."

"That's wonderful!" he said. "Oh, I can't wait. It will be so nice to have you right in town."

"It's not like I was that far away before."

Tom nodded. "I know. It's more of a mental thing."

"So are cardigans," Taylor warned.

Gen appeared at the door and knocked on the frame. "I'm looking for Professor McEwan?" she said.

Tom rose and gave her a hug. "Hi, Pussycat," he greeted. Gen just smiled and kissed his cheek. Taylor gave her a look, knowing the wrath he would incur if he called her by her old nickname.

"Tay," she said, giving him a kiss, too. She turned back to Tom. "So, how are classes?"

"So far, so good," Tom said. "Believe it or not, I'm going to have Wayne in my class again. He took Adam's creative writing class."

"Be unmerciful," Taylor advised.

Gen slapped him in the chest. "Do *not* listen to Taylor. You be nice to that boy."

Tom smiled. "I'm always nice to that boy. Whatever Taylor may say, if I was mean to him, I'd be sleeping with Molly."

"It's true," Taylor agreed. He caught something in Gen's eye and looked at her. "What's new with you?"

She squealed with excitement. "Ooo, I have to tell somebody! But you can't say anything to Miguel. Promise!"

"Okay, we promise," Taylor said.

"Tommy?"

"I promise," he agreed.

Her eyes positively sparkled as she beheld her friends. "I had a doctor's appointment this morning."

"Yes?" Taylor asked, leaning in expectantly.

"The doctor walked in with my chart and said I'm pregnant!"

"Really?" Tom asked.

"Yep! He said, 'Gen, you're pregnant. Yep, no doubt about it, there's a little Gen or Miguel hiding down there, in that neck of the woods.'" She used Taylor to gesture toward his abdomen. "He said it's already been a couple of weeks and they'll do an ultrasound in a couple more to verify it. He said my blood work showed it was unmistakable, though."

"Oh my God, Gen, that's awesome!" Taylor said. He pulled her into a hug and kissed her again. Tom hugged them both and got the other cheek.

"We're going to be uncles again," Tom said. "I can't wait."

"So you're, what, six months or so behind Anita?"

Gen nodded. "Probably about that. Believe it or not, the doctor said it may have been relief from winning the election that helped carry me along."

Tom shook his head. "That's incredible. Wow. We're so happy for you."

"Yes, we are," Taylor added.

Gen took a breath. "I had to tell someone. I don't want to tell Miguel over the phone, but he's tied up in meetings until this afternoon. I'm going to drive over and tell him in person, though. I can't wait."

"I don't blame you," Taylor said.

"This calls for a celebration," Tom announced.

"A round of cafeteria milk for everyone," Taylor said.

"Sounds like a winning plan to me," Gen agreed and they headed off, arm in arm.

That evening, Wayne, Eric, and Jason sat at a table in the café, relaxing and watching the flow of customers. As they'd hoped and anticipated, the return of students to the college only added to their customer base.

"So, how was it?" Jason asked.

Eric shrugged. "It wasn't bad. They've got me designing a part that will be used in the North American product platform. The people in the office seem pretty friendly, though I'm fairly sure one of the secretaries has her eyes on me."

"How could she not?" Wayne chided. "You're such a catch."

"Thanks, babe," Eric retorted.

Jason continued. "Do you think you'll stick with it?"

"Who knows? I haven't even gotten to see the project yet. Today and tomorrow they're just having me sit through a bunch of HR stuff. It's totally mind numbing, but corporations seem to think it's important."

"What about you?" Jason asked, turning to Wayne.

Wayne laughed, sitting back in his seat. "Check this out. I had Adam for a creative writing class. Guess who's teaching it now?"

"Tom?"

Wayne nodded. "You know it. And, of course, everyone in the class already knows I work with Tom here and that we're family. So, they all want to work with me in the hope that it will get them a better grade."

Eric sipped his Coke. "Maybe you'll finally make some friends."

His comment earned him a punch in the arm. "Careful, buddy, or you may get to try out that couch tonight," Wayne said.

"Feisty this evening," Eric observed.

"I have to condense it down to when you're around," Wayne countered.

"Funny."

Wayne turned to Jason. "How were things here? Did the replacements keep things covered?"

Jason nodded. "We had a few bumps, but by and large, everything was okay. Dan came in for a few hours mid-morning, and Emmy covered the afternoon. We'll get it worked out. I took about ten applications, too. Most of them want to work in the café, but several said they'd work in all three stores."

"Are Liz and Sherry having you staff the bookstore now, too?"

Jason again. "Liz talked to me a few weeks ago, when I mentioned we were going to try to pick up a few students to help out. They're really happy with the increased traffic they've gotten from the café and the later hours, but they needed more people, too. She asked me if I'd be interested in 'renting' some people to them. I told her the computer system actually makes it really easy to just charge the payroll back to them. We agreed to give it a try. Ethan is going to be our first candidate. He said he'd like to work between both stores, so I said we'd give it a shot."

Eric shook his head. "Things are already changing."

Sally appeared behind them, a tray in hand. "Two ham and cheese croissants, and a chocolate croissant?"

"Chocolate," Eric said, holding up his hand. She handed him the plate, then placed the others in front of the two remaining "customers."

"Can I bring you anything else?" she asked sweetly.

"We're good, thanks," Jason said, smiling.

"Great," Sally said. "You're not very observant, though."

"Huh?"

She discretely pointed to the far corner, where a young man sat with a laptop perched on a small table. "He's been checking you out for an hour."

Jason reddened slightly. "I doubt it."

Sally nodded. "Trust me. Gaydar has nothing on woman's intuition. I've been watching him…and he's been watching you," she said, eyeing Jason with a raised pierced eyebrow. She turned and walked away, leaving Jason alone with Wayne and Eric.

"Hey, he's cute," Wayne observed.

Eric got in a quick look, but averted his eyes when the guy looked up. "He is," he agreed, biting into his chocolaty treat.

"Go talk to him," Wayne insisted, eyeing Jason.

"No way. I hate just walking up to guys."

"Come on," Wayne said. "How will you ever meet anybody sitting with a couple of old maids like us?"

"Yeah, like Wayne," Eric echoed. Wayne smacked him in the shoulder again. Eric continued, "Go on."

"I can't," Jason insisted. He leaned into the table and took a bite of his croissant.

Wayne looked at him, a thin smile on his lips. "Well, it looks like you're not going to have to."

"Huh?" Jason said, mouth full of ham and cheese.

The man stood beside their table, his laptop folded in his left hand, his right hand out. "Hi, I'm Jacob," he greeted. "Sally said I should come say hello."

Jason looked stunned, as he slowly chewed his croissant. "Thathun," he said without thinking.

Realizing what he'd done, he put a hand to his mouth and swallowed. Embarrassed, he held out his right hand. "Oh, I'm so sorry. Pardon me."

"It's okay," Jacob laughed, taking his hand. "But I didn't quite catch your name…"

"Jason."

EPILOGUE

Hope Springs Eternal

Tom deftly dropped the bagels into the waiting baskets as Taylor arranged the baked goods on the display case shelves. It was a beautiful Saturday morning, the sun beaming through the windows, giving the duo much needed energy after so many long weeks.

"Is this like old times or what?" Tom asked.

"It feels great," Taylor agreed. It was the first time in weeks that they'd run the place all by themselves. The night crew had prepared some early stock to put in the café, but otherwise, they had been on their own.

In her excitement over her newfound pregnancy, Gen volunteered to take the kids Friday night and have a campout at her house. Never ones to turn down a night to themselves, Tom and Taylor accepted, then volunteered to take the morning shift from Wayne and Eric, spreading the wealth a bit. Emmy, grateful to have a weekend off with Dan, offered them the use of her family's lake cottage the following weekend. Taylor was very satisfied with the chain of events.

The front door opened and their most regular customer made her customary Saturday appearance.

"Tommy! Taylor!" she exclaimed. "I am so *glad* to see you boys! It's been so long!"

"Hi, Mrs. Jensen," Taylor greeted, starting her order from memory. "How have you been?"

"Oh, very well, thank you, Taylor," she said, smiling her bright, happy smile. "How have things been for you boys? It's been so long since I've seen you here together, I was afraid something was the matter."

Tom shook his head, helping Taylor with the order. "Nothing could be farther from the truth, Mrs. Jensen," he said. "We've just been so wrapped up with everything happening this summer, our schedules didn't usually mesh."

"I understand," she said sweetly. She pointed to the café. "There's no doubt you've been busy this year."

"And how," Tom agreed. Taylor took the bag to the register and undercharged her, just as he had the entire time he'd worked there.

"I had a chance to go into the café a few weeks ago," Mrs. Jensen confided.

"How did you like it?" Tom asked, standing with Taylor.

She nodded approvingly. "I liked it very much. I went in trying to find my granddaughter, but she wasn't there."

"You were meeting her there?"

Mrs. Jensen waved her hand. "Oh, heavens no. I was just in town and thought I'd drop in and see her."

Tom and Taylor exchanged a look. "Mrs. Jensen," Tom asked. "Who is your granddaughter?"

"Sally Carney, of course," she said. "Didn't she tell you we're related?"

"*Sally* is your granddaughter? The one you've told us about for so many years?"

Mrs. Jensen nodded. "Of course."

Tom shook his head. "She never told us."

Mrs. Jensen made another face. "Oh, that girl. She insisted that I not say anything to you. She didn't want you to know we were related and only hire her because of me. But I thought she'd have told you by now."

"Maybe it slipped her mind," Taylor offered.

"Maybe," Mrs. Jensen said, taking her change. "I keep telling her if she doesn't stop putting holes in her body, all her sense will leak out."

Tom and Taylor both laughed at that, having shared similar conversations since they'd known Sally. "That's good advice, Mrs. J," Tom said.

"I hope so," she nodded. "Well, you boys have a wonderful weekend and I hope to see you again soon."

"Same here, Mrs. Jensen," Taylor said.

She walked to the door, then stopped at the screen. "Oh, and tell Mayor Pouissant I said congratulations. I voted for her."

"Thank you, I will," Taylor said.

"Bye, then," she said and walked back out to her car.

"*Sally?*" Tom exclaimed. "No way!"

"Apparently," Taylor said.

"That's too much," Tom said. "Wait 'til Jason hears this one."

Later that morning, as Jason opened the café, they recounted the story to him. He'd worked enough time in the bakery to have an idea of who Mrs. Jensen was and he was very surprised at the connection.

"I remember her saying her granddaughter was a lesbian," Jason said. "I just never had any idea she was *our* lesbian."

"It's wild, I know," Tom said.

The bakery rush had slowed and Ethan was helping to cover their store. Jason was managing the café himself, since it wouldn't pick up for a little while longer. While Tom and Taylor were there, he went back to bring a fresh stack of cups out front.

The door to the café opened and a young man made his way in, laptop in hand. When he saw Taylor, he smiled and waved a greeting.

"Good morning, Mr. Connolly," he greeted. "What has you up so early?"

"Good morning," Taylor greeted. "You don't need to call me Mr. Connolly. It's just Taylor."

He smiled. "Sorry. I'm so used to meeting people in offices."

"No problem," Taylor said. "We're just a little more casual around here. To answer your question, Tom and I own these stores."

"Oh! These are the ones. Very nice," he said.

"Taylor?" Tom asked, gesturing to the man.

"Oh, sorry. Tom McEwan, Jacob...Rubenstein?" Taylor introduced.

Jacob's face brightened. "Very good of you to remember," he acknowledged. Shaking Tom's hand, he said, "Nice to meet you."

"Likewise," Tom replied.

"Jacob is a forensic accountant. He's investigating our old friend Stuey."

"No. Really?" Tom asked.

Jacob nodded. "I can't really talk about it, but I talked to Taylor about a few things earlier this week."

Jason reappeared from the back, arms full. He set the cups on the counter and walked to the register, seeing someone was there. In the glare, he couldn't make out who it was until he was at the counter.

"Jacob!" he greeted. "Good morning."

"Hi, Jason," Jacob replied. He walked over to place his order and started a conversation.

"They know each other?" Tom asked quietly.

"Apparently," Taylor replied.

They turned to go and Taylor called over to him. "Good to see you again."

"You, too," Jacob waved, then turned back to Jason.

Back in the bakery, Tom said, "Well how about that?"

"Maybe he'll get Adam out of his system sooner than we thought," Taylor observed.

"That would be good."

Standing in front of the large picture window at the front of the store, Taylor looked at the town they'd helped to save from evil's clutches and smiled. Tom came up behind him and rested his chin on Taylor's shoulder, putting an arm around his waist, and held him close.

It had been a good summer indeed.

BONUS ITEMS

I am an unabashed movie and DVD fan. I have a huge personal library that could honestly give my book library a run for its money. One of the things that I've really come to enjoy is the added "Bonus Items" most companies offer with their DVDs.

In most cases, the Bonus Items are just little tidbits or features that might be interesting to the viewer who wants a little more from his or her movie. Most of the time, books are just the novel itself, with maybe a brief Afterword by the author. The new publisher I selected for *Finding Hope*, however, allows for more items in the book than just the text. So, for the first time, I can offer additional insight into Tom and Taylor's world, as Bonus Items.

Included for your entertainment are several deleted scenes, as well as some of the supporting materials I use to keep track of everything.

Enjoy!

DELETED SCENES

I can't speak for all authors, but when I write, sometimes there are scenes that just don't quite fit with the plot when it's all said and done. Sometimes, as in the case of *Finding Hope*, they can even be whole chapters. (I originally had a different plan to start the book, but it didn't quite work out the way I'd intended, so I scrapped it and started over.)

As I prepared the book for publication, it occurred to me that some of the scenes written for those old chapters might still be interesting in the context of the new book. Then I realized it might actually be kind of fun to include them at the end of the book, much like a movie, as deleted scenes.

So, I offer the following four scenes, removed from *Finding Hope* for pacing or content purposes.

Eric's Departure

This is actually two scenes. In the original draft of the novel, the action was set to pick up a few weeks after the end of Finding Peace. *At that time, Taylor was still the Mayor and everyone was settling into the new lives they had found at the end of the last story. Jason was introduced in an earlier*

scene, and was set to move into his grandfather's house, as Mr. Olsen moved
to Arizona. Taylor had a conversation with Jason, then turned to find Gen
on her way home from the bakery…

As he looked back to the street, he saw Gen coming up her driveway, then through the bushes that separated their two properties. In her arms was a large brown bag, and he knew very well where it came from.

"Genevieve, my lady, how are you this fine morning?" Taylor greeted.

She shook her head. "Oh, no, I'm not sure I'm ready for Taylor-in-a-Good-Mood this morning."

"Such a pessimist."

She laughed, reaching into the bag. "Here, your hubby sent you some breakfast." She handed him a small bag, reaching in to extract one herself. "He sent some sandwiches for the kids, too."

"I love the delivery service," Taylor said, taking a bite from the chocolaty treat.

"Don't get used to it. I was just helping Tommy. He's swamped down there."

Taylor frowned. "Where's Wayne?"

"Wayne's there. Eric isn't, though."

"Where is he?"

Gen gave him an I-don't-know face between bites. "Tom said something is going on between the two of them and Eric didn't come in. He tried calling Emmy, but her family went to the cabin for the weekend." She looked across the yard to Jason's house. "So, he's finally moving in, huh?"

"Yeah," Taylor answered absently. "So, it's just Tom and Wayne there?"

"Mrs. Johnson came in, but they were still pretty busy."

Taylor sighed. "I don't suppose you'd want to babysit?"

Gen gestured to the bag. "You think I brought all this food here for my health? Honey, I've put on ten pounds since you guys took over that place."

Taylor leaned over to give her a kiss on the cheek. "You look all the better for it." He stood, straightening his T-shirt. "I'll try to be back in a couple of hours."

Gen shook her head. "No hurry. I need to go to the store. Once the kids are up and fed, I'll take your car."

Taylor nodded. "You know where the keys are. Thanks, babe."

"Just go help out Tommy."

"Yes, ma'am," Taylor said. He opened the door to take a pair of shoes from the closet, then set off down the street, wondering what was going to happen next...and instantly wished he'd learn not to ask that question.

Even after more than three years, Taylor still enjoyed the walk to the old downtown. He found himself smiling at the smallest things—the clear blue sky, the sound of birds in the trees, the trees themselves. His family had moved a fair number times as he grew up, and always to more and more prestigious locales as his parents' businesses prospered. Truth be told, Taylor had never thought of living in a small town—it just never entered his mind. As always, he found himself grateful for whatever twist of fate had left Gen in such an unusual community, and for bringing him to her.

It was late enough in the morning already that both sides of the street were alive with activity, as usual. From between the old oaks and maples, Taylor spied families in their yards, weeding planting beds, washing cars, or just enjoying the late summer weather while they could. Many greeted him with a smile and a wave, often simply calling out, "Mornin', Mayor!"

Taylor chuckled at that—the office no one wanted, but all were glad he'd taken. It required virtually no work on his part, except to show up at the occasional town functions and a school athletic event now and then. Fortunately, Tom continued to coach a junior softball team, so he was very well connected among the parents in their community. That, combined with their bakery, made them a veritable fixture in the small town.

As he crossed to the last block before Main Street, a dark car turned the corner and promptly beeped its horn, slowing. The driver window lowered and a familiar face leaned out.

"Hey, Taylor!"

"Hi, Rob," he greeted. "What's new?"

Rob shook his head. "Not much. On your way in?"

Taylor nodded. "Yeah, Gen said they're a little short staffed this morning."

"Yep. Ethan just came in, but it's a busy morning."

"I'll probably just add to the confusion," Taylor said.

Rob laughed. "It's our lot in life, my friend."

"Good point," Taylor agreed. "We'll catch up with you later."

"Sounds good," Rob said, then continued on to his house.

Rob and Mel had continued to be exceptionally good friends to Tom and Taylor. Rob had been the first person Taylor met upon arriving to his new home with Gen. In short order, it had been as though they'd known each other for years. Rob was one of Tom's teammates on his Sunday night baseball team, and he had gone out of his way to be supportive the night when Faith Roberts inadvertently "outted" Taylor to the town. In the years since, they had gotten to know each other even more after Pete and Anita moved into a house across the street from them and invited them to many of their social functions.

Finally reaching Main Street, Taylor turned and made his way to the bakery, noticing the usual lack of vehicular traffic. Most of the stores wouldn't open for another hour, leaving their bakery,

Downey McEwan's, as the only draw. Unlike the rest of the street, all of the available spots in front were taken.

The warm weather meant the front door was wide open, with only an old wooden screen door to keep the few bugs at bay. Taylor pulled it aside and was quickly assailed by the warmth of the space and the smells of fresh baked goods, along with the sound of conversation as the table occupants chatted with each other.

Taylor greeted the several people waiting in line by the door, then made his way back behind the counter, stopping to quickly wash his hands at the small sink. Tom turned from the bagel racks and caught sight of him, giving Taylor the smile that could still take his breath away.

Since taking over the bakery from its previous owners, Tom had made some changes to further increase business and traffic from the town residents. He had rearranged the baking room to free up the wall nearest the front, then had a window installed, along with a grilling area, allowing them to offer hot breakfasts and lunches. He'd rearranged the front of the store, taking out a section of cabinets to make more room for tables, and hired additional staff to manage the extra work. Downey's was now considered one of the "cool" places to work, for both the high school students and some of the college students. Tom tended to favor the older kids for management functions, while the younger ones bussed tables and worked in the food preparation area. It could still be a little hectic when things really got busy, but there was usually a line during peak times, so they knew they were doing something right.

Tom made his way over to Taylor. "Hi, you," you greeted. "Thanks for coming down." He put a hand on Taylor's arm, leading him down the hall toward the baking room.

"Gen's going to watch the kids for a few hours," Taylor said. "What's going on?"

Out of earshot from both the store and the baking area, Tom spoke quietly. "I don't know the specifics, but Wayne and Eric got into some kind of argument last night and Eric left."

"He left?" Taylor asked, incredulous. "Where did he go?"

Tom sighed. "Wayne isn't sure. He thinks he went home, but he won't answer his cell phone."

"Are we sure he's okay?"

Tom nodded. "I checked with the Chief. He said nothing has come in since last night."

"Small favors," Taylor said, leaning back against the wall. "How's Wayne?"

"Upset, but working. You know him—the more upset he is, the more he works."

"True," Taylor agreed. "What do you think we should do?"

Tom shrugged. "What can we do? Whatever is going on is something they have to work out. All we can do is listen and offer advice if they want it."

"Eric didn't say anything to you?"

"Nope. This came as a complete surprise to me. I guess it happened around dinner. Wayne said he just got in his car and left."

Before Taylor could respond, Wayne appeared at the door to the baking room, T-shirt and apron covered in flour. He dusted his hands on his apron, a guilty expression on his face as he saw Taylor there.

"I guess you heard, huh?" he asked, his dark jade eyes awash with sadness.

"Yeah," Taylor confirmed. "You wanna go for a walk?"

Wayne gestured to his clothes. "I'm kind of a mess."

Taylor laughed. "I'm used to it by now. Come on, let's go outside for a couple of minutes." He put a reassuring arm around Wayne's thin shoulders, guiding him to the back door.

"The bread," Wayne said, stopping.

"I've got it," Tom said from behind him. "Take five."

"Okay," Wayne said, allowing Taylor to lead him out.

Behind the bakery, Wayne sat on the stairs leading to his apartment above the store, while Taylor sat on a milk crate. The back of the store was in shade most of the day, leaving it noticeably cooler than the front. After the warmth of the bakery, it felt positively cold on Taylor's bare legs. One glance at Wayne pushed the thought from his mind, however, as he saw the torment in his young friend's eyes.

"So?" Taylor asked. "What's the scoop?"

Wayne shook his head, exhaustion showing through in his face. "It's just been one thing after another, Taylor," he said.

Taylor frowned. "Like what? I thought you guys were doing well."

Wayne shook his head. "It's been hard. Eric is a great guy, but he kept complaining about everything. I mean, I know he cares about me, but I don't really think he wanted to be here."

"Here, the bakery, or here, the town?"

"Probably both," Wayne admitted. "He kept talking about the university and how limited he felt here and how he was going to have to retake a bunch of classes and it would put him behind." He looked up. "All he's been doing for the last week is sitting on the couch, watching television. He hardly talks to me at all."

"And he blamed you?" Taylor asked.

"He never actually blamed me," Wayne admitted, "But let's face it, he wouldn't have come here if not for me."

"So you blame yourself?"

Wayne looked away, expression uncertain. "Maybe a little."

Taylor leaned forward, looking at Wayne closely. He could scarcely believe this was the same young man he and Tom had taken in a year ago. The uncertainty and fear had largely been replaced by blossoming maturity and self-confidence. Where Eric's departure would have sent Wayne to tears of despair even a few months before, he now dealt with the situation in a more detached way—he was upset, but his world wasn't crashing down around him. The fact that they had apparently been fighting for more than just the one night no doubt helped prepare him for the possibility that he now faced. Taylor had to admit he was more than just a little annoyed with himself that he hadn't seen that one coming.

"It's not your fault."

Wayne looked down. "I talked him into coming here. He kept saying he wanted to stay there."

Taylor smiled thinly. "He's a big boy, Wayne. He knew what he was doing. He came here by his choice." Wayne looked up, questioning. "Really," Taylor confirmed. "You told him you wanted him here and he wanted to be with you."

"I guess not enough."

Taylor moved to sit on the step beside him, putting his arm around Wayne. "You guys are still very young. I know you think you're ready for all this, but you're just starting out."

"Doesn't love conquer all?" Wayne asked.

Taylor shook his head. "Unfortunately, not always. Do you know if he's gone for good?"

"He took most of his stuff," Wayne said. "He left a few pieces of furniture, but he took his clothes and his computer."

"What do you want to do?" Taylor asked.

Wayne thought for a moment, taking in a few deep breaths. He leaned forward, resting his elbows on his knees. "I don't know. He's been so miserable lately, I told him to just go if he wanted to. I don't know why he's so miserable—the college is fun and he knows everybody there."

Taylor watched him. "Maybe it's just not the place for him. I remember him telling me how much he wanted to stay where he was."

"Then why did he come here in the first place?" Wayne asked.

"He didn't want to hurt you."

"Like it doesn't hurt now?"

Taylor shrugged. "He tried, kiddo. You guys are young. Even going to separate schools doesn't have to be the end of the world."

Wayne looked up, and for the first time Taylor saw anger in his eyes. "I think we're pretty much through."

"Don't be surprised if you feel differently later," Taylor said.

"Maybe," Wayne said.

"So what do you want to do?" Taylor asked again.

Wayne met his gaze. "I want to go to school and get my education."

Taylor smiled broadly at that. "That's what I want to hear," he said.

"I can do it, Taylor. I can do it on my own."

Taylor nodded. "I know you can, but you're not on your own. Eric may be gone, but you've still got Tom and me. And Gen. And Emmy and Dan. And the kids. We're still here and we're not going anywhere."

"I know," Wayne said, looking away shyly. It had taken Taylor many weeks to convince him his new family wasn't going to abandon him. "You guys are the best."

Taylor hugged him tight. "So are you. You watch, this will be a good thing. It'll be good for Eric, too. Don't be surprised if you wind up friends later."

"Don't count on it," Wayne grumbled.

Taylor laughed. "That's okay, too. It'll work out. I promise."

Wayne turned and hugged him back. "Thanks, Taylor."

Taylor looked him in the eyes. "And you know you can come to us when you're having trouble, right?"

Wayne looked away again. "I know. I just didn't want to talk about it. I thought we'd work it out. I guess not."

"As long as you know you're not alone."

"I know."

They stood and Taylor looked up the stairs.

"Do you want to stay here? You can come back to the house, you know."

Wayne nodded. "Thanks. I think I still want to be on my own, though."

"Okay. Tom and I will help you move Eric's stuff to the storeroom for now, then. He can come pick it up whenever he wants."

"Actually," Wayne said, "I think Dan may come move in."

"Emmy's Dan?"

Wayne nodded. "I was talking to him about everything the other day and he mentioned he'd been wanting to find a place so he didn't have to live at home."

For the first time, Taylor began to see the man Wayne was becoming. Not only was he handling the separation from Eric, but he was building his own support network, separate from his family. Emmy had been his best friend for some time, but her boyfriend, Dan, had become a very close friend, too. Taylor was glad to see he wasn't afraid to make new bonds and trust people.

"Sounds like you've got it pretty well worked out."

"I hope so," Wayne said. He gestured to the door. "We should probably get back in there. Tom was running around like a chicken with his head cut off before you got here."

"How's the new guy doing?"

"Ethan?" Wayne asked. "Well, so far he burned eggs for three different sandwiches, and completely lost another order." Taylor rolled his eyes and sighed. Wayne continued, "He should be fine in another week."

"Really?"

"He can't stay bad forever, right?"

Mandy McEwan Supports Eric

As readers of Finding Peace *will recall, Wayne originally met Eric because Eric was a friend of Tom's sister, Mandy, and came to spend the Thanksgiving holiday with them. In this scene, Eric returns to Ohio State to finish his education and explains part of his decision to Mandy...*

Eric dropped his bag at the foot of his bed and set his laptop case on his desk. He was back. It was like nothing had changed. His roommate had the same posters on the wall, same maps taped to the ceiling, same clothes in the closet. It was all the same—except for the the pit that had taken up permanent residence in his stomach.

Thankfully, Kevin had been willing to share the room again. He'd been surprised by Eric's sudden decision to leave school at the end of the winter semester. As they parted ways, he told Eric he'd be welcomed if he changed his mind. Otherwise, Kevin was just going to keep the single and be on his own.

Eric shook his head. Not only had he left Wayne, he'd had to go back to a *dorm*. Could there be a greater injustice?

He lowered himself to the bed and brought his knees up under his chin. He'd done it. He'd given in. His father had won, once again. Eric felt like he was twelve. Would he ever be in control of his life? When was it his turn?

There was no way to argue with his father. He and Wayne couldn't afford to put him through college themselves and he was not about to accept charity from Tom and Taylor. He had no doubt they would find a way to help him if asked, but Eric didn't want that.

It was only two more years. The words echoed through his mind for the millionth time, and then the millionth and first. It had taken him a few days, but he worked it out so he could finish in two years. Between the advanced credits he'd already collected and summer classes, he could do it.

Wayne should know. He wanted so badly to say something to Wayne, but he knew if he did, his resolve would falter and he'd wind up right back where he had been—where he wanted to be—back in that town, working in that bakery, with the only person he'd ever loved.

There was a knock at the door and Eric sighed. Word had no doubt spread that he was coming back. The last thing he needed was to face the throngs of questions that would ensue. It was nobody else's business what was going on with him.

The knock sounded again and the door creaked open an inch or two.

"Eric?"

The voice was hesitant and tentative, but it was one he recognized and he leaned his head around the partition to see the face in the mirror.

"Mandy?"

"Hey, buddy," she said. She walked into the room, quietly closing the door behind her. "You look like hell."

Eric choked a laugh in spite of himself. "Tell me how you really feel."

She smiled and sat on the bed next to him, wrapping an arm over his shoulders. "Tommy called and said you'd left."

He hung his head lower, knowing Tom and Taylor would be worried as well. "What did you tell him?"

"Nothing," Mandy said. "All I said was Kevin had mentioned you were coming back and that I hadn't talked to you yet."

"What are you going to tell them?"

Mandy shrugged. "I don't have to tell them anything. It's not my job to get in the middle of what's going on in your life. Unless you want me to."

Eric shook his head, resting his forehead in his hand. "I don't know what I want."

Mandy watched him. "Don't take this the wrong way," she said, "but why did you come back?"

Eric explained the situation to her, how his father told him he expected Eric to do what was best for *him*, for *his* future, for *his* career. When Eric resisted, his father said he had no intention of paying for a substandard education from some little college in the middle of nowhere. He told Eric it was time to do what he had to do and go back to the university to complete his education.

"That's terrible," Mandy protested. "What difference does it make to him?"

Eric shook his head. "You don't understand my father. I'm the last son. My brothers are a baseball player and a priest. I'm not exactly the star of the family show."

"Because you fell in love with a boy? That's ridiculous."

"That's easy for you to say. Your family isn't like mine."

Mandy nodded. "I'm not going to tell you there wasn't some shock when Tommy came home with Taylor, but my family feels it's about the person and about staying a family."

"My family feels it's about not making waves that make us look bad at parties."

"That's terrible, Eric," Mandy said. "I'm so sorry."

Eric nodded. "I can't say anything because I know if I do, Wayne will find some way to convince me I'm wrong."

"So what are you going to do?" Mandy asked.

"I don't know," Eric admitted, grief on his face. "For now, we're just going to have to be friends, if he even wants me for that anymore, and then we'll see where it goes."

Mandy hugged him closer. "Well, you know I'm there for you if you need me, and I'm sure Tom and Taylor will be too."

"Don't say anything to them. At least, not now."

"Okay," Mandy agreed. They sat together, into the night, in silence.

Jason Comes Out

One of the challenges an author faces as a series of books grows is character overload. Main characters tend to stay the same, with one or two added or removed, but background characters can start to grow like rabbits. Part of good editing is trying to keep the cast down to a manageable number that readers may have a chance of remembering.

In this scene, we meet Jason's best friend, Natalie Ganesan, as she joins Tom, Taylor, and company for dinner. Natalie would have been an interesting character to include in the story, but the plot grew too complicated to have her there without being a distraction. Perhaps at some point in the future, though...

Jason and Natalie roared with laughter as Gen told the story of her most recent trip to her favorite bakery for breakfast. In the background, her story was accompanied by music from the hastily setup stereo. To the side, a few remaining patties sat on the grill, having long since cooled.

The group surrounded Jason's round table on the patio behind his house. Taylor had stopped by earlier in the afternoon to drop off the Kaiser rolls for the burgers and mentioned Gen was watching the kids. Jason had promptly offered to have her join them for dinner, then added an invitation for Miguel when he learned she was married. For someone who had just moved in that morning, he prepared quite a spread.

"...So instead of sending back for a third time, I finally just got up and walked it back there myself," Gen continued.

"You didn't!" Jason gasped.

Gen shrugged. "I have privileges."

"What did he say?" Natalie asked.

Gen smiled. "I couldn't really give him a hard time. He was covered in food, trying to keep track of everything, and there was no one to help him. Wayne was trying to keep the baked goods moving and Tom was out front."

"It was a tough morning," Tom agreed.

"So I introduced him to the temperature control knob," Gen concluded.

"Temperature?" Jason asked.

"Yeah, he had everything on high. It was no wonder I was getting charcoal instead of eggs."

"But really, the food is great," Miguel argued from beside her.

"I can't wait," Natalie said, a little uncertain.

"Hey, at least if it's bad, we know who to complain to," Jason said.

"You've got the idea," Taylor agreed. As usual, the kids were more interested in playing with Molly, who chased them around their own yard. Tom and Taylor had positioned themselves to be able to watch the children, keeping them just in their line of sight.

"So, if I may ask, how did you come to be parents?" Natalie said, watching the kids terrorize the eager golden retriever.

The friends all glanced at each other, and it was finally Tom who spoke up. "Uh, well," he said, "When two people love each other very much—"

"Tommy!" Gen exclaimed, smacking him in the arm. Everyone laughed, and she took over the explanation. "Their parents were very close friends of ours. Last New Years's Eve, they were hit by a drunk driver. Their mother, Sandy, was killed instantly, and their father died the next day."

Natalie's face paled a bit as she realized she had touched on such a painful topic. "I'm so sorry."

"It was a difficult time for us," Taylor admitted, his hand resting lightly on Tom's arm. "We didn't even know John and Sandy had listed us as the children's guardians. We were away on vacation and Gen called us."

"That must have been awful," Jason commented.

"Very," Tom agreed. "But we've done the best we can for the kids. They live with us, but Gen and Miguel are like surrogate parents to them as well. In a lot of ways, it's like they lost their own parents, but got six or eight in return."

"That many?" Natalie asked.

Taylor nodded. "Tom's parents moved here early in the summer. They babysit while we're working. Then Gen and Miguel watch them quite often, as do our friends Pete and Anita, who live down the street. Amanda, who is Rob and Mel's daughter, usually babysits at least one night on the weekend."

"It takes a village," Jason observed.

"So it does," Taylor agreed.

"Have the two of you thought about having children?" Gen asked.

Both Jason and Natalie looked up sharply, surprise on their faces. "Us?" they asked at the same time.

"No?" Miguel asked, sipping his iced tea.

The two glanced at each other confusedly, and Jason turned to Gen. "We thought you knew. We're just friends. Roommates. We're not a couple."

"Oh," Gen said, slipping the quickest of glances to Taylor. "Sorry, I just assumed."

Natalie laughed. "No, Jason doesn't want someone like me."

"Young and beautiful?" Tom asked.

"A woman," Jason confirmed. "I was sure my grandfather would have said something."

Taylor shook his head. "Your grandfather was never one for discussing personal matters."

Jason sat back, his dark eyes twinkling with the light of the candles on the table in front of them. "You noticed that, too," he observed. He smiled thinly, watching Tom and Taylor. "Actually, I just broke up with a guy I'd been with for about the last year," he said. "He disappeared while I was out of town, about two months ago. Took a bunch of my stuff and was gone. About the same time, grandpa called and said he was thinking of moving to Arizona. Nat's lease was coming up on her place, too, so we decided to just shack up out here for a while and see what happens."

"You're single, too?" Gen asked.

Miguel rolled his eyes. "Oh, here we go again," he said. "Don't you start."

"What?" Gen defended.

Miguel looked at Natalie. "She is forever trying to marry everyone off."

"I am not," Gen defended.

"Are," Taylor confirmed. "Sorry, kiddo."

Natalie watched them, smiling. "Actually, I wouldn't mind being fixed up," she said. "My track record lately has been pretty bad."

"I'll say," Jason seconded.

"Like you've been doing so well yourself," she countered pointedly.

Tom watched them all. "Well, you're in the right group. Frankly, none of us are real good at letting someone just stay single."

Jason held up his hands. "I'm okay with staying single for now."

Taylor shook his head. "It won't matter. They can't help themselves. Miguel and I are the only sane ones in the bunch."

"Ha!" Gen and Tom intoned simultaneously.

"Certainly sounds like you'll fit in, Nat," Jason said.

"Don't push your luck, Harper," she said, rising. Before he could retort, she turned to their guests. "I'm going to get another Coke. Can I get you anything?"

Tom and Taylor exchanged glances and rose themselves. "Actually, we should be going. We've gotta get the kids ready for bed," Tom said.

"Thanks for the great meal, though," Taylor said. "I think it's supposed to be the neighbors who cook for the new people, though."

Xanderon Attacks!

This was the scene that was hardest for me to cut from the final book. In the original version, it was the title of the second chapter. It started as a joke with a friend of mine, when I was trying to come up with ideas for Finding Hope. *I decided I would write a sci-fi book where big ugly space aliens come along and sweep our heroes away to another planet.*

I wrote the piece "Wayne" writes below as a sample. I liked it so much, I framed it into a chapter, as a paper Wayne wrote for Tom's class. However, it really just didn't fit the context of Finding Hope *as it evolved, so I was forced to omit it. I include it here for your enjoyment and amusement.*

Later that evening, Wayne relaxed on his sofa, home from dinner and spending the evening with his friends. Unlike the high school comparison he had made over dinner, he didn't have a college class in the morning until ten-thirty. Tom had recently hired a second baker to give Wayne more time to focus on his schoolwork, meaning he didn't have to be at the bakery the following morning. Unused to having an evening where he didn't have to rush to sleep, he decided to look over the homework assignment Tom had given his class.

Reviewing the handout, he wondered how well he would really do. As much as he liked to kid his friend, creative writing really had never been his forte. He excelled at journalistic writing, but creating characters and environments from scratch had always been very difficult. The green photocopy held what were actually fairly simple instructions: *taking real people and events from your own life, create a fictitious story about something that might have happened. Be as creative as you like, but be sure to include clear imagery to answer the basic plot development points of who, what, where, when, and why.*

On the television, Eric had tuned in to one of his favorite science fiction dramas about a group of people who traveled all over the universe, using some ancient ring-shaped relic that flushed sideways, and encountered all kinds of pretty over-the-top bad guys. As Wayne watched, they were hurtled off to some distant world, and immediately surrounded by enemy soldiers who kept hollering, "Kree!" He didn't really know much about the show, but it got his imagination working a little. He picked up his pen and started making some notes...

The alien commander watched as his attack fleet approached the puny planet in their sights. Inside, he felt pleasure as he pondered the fate that awaited these hideous "human" things.

Ever since one of their research drones had detected the probe leaving the human solar system, the position of the Xanderon Royal Court had been clear—the people of Planet Earth must be eradicated. Their continued existence in the universe could not be tolerated.

It wasn't like Xanderoneons hadn't tried. They sent one emissary after another to try to persuade the Earthling governments to adopt more Xanderoneon moral and ethical standards, but they had been blocked at every turn. First, the xenophobic Earthlings attacked them because they looked different. The commander had to admit his green slime covered scales were considerably more attractive than the puffy, squishy skin of the humans, but those creatures had the temerity to consider their appearance preferred. The commander scoffed at the thought. Then, when they learned to disguise themselves as humans, the Earthlings still would not heed their warning.

Now, with the war fleet approaching the planet from all angles, time had run out. One human month before, their operatives on the planet had revealed their existence in every country on the planet, announcing the Xanderoneon plan to exterminate humanity if Earth did not immediately capitulate to the will of the Royal Court. Finally, the stinky little pink aliens would get what they had coming to them.

At the control tank in front of his command bath, the communications minion turned and raised a tentacle. The commander blinked at him and the minion spoke. "My most holy and righteous commander, the unclean and swarthy Earthlings beg your consideration and ask that you lower yourself to hear their words. On your order, I will place their vile, stomach-contents-emptying image on the viewer, but I warn your radiating brilliance once again how truly revolting they are."

"Well said, Worker Unit," the Commander responded. He expected nothing less than complete evacutorium kissing from his crew and they always exceeded his expectations. "Display their message."

"On your order, most veritably profound one."

On the screen, the growing image of the doomed world was replaced by the visage of one of the bloated, sickly dry Earthlings. Though the commander would never deign himself to admit it, this Earthling was somehow less disgusting than many of the others.

"Speak, human," he ordered without ceremony.

"Sir, my name is Taylor Connolly, of the planet Earth. I have been appointed representative of our world to your fleet."

"Uninteresting."

The human—Taylor—nodded. "Sir, our people have only recently come to understand what has caused the great rift between our two worlds. I have been asked to bridge the divide that now separates us."

"A fruitless task." The commander reached to terminate the ugliness from his vision.

"Sir!" Taylor called, raising a hand. "There are homosexuals on this world!"

The commander's tentacle froze. Could it be true? Their intelligence personnel had assured them the Earthlings were doing anything in their power to suppress the homosexuals of this planet. The war fleet had been dispatched to eradicate the heterosexual infestation. Could it be true one of the Earthling homosexuals now spoke on behalf of the planet?

"You jest. Your people are merely pretending to be homosexual for the purpose of averting your own destruction and imminent demise. We are not fools."

Taylor turned and the image widened to take in the person beside him. Like Taylor, his skin was pink and puffy and dry, but also like Taylor, he was somehow less hideous than many of the others.

"This man is my spouse, sir. His name is Tom. We have been together for many years. He is a professor of language and I am the head of our town. We have positions of prominence and power."

The commander's eye slits thinned. Now, at the fourteenth hour, the Earthlings would have him believe they were not suppressing those like his kind? Dare he consider calling off the invasion? Would the Royal Court share his interest?

"I must consult my superiors. What may I take them to show your words are genuine?"

Taylor pulled the other man to him. "My spouse and I volunteer to accompany you back to Xanderon. To appease the Great Queen, we offer a supply of chocolate croissants. Our operatives here on Earth assure us they are a most royal and well-approved delicacy on your world."

Croissants! Surely not! No *Earthling* could understand the most ubiquitous and regal of all refreshments. To understand that, the human *must* be a homosexual. But if homosexuals occupied Earth, then it would be a high crime to attack them. Quickly, the commander issued orders: stop the invasion; bring the human representatives to meet with him.

As always, his crew was fastidious and answered his orders with all possible haste. In short order, the lightwave transport zapper placed the two creatures before him. They watched his graceful elegance with a mixture of awe and jealousy, knowing they could never hope to achieve even a fraction of his beauty.

"You are the homosexuals?" the commander asked.

"Yes," Taylor confirmed.

"Where is your Queen?" He waited to see if they would pass his test.

"She was with us. She is prepared to come aboard as well."

The commander twitched a tentacle and the zapper deposited another human before him.

"Sir, I present Genevieve Pouissant."

"Your worship," the commander greeted, inclining his massive head. Human or not, she was still a Queen of the Realm of Homosexuals.

"Sir," she responded simply, inclining her head as well. "We ask that you not destroy our planet. We did not understand the nature of your complaint with humanity before. Now that we do, all heterosexuals in positions of power have begun training and the republicans have been removed from office. We will coexist with your worlds peacefully."

The commander released air, tension passing from his scales. "A most welcome outcome, your Grace. We welcome your delegation to the Xanderon Royal Court."

And they lived happily ever after...

"Oh my God," Taylor gasped between fits of laughter. "He honestly thought you wouldn't like it?"

Tom lay on the couch beside him, his feet under Taylor's thigh, a pile of student papers on the floor. He had given the class until the end of the week to produce their first creative writing sample for him. He told them a couple of pages would be enough—he only wanted them to start thinking.

When Wayne handed him the typed, double-spaced pages, he'd said simply, "It's not very good. Be gentle."

Tom made a point of reading Wayne's piece first. All kidding aside, he would grade him honestly, but he *was* a member of their family, and Tom would do whatever he could to help. He had to pick his jaw up off the floor when he read Wayne's use of language. Most kids struggled just to use an occasional adjective.

"You know Wayne; he's doing very well, but his self-confidence is still low in new situations."

Taylor handed the pages back to Tom. "Well, Professor McEwan, I don't know what you're looking for, but I'd give that an 'A'."

Tom nodded. "I can tell you it's at least two years ahead of almost anything else in that pile. The kids are talented, but Wayne has been writing for years. He's just not used to having anyone else read it."

Taylor patted his leg, resting his arm across Tom's knees. "He's lucky to have you for a teacher."

A knock sounded at the door and Taylor rose to answer it.

Pine Creek Map

The more complex the story, the harder it is to keep up with all the details. I finally decided it would be a good idea to create a map of town, so I could remember where everything was relative to everything else. Since I can include it in this volume of the series, I thought, why not?

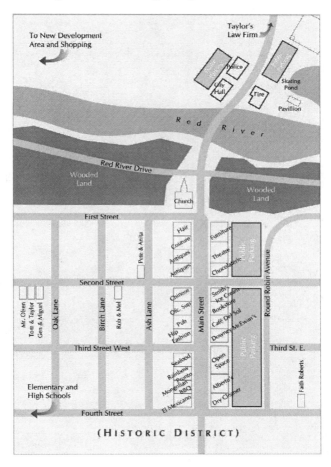

Taylor's Office Floor Plan

Though it never really mattered all that much, I decided it was a good idea to know where everyone sat relative to each other at Taylor's office. The space never figured that prominently into the other stories, but this time it was necessary to spend more time there. This is just a rough sketch I knocked out quickly one night, when I was getting confused myself.

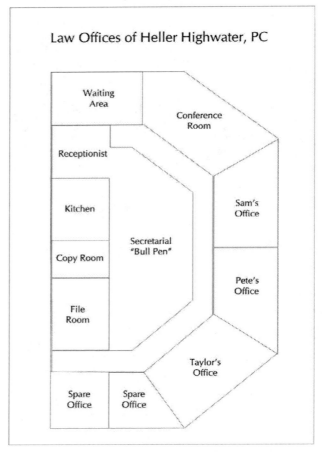

711824

Made in the USA